TAKEN BY THE HORDE KING

ZOEY DRAVEN

Taken by the Horde King

Horde Kings of Dakkar

Book Five

Zoey Draven

Taken by the Horde King

To save Dakkar, she must lure him to his deadly prison. Instead, she finds herself wearing *his* chains...

As a fatal curse continues to spread over the planet of Dakkar, I make a deal with an alien witch who claims she can stop it.

Her price?

The heart of a horde king.

Only the horde king in question is the fiercest male I've ever seen, with glowing demon eyes, a god-like body crafted in battle, and a cold, cruel grin that promises destruction.

Yet when I offer myself to him, all under the premise of luring him back to the witch, his touch sets my blood on fire. His dizzying kiss makes the world spin. Instead of fear, I feel hot and unwanted desire, awakening instincts that tell me I'm *his*.

When he discovers my ultimate betrayal, the enraged horde king vows he will take me as his prize, that I will wear his chains, and that I will serve him in *whatever* way he wishes.

And as the dangers on Dakkar loom, I find myself craving my wicked, wicked ruin...all at the hands of a horde king I should've never crossed.

Chapter 1

I tried not to stare at the Dakkari witch, even as chills ran up my arms and prickled down the back of my neck.

I failed miserably.

There was fear quivering deep in my belly as her black-rimmed eyes moved over me for a brief moment. Her eyes were a bright red, and the smudged black around them gave them the appearance of being otherworldly. Dangerous.

My hands shook as I poured the boiling water into her goblet, splashing droplets onto her hands, which were covered in golden tattoos. Words I didn't know how to read.

The witch didn't flinch, but her eyes narrowed on me. Unwelcome and alarming, that gaze seemed to rip back the layers of my skin until I felt like she could see all of me. And though I wished to, I couldn't look away.

Please, I wanted to beg. But my tongue wouldn't form the word. It was like a boulder in my mouth, as useless as always. Perhaps it was best if she believed I couldn't speak at all.

Dizzying relief made me feel as light as air when she broke my gaze and returned hers to Benn, who sat across from her at the fire.

"Ignore her," Benn told the witch, dismissing me easily with his glance. "She's a half-wit, can barely speak."

The witch laughed, and I flinched, turning my back as I retreated toward the darkness of the forest, where the others were waiting.

Behind me, I heard, "Careful, *vekkiri*. Kakkari often gives power to those who seem most harmless, to better defend themselves with."

Without seeing his face, I knew that the words had given Benn pause. I could almost see the way his mouth turned down into a deep scowl, the way his brows drew together and his eyes narrowed.

Ducking my head, I ignored the others as I sat close to the second fire, not far away—built to give the illusion of privacy between Benn and the witch who'd come to meet with him.

Wrapping my arms around my knees, I curled into myself and stared at the flickering flames, all while listening.

There were thirty-one of us in total, though not all were present tonight for this meeting. A large group was out hunting, though they'd needed to push farther west than ever before. After the red fog began to spread, the game had left the East Lands. Hunger was constant among us. And we were getting desperate.

The witch seemed to be as well. The fact that a Dakkari witch was meeting with a human at all was proof of her desperation, though she hid it well behind a veil of displeasure and distaste.

"Have you anything to eat?" the witch asked next, her words slow. "I travel all this way to be given boiled water?"

Sitting next to me, Mohamed shifted. I sensed others casting wary, angered glances at each other, lobbing them across the flames. As if their muted outrage would make a difference.

Benn's voice was tight when he barked out, "Get her some food."

Though he hadn't said my name, I knew from his tone that his words were meant for me, and I stood. Others cast me glares of derision, as if *I* had offered food to the witch—food from our already dwindling rations—and not Benn.

Stumbling to our food sack, I fished out the dirtied hide, my stomach growling when I peeled back the layer to expose our dried strips of *rikcrun*. One of them was riddled with blue mold, but I stared at it longingly nevertheless.

Behind me, Benn grumbled, "We have very little food left, witch. Did you come all this way to eat it, or do you actually have the ability to break this curse, like you claim?"

"Feed me now, *vekkiri*, and I will ask Kakkari to bless us with a bounty so that you will not question my intentions again," the witch growled. As I approached with a strip of *rikcrun*, those red eyes were on me again, though they were angry now.

The witch's hand flew out and snagged my wrist when I deposited the dried rations before her. When I winced, she tightened her grip, but her voice was calm.

"Whatever magic Kakkari has given you, whatever it is that runs in this blood"—she cut my wrist with a flick of her black claws to emphasize her point, and I bit my lip as red blood trickled from the small wound—"she gave you an advantage over *us*, her true children."

My heart was beating rapidly in my chest, and fear was making me shake. I cried out when the witch leaned forward and licked the line of my blood from my wrist, smacking her lips together at the taste, her nostrils flaring.

"I have come to honor her wishes. I have come to find out *why*," the witch finished, her lips smeared with my blood. Finally, she flung my wrist away, and I stumbled back, the feel of her hot, sticky saliva on my flesh making my stomach roil. "*Why* can humans withstand this curse while the Dakkari and our creatures fall to it? You are weak where Dakkari are strong. Yet perhaps it is the Dakkari that need to realize that *vekkiri* are strong where *we* are weak. And it is only together that we can survive."

"Humans are not immune to the fog," Benn pointed out, though his eyes came to me, briefly, before his mouth pressed and he regarded the witch again.

"Humans are more immune to it than any of us. That is powerful in itself. I am told that even the *Dothikkar* does not yet know this," the witch said, and she brought the dried rations to her lips, tearing at the hunk of meat hungrily. Her teeth were filed and sharp. Some of my blood still decorated the corner of her mouth, and I felt that strange chill again, funneling through my body, making me want to *run*.

But where would I go?

"We can break this curse on the land. Together. I have seen it," the witch said, smiling through a mouthful of dry, chewy, grainy meat. "And once it is broken, we can claim our places on Dakkar once more. We will be worshipped and respected. We will never be hungry again. We will live *gilded* with Kakkari's touch. Even the *Dothikkar*, even all the *Vorakkar* will not be able to strike us down again. It is *us* that will strike *them* down. We will restore balance to Dakkar, and it will be *them* who kneel before us."

The witch's words rang out strong and clear in the dark forest. She'd come alone, but I knew there were others. Hearing her speak, hearing her certainty, hearing the humans behind me go still at her words, mesmerized by what she offered them...I understood why a coven of witches followed in her wake.

"And what do you ask in return?" Benn said, though his voice had gone soft. His gaze was rapt on the witch. "There is always a price."

The witch smiled, and it was blackened with *rikcrun* meat.

"All I ask is that you bring me the heart of a horde king."

There was a gasp behind me, and I stilled, staring at the witch in frightened disbelief.

"To break this curse, that is what I require."

As if sensing my stare, the witch turned to me. Her eyes moved over my body, calculating and assessing. I didn't know what she was searching for, but when she met my wide gaze, her smile widened.

"And I know how we can get one."

CHAPTER 2

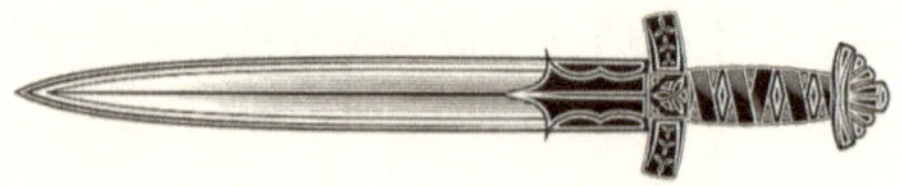

Okan was restless beneath me, stomping his taloned claws into the rocky earth, wheeling around before I clamped his chained reins tighter.

"*Pyroth*," I growled softly.

Hearing no give in my voice, my *pyroki* stilled, obeying the command. I pressed my palm to the side of his long neck, feeling the strong heart beating rapidly beneath it.

"*Pyroth*," I said, though gentler this time, before narrowing my gaze back over the Dead Lands. I could not see a single thing past the heavy red fog that blanketed them. The color of it was like *vekkiri* blood. Every passing day, as it got thicker and thicker, choking all life from inside it, it blackened.

The sun was rising over Dakkar, but the rays of light would not penetrate the fog. Before dawn, I had guided Okan up to the cliffside, one of the smaller mountains that dotted this land but one that offered a view of the East Lands in their entirety. Just like yesterday morning, the sight of the red fog made my shoulders tighten, made a grim scowl cross my features.

I maneuvered Okan to the right, taking the narrow, steep trail that led down toward the fog. My horde lay to the west, enough of a distance away where I didn't fear that it would be swallowed by whatever consumed the Dead Lands.

Once we reached the base of the mountain, I dismounted, swinging down and landing with a heavy thud on the hard earth.

"*Okkai,*" I rasped to Okan, the weight of my sword sheathed against my back comforting. My *pyroki* obeyed me once more, sticking to the black rock of the mountain as I ventured toward the fog.

The edges of it swirled and swayed, as if being blown by a breeze, though none ruffled my hair or drifted across my flesh.

Like little fingers, I thought, watching the fog reaching out toward me, growing in small increments, right before my very eyes. The growth had started slowly when it first appeared. But now, months later, every day it consumed more and more.

I felt the tendrils of the fog reach my legs. Behind me, I heard Okan give a warning, displeased huff, heard the way his claws stomped in irritation.

It felt cool, like it always did. It swirled and drifted through my trews, through my boots and my fur cloak. I gritted my teeth, my hand flexing instinctively for the sword at my back.

This is reckless, I knew. But I had been tasked with keeping watch over the Dead Lands after the *Vorakkar* of Rath Kitala left. He had been the first. I had been next in rotation. And as such, I would do whatever I could to learn about it, even at the expense of my strength.

As if alive, as if sensing what nourishment I could give it, the fog rippled around me. My vision went red with it. I could no longer hear Okan behind me. A dull rushing sounded in my ears. My heart throbbed. My lungs began to squeeze tight. My mind went heavy.

I grunted when my strength left my legs, when they began to feel like they weren't a part of me anymore, when I couldn't *feel* them at all.

I spied movement out of the corner of my eye.

For a brief moment, I forgot that I couldn't stay within the fog much longer. Because for a brief moment, I swore I saw a small figure, silhouetted among the swirling shroud. I stilled, wondering if I was beginning to hallucinate or not.

I blinked, heavy and slow, and then the figure was gone. Melted away—or perhaps it had never been there to begin with.

My limbs were like boulders as I flung myself away from the fog's grip. I surfaced through the other side of it.

Sound and smell and sight returned to me. Okan chuffed upon seeing me emerge and, disobeying my command, sprinted toward my side, my loyal beast quaking the earth with his bulk.

I leaned heavily against his side as I led us away quickly. When we reached the safety of the mountain, I sank down to the ground, my back to the black rock, trying to catch my breath. I felt drained. Spent. Like I'd been on the training grounds from morning to night. Or in the bed of a ravenous female or two, who had been eating away at me bit by bit.

How long was I in the fog? I wondered, furrowing my brow. It had seemed like brief moments, and yet the sun was much, much higher overhead than it'd been before I entered.

My temple began to throb, and with the last of my strength, I drew myself up and managed to climb onto Okan's back.

"*Vir drak ji vorak,*" I ordered him.

We ride for the horde.

"You went inside again," Valavik accused upon seeing me. "Didn't you?"

I grunted, leaning heavily upon the table in my council's *voliki.* Only Valavik, my *pujerak,* my second-in-command, was present.

Slowly, my strength was returning to me. My legs didn't feel like they would give out underneath my weight, at the very least.

"It grew toward me," I told him quietly, staring down at the map of Dakkar spread on the table. "Like it knew I was there. I felt it taking from me. I felt it *feeding* from me."

"*Vok*," Valavik cursed. "You must stop this, Rowin. Send a group of *darukkars* in your stead. They can take the fog in turns. It's too dangerous, too unpredictable."

There were only two beings that I knew of that were immune to the fog. The *Vorakkar* of Rath Drokka—the Mad Horde King, as they called him—and his human *Morakkari*, his queen, the white-haired sorceress that some believed had caused the red fog to billow out from the Dead Mountain.

Both possessed powers of Kakkari. Gifts from her, given to them at birth.

None in my horde, however, were immune to it. I certainly wasn't. And none of our creatures were either. The *pyrokis*. The *thespers*. Or the beasts that the fog had banished from the surrounding land.

I shook my head, reaching out to snag the skin of water on the table. Taking a long swig, I felt it soothe my throat, scratched and bone-achingly dry.

"How are our rations today?" I asked Valavik.

His lips pressed. "We have enough until the bright moon but not much more. The game is gone from these lands. Though we will receive aid from Rath Kitala and—"

"Send our hunters farther north," I ordered him, not liking the idea of relying on other *Vorakkar* to feed my own horde. It built a restless ache in my chest, as did our dwindling supplies. "No more than ten."

This season we had been meant to be far to the west, far from here. Yet duty called on us—on me—to stay in the East, where the land was depleted. Dead. Wasted and covered in a fog as red as *vekkiri* blood.

Valavik inclined his head. "I will."

For a moment, I debated telling my *pujerak* about the figure I'd seen in the fog. A small figure. Not Dakkari, nor Ghertun.

But I held my tongue, not entirely certain I *had* seen anything.

"Rowin," Valavik rasped, spearing me with a look that I recognized. "I know it is not my place to give you orders. But I beg you, stay away from the fog. For all our sakes."

My jaw tightened. It was not in my nature to run. To turn my back on something I deemed a threat. Dangerous. Especially if it was a danger to my own horde, to my own people.

"You are right," I said quietly, meeting Valavik's eyes. "It is not your place."

CHAPTER 3

"We can run, Mina," Tess whispered in the dark. Her words were forbidden and lush and so sweet that I could almost taste them on my tongue. "Before...before they make you..."

She trailed off.

Even Tess knew it was hopeless. I heard it in her voice.

"Whe-Whe-Whe—" I took a deep breath when I saw Tess's lips press. I tried again with, "And whe-where would we go?"

I finished the words in a rush, needing to get them out.

She took my hand, squeezing gently. "Jacob and the others returned north, didn't they? They followed the mountain range. We could find them."

It was dark, deep under the Dead Mountain. We'd gotten used to the stench, to the blackness. But the quiet was almost unbearable. The calm before the chaos.

I blew out a long sigh, disentangling my hand from Tess's before wrapping my arms around my body.

"I don't think we-we would ever find them, Tess," I whispered. "And ho-how far could we run before the f-fog found us?"

Tess leaned back. For a moment, she was angry. I saw it. But then her shoulders sagged. "That wouldn't matter for you."

"And food?" I asked.

She turned her head away, staring at the dark stone of the room we were in. It was damp, humid, which only made the stench all the worse. We'd found decaying Ghertun in this very place. I wasn't certain we'd cleared out all the remains either.

As if on cue, her belly growled. I heard her swallow.

"He would kill you if you left," I told her. I didn't speak his name. I hardly ever could, regardless. His name held my tongue and closed my throat until I felt like I couldn't breathe.

But Tess knew of whom I spoke. Of course she did.

"Benn wouldn't care," she said, but we both knew it was a lie.

Looking at her now, I would think Tess was broken. Her eyes were sunken in, her shoulders sagged. There was a quietness about her that had never been present before. Back in our village, before the Ghertun had destroyed it two years prior, she'd been boisterous and headstrong. *Alive.*

Given the world we lived in, I had often wished I possessed her confidence. Her optimism.

Tess was also smart, both then and now. She didn't show this side to anyone but me. This frightened, exhausted, hungry, vulnerable person she'd become. She hid it well.

Around the others, she drew herself up. She hardened her shell. She smiled coyly at Benn to keep him reined in. She didn't like weakness. And so she did everything she could to rid herself of it when we were not together.

When we passed one another, she pretended not to see me. When Benn struck me, she looked the other way.

Yet it was she who tended to my injuries, and in those moments, I felt her shame. Her helplessness. Because in some ways, she was more helpless than me.

"What will you do?" she asked me, peering at me with solemn brown eyes.

I didn't want to speak because I knew the words would not come out. Shaking my head, I swallowed hard. I gazed around the dark room, my stomach roiling with the thought that not a week ago, there were dead Ghertun here.

We guessed that the Ghertun had fled to the deepest parts of their mountain kingdom. The fog had not reached them here, though it had reached the upper levels. There, Ghertun had been paralyzed where they stood, unable to move, slowly dying from the red mist that suffocated them, that had wound around them like rope, eating from their bodies until there was nothing but a shell left of them.

Down here, however, the Ghertun had starved, unwilling to venture to the surface where the red fog swarmed in their halls and made its home there.

I could only imagine the horror they'd experienced. A part of me felt a tremor of pity, though I then remembered the screams of my village during its last night.

The anger felt good. I would choose anything over fear.

Grasping that anger, I let it lead the words from my lips, clear and even, and said, "I will do whatever is necessary to keep us safe. And once the fog is gone...we will leave this place. Together. And we will find the others."

If they aren't already dead, I added to myself silently.

Tess stared at me. Sometimes she looked frightened of me, and in those moments, I always wondered what she saw.

She shook herself and looked around the room we were preparing. For *him.* There was a stone slab in the center of the room, the reason why we'd chosen this one over all the others. There was a loop carved into the slab at the far end, where we'd be able to attach the chain. The room seemed to have been used for medicines, for Ghertun-made potions and tonics, judging by the vials and vases that lined the walls. Only a few remained, however. Most had been smashed, and I had painstakingly picked up every single shard yesterday so no one would cut their feet.

The Ghertun bodies had been removed. We were giving the room a final sweep to ensure that nothing could be used as a weapon, though Benn would inspect it soon. Black cuffs and a chain sat on the stone slab, a constant reminder of who they were intended for. The Dakkari witch had given them to Benn. They were supposedly made of the strongest metal on Dakkar, the only metal a Dakkari male could not break free from.

Even a horde king.

This will go so horribly wrong, I knew. A haphazard plan that was strung together with desperation and mad hope, sprung to life from the words of a witch.

It would never work. The wrath of a horde king would be immense, even if we managed to capture him. *Keeping* him here until the witches arrived was another mountain of a problem entirely. One we were not prepared to climb.

But it had to work. What other choice did we have?

"I wish I could go in your place," Tess confessed to me. "I wish that I could take that burden from you."

Strangely, her words made me bristle, though I felt her worry for me pouring from them. She had always seen me as weak. Her weakness to bear. Her weakness to protect.

She didn't think I was brave enough. Perhaps a part of her didn't think I was capable. Just like the others thought.

And yet I was the only one of us truly immune to the fog that had blanketed the East Lands.

And yet...even Tess didn't know what I could *truly* do inside the fog.

"Let's fin-finish," I said softly. "Before he comes."

Everything around me was red. Like a sunset had been painted before my very eyes. Streaks and swirls of vibrant color that swam around me, parting for me as I stepped into it. Trying to escape me, perhaps.

Others feared the fog. I knew, logically, I should too. I had seen what it had done to the Ghertun. I had seen what it had done to Benn's wife, to Karr, to Serina, to Matti too. Members of our village that had not made the crossing to the East Lands, who had succumbed to the reddened power.

Yet the fog meant safety for me. Walking into it felt comforting. I felt strong. Because I knew that no one could touch me here. No one could harm me here.

I was safe.

Truly safe.

The only danger to me was getting lost in it, which was why I'd left markers for myself. Peculiarly shaped rocks I'd found, a broken shard from a potion bottle with blunted edges pointing back toward the mountain, a scrap of brown cloth tied to a stick. All led me west. Toward *him*. Toward where we knew he visited every single morning.

We had been at the Dead Mountain for nearly two weeks. All the preparations were done. A group of females had left to hunt and to forage whatever they could find farther north. Mohamed had gone as well, to ensure that they returned. The rest of the men had stayed behind, however, because we might need all their strength to haul an unconscious horde king back to the Dead Mountain.

Tomorrow. We would attempt to capture the horde king tomorrow morning. They wanted me to lure him back to the mountain, which was a laughable idea. I was no siren, no great beauty that could seduce a horde king of Dakkar. But the Dakkari witch seemed to believe that if I came to him as an *offering*, if I told him that I was *his*, a gift from Kakkari herself, then he might be more amenable to my sudden presence.

The fog worked quickly. It fed on strength. The horde king would only need to be within it for mere moments before his strength would begin to leave him, before his mind would begin to blur and soften.

And I knew that this particular horde king entered the fog willingly. Two of our scouts who had eyes on his horde reported it. Just yesterday I had gone to see for myself, slipping from the Dead Mountain when I knew that Benn was sleeping, with Tess no doubt next to him.

I'd seen him. Though not very clearly. My sudden fear at his massive, shadowy size—a body that even the thick fog could not conceal—had me retreating quickly, though I feared he'd seen me.

It had been impulsive and foolish. And a part of me itched to go to the edge of the fog again. To see him clearly. To gaze upon his no doubt fearsome face. For horde kings seemed like mystical beings to us. Gods. Monsters. Devils. Demons.

All our lives, we had been taught to fear them. Now I was supposed to go to one willingly. I was supposed to bare myself to the beast in a ceremonial dress the witch had given me. I was supposed to let him touch my offered flesh, let him do whatever he wanted to me until the fog stole his mind and crumpled his legs under his bulk.

The Dakkari witch had even taught me the words to say to him.

"*Lo rune tei'ri, Vorakkar,*" I practiced.

I am yours, Horde King.

The words were frightening and beautiful. The cadence was soothing. Easy. I didn't stumble my way through them, which was thrilling in itself. I didn't feel them building in my throat, trapped and hammering at my tongue to get out. They released from me easily, as smooth as the words that came from everyone else.

"*Lo rune tei'ri,*" I practiced again.

Before I realized it, the red fog pushed away from me, leaving a bubble of clear air all around me. The fog seemed to hit a boundary, dispersing when it met it. Above me, the fog still shrouded the sky, but I saw its wispy tendrils trailing across the bubble, sliding their way down, as if trying to find a gap to slip inside.

It had happened before. Often, in fact. Possibly even before the fog.

Blowing out a breath, I spied one of my markers just on the edge of the invisible boundary. The glass shard, pointing back to the Dead Mountain. It was covered with a thin sheen of dust, and I crouched to wipe it away, in preparation for the morning.

I needed to get back. And yet a part of me wished to stay within the fog forever.

"*Lo rune tei'ri,*" I whispered, dragging my fingers over the earth. The fog didn't move. It hovered. Waiting. Always waiting.

For what, I didn't know.

CHAPTER 4

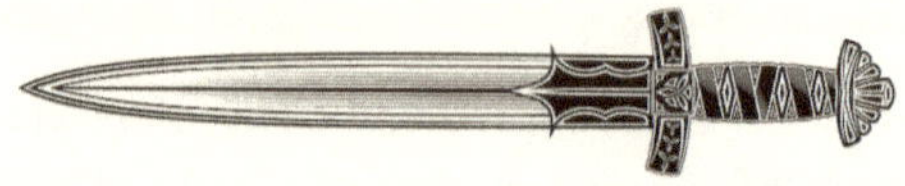

I rode from my encampment before the sun rose. The path toward the fog was so familiar to me now—and to Okan beneath me, for he traveled it without my lead.

How long will you continue this, Rowin? I pondered to myself.

I didn't know. Until I had answers, at the very least. The fog was an enigma. Never had one been reported or written about in our planet's history, as far as the *Vorakkar* knew. The priestesses of Kakkari, who lived in their mountain far to the north, where no male was allowed to enter, would know. They could give guidance.

But our messages to them had gone unanswered. As such, the horde king of Rath Okkili was traveling north this very moment, to speak with them. But the pass to their mountain was treacherous. It could be weeks before he reached them.

And they did not always respond to our calls for aid.

When I reached the edge of the fog, I didn't hesitate. I walked into it until it enveloped me, like walking into a lover's embrace. I felt it feeding off me the moment I entered.

Was Rath Okkili right? Was this Kakkari's punishment? Or was it Drukkar's wrath?

But for what? For the blood that was spilled at the Dead

Mountain? For the white-haired sorceress that had used Kakkari's heartstone? Or was our world out of balance? Was the earth sick?

"What is it that you want?" I growled softly, gritting my teeth, desperate for answers. "What do you seek from us?"

There was a rushing in my ears again. A buzzing sound that grew and grew.

Nik.

Voices, I realized, my heart thundering at the discovery. Or one voice speaking in many tongues at once.

I couldn't be certain. I stilled, closing my eyes to better discern what it was saying. I thought I caught a thread of one, but it slipped from my mind's grasp, skittering away. I swore I caught familiar words. Familiar words in the old language. The old language which hadn't been spoken for many, many ages.

A ragged breath escaped my lungs.

Whatever the fog was, whatever it was made of...it was an *ancient* thing. The thought sent a chill running down my spine.

Then I grunted, feeling those voices swarm into me, seeming to slide around my bones, to speak to me from the inside out. The sound was deafening. Almost unbearable. Then came the pain of it. Jagged and hot.

"Tell me what you seek!" I roared, though I couldn't hear my own words.

All at once, it went silent. The pain disappeared. In front of me, the fog had *retreated* from around me, leaving me standing in a small clearing, making me blink in dazed confusion even as I drew a lungful of much-needed breath.

Movement came to my right.

I whipped around, though disbelief made me freeze briefly.

On the edge of the fog, shrouded in wispy red tendrils, stood a female.

A *human* female.

My hand shot for my sword on instinct, gripping the hilt

where it was strapped behind my back, a growl rising from my throat.

I heard a hitched breath, and the female stepped back quickly. Around me, the fog began to close in again.

"*Pyroth!*" I rasped, trying to center my thoughts, for they were still jumbled from the fog. "*Okkai, kalles.*"

The fog stilled around me once more. I spied a shadow within, watching me. Waiting. Her figure was familiar to me. Achingly so.

"*Jiria,*" I ordered. In the universal tongue, I said, "*Come. Come to me, kalles. I mean you no harm.*"

On the edge of my vision, I saw the fog begin to travel toward me once more. Slowly. Creeping.

What was happening? I'd never seen it react like this before.

The fog swirled, and the human female stepped into the clearing. Over my head, my hand flexed on the hilt of my sword, my gaze dropping to the ceremonial dress that did nothing to conceal her body, my jaw slackening.

Like most of their race, she was bony and thin. Undernourished and lacking in apparent strength. And yet her skin was luminous, her eyes seeming to glow a light green, the color of which I'd never seen before. Her hair hung in a dark, wavy curtain around her, as black as night—like my own. Her small lips were parted as she stared at me, though her expression was unreadable.

Underneath the translucent Dakkari-made dress, spun from *Ulloi* silk, her full breasts were tipped with dark nipples. Large enough to fit within my palms perfectly. Her ribs were prominent, as were her hip bones, though her hips flared wide. Between her thighs, dark curls hid her *melir* from my gaze.

My blood began to rush, my heart speeding at the mere surprising sight of her. Slowly, my hand dropped from the hilt of my sword, and I saw her straighten slightly, which caused her breasts to tip up toward me. I preferred my females with lush curves, with evident strength that could handle the lusts and attentions of a horde king. Not small little creatures who I could break in half.

But there was no denying the heat in my *deva*. The fog in my mind, my slack jaw, my bated breath.

I shook my head. Was this another hallucination? I thought I'd spied a figure in the fog a couple days prior. But surely it hadn't been her? This waif of a creature.

Nik. With the exception of the white-haired *Morakkari* of Rath Drokka, no humans were immune to the fog. Yet this female was not buckling under the weight of it. Her chin was lifted, her eyes bright. With fear? With interest? *Lysi.* But certainly not with pain.

"You're not real," I murmured, my gaze rapt on her. I couldn't look away. I never *wanted* to look away from her.

She didn't say anything in response, though she took a step toward me. The fog billowed behind her. It began to close in around me once more. I felt the shadowy caress of a tendril against my clenched fist.

"Who are you?" I rasped, my brows furrowing. Her eyes were a shimmering green. *Mesmerizing.* Looking into them, I realized that I felt the sensation of spinning. "Are you her? The one I heard speaking?"

The ancient being in a human form? But why?

Nik. It couldn't be. None of this was real. The fog could conjure beings, voices. I needed to tell Valavik and the other horde kings—

"*Lo rune tei'ri, Vorakkar.*"

A gruff sound escaped my throat, my eyes going wide at the tempting, bold words that fell from her lips.

Her voice was...*vok*, like I always imagined Kakkari's voice. Pure and lyrical. Clear and sensual, given the words she offered to me so freely. Otherworldly.

Powerful.

Her steps toward me were hesitant. Though her last one, which brought her within a hand's span of me, seemed purposeful. The fog closed around us, though it didn't touch me or her. Like a cocoon.

The top of her head came up to the middle of my chest, though she was tall for a human female. Up close, I saw swirls of gold in her eyes. Kakkari's gold. She'd been blessed by the goddess. Dark lashes rimmed those eyes, long and thick. A smattering of small, brown spots were dotted across the bridge of her nose and the tops of her cheeks.

Enthralled.

I didn't want to look away from her, especially when her eyes captured mine so completely.

"Who are you?" I murmured, though my voice had softened considerably, an edge of wonderment creeping into my tone. My hand flexed. I *needed* to touch her.

"*Lo rune tei'ri,*" she told me, those full lips forming those perfect words.

I am yours.

My blood *throbbed* at the rightness of those words. They broke something free inside of me. Something forbidden, something ancient and ancestral that continued to course through my blood, after all this time.

A knowing, a *rightness*.

I wondered if *this* was what the *Vorakkar* of Rath Kitala felt when he stole a human female from her village and made her his queen. His *kassikari*. His fated one. A gift from the goddess herself.

Ever since, I had thought him undisciplined and weak. He'd chosen his selfish needs above what was best for his horde. For what did a human female know of being a queen to the Dakkari? I had decided long ago that I would not bind myself to a female for love or pleasure or temporary madness. I would only take a *Morakkari* for my horde who would strengthen it, who would bear me strong heirs that would continue to rule the wildlands long after I passed into the next world.

So why was I so incredibly tempted by the human female before me, who offered herself to me in the old way, with words that made my cock rise and my strength leave me?

Like the fog, she was making it difficult to think. Like the fog, she was feeding off me. That was my first clue that something was wrong.

She's not real, I told myself. Only a fantasy. An imagining.

I shook my head, feeling the fog creep closer.

Nik. This was wrong. It wasn't right. I only needed to clear my mind and—

Her touch was cool and electric. Her fingers grazed the back of my hand, tracing the thick veins that ran across it, mingled with the scars.

I shivered, a rough guttural growl falling from my throat. Her touch made my tail twitch, made my *deva* pulse.

"*Lo rune tei'ri, Vorakkar,*" she said again in a whisper.

The fog began to shroud my vision once more. She guided my hand to her waist, and the warmth of her flesh heated my blood. Instead of pulling away, my palm gripped her tight, as if I was afraid she'd disappear entirely, as quickly as she'd arrived.

Her touch found my other hand, and I watched with hooded eyes as she brought it up to her lips. With gentleness, like I was a beast that needed taming, her lips brushed a scar I'd received during the *Vorakkar* Trials, and I felt my cock throb with that softness.

She took a step backward, but since I was loath to release her, I followed her. My grip tightened. Was that a flare of alarm I spied in her eyes?

"What are you doing to me?" I demanded, though my tone was as gentle as her kiss as I followed her every step. I couldn't look away. Nothing could pull my gaze from hers. If she took it from me, I would do anything to reclaim it.

Again, she didn't speak, though her lips parted as though she was about to.

"You are mine, you say?" I rasped, my voice darkening. "Then give me your words again, *kalles*."

I tugged my hand away from her grip and cupped her jaw, tilting her small face up toward me. She felt real enough, warm and soft. But I still felt like my mind was swirling, like I was deep within a fog.

The fog...

What was I supposed to be remembering? The buzzing was starting again, though not as loud as before.

Nik, this wasn't right, this wasn't—

"Will you help me?" she asked, that goddess-like voice drawing my rapt attention.

She spoke in the universal tongue this time, and my brow furrowed in confusion. She saw the small movement and reached out to grip my wrist, stroking over the golden cuffs that bound my wrists. My *Vorakkar* cuffs.

"What is it that you need, *kalles*?" I asked. "Tell me, and I will give it to you."

"Take me back to your horde," she murmured, her eyes glowing. An expression flashed over her face. Surprise? "Please?"

Lysi.

Take her back to the horde. Back to my furs. And keep her there, came the thought, primal and so *vokking* right.

"I will," I vowed to her. Something nudged forward in my mind, just as the buzzing grew to dizzying heights. "I swear it to you, *kalles*. I will keep you safe."

Vok, how long had I been within the fog?

My head snapped up, though the movement felt slow, and I peered around us. A thin barrier of clear air kept the red fog at bay, but I realized...I realized I had gone too far inside it.

"This way," she whispered, stepping back again. My legs felt heavy, but I followed.

I shook my head. "*Nik. Nik, kalles*, my horde lies to the west."

"That is where we are going," she replied, her voice so beautiful to me that I nearly accepted her words as complete truth.

My brow furrowed. My temple was beginning to throb, even as my blood ran hot in my veins for this female, thickening my cock, making it hard to think, to *breathe,* even.

Nik.

My instincts rose, and I began to pull my hands away from her, disentangling myself from her enthralling touch. I heard her breath hitch.

"*Nik, kalles*, my horde is behind us, and we must hurry to—"

Her lips met mine.

Soft and warm and full and sudden.

Her kiss momentarily paralyzed me.

Then my hands returned to her, a savage groan pulled from my throat, as I crushed her to me, gripping her hard. Something was happening. Something I didn't have control over. Something I didn't understand.

All I knew was that *she*—whatever or whoever she was—was the cause.

I heard her shuddered gasp as I took what she freely offered me—no matter how foolish—lapping at her tongue as I felt her tight nipples drag against my chest. This was *right*. The feel of her in my arms, her warmth against me was perfection itself. *Sublime.*

My hands moved, pulling her closer. One hand slid into her wavy hair, tugging her head back so I could kiss her harder. I heard her gasp. Her heart raced against my flesh as I cupped my hand over her breast, squeezing and stroking, as I succumbed to my desire, as mad as it was.

"*Lysi*," I growled against her, my voice thick, sounding far, far away. "*Vok*, I want you, *kalles*."

A rush of cool air came.

My eyes snapped open, and all I saw was red.

In the next moment, the roaring of the voices returned and my head felt like it would split wide open. Stunned and groaning, I stumbled back from the female, my legs finally relinquishing their strength.

They buckled underneath me, pain scraping me from the inside out, my lungs so tight that I couldn't breathe.

And yet my gaze never left hers. Even as more figures appeared on the edge of the fog. Dark figures. Males.

Human males.

In the fog.

Near *her*.

Mine.

I growled, trying to reach for the hilt of my sword. But my arm didn't move. I had no strength left.

"He's not out yet," one of the males said, hesitant, fear evident in his voice.

I snarled, trying to kick out with my useless, unresponsive limbs.

One of the males tossed the female a dark cloak, and I watched as she drew it around herself, shielding her body quickly.

Realization shot through me, just as the edges of my vision began to blur.

"Don-Don-Don't h-hurt him," I heard her say, though her voice was changed. Tinged with fear and hesitation, nothing like the calm, gentle words she'd spoken before.

She'd done this to me, I realized. Enthralled me with something unseen, until all I saw was *her*. Until all I could think about was *her*.

Sorcery.

I roared with the last of my strength, enraged with that knowledge. Enraged with my own weakness, a weakness I had never known I possessed.

My father had been right. Females brought about the downfall of males. Females were the most powerful beings in this universe.

And I had walked straight into one's clutches, turned my back on my horde—and everything I had worked so hard to build.

Gone in a moment. A single moment of madness.

As I glared into the female's eyes, I watched her take a step back, as if she saw my hatred, my loathing within. Her lips were still reddened from my kiss, and the thought made my belly roil, that she had had her claws so deep into me.

With my remaining breath, I vowed, "I will make you regret this, *sarkia.*"

Witch.

"I swear it on Kakkari."

Her eyes widened.

"We don't have time for this! Take him," came a dark voice. "*Now.*"

Something heavy crashed against my temple.

Those luminous, fearful green eyes were the last thing I saw.

Chapter 5

I was shaking, my heart thundering in my breast, so quick and hard that I feared it would beat right out. Was that possible? Was that a thing that could happen to humans?

I was about to find out.

"Grab him on the other side," Kyl ordered Jacques.

The men could barely lift the horde king from the ground. The Dead Mountain still lay a distance away, and they were running out of time to bring him there. Before the fog wove into their own bodies and began to feed.

Kyl, Jacques, Emmi, Taylor, and Benn all crowded around the horde king. They managed to get him up—Kyl slinging one of his arms around his shoulders, Jacques taking the other side. With the others' strength, they managed to begin moving him, though his long, heavy legs dragged across the rough terrain behind him. He was bleeding from his temple where Taylor had brought the blunt end of his spear down to knock him unconscious.

His head was rolled back, his eyes closed, though his expression was still fearsome.

"Shit," Emmi murmured in disbelief. "We actually have a *horde king*. We actually did it."

"And we better hurry to get him chained up before he wakes," Kyl growled in annoyance, especially since he was bearing most of the male's weight. "Or else we're all dead."

Those words sobered them all. I stood rooted in place, still clutching the cloak around my body, feeling my heart in my throat. The fog swirled around me, and I watched them disappear into it.

I realized I wasn't alone when Benn's footsteps crunched toward me. He held a cloth over his nose and mouth but those eyes were rapt on me, and I could see that he was pleased.

"Perhaps you have your uses after all, Mina," he said. I barely concealed my flinch when he ran his fingers over my cheek. "You nearly got him all the way to the Dead Mountain."

My lips felt swollen from the horde king's kiss. My skin was so sensitive that I could feel the rough scrape of the old, ratty cloak against it. My senses, despite the fog, felt overstimulated.

And underneath it all, I felt a deep sense of shame. Of dread. Because in that moment, I realized that I had set something into motion that I wasn't entirely certain was the right path.

"I wonder what it is he saw in you," Benn continued, his voice a rumble, and I tensed when his fingers loosened my cloak. I felt the tendrils of the fog rush in, over the transparent dress I wore. A rough sound emerged from Benn's throat as his gaze roved over me. "I think I know, however. The mind of a child and the body of a woman."

I saw his hand move.

In a rush, before he touched me, I began to ask, "Can I-I-I go ba-ba-ba—"

With a sound of impatience, of disgust, he withdrew his hand from the edges of my cloak, and I wrapped my body tight once more. Benn hated when I spoke. It was why he'd never touched me, not in the way he touched some of the other women. And mostly Tess.

For that alone, ever since Benn had taken over leadership of our group, there was a part of me that was thankful for the way I spoke. I saw a blessing there that I'd never seen before.

And yet when the horde king touched me, I spoke more clearly than I ever had before, I couldn't help but recall.

I didn't know what that meant. Or why, considering my nerves had been jumbled and my fear had been high during those moments with him. At least at first.

Benn turned to leave, back toward the mountain, and I waited briefly before I followed.

When I reached the entrance, my head tilted back. I saw the yawning open mouth of the Dead Mountain with red fog billowing in and out. There was no soul in sight.

As always, a chill raced up my spine when I looked up at the mountain looming before me. It had been at the Dakkari witch's insistence that we keep the horde king here. She claimed it was where this all began and it was here that it needed to end.

Benn had been worried about the Ghertun when we first entered. But none within the mountain had survived. The fog had roamed the land for many moon cycles now. It had killed Ghertun in the upper levels quickly. The ones who'd gone below, where we all now resided, had been taken by hunger and thirst and darkness.

It might not be long before we suffer the same fate, I thought.

And I didn't want to die in a place like this.

Not with fear and horror constantly curling in my veins.

Quickly, I rushed inside, drawing the cloak around me tighter and tighter, as if it could make me disappear. The Dead Mountain was a kingdom of mazes. The upper floors were labyrinths of long, tunneled hallways, which all led to a vast throne room, where we'd found piles and piles of decaying Ghertun.

The lower levels were connected by chiseled stairways, some

impossibly wide, some so narrow I couldn't imagine Ghertun squeezing through them. This place was littered with them, and it had taken a few days to remember the correct pathways down to where we lived, where the fog did not reach. It was there that we would keep the horde king until the Dakkari witches arrived.

I wound my way down, the darkness overwhelming as I didn't have a torch with me. When I descended the fifth set of stairs and stopped on the landing, I saw a glow of light at the end of the hallway and I hurried toward it. The medicine room. Now it would be a prison.

Tess found me first. Her eyes were wide and worried, though relief shone in them when she saw me unharmed. She'd been waiting for me, it seemed.

"You did it. Oh, I've been so worried," she whispered, taking my hands in her own, rubbing warmth into them. She frowned. "You're shaking, Mina."

I hadn't been able to stop.

My eyes didn't leave the doorway of the medicine room, where a vibrant, golden glow from the torches shone within.

"Is...is h-he all right?" I whispered quietly.

Her brow furrowed.

"The horde king?" she asked carefully, peering at me closely.

In the next moment, Benn strode from the room, and Tess stepped back from me quickly. Dangling from his grip was the horde king's sword, though I didn't linger on it. I didn't meet Benn's eyes either. Instead, I directed my gaze to the floor, at the smooth, softened edges of the stone.

"Is he secure?" Tess asked, stepping toward Benn. I didn't know how she did it. I didn't know how she smiled as she touched him, how she sighed as he kissed her.

I rubbed my lips with trembling fingers, remembering the horde king's heat there, remembering my gasp meeting his deep groan. Then I clenched my fist, lowering it back to my side as I shivered.

Foolish girl, I thought, my jaw tightening.

"Yes," Benn grunted, just as the other men trickled from the room, Kyl sagging against the wall, trying to reclaim his breath. "Kyl, go inform the others we have the horde king. Emmi, take the first watch."

"Now comes the hard part," Emmi grumbled, crossing his arms over his chest, leaning against the wall.

"You," Benn growled, and I knew that his eyes were on me. When I lifted my chin, he said, with a slight tone of delight in his voice, "When he wakes, you will tend to him."

I froze, remembering the hatred I spied in the horde king's eyes, just before Taylor knocked him unconscious.

Jacques shifted in the hallway, straightening, and I sensed Emmi exchanging a look with Taylor.

Jacques said quietly, "Perhaps another of the women, Benn. You heard him—it sounded like he wanted to kill her where she stood. Once he wakes, he will remember her."

"The rest of the women have other duties," Benn said. "Most of them are on the hunt, regardless. I forbid Tess from going near him. And I don't think you want Kaila going near him either, do you, Emmi?"

Emmi's lips pressed together tight at the sound of his lover's name. His pregnant lover. He looked at me...and then looked away, down the darkened hallway, acknowledging Benn's words without saying anything.

My wild eyes met Jacques's. His lips parted before he raked a hand through his graying hair. "I'll look after him, Benn. The women shouldn't be so close to him anyway, and—"

Benn stepped toward Jacques, cutting off his words abruptly. Though Jacques was only a few years older than Benn, he was no match for his height and strength.

"I say that *she* goes to him," Benn said softly, the quiet

words deadlier than any curse or shout. Jacques's jaw clenched. "And if he kills her, then that's one less mouth to feed."

"And what about her immunity to the fog?" Jacques asked. I was surprised he dared to speak again. "We might need her again."

"You were perfectly fine with letting her walk right up to the horde king not long ago. We were *all* fine with it. He could have killed her in a single moment. So what's changed now?" Benn asked, opening his arms wide, his face taking on an expression of careful confusion. The tip of the horde king's sword dragged across the stone, making a scratching sound that made my spine tingle. "She's expendable. The other women are more valuable to us than she is. And soon the fog will be gone, so what use is she, really?"

Jacques didn't speak again. He didn't look at me again, while I still stood trembling.

The confusion dropped as suddenly as it arrived on his features, and Benn grinned, clapping Jacques on the shoulder. "It's settled, then."

My fist clenched again.

"Come, Tess," Benn barked out, sliding his arm around her waist and pulling her against his side. He started down the long hallway, the one that led to a short flight of narrow stairs, down to where he'd claimed his private quarters. "Alert me when the horde king wakes," he tossed over his shoulder to the rest of the men.

Tess held my eyes for a brief moment, but then she left with Benn, turning her back. I was rooted in place as silence stretched, long and thick. Then my feet were moving. Jacques's head turned to watch as I moved to the threshold of the door.

And there he was. Stretched out on the cold slab of stone in the center of the room, the horde king lay. He was on his side, his hands cuffed and pulled over his head, leading to a single, short chain attached to the chiseled loop in the stone. As thick as it was, I wondered if he could break the carved loop. Because the Dakkari witch assured us the metal chain links were unbreakable, but what about the stone?

For good measure, his feet were cuffed too, though they were not attached to the slab like his hands were. He would still be able to stand, to move around—though not far given the short leash of the chain.

Long black hair obscured most of his face from view, but I shivered, remembering his features in my mind's eye. Glowing red eyes, high cheekbones so sharp that I wondered if they could cut like a blade, a broad nose which gave way to a serious, full, wide mouth.

His massive body, constructed with thick slabs of muscle, was one made for war, for violence. I remembered looking up at him when we were surrounded by the fog. I remembered thinking that he seemed like the mountain ranges that dotted this land, unmovable and endless and unforgiving.

Darkly handsome and grimly beautiful in a way I hadn't expected, he'd stolen my breath straight from my lungs. I'd never seen a Dakkari male up close before, much less a horde king. And I could understand why *this* male had been given such a title of power over the others.

I watched his chest rise and fall, and I felt a strange sense of relief course through me. Only until I saw the state of his legs. He was wearing a black hide tunic that covered the bulk of his chest, but his legs were bare, his lower region covered with a long, triangular fur cloth that hung to his knees, tied around his hips with a thick, woven strap.

When the men carried him toward the Dead Mountain, his legs had been dragging on the ground, scraping against rock and debris. From his knees to his booted feet, the skin was broken and ravaged, black with blood and smeared with the brown, clay-like dirt that stretched across the East.

I couldn't refuse Benn's order. That I knew. Even as certainly as I knew that the horde king might try to kill me once he woke.

I will make you regret this, sarkia. *I swear it on Kakkari,* he'd told me. A vow. An unshakeable promise. The words had been soft yet dangerous. I'd heard his roar of outrage and fury when he realized that I'd led him toward the others. He'd told me he would keep me safe—words that nearly made me cry, that filled my breast with such longing and grief—and in the end, I'd betrayed him without hesitation.

That *glare*—filled with his derision and hatred and sudden understanding—would haunt me even in sleep.

I didn't know him. He didn't know me. So why did it feel like I did?

I set my jaw.

I turned from the room, making for the upper levels where a well of water still ran, clear and full. I felt Jacques's gaze on my back as I left.

The horde king's wounds needed tending.

And I better tend them before he wakes, I knew.

CHAPTER 6

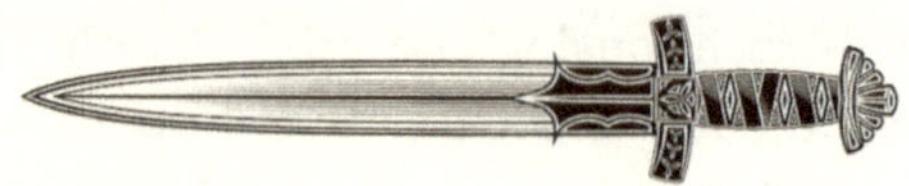

When I came awake, I swore I could smell the scent of the North Lands. The icy, unforgiving land where I'd been born, where I'd grown. The North Lands that had nourished me while also taking from me.

I swore I could smell the land—the crisp air that seemed to spear one's lungs—just after a storm. The violent pellets of rain that released a fragrance, perfuming the air with a refreshing scent of *luria* blooms and the musky smell of *kenuv* oils.

I both loved and hated when it stormed in the North. I loved the calmness, the quiet reverence that seemed to descend among our *saruk*. And yet after a storm, my father had always trained me hardest. He hated the rain. It made him remember his days of war in the Southeast.

After those stormy days, when the air was chilled and hushed, he battled me to a bloody pulp and wasn't content until my sword was dulled from his strikes and my body was battered.

The *Vorakkar* scars from the Trials in *Dothik* were nothing compared to the scars my father had given me.

When my eyelids lifted to darkness, I sensed movement at my legs, but I held still. My temple was throbbing, my mouth was dry, and my strength was gone. Exhaustion pulled at me, trying to lure me to sleep once more, but I fought to process what had happened.

When I lowered my gaze down the stretch of my body, I saw *her*.

The female.

The *vokking* witch.

I felt rage swell like a wave, but I kept it close and tight. Emotions were a weakness. Stronger ones even more so.

She didn't know I was awake. She was standing, hunching over me, and was...tending to my legs. I felt the sting of them before my gaze adjusted to the dim light, and I saw the skin was torn and bloodied. I didn't know how they'd gotten into such a state. I didn't remember anything after...

The fog. *Her*, with her bewitching gaze and beautiful voice.

She'd set a trap for me. And like an unwitting beast, I'd followed her into it without hesitation.

Me.

The *Vorakkar* most considered cold to the point of cruelness.

Nothing about me had felt cold in the fog, when I'd been with her, however. My body had burned, my blood had rushed hot.

Her touch was gentle as she blotted a gray cloth against my wounds. The water was ice cold, but I was glad for it. It helped numb the flesh.

My wrists were shackled in cuffs, but I didn't want to move my head to see where they were tethered. I was in a dark, circular room. The air was cold yet...damp. Humid. Only a single torch was lit, casting the room a soft gold, the light flickering off walls of stone. Black stone. Like the mountains that littered this Kakkari-forsaken land.

I was lying on a table of sorts in the center of the room. Hard and unyielding underneath me. My gaze darted to the left, and I saw horizontal rows had been chiseled into the wall. They were mostly empty, though a few vials and bottles were nestled comfortably there. Underneath the chiseled rows, there was a long stone table, though it was lower in height than the one I currently lay on. A workbench, I realized.

There was nothing else in the room, as small and circular as it was. Not even a fire basin to warm it.

My gaze flicked back to the human female standing near my legs. I watched as a long tendril of black hair escaped from behind her ear. I felt the brush of it tickle my bare thigh, felt the icy cloth freeze on my skin, and heard her breath hitch. In fear? Fear I would wake?

Too late, sarkia, I thought.

Her eyes darted to mine. I watched them widen in realization. Realization that I'd been watching her. Did that make her uneasy?

Good.

"Who are you?" I asked quietly, narrowing my gaze on her, watching as she stumbled back from the table, her backside hitting the workbench a few paces away.

I remembered males with her. Males that had no doubt dragged me here, where they'd shackled my wrists.

Where were they now? And how many of them were there?

"M-Min..." She took a deep breath, cutting off whatever she was about to say. Then I saw her gaze dart. To the door.

When I tilted my head downward, I saw the door was wide open. Beyond it was more torchlight, and I swore I caught the snores of a slumbering male. A guard?

Now that I moved my head, I saw that my feet were shackled. My eyes narrowed further when I saw it was Dakkari steel. *Blackened* Dakkari steel.

Vok.

I looked at my wrists. The same.

A short chain ran from the cuffs, and I pulled, feeling it snap taut. They were anchored around a loop in the stone.

Angered disbelief coursed through me. They thought to *imprison* me?

My tail flickered in irritation—

They didn't secure my tail, I realized.

Vokking *fools,* I thought next.

"Mina," came her quiet voice.

I almost growled when I met her eyes again. I saw her hand was placed over her breast and realized that she'd just told me her given name.

I almost grinned, though I felt no such amusement.

"You think I give a *vok* about your name, *sarkia*?" I asked. The word meant *witch* in Dakkari. Her lips parted, and she moved to take another step back, as if sensing the venom in my otherwise even tone. "What I truly want to know is why a group of *vekkiri* think they can capture a *Vorakkar* without retribution?"

Her breaths came faster. I heard her swallow in the quiet.

"What I truly want to know is who wishes to die first?" I asked, my voice softening into a purr.

It surprised me when she took a step *toward* me. It surprised me when she didn't scramble for the door like I'd expected her to, this skittish, fearful creature.

And yet...she hadn't seemed afraid earlier. When she'd come to me wearing next to nothing and dragged me toward her for a kiss...

That was when I remembered.

The fog...it had *moved* around me. There had been clear air between us, as if she'd controlled the movements of the fog.

Had she been *shielding* me from it?

Perhaps she had. And yet she'd let it close around us the deeper she'd ventured inside it. Until I was trapped. Until it was too late.

Lo rune tei'ri, she'd murmured to me in that sinful voice.

My fists clenched in the cuffs.

Perhaps I would hold her to her ancient vow.

I almost felt the restlessness softening within me at the thought. *Lysi,* I would get my revenge. And she would be the last one to feel my vengeance once I slaughtered all the rest. And it would be *her* that I would savor even as I brought about her destruction.

"You-Your legs..." She trailed off. She seemed to pull herself up, and I watched—in mild fascination, as I would study any enemy—as her chin lifted and her words came strong. "I need to finish cleaning them. And your head...you're bleeding there too."

Was I?

Maybe that accounted for the splitting headache.

Do not give in to anger, I reminded myself. What had my father always taught me to do?

Observe, assess, and then act.

I'd survived the *Vorakkar* Trials because of those very words. I'd successfully led a strong horde across the wildlands for *years,* centering my core principles on those very words.

Those green eyes tore into me, and I stared right back into them.

Again, I felt something between us. That undercurrent of energy I'd felt before. *Recognition.* My nostrils flared. Kakkari's guiding hand.

When the males had approached us in the fog earlier, she'd pleaded with them not to hurt me. For a reason? Because I had a greater purpose here?

Or...was it because she felt that same vulnerability with me? That same feeling of *knowing?*

I can use her, came the thought. *Easily.*

But I would have to tread very carefully. I could be a patient male. I would have to be if I ever wanted to determine what the *vok* was going on here.

When I didn't respond to her soft words, she moved toward

my legs once more. I saw her cast another long look at the door, which was slightly slanted on crooked hinges, not unlike the doors in the *saruk* where I'd grown up.

Where is this place? I wondered again, brow furrowing.

The *sarkia* took up the gray cloth once more, swished it around in a small basin of water, which sloshed over the sides, and pressed it against my battered shins. I ignored the pain, using the time to study the female who had so easily led me to my own prison.

And I wondered what I had ever seen in the first place. The female was changed. She wore a drab tunic that at one time might have been white and loose, dark trews that she kept on her hips with a rough, tan cord. In that dark, circular room, the shadows under her eyes seemed prominent and the color was leached from her face, making her appear ashen and sickly.

She seemed scared of her own shadow. Her hands trembled as she brought the cloth to my fresh wounds, and I got the sense that she was keeping an eye on the door. For whom? Or what?

To be brought so low by a female like *this*—this timid, wretched creature—it was a humiliation I didn't think I would ever see past.

And yet...

My jaw clenched remembering the shock of seeing her emerge from the fog. Her lush breasts, her flared hips. Those glowing eyes, the color of which I'd never seen before. Her skin had seemed to radiate the sun, and her touch had sped my heart in my chest.

It had to be sorcery of some kind. She'd walked within the fog freely. Was there a magic that the humans, the *vekkiri*, had discovered to make them immune? Was there a magic they'd discovered that enabled them to *control* the fog?

Perhaps my being here was more of a blessing than I'd first realized. Perhaps *this* was what I was seeking. Answers.

And I wondered if the little creature at my feet could tell me what I wished to know.

If she has incentive, perhaps she will, I thought.

The female—Mina—worked in silence, tucking her dark hair behind her ear every time it slipped down. A little frown of annoyance—one she probably didn't realize she was making—crossed her features whenever it did.

Every few breaths, her gaze would flick up to me. I tried to soften my glare each and every time, reminding myself that I could use this female. I needed her trust.

When she finished with my legs—though they were clean, she didn't wrap them in bandages, instead leaving them open to the damp air—she hesitated.

"Your...temple," she murmured, the words rushing out quickly, though they sounded oddly stretched out.

My eyes narrowed as I watched her approach. She stutter-stepped when she heard my chain links jingle together, but I forced my hands to still.

"Yes?" she whispered.

A small grunt came from my throat. I didn't want her hands on me, but what choice did I have?

Her touch was gentle, though her expression was frightened. As if I'd bite her the moment I had the opportunity.

When I drew in a breath, I stilled. Because I realized that the scent I'd recognized before—of *luria* blooms and storms—was from *her*. My gaze flashed to hers, and I fought the impulse to drag her scent into my lungs once more.

"Where are we?" I asked when she dabbed the cloth at my temple, where I felt a stinging sensation.

She froze. She didn't meet my eyes. A moment later, her hand moved to dip the cloth in the water basin once more, and I felt an icy drop of water slide down my cheek before traveling behind my neck.

Without thinking, I caught her wrist when she moved

toward me again. Though my hands were cuffed, the chain running from them allowed a decent amount of freedom.

She didn't gasp or cry out, like I braced myself for. Instead, she stilled. Instead, her other hand came to rest on my own, like she would attempt to pry off my grip. Only...when our flesh met, her fingers gentled. I felt the pad of her thumb rest over an old, raised scar on the back of my hand.

For a moment, I forgot what I'd intended to do. Her skin radiated warmth. Her scent was...*vokking* divine.

When our eyes met, I saw her lips were parted. Surprised too? I felt my heart begin to pump mightily in my chest.

This is why I'm here, came the realization. One touch from her and I was...*weak.*

Why?

The mere idea made me furious, that this slip of a female had control over me in ways I didn't understand. Yet my grip around her wrist gentled.

"Where are we?" I tried again, my tone soft. Unrecognizable.

Her throat worked. I saw her pink tongue dart between her parted lips. A tongue I had stroked with my own when we kissed.

My teeth ground together at the memory.

Finally, she answered.

"Dead Mountain."

This time, it was I that froze.

Then I heard her gasp, saw her head whip toward the door, where I heard footsteps echoing.

"Emmi," came an annoyed voice. "Wake up! What the hell are you thinking?" A pause. "Shit, where's Mina?"

Then the owner of that voice stood in the threshold of the door. A dark-haired, slim human male. His face looked gaunt, the hair nearest his temples graying. Like Mina, he wore a dirtied tunic and trews, though his didn't seem as loose on him.

"Mina," he rasped out, his eyes widening when he saw me awake, with her wrist in my grasp. "Let...let go of her! *Now*."

I bristled at the order in his tone. This human thought to command *me*?

When I looked back to the female, I saw that her eyes were wide with panic. But I didn't get the sense that she feared *me*.

"P-Please," she whispered.

My brow furrowed, and with flared nostrils, I released her wrist. She stumbled away, the basin of water tumbling over the edge of the table I lay on. She didn't make a sound as the bloodied water rushed over the floor.

"Mina," the male hissed, prowling toward her. "Stupid girl! What the hell were you thinking, getting that close to him?"

I growled when the male reached for her. Loud and rough. A warning.

The male froze, his hand hovering in the air. Mina's head snapped toward me from where she'd tucked herself against the workbench. I heard her swallow and then saw her gaze dart back toward the male.

"I-I-I'm so-sorry, Jacques," she stumbled out.

The male glowered at her.

"You're as half-witted as Benn says," the male continued. "Clean this up and then get out."

I watched the exchange with curiosity even as restlessness rose in me. The careful, blank expression the female wore told me this was no odd occurrence. Her movements were quick and efficient. She didn't utter a single sound as she collected the water basin, soaking up the majority of the water with the cloth. It landed in the empty bowl with a wet sound, but then she hesitated.

Her eyes darted to me. I saw her throat bob with her swallow as the human male watched on from the corner.

"*Now*," he said, though his tone was a little gentler than before.

"I'm sorry," Mina said, her eyes catching mine.

A long sigh came from the male she'd called Jacques. "Just go, Mina. Go eat. There's some rations left for you upstairs."

The male thought she'd apologized to him again.

My brow furrowed when I realized she'd been apologizing to *me*.

She felt...guilt. For her deceit? For leading me here?

And where there was guilt, there was weakness.

I nearly grinned, but I watched with narrowed eyes as she darted from the room, not looking at me again. Weakness I could exploit. That weakness would be what freed me from this prison.

Turning my head, I saw the human male watching me. I showed him my teeth, especially considering he looked wary. His nostrils flared, he took a step back and then seemed to catch himself.

Another male appeared behind him. The one who I assumed had been snoring in the hallway, the lazy guard. In my horde, he would have been sent back to *Dothik* had I caught him.

They were undisciplined. Disorganized. Leaving the door open to my chambers and not chaining my tail. Letting a female of theirs freely enter without supervision, when I could have easily killed her.

What kind of place was this? And who was the leader that took responsibility for this?

"Send for Benn," Jacques told the bleary-eyed male. "Tell him the horde king is awake."

It seemed like I was about to find out.

CHAPTER 7

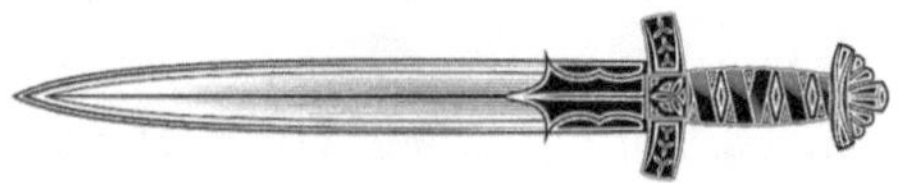

Now that I was alone, I tested the cuffs encircling my wrists. They were tight around my own *Vorakkar* cuffs, the golden metal that the *Dothikkar* had placed on me shortly after completing the Trials. A symbol of service to Dakkar, to my horde.

Just as I suspected, the chain was blackened Dakkari steel. Unbreakable. Next, I tugged on it. It attached to a thick loop in the stone table, which was situated just above my head. Tugging hard, I felt the cuffs bite into my flesh and felt the tension of the chain snapping tight—but the loop didn't give. With time, however, perhaps I could weaken the stone.

Examining my shackles, I saw that they could only be released with a key. But the weapons master at my horde, the *mitri*, worked with Dakkari steel often. Perhaps he could release them if I managed to escape the chain.

I paused.

Then again, if what the female said was the truth, I was in the Dead Mountain. Likely deep underground.

At first, I had dismissed her words.

Surely the humans would've succumbed to the red fog long before we reached the entrance of the Ghertun's stronghold.

And even then...where were the Ghertun? We had long suspected them dead...or that they had gone deep underground to hide from the fog. We didn't know how it affected them, but many died the day that the human queen of the *Vorakkar* of Rath Drokka used Kakkari's heartstone here.

None had spotted a single Ghertun since.

Had they truly been wiped out? Had the humans found a tunnel that led inside the mountain and decided to make their home here in the Ghertun's absence?

That seemed the likeliest of possibilities.

It still didn't explain why *I* was here, however.

Escape would be difficult if we were in the Dead Mountain. Because endless fog blanketed this place and these lands. Just like it had earlier, the fog would take my strength quickly. I would never reach the edge of it before that happened.

And my horde...

Valavik, my *pujerak*, would realize that something was amiss when I didn't return for the morning training session. Or if Okan returned without me. He probably knew already, was probably rounding up *darukkars* to lead a search for me.

I growled in frustration, pulling at my chain. The last thing I wanted were my *darukkars* venturing into the fog for me, risking their lives for me. Valavik had warned me to stay away from this place, and yet I had done what I thought would serve us best.

In the end, I'd doomed myself.

I thrashed at the chain, twisting and pulling for long moments. My nostrils flared with the effort. The majority of my strength had yet to return to me. My head was throbbing and my throat felt like I'd swallowed a mouthful of sand.

Save your strength, I told myself, forcing myself to still when the chain didn't budge.

I would need it.

My skin prickled just then, and my gaze flashed to the door.

Torchlight flickered underneath it, and a moment later, I heard the handle unlatch and then the door creaked open on old hinges.

The first thing my gaze zeroed in on was *my vokking sword.*

A low growl escaped me when I saw a human male's hand around its hilt. The sword made for me. The sword my father had marked with his blood. He'd purposefully made it to match the size of a *Vorakkar's* sword. When he'd gifted it to me, I could barely lift it, as young as I was. He'd told me I would grow strong enough to wield it, and he'd been right. I knew that sword like it was a part of me, like it was an extension of my own soul.

The handle was smooth from years of use. Every night, I cleaned its blade. Over the years, it had been soaked with Ghertun blood, with Dakkari blood, with Kakkari's earth, with the rain, with the frost, with the desert.

The male that was wielding it was unremarkable. If I had seen him in one of the human settlements before, I would have forgotten his face the moment I looked away. His skin was almost the same color as my own, nourished from the sun, and yet that was where our similarities ended. He had eyes so dark they appeared black and brown hair, cropped short to his scalp. Dakkari males with short hair were either young boys or disgraced *darukkars,* and my lip curled with distaste.

He appeared stronger than the other two males I'd seen. At least, his face wasn't gaunt and sunken with apparent hunger. His chest was wide and his trews fit snugly on his legs.

I assumed this was the humans' leader. A leader who ate before his own people was no leader at all, however. Not in my eyes.

Benn, they'd called him.

He walked to the edge of the table where I lay, though he had the good sense to stay out of reach. My sword flashed in the torchlight, and he dug the tip of it into the stone floor, twirling it like it was a cane.

My ire grew, my claws digging into the flesh of my palms.

With my tail twitching, I was half-tempted to snag my sword from his grip with it. My tail would curl around the handle, and I'd plunge it into his belly, just for daring to take it from me.

Patience, I reminded myself. Somehow, they had Dakkari-steel cuffs in their possession, but they didn't know about a Dakkari's tail or the strength of it. I needed to save that advantage for later.

"You are not as formidable as I thought you'd be," the human male started, his voice soft and echoing around the tall room. "I expected much more fight from a horde king."

I grinned, which seemed to take him off guard for a moment.

"And yet," he continued, "our weakest woman managed to capture you quite easily. Then again, I've seen Dakkari females. I shudder at the thought of bedding them too."

The grin slid from my face, a growl rising in its place.

"What is it that you think to do with me, *vekkiri?*" I asked, no longer feeling the amusement I'd felt moments before. This human was alive right now because I allowed it. But if he pushed me too far, I might do something that would prove foolish later.

Though I'd never *regret* killing a human like this, I would regret the error in judgment from killing him too soon.

"You think to trade me back to my horde for...*neffar*? Food? Weapons?" I asked, narrowing my gaze. That was the only reason for my capture that I could think was plausible. They were obviously hungry. And desperation was unpredictable.

The human male smiled. "Now, why hadn't I thought of that?"

Ah. Perhaps he was more cunning than I gave him credit for. His answer gave nothing away.

Very well. Next, I wanted to see his reaction to anger.

"A male like you is not worthy of a sword like that, *vekkiri*," I said, keeping my voice even. "Do you know what it is that you wield?"

"Yes," he answered, though I saw his jaw grit slightly. Good. "*Your* sword. Does it frighten you that I took it?"

"Frighten?" I asked, my tone incredulous. "Frighten me of what? Of *you*?"

He glowered at that, his hand tightening on the hilt of my sword. His skin around his smooth knuckles lightened with the tension.

"It takes much to kill a *Vorakkar*," I informed him. "Strength that *vekkiri* simply do not possess."

"And yet," he started, his tone clipped, "it is *you* chained before *me*. I could gut you right now, and you would not be able to do anything about it, Dakkari."

"*Lysi*, a dishonorable advantage," I said. "The only way you would draw my blood is if I were chained like this. If I were not..." I bared my teeth at him. "You would already be dead at my feet, and I wouldn't even need to lift my sword. I would rather it not drink in a coward's blood, regardless. Even your blood is not good enough for my blade."

That angered him. I saw the wild flash in his gaze and the way his features morphed into a still, pinched expression.

"Then what about yours?" he asked next.

His arm lifted, the tip of my sword scraping across the stone of the mountain. It pleased me to see his obvious struggle, which he fought to hide. Yet he couldn't shield the way his arm shook under the weight of the steel.

I stilled when he laid it across my chest. The blade dug into the tunic I wore. I had just sharpened the edge last night, in the warmth and quietness of my *voliki*, and now it would drink from me when it had never tasted my blood before.

As if to himself, he said, "They said nothing about keeping your body whole. All they need is your *filthy* beating heart."

My brow furrowed grimly, a memory pushing forward from the recesses of my mind at his quiet words. But in my weakness, it eluded me.

With that, he dragged the weight of my sword across my chest. The steel cut through my tunic easily, like parchment, and I felt the warm slide of the pain as it split my flesh.

I didn't make a sound as the blood welled in the new wound and trickled out, wetting my tunic and seeping underneath it. The cut wasn't deep. He'd meant it as a warning.

And it told me three things.

That he could be controlled with anger. That he thought he could control *me* with pain.

And lastly, that the *vekkiri* were working with someone else to keep me here. Was it the Ghertun?

I saw the glint of black blood on my sword as he lifted it from my chest. My own blood. Benn was breathing hard, his eyes gleaming with something that gave me pause. Delight.

In a leader, that was a dangerous thing. That he reveled in pain and power.

"Blood keeps us strong, does it not?" Benn asked me, turning toward the door, turning his back on me. "And I like you weak. I think your sword will get used to the taste of your blood while you're here, Horde King."

My nostrils flared.

Before he left, however, I murmured quietly, "You just sealed your own death, *vekkiri*."

He paused at the threshold of the door. Perhaps he heard the truth of my words in my voice.

I grinned.

"And I will *relish* it."

CHAPTER 8

When my eyes opened, I stayed still. Benn's murmuring voice reached me, carrying over the snores of the others. All of us, with the exception of him, slept in the same room. Curled up on the floor, padded with whatever we could find.

A short distance away, I saw Emmi asleep, his hand curled over Kaila's growing belly. A child hadn't been born since long before our village burned to the ground. The youngest among us was Hassan, a young boy of eleven, who wore the expression of a jaded warrior, much too grim for one of his age. He was sleeping now next to his mother, his hand holding hers.

When I was eleven...

I couldn't actually remember what life had been like then. The same as it was now and yet completely different. Happier. Sadder. And yet I hadn't been nearly as lonely then as I was now. Father had been alive. And my aunt.

"We will just need one guard on him," Benn was saying, his tone hushed. I heard something scrape against the ground, and I knew instantly what it was. The horde king's sword. "He's not nearly as strong as I expected."

Because the fog stole his strength. And then you chained him in unbreakable bonds, I couldn't help but think.

"Rest tonight," Benn said. "Taylor is on guard now. You can relieve him in the morning."

And when was morning, exactly? Under the Dead Mountain, keeping track of the sun was nearly impossible.

We all slept when Benn told us to. And morning was when he woke. I marveled at how much power he had amassed over us in such a short amount of time. I wondered if it bothered the others as it bothered me.

But was he so different than a horde king? I'd heard unspeakable things happened within a horde. Torment and tortuous punishment for those who went against their king, who dared to defy him. I'd heard a *Vorakkar* could have his pick of the females and that they could not deny his advances. The horde members died for their king, went to battle for him, and obeyed his every order.

Was Benn really so different, then?

I chanced a peek toward the voices. In the hallway just outside the open door, I saw the flickering of torchlight. Benn stood there speaking with Jacques, who looked spent. His shoulders were sagging and his head hung heavy. The events of the day had finally caught up with him.

My heart thundered when my eyes caught on the sword. Something dark slid down its tip. Thick and black.

Blood.

Dakkari blood, I knew.

Had Benn…

My eyes quickly snapped closed when Benn turned to regard the room, the torchlight shifting with his body.

"The horde king's wounds were cleaned," I heard him comment.

Jacques hesitated but then said, "Mina."

A grunt.

"Tell her that if she tends his wounds again, she will be punished for it," Benn said. "I want him weakened. It is safer for all of us. And if his wounds fester…well, we only have to keep him alive until the black moon. The witches will be here by then. And then it won't matter."

"I'll tell her," Jacques said quietly.

Shortly after, Benn's footsteps faded away, walking toward his private quarters, and I heard Jacques sigh. He went to the little corner he'd claimed for himself and lay down. He wasn't that far from me, and I focused on the sound of his breathing, trying to block out Jerrod's loud snores.

Almost as soon as he lay down, his breathing went even. He'd not slept the night before either, and I knew that nothing would wake him.

With a deep breath, I slid up from the ground, my bare feet padding across the stone floor, hopping over still, slumbering bodies. It was dark in the hallway, nearly pitch black, but I knew that a torch was kept lit down the corridor. My eyes adjusted to the dark as best as they could, and I slid my hand along the stone to help guide me.

When I reached the torch, I plucked it from the wall. Then I went to get water from the well along with the gray cloth I'd done my best to wash earlier.

Navigating the maze of the Ghertun's kingdom, I soon reached the hallway where the horde king was held. A sigh of relief emerged from my throat when I peeked around the corner and saw Taylor against the wall, his head bobbing as he valiantly tried to stay awake.

It didn't take long for him to doze off completely, and I hurried to the door, slipping inside and gently closing it. *Hoping* he was none the wiser.

When I turned, I saw the horde king, sitting on his bed of stone, his feet firmly on the floor, though its height was high. His strength must be returning if he had the energy to sit up, but then I saw the way his shoulders were curved in and a steady trickle of blood that stained the front of his tunic.

His head turned slowly to regard me when I entered, those red eyes narrowing on me.

I didn't speak. Instead, I went to him. And maybe I wasn't afraid because I didn't care what happened to me anymore. All I knew was that...

All I knew was that when the horde king was captured, I'd gotten a chill up my spine. In that moment, everything in me *screamed* that we had changed something that wasn't meant to be changed. That the horde king's capture was not...it was not *written*. It should not have happened.

And now I didn't know what to do about it. He was here because of me. Maybe the others would have eventually figured out a way to bring him to the Dead Mountain. But ultimately, it had been *me* to lure him close enough to be taken.

Standing before him, I held up the basin of clean water. He turned his face away, and I whispered, "Water. From the well."

A muscle in his jaw jumped. His nostrils flared. But when I tipped the basin toward his mouth again, he drank from it. Slowly, I aided him, taking it away before he drained the whole thing.

Our eyes held as I set the basin next to his hand on the table. I caught movement there and saw that his tail was flicking, the tip tufted in dark, silky hair. When he saw me looking at it, it stilled immediately.

"Why are you here, *sarkia*?" came the rumbling question, and I worried that his deep voice would carry through the thick door and wake Taylor.

I placed my finger over my lips, and his brow drew together. His head tilted toward the door, but I remained quiet as I dropped the cloth into the basin. There wasn't much water left, but it would have to be enough, considering I didn't want to chance waking Taylor if I returned to the well.

"Why are you here?" came the question, only his voice softened considerably and I had to lean close to hear it properly.

I looked down, moving the torch closer to him. Immediately, I saw the long horizontal wound across his chest. The sword had cut through his tunic, revealing golden, scarred, hardened flesh beneath.

I didn't answer him. I squeezed the cloth and brought it to his chest.

My breath hitched when he snagged my wrist, his hand curling tight. My gaze flashed up to his.

"Why bother?" he growled softly. "There will be more soon."

More wounds? I remembered what Benn had said about keeping him weakened. Was this what he meant?

"Then I will clean those too," I informed him.

His hand tightened on my wrist briefly, a thunderous expression on his darkly handsome face.

For a single moment, I was struck by that expression, and the whispered words escaped me before I could stop them, "We have heard tales of horde kings all our lives. And I can see why they portrayed you as gods in your own way. Monstrous, powerful gods."

It struck me a moment later that I hadn't stumbled over my speech once. The words flowed from me freely. Effortlessly. My throat hadn't tightened, and the words didn't get trapped as a result.

"Monsters?" he murmured, his fingers sliding along my wrist, prickling my flesh. "I see only one monster here."

I felt the words like a slap across the face. I jerked with them, the shame in my belly bubbling up because of them.

"Is that why you're here?" he questioned. "Why you think tending to my wounds somehow assuages your own guilt? Because I can see it. In all your stories of the horde kings, did they ever tell you that we are vengeful beasts most of all?"

I pulled away from him, and he let me go. I didn't have illusions of my own strength when it came to him. He released my wrist because he no longer wished to touch me.

Was I a monster to him? I wondered. Why did the thought make my belly roil?

"What did you do to me in the fog, *sarkia*?" he demanded next, and I bit my lip, looking toward the door. If Taylor woke and heard a single noise, he would come investigate. He would report it to Benn, and I would be punished. Then again, I'd known I would be regardless, coming here. "What spell did you place over me?"

My brow furrowed.

"Spell?" I whispered, shaking my head.

"You shielded me from seeing who you truly are," he said. "But I see you now."

We stared at one another. His was a thunderous glare. Mine was, no doubt, wary.

"And what is it that you see?" I couldn't help but ask.

His tone was cold, his face impassive as he listed out, "Cowardice. Weakness. The fact that I ever desired you in the fog is proof in itself that there was sorcery in play. Because who would ever desire you otherwise?"

I wanted to laugh in his face. Or cry. I wasn't certain which.

He thought the only way he would have possibly desired me was if I bewitched him?

Was he trying to anger me? If he was, I couldn't see his purpose in doing so. I was here to help him, not wound him further.

"Your wound needs cleaning," I told him, feeling a strange sensation come over me.

One of...invulnerability. Detachment.

I had heard it all already. Everyone underneath the Dead Mountain—with the exception of Tess—considered me a nuisance. Like a stray animal. They fed me the scraps, they ordered me about, they laughed when I stumbled over my words until I grew so flustered that I simply couldn't speak.

Ugly. Half-witted. Weak. Spineless.

The horde king's insults were nothing new.

Only now I could add *undesirable* to that long, ever-growing list.

If I surprised him with my steely words, he didn't show it. The only clues that he'd even heard me were that his jaw tightened subtly and I caught a short flick of his otherwise limp tail.

Perhaps he *had* been trying to get a rise out of me. Had he goaded Benn the same way? Was that why he was now adorned with a long wound from his own sword? Unlike Benn, the horde king would find that I couldn't be stoked to rage. I was mild tempered, which I considered a blessing after all the shit I'd dealt with in my lifetime.

The horde king looked away from me, and I took that as his answer. If he didn't want to look at me, fine. I would be quick about it.

The wound was deeper than I thought when I hunched over to peer at it. Still, I had nothing to stitch it with. I hoped Dakkari were the fast healers that stories made them out to be. Once, I'd heard of a Dakkari warrior taking five spears to the chest and he still walked from that battle alive.

Quickly, I cleaned the blood away and used most of the fresh water to cleanse the wound. Infection here was highly probable, given the damp, wet state of the Dead Mountain. I worried if I got the smallest of scratches. I'd watched many die from lesser infections over the years, my father included.

"Are you their healer?" came his question.

I was surprised he was still speaking to me. When I looked up at him, I realized that our faces were close to one another's. I could see a faint scar along the bridge of his nose and a wider one, raised and golden, near the back of his jaw.

In the end, I didn't answer him. What did he care anyway?

To him, I was nothing. I was practically a ghost to everyone else too.

A short grunt emerged from his throat at my silence.

"I've angered you," he commented quietly. "Even human females can kill with their scorn."

"You can think what you wish, but I am too tired for scorn," I said softly, deciding not to give him anything more than that. Surprise alighted in his gaze before his seemingly ever-present scowl returned. I dabbed the last bit of his wound and straightened, dropping the bloodied cloth into the basin.

I stepped away, cradling it in my right arm and snagging the torch with my left.

As I stepped toward the door, his voice stopped me.

"Just tell me one thing, *kalles*," he said. I stared at the door in front of me, at the shadows playing there. "How did you do it? How did you control the fog?"

My lips pressed together. He remembered the way the fog had pushed away from him then. I hoped he wouldn't let that slip to anyone else. It was safer for me if no one else knew.

"I didn't" was all I said.

His slight scoff told me he didn't believe me.

My jaw clenched. I looked at him over my shoulder, only to see his glowing red eyes fastened on me.

"The stories were wrong," I whispered. "Horde kings aren't gods or monsters. They're just like everyone else on this planet."

His brow quirked, his sardonic interest clear. "And what am I, *sarkia*?"

"I think you're scared."

The tension in the room snapped tight as my accusation hung between us.

"Maybe not of us, of him," I whispered. "But I think you're scared of what's out *there*. Is that why you went into the fog every morning? Because you were trying to figure out its weakness?" I shook my head. "It has none."

His chain rattled. I watched as he stood from the stone table, though the short leash of his chain prevented him from taking more than a step or two. Still, it drew him closer to me.

That massive body would have towered over me had I not been near to the door. I couldn't see beyond his wide breadth. Only him.

And I saw it then. His rapt gaze on mine. His furrowed brow. He'd worn the same expression in the fog as he studied me. When he'd claimed, by his own confession, to *desire* me. As if he couldn't understand what I was made of and he *needed* to uncover it.

"And you don't?" he asked quietly. "You don't fear it?"

"No," I whispered. "I don't fear what's beyond the Dead Mountain. I fear what's within it."

On my way back to the sleeping quarters, I spied Kaila carefully stepping from the room. She hadn't seen me. She moved along the corridors with a stable hand against the wall to act as her guide.

She wove a familiar path, one I was certain we all knew, and I followed her with a sinking feeling in my belly. She turned into a dark room, and I saw the flare of a small torch coming to life. I waited a moment and then crept closer.

Peering inside, I saw what I feared. Kaila had the chest open —the key to which only Benn had—and was rummaging through our rations. I watched as she dug out a long strip of *rikcrun* meat, dry and crumbly, and brought it to her lips.

Her teeth gnashed at the meat hard, and it was only after she swallowed her first bite that she looked over her shoulder.

She froze, her eyes going wide, when she saw me standing there.

"Mina," she whispered in astonishment. Then came the anger, her shoulders going back. "Did you *follow* me?"

She was the one sneaking rations while the rest of us slept, and she was angry with me? She was taking food from us all when there was so little of it left. The women and Mo hadn't returned from the hunt, if they even found any food.

When I didn't flinch away from her anger, I watched her shame begin to take root. I wondered if that was what the horde king had seen in me tonight, when he said he could see my guilt.

It was a pitiful sight. One that made me uncomfortable to witness.

Kaila came to me, taking my hands in hers.

"Please Mina," she whispered, her eyes pleading with mine. "Don't tell anyone, all right? It's just...the baby..."

One of her hands left mine to curl around her belly protectively.

"I don't want to lose another one," came her soft confession.

My throat went tight with memory.

"She was so small," Kaila whispered raggedly, though her eyes remained dry. Many of us had listened to her sob for days after her last miscarriage. We had all watched Emmi bury the lifeless girl, who had come much too early. "She didn't have a chance. But this one will. He's stronger. And I swear I will give back what I take here. Emmi will double his hunt rotations once the women return. Just don't tell anyone."

"He-He will kno-know," I told her. "He co-counts it."

Her grip tightened on me. "He won't find out."

But it sounded like she was trying to convince herself. And once Benn discovered that one of us was taking more than our share, he wouldn't rest until he knew who it was—and until they were punished, pregnant or not.

"Will he, Mina?" she asked, her question pointed. "Don't tell him."

She said the words slowly, like I wouldn't understand them otherwise.

I didn't see what choice I had. I had sympathy for Kaila. I knew that she needed more nourishment right now than me, at least.

"Please," she whispered, her tone softening.

There was a crumbled bit of *rikcrun* on the edge of her mouth. I caught sight of the opened chest behind her, the key sitting neatly in the lock, Ghertun in make. I wondered if Emmi had stolen it for her.

"Will you tell him?" she pressed.

In the end, I shook my head. Only because I didn't trust my voice.

"Thank you," Kaila breathed. "Thank you, Mina."

CHAPTER 9

"Mina," came the sharp bark.

Immediately, I stopped scrubbing the clothes in the small stone basin next to the well. I was huffing with exertion, my arms trembling from the lack of food this last week.

Benn stood in the hallway. Taylor was next to him. For a moment, I feared that Taylor somehow discovered I'd been inside the horde king's room last night. But the other male simply looked tired, and his gaze was more rapt on Shayna, who was on the other side of the well, hanging up the freshly washed clothes to dry on snags in the mountain wall. They would take days to dry in this humid environment and always smelled like a swampy bog once they did. Like the one we used to live beside.

The others grumbled and complained when they pulled on the washed clothes, but I wondered if the smell brought a sense of comfort to them, like it did to me.

"Come," Benn ordered. The horde king's sword was in his grip again. Slowly, warily, I rose from the floor, wiping my arm across my forehead. My tunic was drenched in sweat, my hair sticking to the sides of my face. I probably looked as wretched as I felt.

I followed Benn from the well room and wound a familiar path through the Dead Mountain until we stood in front of the horde king's door. Jacques was still on guard from this morning, looking more refreshed than he did yesterday.

My heart began to pound. I cast a look at Benn, wondering if he'd seen the cleaned wound across the horde king's chest already.

When Benn unlatched the lock and the door creaked open, I saw a dark, looming figure pacing back and forth. More like shuffling, however, considering his feet were shackled in the same cuffs that adorned his wrists.

The horde king's red eyes glowed in the darkness. Those eyes promised pain, even though his expression was cold and impassive, revealing nothing.

He stilled when we entered, straightening to his full height. Even I could see the way that made Benn pause and scan the length of the chain, just to ensure it was still attached to the stone loop on the table.

He relaxed when he saw it intact, though his gaze then went to the wound on the horde king's chest. To my astonishment, I saw that it was already healing over. When I looked at his legs, it looked like the wounds there had been healing for close to a week, not a single night.

His strength seemed to have returned. His body was healing. I saw Benn process this information just as quickly as I had.

The horde king's eyes narrowed on me before they flicked to Benn, who I hovered behind.

"How long do you think you can keep me here, *vekkiri*?" the horde king asked. "How long do you think this chain will hold me?"

His words made Benn pause, but he covered it quickly with, "Do not think to trick me, Dakkari. I know what those are made of. Blackened steel, yes? The strongest substance on this planet, and unbreakable by any beast."

"Whoever told you that," the horde king started, "is wildly misinformed."

My heart throbbed. The chain could be broken? Had the witches told us a lie? Or did they simply not know?

Or was the horde king bluffing? It was possible he wanted to get under Benn's skin, make him doubt what he'd been told.

"Not only that, *vekkiri*, but my horde will be searching for me," the Dakkari male said. "Tirelessly. They already know that I am gone. And they will slaughter every living soul who had a hand in my capture."

His eyes cut to me then. Seemingly on purpose.

Benn noticed, and he hid his trepidation at the horde king's words with disguised glee as he said, "Oh, do you recognize her, then?"

The horde king's expression darkened.

Lowering my gaze, I looked down to the floor. I realized then why I'd been summoned here. Benn wanted to see how the horde king would react to my presence. To see if I could be used further.

The horde king didn't rise to the bait. Instead he bit out, "If what your *witch* there says is true and we are under the Dead Mountain..."

I felt the blood physically drain from my face, saw the way Benn's head cut to me at the words. Swallowing hard, I bit my lip to keep it from trembling.

"...then know that my horde will figure out a way to reach me. It is only a matter of time."

Without another word, Benn left the room, pushing me out into the hallway. Jacques caught my arm before I fell to the floor as Benn shut the door firmly, latching it once more.

"What's wrong?" Jacques asked, though I knew he suspected since he must've heard the brief conversation.

Benn's hand lashed out, and a burst of light flashed in my vision. I fell to the floor, my knees scraping against the stone.

When the side of my face began to throb, I cupped it. I tasted blood and realized I'd been biting my lip when Benn struck me.

"Who let her inside with him?" Benn growled.

Jacques swallowed. "You—you said to let her tend to him. She cleaned his wounds."

"She spoke to him," Benn said. "And like the fool she is, she told him where we are!"

Jacques was breathing heavily, but he kept his voice calm, trying to defuse the situation. "It doesn't matter, Benn. They can't move through the fog like we can. It's all right."

Benn cursed, raking a hand through his hair. "His horde is not far away. What if they do manage to find the other entrance? The Ghertun made tunnels all over these lands!"

"And the fog covers most of them. And if the witches don't hurry, their only entrance will be blocked soon too," Jacques reminded him. "We've had scouts watching his horde. They've sent warriors into the fog searching for him, but they return quickly. They'll never reach us. They don't have the strength to."

Kneeling on the stone floor, I watched a drop of my blood drip onto the floor. I didn't dare move. Everyone knew Benn's temper was legendary. It was best to let him calm down without drawing his attention.

Luckily, Jacques's words seemed to soothe Benn's sudden fears.

A long stretch of silence consumed the hallway. Then Benn said, "Gather the strongest of the men."

"For what?" Jacques asked.

"We need another way to keep him secured. The chain is too long. He's recovered his strength much too quickly. We can get him chained to the pillar underneath the table and keep his hands behind his back. That way, we can keep him weakened if we need to."

"You want to take the cuffs *off* him?" Jacques asked in disbelief.

"Just gather the men," Benn snapped.

Jacques went quiet.

"And as for you," came Benn's voice above me. I didn't dare look up, but I knew he was speaking to me. "If you say another word to him, I'll cut that tongue from your mouth, do you understand me? Maybe I should've done that a long time ago. It would have been a favor to us all."

The fury that began to burn in my chest surprised me, but it was a welcome feeling. He thought me nothing more than a slave to him. Something that wasn't even human. Something that he could hit and take his frustrations out on, that was simply alive for his amusement.

Benn wasn't angry that I'd told the horde king we were under the Dead Mountain. He was angry that he hadn't known about it. His control over us was a tenuous thing, built more on fear and desperation than strength or loyalty. And he held on to that control with a tight fist. But didn't he realize that his temper and his outbursts only made us more wary of him, more mistrustful?

I was starting to see it within the others. Their growing restlessness. And I knew that Benn sensed it too.

"Mina," Jacques said, a long moment later. "He's gone. Come, let's—"

"Don't," I whispered, shrugging from his grip when he tried to help me up. I sat up and then stood on my own. Jacques's gaze went to the side of my face and then to my split lip. I swore I caught a flash of pity, and I couldn't stand to see it. A part of me hated that sometimes he was kind to me. A part of me hated his cowardice when he let Benn's abuse happen.

It was the same with Tess. I loved her like a sister, for that was what I'd always considered her. And yet I was hurt when she turned her back on me when it came to the others, even though I understood why she did it.

For once, what would it be like to be *chosen*? What would it be like to be loved and protected and safe?

Walking back down the hall, with fury burning in my breast, I realized that I didn't want to live like a slave anymore. I didn't want others' pity. I didn't want to live in constant fear.

My small laugh echoed around the dark hallway, even as a sob bit its way up my throat.

I like who I am in the fog, I thought. Because I felt no fear there. *I* held the power there. No one else. It gave me strength—whereas in others, it made them weak.

And the heart of a horde king would take it away from me.

Chapter 10

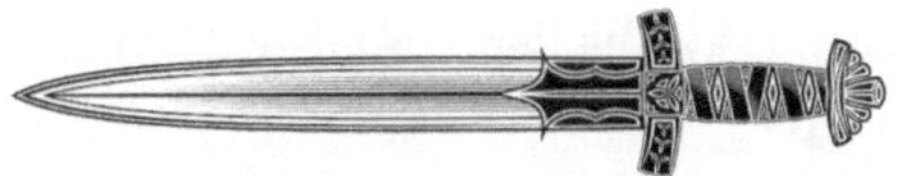

My eyes snapped open when the latch lifted and the door creaked open.

All at once, the light of multiple torches flooded the dark room as a group of bodies strode forward quickly.

Reacting on instinct, I leapt from the table, but my body jerked when the chain went taut, securing me in place. There were seven males in total, I counted, and all of them either wore grim expressions...or fearful ones.

Nik, there were eight males, I realized when I saw Benn hovering in the doorway.

One male I recognized from the fog held a spear, though the blunt end was pointing toward me.

"Secure him," Benn ordered the others, reaching inside his tunic pocket for something. They fanned around me in a circle, and my gaze darted as I tracked their movements. Ordinarily, I could take down seven human males without a weapon relatively easily. But right then, I was chained, my wrists and ankles bound tight.

Even still, I'd take the odds I could succeed.

A golden-haired male closest to me rushed my left side just as another darted to my right. In a flash, I caught the golden-haired male's arm beneath my palm, and I bared my teeth at him when I snapped the bone.

His howl momentarily made the others freeze, and he stumbled away, his back hitting the wall, his chest heaving as he cradled his broken arm.

I huffed in derision. Humans could be hurt so easily. Had *this* been their plan all along? I leveled my gaze at Benn, eyes narrowing when I saw the item he'd fished from his pocket was gold. Kakkari's gold.

The key.

And it was Dakkari-made.

Movement to my right.

Two males lunged for me, and I spun to evade them, ramming my elbow into one's face before I scented a rush of metallic blood. The male, with blood pouring from his nostrils, cradled his face, but then a frustrated yell burst from his throat. He leapt at me again just as the male with the spear jabbed it forward, making my head whip to the side from the force as it connected with my temple.

They want me unconscious again, I realized, gritting my teeth when my vision momentarily went blurry.

As I shook my head clear, two other males took their opportunity, grabbing my arms, forcing the strength of their entire bodies against me. A third joined in when he saw the other two had found purchase in their footing.

Another hit of the spear landed on my temple, narrowly missing my eye. With a roar, I felt my strength surge, and I shrugged off all the males trying to secure me, spinning to whip one across the face with my bound fists, another in the belly, and the last in the groin. He fell to the floor, groaning in front of me. I raised my fists to finish him—

A cloud of grit burst in front of me, and I hissed, feeling rough particles enter my eyes, momentarily blinding me, and I raised my hands to wipe whatever it was away.

That was all they needed. The spear rammed my head again, and I stumbled. Then came another hit. I cracked my eyes open briefly, only to see a rush of dark bodies and the glint of my sword in the torchlight. My hand was already curling for the hilt, as if on instinct.

"He's down!" came a voice to my left. "Taylor, grab him!"

A crush of bodies rushed me, piling on top of me as I bucked underneath them. I threw a few off, but they rebounded quickly, save for the male clutching his arm in the corner, moaning and cursing.

"*Shit, Bray, hold him!*"

"*I am!*"

"Move out of the way," came Benn's voice.

When I opened my eyes again, I saw the blade come down. I felt the edge of my sword enter my right shoulder. I kept it sharp, so it slid into me easily, despite Benn's obvious lack of strength.

The bright burst of pain came next. I felt the males' huffs of exertion drift across my flesh, and my belly roiled at the sensation. Out of the corner of one bleary, gritty eye, I saw the blunt edge of the spear flash.

It hurtled down toward me.

When I woke, it was to darkness.

My nostrils flared, and I blinked, still feeling the grit in my eyes, though it was considerably better. Sand? Had they thrown sand into my eyes?

When I moved to wipe at them, I realized my hands were shackled behind my back. Something hard and cold was running along my spine, and when I moved my hands around it, I discovered it was one of the stone pillars underneath the table, one of its legs. Solid and heavy and carved from the mountain, so there was no way to move it.

My legs were stretched in front of me, the skin on my shins continuing to heal.

When I adjusted my position, I felt a sharp sensation that momentarily stole my breath. And I remembered. My sword.

As my blurry eyes adjusted to the darkness, I lowered my head down to inspect the wound.

Vok.

He'd nearly run me straight through with my own sword. When I lifted my shoulder, shrugging it along the pillar, I grunted, gritting my jaw with the pain. It felt like he'd nicked the bone, like he'd twisted the blade when it was inside me to cut through muscle and tendon.

My right arm was my sword arm. My strength. Benn couldn't have known that, but it still made my ire toward him grow. The last thing I would do here was ensure that he was dead at my feet. And I'd kill him with my sword just for good measure.

As for the others, I only regretted that I hadn't wounded them more. They'd moved me because Benn realized I was still a danger to them, even chained and cuffed. Now I couldn't stand. And with my hands cuffed around the pillar, I was robbed of opportunity to strike first.

Only my tail was free. I used it right then, dragging it up around my back, and I leaned away from the pillar as far as I could. I touched the tip of my tail to the back of my shoulder. It stung, and my lips pressed together. When I lowered it, I maneuvered it closer to my face and saw the tufted end was covered in blood.

Vok, he actually *had* run my sword right through me.

One thing was for certain: they wanted me alive. He'd chosen my shoulder purposefully, as if he knew I would survive it. They'd only wanted to weaken me further.

I tilted my head back, my mouth dry, my throat scratchy. Looking at the dark ceiling, I realized I couldn't actually see where the room ended.

Perhaps I shouldn't have taunted the human male so much. Perhaps I shouldn't have pushed him to anger. I should have remained lying down, and I should have made him think I was still wounded, that I was still robbed of my strength. Instead, I'd given in to my pride and ego.

I thought my father had long beaten both those things out of me.

A humorless, dark laugh rose in my throat.

I needed to make a plan.

That much was clear.

Within moments, I knew what direction that plan was heading in. I think I'd always known, I just hadn't wanted to give in to it.

The female.

The *sarkia*.

The witch.

Logically, I knew that she was my best chance for escape. Despite what I'd told the humans' leader, I knew the Dead Mountain was too far into the fog for my horde to reach. I couldn't depend on Valavik or my *darukkars* to come. Nor did I want them to. It was too dangerous.

But the female...she could bend the fog to her will. I'd seen it, hadn't I?

She had all the answers. Why I was here. What purpose I was supposed to serve. Where the Ghertun were. And most importantly, how to control the fog that had begun to plague our lands.

Though it would further wound my pride, I would need to appeal to her. I could *use* her. I already knew she felt shame and guilt for my being here. She'd *apologized* to me.

I was a callous, cold bastard. And I would do whatever I

could to protect myself and my horde. As such, I had no misgivings about using her for information, for playing upon those emotions to guide her toward freeing me.

Thus far, however, I had not been kind to her. That would need to change. Trust took time to build. But how long did I have left?

The next time she comes, I vowed quietly.

The next time she came, I would put my plan into motion.

I only prayed to Kakkari that it wouldn't be too late.

In the end, I didn't need to wait long.

Later that night, I was jolted from sleep when I heard the door. My head felt cloudy from sleep and the loss of blood.

But when her scent reached me, it cleared most of the fog away, and I straightened, my chain rattling behind me.

I caught a flash of her green eyes before she shut the door. Tonight, she wore a long shift dress, gray in color, that brushed the tops of her bare feet. It hid her form well, as baggy and loose as it was. She pressed her ear to the door, listening, and then she let out a soft sigh, turning toward me.

Another basin of water was cradled in one arm, and she held a small torch in the other, which she perched in the holder along the wall.

Then she was drawing closer. She gasped when she saw the wound in my shoulder. The side of my face felt tender and hot from the spear strikes. And my abdomen felt tight and bruised, as if I'd been kicked, though I hadn't been, at least when I was conscious.

But all of that flew out of my mind when she crouched before me.

Because when my eyes fastened on her face, when I saw the blue ring that lined her eye and a swollen, puffy lip, which had scabbed over in deep red blood, I growled. The chain rattled when I leaned toward her.

And I didn't understand it, the rage that I felt coursing through me at the sight of her bruised face. I shouldn't feel anything for this *sarkia*. She'd tricked me. She was the *reason* I was here, chained and battered and *caged*.

Only, there was no denying the fury I felt rising in my blood at the sight of her.

Perhaps a part of me still recognized her oath to me. That she was *mine*.

Lo rune tei'ri, Vorakkar.

That ancient vow ran deep, stroking instincts inside me I hadn't even known existed. I remembered the *rightness* at hearing those words escape her lips, the maelstrom they had unleashed within me and the *need* I'd felt for her in those moments in the fog.

"*Who struck you?*" I growled.

CHAPTER 11

The horde king had a fist-sized wound in his shoulder, and he looked...*angry*? For *me*?

Without thinking, I reached forward to touch the fabric of his tunic—a thick, dark hide—and my fingers came away hot with black blood. I was crouching beside him since they'd moved his position within the room. Now his hands were bound behind his back, the cuffs securing him against one of the thick, rocky columns that supported the stone table's weight. He was slouched against it, his long bare legs stretched out in front of him.

Without a word, I dragged the basin of water over. Just like last night, I lifted it, struggling slightly under its weight as I brought it to his lips.

The horde king turned his head to the side. Those red eyes bit into me as he growled, "Tell me who struck you, *sarkia*."

"Drink," I told him.

He held my gaze, and I didn't understand his fury. My patience was thin that night, however. I was tired from the day. And I'd already helped patch up a few men from their encounter with the male in front of me. Jos's arm, however, had been beyond my capabilities. Jacques had held Jos down while

Shayna and Emmi set the bone. I swore I could still hear his screams echo around the Dead Mountain even now.

"How do you say *stubborn male* in Dakkari?" I asked, my tone hardening.

His gaze flashed. Again, a peculiar expression came over his face. Like he was trying to read me, trying to figure me out.

"So she has claws," he murmured, the chain rattling behind him as he shifted. "Dull ones. So soft they wouldn't even break human flesh, much less mine."

I dragged in a deep, steadying breath. I lowered the basin into his lap because my arms were about to give out. The lingerings of my bad mood had followed me even here. And perhaps I should think twice about giving this horde king my temper because I'd seen what he'd done to fully grown men while he was cuffed and chained and weaponless.

So why didn't I fear him?

Why didn't I fear being *here*?

And when I thought about Benn catching me, when I thought about what he might do to me...I only felt a dull throb of indifference.

Pain was pain. I'd felt it all my life. We all had. And I would continue to feel it, perhaps every day for the rest of my existence on this planet.

I better get used to it, then, I thought.

I believed I already was.

Briefly, I looked down at my fingers, long and bony, leading to bitten nails. No claws there. Not like his at least.

"Does it hurt?" I whispered.

In the basin of water perched in his lap, I could see his reflection. He was still gazing at me, and I saw his lips pull down at my question.

"I've been wounded like this before," he murmured. His voice hardened. "Though not with my own sword."

Dragging over the clean cloth I'd brought with me, I told him, "Last chance to drink."

His head tilted back, leaning the back of it against the column of the table, exposing his golden throat. We stared at one another for a long moment, and finally, he inclined his head subtly.

Dropping the cloth into my lap, I brought the basin up to his lips again. He tilted forward, and I watched his lips as they parted, remembering them well. I swallowed, ignoring the spark of uncomfortable desire, shifting on my knees a little, just as he got a mouthful.

I helped him drink until half of the water was gone, and then I set it down in front of me.

"I—I brought you some food too," I whispered, feeling a little shame when I hesitated in telling him. Pulling out the wrapped bundle I'd stuffed into the pocket of my dress, I opened the cloth to show him a single strip of *rikcrun* meat, no larger than my middle finger.

I'd saved it from my own rations that evening. This had been the larger of the two strips, and my mouth watered just looking at it.

The horde king's gaze flashed down to it before it snapped up. Those eyes darted back and forth between mine, his jaw tightening at whatever he found.

"You eat it, *sarkia*," he murmured. "Dakkari can go over a week without food."

"You need the nourishment to heal," I said. "I know it's not much...bu-but anything will help."

The horde king leaned his head back once more, and I swore I saw his expression soften at my words. But then a muscle in his jaw flexed, and it was gone.

"Eat it, *kalles*," came his gruff order. And even chained and wounded, I had the strongest urge to obey him blindly. When I didn't move, his eyes narrowed and he said, "And you think I am the stubborn one?"

"I'll save it for you when you are hungry," I told him, wrapping the dried meat tight and bundling it once more. I placed it back into the pocket of my dress. Before he could say anything, I dipped the cloth into the remaining water and squeezed out the excess.

I bit my lip with indecision before I remembered that I'd split it earlier. Flinching slightly, I felt a flash of my anger from earlier return to me, and my spine straightened in defiance. Without hesitation, I moved forward, gently pressing the cloth to the horde king's temple.

The skin was darkening with bruises already, and a long gash was crusted with dried blood.

"Does it hurt here too?" I whispered, dabbing with the cloth which was helping to loosen the blood, though I was highly aware that he was studying me in the darkness.

"I hardly feel it" was his soft answer.

"Do you feel anything at all?"

The soft question escaped my lips before I could stop it. Right now, he was holding himself as still as a statue and his expression gave nothing away. Not pain from his wounds, not disgust at being this close to me, not even anger.

"Or are you made of stone like this mountain?" I finished, before I lost my nerve.

A soft huff escaped his lips. We were close. I'd leaned toward him to better clean his wound, and I realized that I could see strands of black in his red eyes.

"More times than not, emotions get you killed, *sarkia*," he informed me. "Rage overcomes you. Happiness lowers your guard. Love is for fools. And lust only blinds you."

There was a hint of bitterness in his tone, and my cheeks heated, remembering those brief moments in the fog.

Still, his words surprised me.

"You're a horde king of Dakkar," I whispered, taking the cloth away and dipping it back into the water. "You have the world at your feet. And still you are this jaded? I thought that particular emotion was reserved only for the rest of us wretched, lowly beings."

The horde king shifted, moving his head away from the cloth so he could peer at me closely. The weight of his full attention was...dizzying. As dizzying as the endless stream of words that escaped my tongue. I had more words, it seemed, pent up over my lifetime than I knew what to do with.

And it was onto a horde king that I would release them.

"To live is to suffer, *Vorakkar* or not" was all he said in response. "I do not have to tell you that."

My jaw tightened, and I leaned back on my heels. "And I wish that there was a world with no suffering. No pain. Only peace and...safety."

A sharp scoff burst from him. "When you find that fantasy universe of existence, do inform me, *sarkia*. I know many that wish to find it too."

"You think me naive," I guessed. "Don't you?"

His nostrils flared. For a moment, he went quiet, and I took the time to clean the cloth, wringing it out.

"I think for all your suffering, *kalles*," he started quietly, "there is still a world that you know nothing about. Of greed and politics. Of war and bloodshed. Of recognizing the darkness in every living soul on this planet and realizing that no one is untouched by it."

A small, quiet laugh escaped me, which made him still.

Then I sighed, bringing the cloth to his shoulder.

"You don't have to tell me about darkness, Horde King," I murmured to him, bending so close that I could *almost* rest my cheek on his upper arm. "I live in it."

Whether he stiffened at my proximity, my words, or the press of the cloth to his wound, I didn't know.

The silence was broken only when I wrung the cloth out, trickling water counting the seconds as they passed. He leaned forward at my urging so I could inspect the back of his shoulder. My lips pressed when I saw the sword had gone through, though the exit wound wasn't as wide.

As I tended to him there, I heard him ask, "Which village did you belong to?"

Once I was finished cleaning the blood away, I pressed a hand to his chest to gently lean him back. The wound had stopped bleeding. Dakkari healed fast, which was fortunate for him. This wound would have been fatal for a human, from the blood loss alone.

"We lived in the North," I whispered, wondering how hard Benn would strike me if he ever found out I was here tonight. A part of me almost...*welcomed* that pain. "Near the bogs."

"The Orala Pass?" he questioned. I shrugged. I didn't know what the Dakkari called the area. Then he commented, "That village burned two years ago. We thought none survived."

So he knew it.

"Yes," I whispered, my throat suddenly going tight. "It did."

The Ghertun tunnels stretched far and wide. Some had been made before the humans even settled on Dakkar over thirty years ago.

Unfortunately for our village, the Ghertun had ended one of their newest tunnels close to our settlement. There had been reports of Ghertun sightings in the tall, swampy forests of our land, though not many had been taken seriously. Until it was too late.

"Many were lost," I said quietly.

"Perhaps I have seen you before," he commented. The words made me pause. His tone was musing and soft. Had he thought before that I seemed familiar to him?

"Why do you say that?"

"I went to that village once," he told me.

My eyes met his, and I frowned. The only horde king that had ever come had...

"The funeral pyre," I murmured, my eyes widening.

An older woman in our village had taken ill. She'd died shortly after, and we'd held a funeral for her. The ground had been frozen over, however, leaving us with the only option of burning her body, which we often did in the frost season. We only prayed that no *Vorakkar* were nearby to see the smoke because unconfined fire was forbidden to us. The Dakkari viewed it as an ultimate insult to Kakkari, their earth goddess. Fire was never meant to touch her earth.

That frost season, our luck had run out. A horde king *had* been nearby to see the dark smoke that curled into the still sky, and shortly after the ashes had blown away, we'd been faced with a group of Dakkari at our gates.

Song, our village leader, had walked out to meet them. I remembered his head held high though his fate was evident. He'd been willing to sacrifice himself for the sake of his village.

My father had taken me back to our little house, which we shared with my aunt. The Uranian Federation had given each settlement building supplies, but the wood of our house still let in a terrible draft and it went damp with the cold. Father had often been sick during the frost—plagued with a deep, rattling cough—because he bundled me up in most of our furs and gave my aunt the rest.

In the end...the horde king had been *merciful*.

He'd investigated the pyre and left as quickly as he came. The words he said to Song that day had quickly traveled through our village, whispered with disbelief and a small smile among many.

May Kakkari guide her way in death, the horde king had said.

But be cautious during the frost, vekkiri. *Another may not choose mercy.*

The next day, the fresh carcass of a massive beast had shown up at our gates, along with bundles of dried meat.

"During the frost," I whispered to the horde king, my eyes widening in quiet realization and memory.

I'd nearly forgotten it. It had happened so long ago. In that memory's place, tales of vengeful *Vorakkar* across Dakkar had risen. Tales so soaked in blood and horror that I'd forgotten one horde king's act of mercy, the only horde king our village had ever known.

He inclined his head.

"Yo-You fed us," I said. "Why?"

He turned his head away, a tendril of his dark, long hair falling forward to shield his expression.

"That frost was brutal for us all," he murmured. "I know how difficult the North Lands can be."

I didn't know what to say. But I did remember the food. It was the first time I'd ever had meat so tender. It was the first time I'd ever felt *energized* from a meal. Everyone had been in high spirits that season, despite the bone-aching cold.

I'd been sixteen then. I'd just started my bleeding rotations, and when the horde king came that day, I'd been nauseous from the aches in my womb.

And still...

"My father took me away when you came to the gates," I told him, dropping the cloth into the bowl with a wet thud. When I looked down at my hands, they were tinged black with his blood, and I rinsed them in the basin. "I remember being so angry with him because I wanted to see the Dakkari. I wanted to see *you*," came the quiet confession.

He met my eyes again. I wondered if any of the others who'd been there that day recognized him.

"So you couldn't have seen me," I said. "But I remember the day well."

Understanding seemed to pass between us, the longer we held one another's gaze.

"Is your village leader still alive?" he asked.

Song.

I rocked back on my heels. "No."

He'd been killed.

"Where's your father now?" he asked next, his gaze searching. Seeking something that I knew was long lost.

I swallowed. Looking down at the basin, I gathered it up, knowing I couldn't do anything more for him with what I had available to me.

"Buried in the North," I whispered. I hadn't spoken for weeks after his death. "I marked the place with a piece of gold shaped like a star. I found it while digging his grave. I like to think your goddess gave it to me for him. But I'm certain it's long gone now."

I stood and turned toward the torch, reaching out for it in its perch on the wall.

"We call the North the *orala sa'kilan*," came his quiet words. "The frozen haven. Time stops there, as I'm sure you know. But if you ever return, you will find his grave just as you left it, the star of gold and all."

The words were beautiful. My heart ached with the sentiment behind them. The thought that, in the North, my father was at peace and his rest was undisturbed and unbroken. With Kakkari's gold protecting him, as if the Dakkari's goddess cared about *us* too.

"*Orala sa'kilan*," I whispered, turning to look over my shoulder at him. I'd been speaking too much. I tasted the blood from my lip, which was beginning to split again.

The horde king inclined his head, his eyes glowing in the darkness.

I...hadn't known what to expect this night. I'd expected his anger. His barely concealed hatred. His seeping coldness. In my foul mood that evening, I'd even welcomed it.

Instead, he'd surprised me in the most unexpected of ways. He'd almost been...*kind* to me.

"I'll return tomorrow night," I told him. "Try not to enrage him before then. I'm running out of cloth."

I didn't need to say Benn's name aloud. The horde king's tail flicked across the ground.

"No promises, *sarkia*," he said.

Now that I had tasted some of his words, I was greedy for more.

"What does that mean?" I asked, tugging the torch away from the wall. "*Sarkia*?"

Only this time, he didn't tell me. His silence stretched toward me, and I realized he wasn't going to answer.

Before I left, I pressed my ear to the door. It was thick, however, and there was no guarantee that Emmi wasn't awake just outside of it.

"Who struck you?" came the quiet question. The first one he'd asked me tonight, repeated again.

"Who do you think?" was all I asked in response.

"Why did he do it?"

I blew out a small breath.

"Because he can," I said softly.

After one last look back at the horde king, after seeing his expression darken, I slipped through the door. My heart leapt in my chest when I saw the hallway empty, no signs of Emmi anywhere. Which meant he'd woken.

Quickly, I shut the door, praying that Emmi hadn't seen the door unlatched as I locked it again.

I needed to leave before he returned. Quickening my footsteps, I made for the end of the darkened hallway.

Just as I was snuffing my torch out on the wall—deciding to

keep to the darkness to stay out of sight—a hand snagged my arm, and I bit my lip hard to keep from crying out in surprise. A sharp sting and the metallic taste of blood came next, and I looked back, only to see a narrow-eyed Emmi.

"What the hell do you think you're doing with the horde king, Mina?" came his soft growl, shaking me. "Give me one reason why I shouldn't take you to Benn right now."

CHAPTER 12

All the ease I felt in talking with the horde king was extinguished like a flame the moment I saw Emmi. My tongue felt as heavy as a boulder in my mouth.

"Be-Be-Becau—" I started, but the word was lodged in my throat.

"Be-Be-Because what?" Emmi mocked.

My nostrils flared. In a rare moment of frustration and anger, I pushed at his chest. His eyes went wide with astonishment as I tugged my arm out of his grip, some of the blackened, bloodied water sloshing over the sides of the basin, splashing onto Emmi's worn boots. He cursed, jumping back.

Swallowing the lump in my throat, I said, "*Because* I-I know about Kaila." I was immensely proud that I hadn't stumbled over the first word again. It felt like a small victory. It felt *good*.

Emmi went still. So still that I knew my words had frightened him.

Good, I thought.

"W-We all ha—" I started, before drawing in a deep breath. "Have secrets. It's best if w-we keep them."

Emmi's lips parted, but then he closed them, his jaw tightening. He glowered at me but said nothing. That was how I knew I'd shocked him.

I turned my back on him then, continuing on my way. Only when I reached the well and quickly washed out the basin did I realize that my hands were trembling and my nerves were frayed.

Or maybe it's because I didn't eat much, I thought, feeling the pit of my stomach pinch with hunger. I thought of the *rikcrun* strip in my dress, thought about the horde king rejecting it, telling me to eat it instead. Did he guess that we had very little food here? Had he...*wanted* me to have it instead?

But that would imply that he cared about my well-being, and I wasn't foolish enough to believe he did. Tonight was an anomaly. He'd probably spoken with me because he was a little delirious from his wounds. Perhaps he hadn't been sleeping.

It didn't change the fact that I needed to decide what to do and how I was going to do it.

The witches would come soon. Once the moon was black and darkness blanketed the land. That was when the ceremony would be performed. That was when a heartstone would be made.

The question was...would the horde king be here when they arrived?

Or would the curse continue on? Would Dakkar survive in an endless, growing fog?

"*Orala sa'kilan,*" I whispered to myself, feeling the words flow from me easily and effortlessly.

Would the fog reach the North Lands? Would it suffocate my father's grave, spreading its long tendrils across the earth where he rested? Or would my homeland freeze it in its tracks and remain a frozen haven for the rest of time?

The only thing that was certain was that the horde king's fate would determine everyone else's.

That night, I barely slept. The gnawing ache in my belly and the horde king's words kept me awake.

And in the morning, I rose as everyone continued slumbering and quietly snuck from the dark room, weaving through the labyrinth of the Ghertun's fallen kingdom, climbing empty, eerie stairwells and echoing chambers, until a gleaming hint of sunlit red beckoned me from the Dead Mountain.

The mist reached for me, and I went into it, determination steeling my spine. Like a friend, it embraced me. I breathed deeply, and my fear melted away. The tension in my shoulders released. The clenched knot between my brows smoothed.

Behind me, the Dead Mountain loomed though I walked forward. I walked for a long while until I knew that I would be completely safe. So deep inside that even Benn wouldn't be able to survive the journey.

"Help me understand," I whispered, stopping. "Please."

The horde king had been correct. I *had* controlled the fog. I'd shielded him from it, and I'd been able to easily manipulate its distance from him. It had been the only way to lead him to the Dead Mountain.

Closing my eyes against the endless sea of red, I curved my palms near my belly, imagining a small ball between them.

I'd practiced this before, but it had always been...unpredictable.

I blew out a long breath and imagined the small ball growing with energy. I fed it, giving it myself, letting my own strength nourish it. My body tensed, and I felt something push against me, something familiar. But it fought against me—it was struggling. I gritted my teeth, my nostrils flaring, focusing on building it, building it. I imagined it spreading from me, like a halo of safety. Of protection.

I only want to protect, I thought. Or perhaps pleaded. But pleaded with what or who, I didn't know.

When I opened my eyes, I saw that I had created a barrier around myself but it was small. Still, the fog couldn't reach me. It slid across the bubble, seeking an entrance, but there was none.

But it didn't feel as effortless or easy as it had before. With the horde king, I'd simply...

Asked.

I hadn't forced it then.

I slashed out my hand, cutting through the edge of the barrier, and it crumbled, dropping like rain.

I would try again.

Only this time, I wouldn't fight against the fog. I would work with it.

Give me the room to breathe freely. Give me the clarity to understand. Give me aid so that I might make my choice clearly and without fear, I thought silently.

Then, tentatively, I imagined the shield around me again. I imagined it spreading out from my flesh, from the strands of my hair, from the tips of my fingers.

Like the fog, its spread was gentle. Soft. Like a ripple across a pond.

It was a question, I realized.

And then the fog gave its answer.

The shield pushed out from me, and with a surge of energy, I envisioned unleashing it across the plains.

No, that wasn't quite right. I envisioned unleashing it *west,* hurtling it like a spear toward where I'd first encountered the horde king. I didn't know why.

And then something happened.

That energy buzzed under my skin as I watched the barrier push wider and wider, until there was a clear path for me. West.

My eyes went wide as I watched it continue, as I focused on that energy, feeling it begin to snap and pull and *hurt*.

Then it burst.

The barrier reached the end of the fog, and it had nowhere else to go. The energy continued *rushing* out of me. I couldn't control it any longer! It was growing too fast and—

In disbelief, at the end of the path, on the western edge of the fog, I saw Dakkari males.

Tall, bare-chested, strong Dakkari males.

At least a dozen, and I gasped when my barrier rushed at them and flung back the closest two. They went flying, knocked into the air for a brief, breathless moment, before they thudded to the hard, compact earth *hard*.

Stop, I commanded. *Please stop!*

I gritted my teeth and pulled the barrier to a stop, my fist clenching out in front of me as if I could grip it. My forehead was dotted in sweat and my breaths were shallow. My arm was shaking, my knuckles white.

There was a clear path before me. A *break* in the fog. The Dakkari males seemed just as in shock as I was, but it was a broad-shouldered male with yellow eyes that stepped forward first. The two males that I'd knocked over clamored to their feet, and immediately, I heard the hiss of swords being pulled from sheaths.

That sound startled me from my stupor. With a gasp, I began reining in the barrier, though I didn't know if I had the strength to.

"*Pyroth!*" came a panicked voice. "Wait, *kalles!* Cease, *darukkars!*"

The male with yellow eyes held his hands out in front of him as if I were a spooked beast that needed taming. We were a long distance away from one another, and yet I could see his eyes clearly. If they rushed at me, I'd have time to run, time to pull the fog back over their heads like a tidal wave.

I hadn't known I'd walked so far west. I'd nearly been on the edge of the border when I began testing my control over the fog. And I hadn't expected a small horde of Dakkari to be just on the other side of it.

These males were looking for the horde king. That much was obvious.

"Wait, *kalles*," came the yellow-eyed male's voice again, though it sounded softer. "*Hanniva*. Please."

His voice accented the universal language more than the horde king's.

"Please," the male started again, and I stumbled a step back when he took a step forward. The male immediately froze. "We just seek our *Vorakkar*. Where is he? Do you know?"

My lips parted. My tongue tapped at the roof of my mouth. And it wasn't that the words were trapped. It was that I didn't know what to *say*. What to *do*. If Benn knew about this, if he found out, he'd kill me. I knew that as certainly as I knew that these males would do anything to find their lost horde king.

Taken. Their taken horde king.

Perhaps it was my shame, but I began to turn away, suddenly panicked.

"*Nik*, wait!" came his urgent voice. "*Please*. At least—at least tell us if he lives."

It was the desperation in his voice. Desperation I recognized well.

I looked at him, my lips parting. I tugged on my barrier. The fog crept toward the male, and he cast the barest of glances toward it, his jaw tightening, but he continued to hold my gaze.

Who was this male? His friend? A brother?

"He lives," I rasped to him, the words falling from me like a rough pant.

The male's eyes went wide just as his brow furrowed. He took a step toward me again, and I knew that it needed to end.

With a gasp, I pulled on my barrier, and it collapsed all

around me. I saw a blinding red as the fog swarmed, like a swirling cloud. An angry one.

I heard a cry of ragged frustration from the male's lips, though it was muffled and muted.

I turned to run, just in case the male took his chances and gave chase within the fog.

"*Rowin!*" came his cry. "*Rowin!*"

The male was calling for the horde king, the name ringing out in the dense fog.

His name is Rowin? I wondered.

My lungs were burning by the time I reached the yawning mouth of the Dead Mountain open before me. Collapsing near the entrance, my back to one of boulders, I heaved in long breaths, feeling my arm tremble when I reached up to push back my hair, which clung to my forehead.

I felt *spent*.

Was this how the others felt when they ventured inside the fog for too long? This lack of strength?

And I'd come so close to the horde. I'd spoken with a Dakkari male.

And I could push my barrier as far as my strength would allow, I thought, pressing my lips at the knowledge, not entirely certain what to think about that. The barrier didn't *abolish* the fog. It simply pushed it out of the way, creating clear pathways at my beckoning.

Still...that was powerful in itself. I thought back to the conversation I'd had with Tess a few days prior. About her suggestion that we leave the Dead Mountain. Together. Now I knew I could lead her through the densest areas of it, where even Benn could not follow. I could keep her safe. Protected. Would that give us a chance to escape?

But then where would we go? came the sobering question.

Tess wanted to find the others. The small group that Jacob had led back north, back home. A part of me still resented him for leaving us behind, Tess and me. But Benn had nearly killed him and time had been running out.

"There you are," came her voice, bright with relief and something that was tinged with excitement.

Tess emerged from the Dead Mountain. The fog was lightest here, however, pushed in and out of the Dead Mountain's entrance, which acted like a wind tunnel. Like the mountain was...breathing. Inhaling and exhaling. A chill pricked the back of my neck at the thought.

Tess crouched in front of me.

"I couldn't find you anywhere. I was worried," she told me. She touched my forehead, and her brows drew together in concern. "What's wrong? Are you sick?"

"No," I whispered, not trusting my voice. "No, I...I'm just tired."

I didn't stumble over the words once, and Tess blinked.

There was still a spark in her gaze, however, and I swallowed, finally feeling like I had caught my breath.

"What is it?" I asked.

Tess smiled wide. She took my hand and helped me stand.

"The hunters returned," she murmured. "Just now, through the north tunnel."

My heartbeat quickened. "And? Did they—"

"The women brought down a huge beast, Mina," Tess said, her eyes glistening with her excitement as she led me back inside the mountain. "They managed to bring back most of the meat and hide! *Satchels* of it."

That would feed us for...weeks. And it would feed us *well*.

"Truly?" I whispered.

"Don't you know what this means?" Tess asked, taking my hands, rounding on me with wide eyes. "The witches were right."

I stilled, something in my belly souring at her words.

"You heard her, didn't you?" Tess asked. "You were right

there! She said if we fed her, she would have Kakkari bless us with a bounty so we do not doubt her powers again."

"Tess..." I started, swallowing. "That...that was—"

"She was right. She gave us a bounty, Mina," Tess said, laughing, bubbly in her exuberance. "It's *unbelievable*, isn't it? But it's true. She has powers. Now we've all seen it. We shouldn't have doubted him. And now I won't doubt the witches either."

I focused on breathing through my nostrils because the world swayed again.

"Benn?" I asked, managing to spit out his name before I could even think about stumbling over the word. "How can you say that? How can you say that he's right? You know who he is. You know what he's *done*."

If Tess was surprised I spoke the words clearly, she didn't show it. Or perhaps she hadn't even realized it.

"He wants what's best for us," Tess told me, her voice tightening. "I know how he is. But I feel like things are starting to change for us. Our lives are starting again. Don't you feel it too?"

How could she defend him after everything? After what he did to Jacob? To *Song*? After his abuse yesterday, when my face was still tender and bruised? Just a week ago, she'd wanted to run from him.

And now everything was changing because of *food*? Because of the brittle words of a witch? If the witch was so powerful, why didn't she ask Kakkari for her *own* bounty, as starving and desperate as *she* was?

Benn was a monster. He embodied the darkness that the horde king had spoken about last night. And with a sinking feeling in my gut, I realized that Tess was vulnerable to him again. Their relationship had always been volatile, even when Benn's wife was still alive. It swung from the highest of highs to the lowest of lows.

And now I knew which way her feelings were swinging again. The disappointment and hurt made my jaw tight and my heart thunder in my chest. It made my cheeks heat and my blood rush.

Right before we were swallowed up by the darkness of the Dead Mountain, I looked behind me, looking west as Tess's words rang in my ears. Only they felt so incredibly *wrong*. Like the sensation I'd felt when I saw the horde king lying motionless on the earth after his capture.

A chill raced up my spine, thinking about the Dakkari male's calls for his *Vorakkar*.

Rowin.

Wrong, wrong, wrong, my gut told me.

I needed to make it *right*.

I knew what I needed to do.

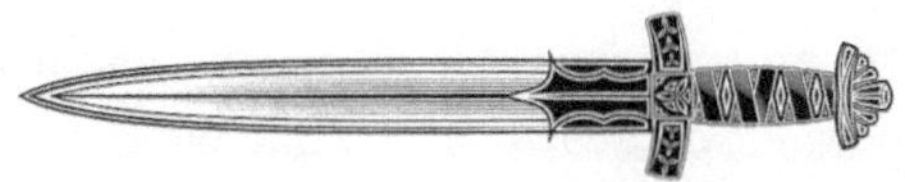

Arms aching in protest and with my shoulder throbbing, I continued the sawing motion against the stone pillar of the table. The cuffs grated across the stone. Blood ran from my wrists where not only the Dakkari steel cut into them but also the golden *Vorakkar* cuffs underneath them.

Blackened Dakkari steel was nearly impossible to break. But the stone of the mountain was not. The Ghertun had carved up their kingdom from it after all, hadn't they? And already I could feel the deep notch I'd made in the pillar with the tip of my thumb.

If I could break free from the pillar, I might be able to take that smug *vekkiri* by surprise the next time he entered the room. I would use his life to bargain for my release from the cuffs...and then I would slaughter him with my sword regardless.

Only it was slow work. And the repeated motion was only aggravating my shoulder wound, delaying the healing process, which was risky for infection. Even still, I worked at the pillar every moment I was not sleeping.

The latch on the door lifted from the outside, and I stilled immediately. A moment later, the door opened, allowing in a shaft of golden light from the blaze of a singular torch.

I heard the door close, and then I scented her. The female's tantalizing, almost comforting scent, and again, I fought the urge to inhale too deeply. Just in case the witch wound herself into me and made a place there.

She'd been true to her word. She'd returned this night, and it wasn't the first time that I wondered what she risked in being here.

Tonight, there was something changed about her. It took me a long moment to realize what, but when I did, my gaze narrowed. Her expression was hardened, and yet there was a tiredness about her. As if she was a moment away from crumbling to the floor in exhaustion.

A familiar water basin trembled in her arms as she approached. But her small eyes darted over me, as if seeking a new injury that she could tend to. Only my wrists bled this night, but I wouldn't bring them to her attention. She couldn't know. Her loyalties were still with the human male, were they not?

She seemed relieved to see me relatively unharmed, though her gaze zeroed in on my shoulder, frowning. It probably hadn't healed as much as she'd expected.

As she sank down to the floor next to me, my gaze caught on the hem of her dress, the same one she'd been wearing yesterday. My jaw tightened when I saw the edge was smudged with a familiar-colored dirt.

She'd been outside in the fog. Was that why she was tired? And yet I'd watched her control it, hadn't I? It didn't affect her the same way it affected the rest of us.

Though a part of me wanted to demand how she controlled it, I bit my tongue. I needed her trust. I'd started to build it the night before. I'd put aside my resentment, my bitterness toward her. For now.

This human female—Mina was her given name—was useful to me. And I intended to use her. This treacherous little witch—with her haunting voice and her soft, sad eyes—I would use her up until there was nothing left of her.

Only then would I be satisfied.

"Have you been eating, *kalles*? Sleeping?"

Her brittle gaze rose to meet mine. The bruise underneath her eye was still as prominent as it was yesterday, though her cut lip looked less swollen.

I told myself that if I acted like I cared about her well-being, she would soften toward me all the more. So why could I not look away from those mesmerizing eyes?

Is she bewitching me again? came the thought. *Just like she did in the fog?*

"Good news," she told me softly. "Our huntresses returned. They brought down a large beast, and we all ate very well tonight."

She shifted, pulling a familiar bundle from her dress pocket, only this time, I saw the cloth was stained with grease.

"From where?"

"They traveled north."

That was where I had begun to send our own hunting parties. Hopefully my horde would also be blessed with the fresh game.

When she unbundled the cloth, I saw it was *wrissan* meat. My jaw gritted. They were so far north now. Before, they had overpopulated these lands.

"It's still warm," she murmured, "so please eat tonight. You need the nourishment."

I leaned my head back against the pillar. "And what would your *vekkiri* leader say if he knew you were sneaking me food late into the night?"

Her expression was unchanged.

"Did he ask you to come here?"

That made her frown.

"No. Why would he do that?" she wondered.

To make me lower my guard. To try to let this slip of a female get under my skin. *Again.*

Yet...I knew he hadn't. Were the situation reversed, I'd want my prisoner weak and tired if I wanted something from them. I wouldn't let them sleep or eat. I'd keep them on edge. I'd keep them in fear.

She was doing this of her own volition. At her own risk.

"Why are you trying to help me?" I asked her quietly. "Because you feel responsible for my capture?"

She looked down at the opened cloth she'd presented to me. "Because this was not meant to happen."

Her words gave me the urge to straighten, but I held carefully still.

"There's something inside me," she whispered, swallowing. "Something that is *screaming* at me that this was never meant to happen. You or the witches or being *here* or Benn or any of it."

My jaw tightened. "The witches?"

She looked up at me. "The hallways were littered with Ghertun when we arrived. Dead in their tracks, mouths gaping because the fog had suffocated them. Even after seeing my village burn, I don't think I've ever seen anything more horrible."

I'd let the witches slide for now. But it brought information swirling forward, pushing me toward *realization.* An ugly realization at that because I feared I now knew why I was here.

Benn had mentioned my beating heart. Now Mina mentioned witches, though I didn't think she'd meant to.

Vok.

Blood magic.

"So the Ghertun are gone?" I asked, though my voice sounded far away. "Dead?"

"There are none alive here," she told me. She seemed to shake herself, and I watched her sway a bit. I jolted forward, but the cuffs cut into my wrists further and she almost fell over. At the last moment, she righted herself, placing a palm flat on the ground, but the sudden movement made the *wrissan* meat tumble out of the cloth and onto the floor.

Her small gasp had me studying her. She snatched the meat back up, and to my disbelief, I saw her eyes flood with *tears*.

"I-I'm s-sorry," she whispered. She bit her lip, plucking off something black that now coated the meat. "I'm...I'm..."

"*Kalles*," I murmured, my chest tightening when I saw her tears begin to spill over and make long tracks in her dusty face.

"I'll go-go get fresh meat for you," she said quietly, moving to rise from the floor. "I'll return—"

"Sit down, Mina," I growled out.

I watched her freeze, those eyes large and glistening in the flickering light.

Discomfort slid into my gut. I...didn't like seeing her cry. I didn't like seeing any females cry, for that matter.

And I feared that she wouldn't stop until I ate the damn food.

"Ah, *kalles*. Don't do that. Rinse the meat in the basin, *lysi*?" I told her, my voice gruff. "Do not worry yourself over it. I've had much, much worse. I promise you."

She sniffled. There was this little knot in my chest that warmed as we regarded one another. A dangerous little thing, I knew. I had the strangest urge to rub it from my chest, only my hands were shackled behind me.

Finally, she nodded after a small sniffle. But I watched as she placed the meat safely back on the cloth, which she then placed on her lap.

"Drink first before I rinse it off," she said, her voice still quiet and raspy. "The water is fresh from the well."

I...couldn't figure her out. I held her eyes over the rim of the basin as she tipped it up to me. Fresh, cool water slid down my throat, coating it and soothing it, and I only felt relief when I'd drained nearly the entire thing.

With what remained, she rinsed the meat until it was clean of debris before tearing it into smaller chunks, the strands of meat still tender.

"I'm sorry," she whispered again.

Then she held it up to me, offering it to me with tentative hope in her expression. Feeding me?

I paused, but then again, I supposed there was no other way.

It was strange for me, but perhaps *vekkiri* didn't understand the significance to a Dakkari.

For only the wife of a male was allowed to feed him.

And for a *Vorakkar*...well, only his *Morakkari*, his queen, was allowed this intimacy. No others.

My nostrils flared, but I accepted the food, holding her gaze all the while. Her eyes trailed to my lips, which parted for her, and she placed the first bite on my tongue. She snatched her hand back quickly, watching my jaw work in rapt fascination as I ate.

The meat was bland and flavorless—as *wrissan* meat typically was without proper preparation—but it slid down easily enough. By the time I was done, she already had the next bite ready and there was less hesitation on her end than there was before.

We went on like that until the meat was gone. On the last bite, one of my sharpened incisors scraped against the soft flesh of her finger. As she pulled it away, the back of her little finger brushed my lips.

I swallowed, feeling her innocent touch burn into me. Silence continued to weave between us, heavy and thick. With that luminous gaze on me and with her scent filling my lungs, the moment felt oddly...*charged*.

So much so that I felt my cock begin to stiffen under my fur coverings. I shifted my leg up quickly, not wanting her to realize it. This witch might have some semblance of control over my body, but I would be damned if she *knew* she did.

Again, I thought, my jaw tightening.

This little *vekkiri* had had my cock the hardest it'd ever been in the fog, when she'd tempted me toward my prison. Then, all I had thought about was bringing her back to my horde, back to my furs, and burying myself inside her. A temporary madness. All because of *her*.

"I—I'm sorry I didn't bring more," she finally said softly, seemingly oblivious to the reaction she'd wrung from me.

The *wrissan* wasn't much, but I *was* grateful for her bringing the food. Despite what I'd claimed earlier, I would begin to feel the effects of lack of food soon. Dakkari—especially warriors—consumed perhaps twenty times as much every day as the amount she'd just fed me. I didn't have much time left before my strength would begin to wane, so any form of sustenance was necessary.

My voice was dark and husky from my previous thoughts when I said, "You apologize too much, *sarkia.*"

She blinked before her gaze slid away. She balled up the little cloth she'd brought the meat in.

Softly, she said, "Now you know about the hunting. I probably shouldn't have told you about that."

A sharp sound escaped my nostrils.

"Aren't you duty bound to punish us all now?"

She was speaking of the ban placed on all species except the Dakkari. All who sought refuge on Dakkar. It had been an agreement with the Uranian Federation, though it only served to feather the *Dothikkar's* gilded halls. It was *us*—the hordes—that witnessed the suffering instead.

"That is only a law of the *Dothikkar.*"

"Your king?" she whispered, frowning. "But it's not one of yours?"

There were *Vorakkar* still loyal to the king, who would uphold his laws without hesitation.

And while I was known to be unyielding and, at times, merciless, I was not one of them, unless my horde was threatened.

Then I would do whatever I could to protect them—and not even Kakkari could stand in my way.

When she realized I wasn't going to answer her, she asked instead, "How is your shoulder?"

I grunted. "Healing."

She leaned closer to inspect it. "It's still bleeding."

"Leave it, *kalles*," I murmured. "It will heal in time."

She frowned.

"You went out into the fog today, did you not?" I asked her, partly to distract her from my shoulder.

Her brow furrowed. "How did you know that?"

I inclined my head. "The hem of your dress."

Her head lowered, and she peered at the dark-colored dirt, as if surprised to see it. She stared at it for a long moment, unspeaking.

"What do you think it is, *sarkia*?"

"What do you mean?" she asked quietly. "The fog? I haven't the faintest idea."

I needed to choose my words carefully. Perhaps I was planning to lie to her, though those lies were half-truths, but anything that could sow doubt would only benefit me.

"It's happened before," I told her.

Her head snapped up, her eyes going wide. "The fo-fog? It has?"

I nodded, unease sliding within me, but I paid it no mind. "Not in my lifetime, but there are records from our history."

"And—and it can be...erased?" she wondered.

Though my expression was no doubt grim, I inclined my head. "There are priestesses of Kakkari who live in the North.

Inside one of the tallest mountains at the end of the Orala Pass, not far from your village."

Those luminous eyes were rapt on my lips, as if she needed to see the words to understand them in their entirety. She drew closer and closer, drawn to me and what I was telling her.

"They are being summoned down to the East Lands even as we speak. Here. To this very mountain. Where we know everything began."

"*Here?*" she whispered, her lips parting, a flash of something crossing her features. Something that resembled fear. "Priestesses?"

"*Lysi,*" I rumbled, feeling her thigh press into my knee. "They know how to banish the fog from our lands, for their ancestors have been doing it for centuries on Dakkar."

"Truly?" she asked, the word breathless.

My jaw tightened. My chain rumbled when I shifted, as if in reminder of my imprisonment.

"*Lysi,*" I murmured. "Yes," I said in her language.

"Why did everything begin here?" she murmured, though her voice sounded dazed.

It was then I realized how close our faces were to one another. For a brief, mad moment, I nearly succumbed to the desire to kiss her again. To feel those lips on mine, to have her soft sighs weaving down my throat and her scent all around me.

"Why is..."

Mina trailed off, her breath hitching as she seemed to come to the same realization as I.

Quiet descended between us as she held perfectly still. My nostrils flared and, unable to stop myself, I dragged her scent deep into my lungs, nearly groaning at the rightness of it. My cock began to thicken, and this time I didn't think I could hide it from her.

"What spell are you weaving over me now?" I growled at

her, my gaze on her lips. My tone was frustrated. She was doing it again, and I knew I'd be helpless against her pull. Just like in the fog. "Tell me. Or kiss me. I don't care anymore."

Mina's lips parted. Those wide eyes were flickering between mine, and then...and then they dropped to my lips. Like she wanted it too.

Vok, but I wanted her to do it, I realized. Anticipation was rising within me. Desire was mingling with my frustration.

Her head lowered, ever so slightly. I swallowed hard, staring deep into those green eyes, daring her to kiss me, *willing* her to.

The door creaked open, shrill and grating.

Both of our heads snapped toward the sound.

The *sarkia* didn't scramble away as I expected her to. Instead, I watched her spine straighten and her jaw set as if...as if she was bracing herself for whatever would come.

Only it wasn't a male that ducked their head inside the room.

It was a female.

She had dark hair and dark eyes, the color of which I couldn't make out in the dark. Unlike Mina's dress, her own looked freshly washed. The female looked...strong. Stronger than Mina at least, whom I wondered if I would break if I allowed myself to touch her.

Mina rose. I saw the *sarkia* was taller, however, than the dark-haired female who'd just stepped inside, whose fear I could almost *smell* as her eyes went wide at the scene before her.

"Get away from him, Mina," the female snapped. "*Now.*"

CHAPTER 14

"You foolish girl," Tess seethed when she'd pulled us out of earshot of Emmi. The male who'd been assigned the night watch over the *Vorakkar's* prison had only looked at me with a smug expression when we passed him.

Earlier, Emmi hadn't said anything when I approached the room with a fresh water basin. His jaw had tightened and his glare had nearly frozen my heart, but he said nothing as I slipped inside the room. Perhaps my threat had taken root and he knew he couldn't reveal anything to Benn, since I knew Kaila was stealing food from the rations.

Tess took my shoulders and shook me, sloshing the remainder of the water from the basin I clasped to my chest. It wet my dress, freezing my belly.

"Stay away from him, Mina," Tess breathed. "My god, what were you even thinking?"

"Did you fo-fo-fo..." I began, frustration beginning to eat at me when the word wouldn't come. "*Follow me?*"

"I was worried about you," Tess said, glaring at me though she released my shoulders. "You looked so tired today. And when I saw you were gone from the sleeping room, I went searching for you. But never would I have thought to find you *there.*"

She must've asked Emmi if he'd seen me. And he'd only been too happy to let slip where I was.

Tess blew out a long breath, looking up toward the ceiling of the dark hallway we were in.

I knew what was coming.

"I love you, Mina," Tess said, her voice considerably softer. Speaking to me like I was a child, like it was the only way I was going to understand. "You know I do. So why would you put your life in danger, being so close to him? Do you know how terrible I'd feel if something happened to you?"

If she knew what I'd *really* been about to do, she would've fallen over in shock.

Because gods...if she hadn't walked in, I thought I might've kissed him again. I'd *wanted* to. So badly it had *hurt*.

I bit my tongue. All afternoon, there'd been a strange tension between us. Mostly because of me. Because I was still disturbed by our conversation earlier, after she found me outside. When we ate dinner that night, when Benn was dragged into conversation with Taylor, she snuck over to speak with me, but I'd been quiet and she'd given up shortly after.

"I only want you to be safe."

And yet she looked the other way whenever Benn struck me or spit vile words at me or ordered me around like a servant when he was angry. When I worked myself to the bone, to utter exhaustion. Didn't I deserve to be *safe,* then, too?

"He doesn't frighten me," I told her, anger steeling my spine.

Her gaze narrowed. "*What's* gotten into you lately, Mina? You've been so, so...*combative*. It's not like you. You would really risk being near him? *Why?*"

"He's been kind to me," I told her, my voice soft and quiet. "I can't say the sa-sa-same for others here."

Tess scoffed in disbelief. When she saw I was serious, her expression sobered.

"*Do not* mistake his kindness for anything else but manipulation, Mina," she said, her voice carefully clipped and measured. "Don't make a fool of yourself. He is *our* prisoner here. He will do *anything* to gain an advantage while he's in that chain."

"The chain I helped put him in."

I wasn't a fool. Of course it had crossed my mind that he was purposefully being kind to me. It didn't change the fact that our brief exchanges still felt...genuine. It didn't change the fact that I liked speaking with him, even when he was being a little surly.

I didn't fear him. Just like I didn't fear the fog.

Tess blew out a long breath. She took my shoulders again and bent low as she said, "I know your heart, Mina. I've known it nearly all our lives. And I don't want you to get hurt. I don't want you interfering with this. It's much too big now. Even for us."

Something dark was blooming across Tess's arm. I tipped my head down to regard it. And my lips pressed when I saw it was a bruise. There were three of them, the width of fingers.

When she saw me looking at them, she lowered her arms back down to her sides. For a moment, I caught a flash of shame flitting across her features. I blinked, and it was gone.

"Promise me," she whispered. "Promise me you'll stay away from him."

Her eyes were beseeching. In the past, I would've given her my promise. I would have given her any promise she asked of me.

But she hadn't felt what I felt today in the fog. She hadn't felt that bone-chilling realization that we would be descending into something that we would not be able to come back from.

I knew what I had to do. I'd come to the conclusion shortly

after I returned to the Dead Mountain. And that decision was only bolstered by what the horde king had just revealed to me.

I would need to help the horde king escape. Somehow. Someway.

His death would be meaningless. The priestesses from the North already *knew* how to eradicate the fog and were on their way here, no doubt led by hordes to see to their protection. The witches were wrong.

I will free him from this place, I vowed.

And it very well could cost my life in the process because Benn's wrath would be cataclysmic.

"I cannot give you that promise," I told Tess softly.

My words shocked her. I saw her gaze flash and her expression momentarily freeze.

"What?"

"I won't stay away from him. I won't stop trying to help him, in whatever way I can."

Her nostrils flared. She went silent, those eyes flickering back and forth between mine.

"If you continue coming to him," she said, "I *will* tell Benn what you're doing."

The words hit me like a punch in the gut, nearly snatching my breath from my lungs. What hurt the most was not the threat of Benn's punishment...but rather that Tess would betray me in that way.

When she *knew* what that monster was capable of.

"It's for your own good, Mina," Tess continued quickly. "I'm doing this to *help* you."

Something hardened in my chest. I thought of the friend I'd had back in our village, who hadn't cared that I stumbled over words or that the other children shunned me. Who had shared her rations with me when she saw I was hungry. The friend who had comforted me when my father and my aunt died. Who *I* had comforted when Jacob, our friend, was banished.

She'd made me smile when the world made me want to break down, curl into a ball, and simply...melt away.

This wasn't that friend anymore.

And I wondered if I just hadn't noticed until now. I wondered when the changes had begun to happen. The first time that Benn struck me? The times Mo had mocked the way I spoke or told me that I wasn't worth the food they spent on me?

She thought she was *helping* me?

"I think you believe that," I told Tess, stepping back from her, feeling the hurt seep into *everything* I had until I wanted to cry and scream so that I lost my voice completely.

Tess's lips pressed together. For a moment, she looked as if she wanted to snatch back her words...

But the damage was already done. I felt a piece of me break because of it.

She said, "If I have to be cruel to be kind, to *save* you, then I will."

So be it.

Chapter 15

From across the room, I watched Emmi slide half his portion of food onto Kaila's lap, where her own cloth was spread out. It was the following night. Mealtime.

The high of the huntresses' kill had faded. Benn had only allowed the fresh meat the night before and decided the rest needed to be dried so it could be best preserved. Begrudgingly, I knew he'd made the right decision, but for now, it was back to *rikcrun* meat while we waited.

And our supply was getting dangerously low now that the group of huntresses had returned.

Watching Kaila try to push back Emmi's portion made something in my gut go hollow. Her belly was more rounded than it'd been the last time. She was further along. She'd told everyone she could feel that it was a boy, strong and wild as he moved inside her.

And he was hungry. He always was, as were we all.

A part of me wondered how they could bring a child into this life and feel happy and excited about the prospect. They only needed to look at Hassan, at his slumped shoulders and hear the way his belly gurgled in the night, though his mother gave him nearly her entire portion at mealtime.

One only needed to look at the desperation in her eyes whenever she looked at her son.

We were capable of hunting large game. The women had proved that to us. The world was wide. We should not be sitting and rotting under the Dead Mountain. We should be *moving*, like the hordes across the land. For that was the way of *life* here. That was the way to prosperity and a full belly.

We were past the point of fearing the *Vorakkar*. We were all starving slowly.

And instead of *doing* something about it, we waited. Starving all the more. Because Benn told us to. Because most here believed that Dakkari witches would save us all. Most believed that once the fog was gone, life would miraculously get better, as if it hadn't been just as hard before. They'd forgotten that.

Across the room, seated near Benn, Tess glanced over at me. Our eyes met and she stared, but it was I that looked away. We hadn't spoken all day, and I couldn't remember the last time we'd gone as long as this.

My eyes landed on Hassan instead. He'd finished his *rikcrun* and was refusing his mother's portion. Like everyone else, the young boy had begun to notice the gauntness of his mother's face. She'd collapsed yesterday morning, faint and dizzy, while she was hauling water from the well.

Looking down into my own lap, I saw the few strips of *rikcrun* untouched. I picked off the end that had begun to mold. My belly had already soured. And though I should save the pieces for the horde king, I thought of his mercy that frost season in our village. He'd fed us though he'd been meant to punish us.

He was still strong when we were not, and a part of me knew that he'd want the food to go to the boy.

Standing, I walked to Hassan. He stared down at the *rikcrun* when I laid out my cloth neatly in his lap.

When he met my eyes, his were bewildered.

"Thank you, Mina," he eventually murmured, and I thought I caught a flash a shame, as if he knew he would not try to refuse the food. I didn't want him to. I could have given the portion to Kaila, but there was already a child among us who was suffering.

I didn't say anything. Reaching down, I touched his dark hair, thick and surprisingly soft. His mother's eyes were glistening, but looking into them made discomfort slide into my chest. So, without meeting anyone's gaze—though I knew many eyes were on me—I walked from the room, heading toward the well.

I would need to wait until everyone was asleep before I visited the horde king again. But I couldn't stomach being in the belly of that pit of desperation and hunger a moment more.

Emmi's jaw was tense when he saw me approach.

"Next time," he ground out to me, "give your food to Kaila. She actually needs it."

I looked straight into his eyes. Whatever he saw in my gaze—whether it was my disgust or my anger at his demand—made him take a step back. There was a flash of a familiar expression. One the horde king showed me a time or two.

As if he didn't know who I was. As if I'd taken off a mask and revealed someone completely different to him underneath.

Emmi had known me almost my entire life. Though he'd never been cruel to me, he hadn't been particularly kind either. And I was done letting others think I was beneath them just because of the way I spoke.

My words were strong and clipped and clear when I said, "*Everyone needs it.*"

Emmi glowered at me, but I didn't stay in his sight for long.

I slipped through the door, the hinges churning so loudly I feared that Benn would hear them on the floor above.

Closing the door behind me, I went to the horde king, kneeling beside him. With parted lips, I took in the sight of him, my gut roiling with sudden nausea.

His face was bloodied, a large gash across his cheekbone. A blade wound. From his own sword?

His lip was split. Blood was dripping into his left eye from a gash across his brow bone. And his shoulder...it looked raw again.

The expression he wore was thunderous. Black waves of rage seemed to roll off him, and again, I was reminded that this was partly *my* doing. *I'd* led him here. To *this*.

The tears that had threatened to well up in the meal room came now. They made my vision bright and glassy until all I could see was his blood.

It was clear what had happened. Benn had made it obvious he wanted to keep the horde king weakened. In pain. It was the only way to control a being so powerful, so strong.

But another part of me knew Benn. He was cruel. He'd taken it further than another might because he liked to watch others suffer. He liked to feel powerful and in control. To see another weak only served to remind him of his own strength.

Benn must be getting off on the idea of having a *horde king of Dakkar* within his grasp. He must relish the thought that he could strike and cut and kick one, taking out decades of aggression and anger on a male who had fed him for a frost season, a male who'd chosen mercy instead of suffering.

I was glad I hadn't eaten this night. Because I would have vomited the contents of my belly regardless.

His jaw was tense, a muscle jumping. He held himself stiffly against the pillar. It took me a moment to realize that he might be in pain but it was his pride that suffered too. To be tied and restrained and beaten—especially at the hands of a man like Benn—would've made any male seethe.

"Rowin," I whispered, reaching forward to touch the edge of his jaw.

I didn't know why I did it. But I wanted him to look at me.

His head snapped toward me, those red eyes freezing me in place.

"Is that your name?" I asked, unafraid of the withering look he sent me.

"How do you know that name?" came his growl.

Swallowing, I told him, "Because a male from your horde used that name when he was calling for you."

He shifted, leaning toward me. "*When?*"

"Yesterday morning," I told him. "You were right. I did go into the fog. And I walked within it, and before I realized it, my feet had taken me toward the western edge."

"Did you see him? This male?"

"Yes," I whispered.

"Did you speak with him?" he demanded.

I licked my dry lips and watched as he tracked the movement with his eyes. "Yes. He asked me if you were alive, and I told him you were."

His nostrils flared. I watched him process the words, but he never took his eyes off me during it all.

When he spoke next, I had the faint realization that he softened his voice purposefully as he asked, "Why did you not tell me this yesterday?"

I turned to the basin, dragging my gaze from him.

"*Mina,*" came his voice. He wanted my gaze, and so I gave it to him. "Were you alone when this happened?"

"Yes."

"He doesn't know you go into the fog?"

"No," I whispered. "I don't think he cares. I think many here wish that I would walk into it and just...not return."

Those last words twisted from me bitterly. And for a moment, I was ashamed that I said them out loud. Ashamed that I was feeling sorry for myself when I was kneeling next to this horde king, who had been imprisoned and beaten.

And for no reason at all, I reminded myself. The fog would be gone soon regardless of our actions.

The horde king was silent. He watched me dip a cloth into the fresh water I'd brought and wring it out. Gently, I moved forward, dabbing it along his brow before I moved it to the gash over his cheek, right underneath his high cheekbone. I folded the cloth over to a fresher side before I moved to his lip.

The air seemed to grow tighter in the room when I tended to him there. I touched him so gently that I wondered if he could feel me at all.

"Rowin is my name," he finally grated, his voice rumbly and...*soft.* As soft as my own touch.

My eyes went to his. I felt my cheeks heat when I saw he was looking at me intently. All of his attention was on me, and I had no idea what to do with it.

"One of them," he amended. "It is the name of my line, the name of my mother's line, and of my horde."

His mother? I wondered.

"How many do you have?" I asked. "Names, I mean."

"Two," he said. "Though only my father has my given name."

"Does he live in your horde?" I asked, my eyes on his lips, though I'd moved the cloth to the edge of his jaw, where there was a smear of blood.

Those lips moved when he said, "*Nik.* Like yours, he is buried in the North Lands."

My breath hitched. My hand stilled.

"I'm sorry," I whispered.

Those red eyes flashed. "The only thing we are guaranteed in this life, *sarkia,* from the moment we take our first breath is that we will die." I drew away from him. "It is everything in between those two moments that I spend my time dwelling on. My father would not have wanted me to mourn him. He would have wanted me to move forward. For the sake of the horde. And that is what I do."

That sounded...cold.

Then again, I'd once thought it possible this horde king was carved from stone. Perhaps he was, after all.

But who was I to judge that? He had a world of responsibility on his shoulders, and I had none. Of course we would process loss in a different way.

"Drink before I bloody the water," I told him, dropping the cloth to the ground and lifting the basin to him.

He drank easily this time, stopping when there was enough to clean the rest of his wounds. I rinsed the cloth once more and went over his face again in silence, thinking about what he'd revealed to me.

"What is it like in your horde?" I asked, a question I'd pondered nearly my entire life. "What is life like there?"

He swallowed thickly and leaned his head back along the pillar, exposing the wide column of his throat.

For the briefest of moments, I had the desire to press myself there. To curl my own face into the crook of his neck because I thought I might feel...warm there. Safe there.

Then I flushed and chided myself for being foolish.

"Everyone has their purpose. And no purpose is more important than another," he told me. "There is a rhythm in a horde, one that outsiders might not understand. And only when that rhythm is uninterrupted does a horde thrive. The hunters hunt. The *bikkus* feed us with the game they bring home. With that strength they give us, with the nourishment that Kakkari gifts us, the warriors train and grow strong. The *mitri* makes our swords and keeps us protected with his craft. Our *pyrokis* carry us across the land so we are able to survive.

The *mrikro* cares for the *pyrokis*. A young girl trains under the *mrikro* and will one day take his place. Her mother is part of a group who tends to our crops. And another mother processes the fur and hides that the hunters bring in. If a hunter is injured on the hunt, our healer tends to their wounds. So you see? Horde life is all about connection. That is what makes a horde strong."

He spoke of rhythm, and I felt the rhythm of his own voice. It lulled me, and I felt a longing bubble up in my throat. It was so unlike the stories of hordes I'd heard all my life. Of violent, hulking beasts, who reveled in battle and bloodshed.

"Are they happy?" I whispered, my throat tight.

He met my gaze. "I like to think so."

"Are they safe?"

He inclined his head. "*Lysi.*"

Longing built in my breast. He said it with such certainty.

"And are you happy?"

The expression that passed over his features was one of bewilderment, not unlike the one Hassan had worn earlier when I gave him the *rikcrun*. As if...he'd never asked himself that question before. As if his own happiness didn't matter.

"I serve my horde as best as I am able to. That is all I ever wanted."

"I suppose it's a difficult question to answer," I murmured, my eyes fastened on his shoulder wound as I washed it with fresh water. "I suppose happiness is not a state of being. It's an emotion, like you said. Just like anger or hurt or longing. It passes and fades into another emotion."

When had I felt happiness last, that elusive emotion?

The memory that immediately came to mind was a moment with my father and aunt. It had been a beautiful day in the warm season after a particularly brutal frost. We'd been out in the bog, foraging for whatever berries we could find there. I'd been...perhaps ten or eleven. And we'd been making up songs as we were ankle deep in the muck, trying to rhyme words with *swamp* and *mush* and squelch.

I always liked singing because when I sang, I didn't stutter over words. When I was young, all I wanted was to sing. I thought that if I sang, people would think I was like them.

And so we sang that day in the bog.

And Father had made me laugh so hard I couldn't breathe because he had a terrible singing voice, especially when he was rhyming *mush* with *tush* and *squelch* with *belch.* His cough had finally begun to abate for the season. Our spirits had been lifted. Even my normally disapproving aunt had needed to hide a smile or two that day.

There was a bubble of warmth that built up in my chest at the memory. I hung on to it for as long as I could, keeping it close, letting it heat some of the loneliness that plagued me.

"What do you think of, *sarkia,*" he asked, "to make an expression such as this?"

The weight of his stare flustered me when I met it. I realized that I was smiling. Though it was soft and barely there, I was still smiling, and I didn't remember the last time that had happened.

That memory was precious to me, and so I didn't share it. I didn't want to, not with anyone. As if when I spoke it aloud, it would drift away and I'd never be able to recapture it again.

"What would you even look like smiling, I wonder?" I asked instead.

His grim, serious stare made my lips quirk even more.

Eventually, my smile left me. That little ball of warmth faded, and I was left shivering, in the cold darkness of the horde king's cell, with the scent of metallic blood in my nostrils and his terrifying bulk close to me.

But he was warm, and I found myself scooting toward him. His bare outer thigh pressed into my knee. I saw something flicker in his gaze. His eyes went to my lips, and under his stare, they parted. My belly warmed, replacing that warm memory with a heat that I didn't recognize.

"Rowin," I whispered.

At the sound of his name, I saw him tense and move forward, the chain rattling behind him. I studied the wounds on his face, the swollen areas that I knew would smooth come morning. Then I met his eyes. Suddenly I was a bundle of nerves, but I didn't want to be afraid. Not anymore. Like he said, my death was guaranteed in this life. I might as well die for something I believed to be *right*.

I leaned close, so close that my lips brushed the sharp shell of his ear.

"I am going to help you," I told him. "I will help you leave this place before the black moon comes."

His nostrils flared. That was the only indication that he'd heard me.

"I promise you that."

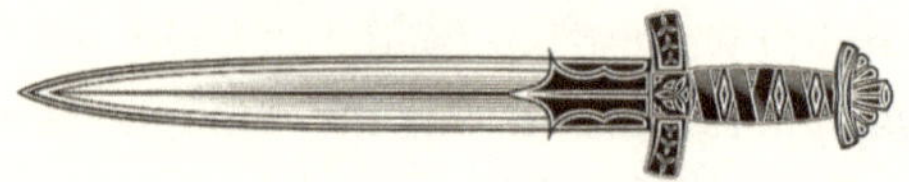

CHAPTER 16

"How exactly do you plan to do that, *sarkia*?" I asked, keeping my voice soft.

I thrummed my thumb across the deepening notch in the pillar. If I worked on it every waking moment, I thought I could cut myself from it within two days.

Mina pulled back, the dizzying sensation of her lips leaving the sensitive flesh of my ear. Briefly, my gaze flickered over her. When she'd been smiling, a quiet, secretive smile just moments before, I'd been...entranced. She'd reminded me of the female who lured me toward the Dead Mountain, that tantalizing female who murmured that she was mine, whose eyes I thought I would die trying to find again.

When she smiled, the *sarkia* was a gentle beauty. She wasn't the frightened, malnourished, broken girl who I caught glimpses of. When she smiled, I saw a hint of the *kalles* she could be. In another life. In another time. In another place.

It...startled me. It made that deep instinct rear up, made me want to fight to see that female again, made me want to battle to keep her safe.

And like in the fog, I did not understand it. Not one bit.

That frightened me. That frightened me more than anything in this world.

But now this gentle beauty was vowing to me that she'd help me escape.

And while it was everything that I'd been hoping for, why did it bring me discomfort? Because I knew what she risked? Because I'd seen how the others treated her? Like she was expendable? Something to be berated and scorned and struck when she displeased them?

So what would they do to her if they knew she'd helped me escape?

"Benn keeps the key to your cuffs in his tunic pocket," she revealed to me. "I think it would be quite simple if I can reach them. Only one man guards the door at night. The others sleep in the room above. I can lead you from the mountain easily, if we're quiet."

One thing I'd learned during my time as *Vorakkar*, during my time warring, was that nothing ever went according to plan.

"And the fog?" I asked. "How exactly do you plan to lead me through it?"

I was curious what she would say, if she would confirm my suspicions or not.

"Leave that to me," she said, disappointing me. "I'll get you through it. And your horde will be waiting at the border for you. I'll make sure they know you're coming."

My brow furrowed. She would approach my horde on her own?

"My horde will capture you if you come close to them. Make no mistake about that, *kalles*."

"Then I won't go close."

"Why are you doing this?" I wanted to know, my gaze narrowing on her.

Those lips lifted a little, but her smile struck me as sad. "You don't trust me?"

"*Nik*. I do not."

She sighed. "I'm trying to make amends with you, Horde King," she revealed. "Before it's too late."

"Tell me about the witches," I ordered. "What is their role in this?"

If she was surprised that I'd remembered them, she didn't show it.

"They claim that they can make a heartstone on the night of the black moon," she said.

"Heartstones are..." I trailed off, guessing what the witches had told the *vekkiri*. "Heartstones are not made, *sarkia*. They have been on this planet since before our time. They are an ancient thing and the most powerful forces on Dakkar."

"They say they are created with the hearts of *Vorakkar*."

"I am certain they claimed that. I am certain they actually *believe* that," I rasped, my nostrils flaring. "But witches practice blood magic. A dark practice that goes against Kakkari. They believe a sacrifice will appease the fog, and they plan to do it here, in the great hall, do they not?"

"Why there?" she asked, her gaze rapt on me.

"Because that was where the last heartstone was used. A *true* heartstone," I told her. "The force of which unleashed this fog over the East. At least, that is what we believe."

"Who used it? And why?" she asked. "Is that why all the Ghertun in there are different than...than all the rest we found?"

"A human female used it," I told her, wondering what she would do with that information.

"A woman?" she asked, her eyes widening in disbelief.

"A sorceress in her own right," I murmured, inclining my head. I licked my lips and tasted my blood. "And she used it to save a horde king. A horde king who made her his queen. His *Morakkari*."

Mina rocked back onto her heels. "I-I-I'd heard that there

were...that there are human queens on Dakkar, but we never knew for certain."

She shook her head, and her gaze appeared brittle and hesitant.

"We truly have no idea what's been happening on our own planet, do we?" she whispered.

For a moment, I felt a wave of sympathy, unexpected and rare.

"Not of your own doing, *kalles*," I told her. "It was by design. You and your people had been dealt a disadvantage from the moment they stepped foot on this planet."

Quiet stretched between us as she processed what I'd told her.

"If there are human queens, does that mean there are humans living in the hordes as well?" she asked softly.

My jaw flexed. "*Lysi.*"

"Humans live in your horde?" she asked, her lips parting.

I inclined my head. I'd taken in a small group of humans that had come from this very mountain. Humans that had been captured and made slaves to the Ghertun. Slaves that the sorceress had helped free.

"*Lysi.*"

Her voice sounded far away, and her eyes had begun to glisten with tears when she asked, "In the fog, did you mean it?"

My brow furrowed. Unconsciously, my body leaned toward her, and when I realized that, I stilled. Even now, she could control me.

"Mean what, *sarkia*?"

"That you would take me to your horde and keep me safe there?" she whispered.

My whole body tensed. Before I knew it, a growl rose from my throat, low and deep. A maelstrom of warring thoughts made my head split anew, throbbing and aching.

Her words brought a sense of *rightness*. I was reminded of my wants and desires. In the fog, I had pictured her in my furs, thought of her sighs as she kissed me so sweetly, thought that I would do nearly *anything* to claim her, to slip between her thighs and rut her until I was satisfied, until I had filled her to the brim with my seed.

That temporary madness might still steal *everything* I'd worked toward.

On the other hand, I thought I would never let this *sarkia* close to my horde. I would never let her ensnare another as she did me. She was dangerous. And though she offered her help now, I would not forget that she was the reason I was here.

"I did," I growled, even though my belly roiled at the words. "And I will, *sarkia*. I will keep you safe in my horde once I return. You have nothing to fear."

The lie was like a husky purr from my lips, and I kept her wide gaze as I made her a promise I had no intention of keeping.

I wondered if this was why she was helping me. Not to "make amends" as she claimed but to try to secure a place for herself among my horde, especially now that she knew there were other humans living there. Anywhere would be better than here.

Perhaps she was far more cunning than I'd originally given her credit for.

She didn't respond. Her gaze shuttered, briefly, as if imagining living in a different place. When her eyes opened, she gave me a small smile—but it also struck me as sad. Her shoulders sagged, though I thought my vow would have given her hope and lifted her spirits.

"I'll figure out a way to get the key," she promised quietly, reaching forward to touch my chest. I felt her words seep into me, like she was pressing them inside me, as did the heat of her palm.

My heartbeat sped at her touch, a reaction I would later curse.

But I was a horde king of Dakkar. I trusted very few, and even then, I trusted no one completely.

So the moment she left the room, taking her bloodied cloth and bloodied water with her, I didn't waste a second.

The chain began to rattle once more. My wound tugged in my shoulder, but I gritted my teeth against it. My wrists throbbed and bled, chafed raw, even under my *Vorakkar* cuffs.

Plans always changed.

So I worked on deepening the notch in the pillar because I would rely on no one but myself. And if the female somehow *did* procure the key, and if she *did* lead me through the fog...

Well, she would be sorry she ever gave me those ancient words.

Lo rune tei'ri.

I scoffed.

She *would* be mine, I vowed.

And I would do whatever I pleased with the treacherous little witch once I escaped from this hell.

CHAPTER 17

I slipped from the Dead Mountain before anyone stirred the next morning. Walking into the fog, I felt it embrace me. Its tendrils roved over my exposed flesh, but I paid it no mind. I needed to make this quick, and I prayed that members of his horde were at the western edge.

When I thought I was close, I breathed in deeply. Closing my eyes, I imagined that shield—small at first, no larger than the tip of my finger. Then I fully formed it in my mind, giving it edges, giving it resistance, thinking that it would protect me, *believing* that it would. And when I felt confident that I could feel it, that I knew it in its entirety, I sent it hurtling out from me, growing and growing and growing.

I felt that familiar explosion of energy. It felt easier this time, now that I knew what to expect. And when I opened my eyes, I found the pathway.

The red around me fell away. I'd felt the *whoosh* of it as it flung itself against the barrier, but I didn't allow it entry. There was a strain behind my right eye, a pinch in my mind at the effort to keep it back.

To my relief, I saw the same male I'd encountered before. He was sitting on a *pyroki*, the Dakkari's battle-bred beasts that roved this land. I'd never seen one up close, and I watched as the *pyroki* reared up onto its back legs, letting out a wild sound, startled by the energy that my barrier had created.

The male kept his eyes on me, even as he urged his *pyroki* back under his control. The moment the beast had settled, he swung off his mount, landing with a heavy thud on the compact earth.

"Who are you, *kalles*?" he asked me, approaching carefully, his hands out on either side of him, as if to show me he wouldn't make sudden movements or reach for his glinting sword.

"Who are you to the horde king?" I wondered, ignoring his question. When he stepped too close to the edge, I remembered Rowin's warning, and I rippled my barrier, closing it off until the male ceased walking.

He was alone this time, as if he'd woken before the other men, hopeful that his horde king would return this morning.

"I am his *pujerak*," the male said.

My brow furrowed. His *pujerak*?

"I am his second-in-command," he clarified. "His general."

"So you lead the horde in his stead?" I questioned, memorizing that word.

Pujerak.

Another Dakkari word that I could add to my growing list.

"*Lysi.*"

"And though you have his horde under your power, you still want him back?" I questioned.

The *pujerak* stilled, though he'd taken another step forward. I didn't know where the bitter question came from. Perhaps because I dreamt of Song last night, though it had been a restless sleep. And it made me remember how Benn had become our leader in the first place. It made me remember Jacob, driven from the people who had turned their backs on his father because of *fear*.

"He is my *Vorakkar*," the *pujerak* replied. "Rath Rowin is *his* horde. It is *his* blood. No one can replace him. I would never wish to."

I...believed him.

We could learn a thing or two about loyalty from the Dakkari.

"*Hanniva, kalles*," the *pujerak* said, his voice soft, though the barrier funneled it to me in a way that made it seem he was standing before me. "Bring him back to us. We will give you whatever you wish."

"I want nothing from you," I told him, feeling the barrier begin to waver. I was weak. I hadn't eaten the night before, after all, and it had been weeks since I'd had a full night's sleep. "But I vowed to your horde king that I would help him escape."

"*Neffar?*" the *pujerak* rasped, his eyes narrowing on me, as if trying to determine if I spoke the truth or, perhaps, if I was trying to deceive him.

"Be here with your men during the nights. I cannot tell you what night exactly, but it will be before the black moon. I will bring him to you. Here."

My grip on the barrier was slipping. Behind the *pujerak*, I saw the first rays of the sunlight glowing on the mountain behind him.

The Dakkari male saw the fog begin to ripple.

"Wait, *kalles*, what—"

With a gasp, I waved my hand before me, the action helping me mentally slice through my weakening control. Between us, the fog swarmed the tunnel, rushing toward me. It blew back my hair once it reached me, and all I saw was red. All I felt was bone-achingly tired.

There wasn't a sound from the other side of the fog, though I thought I heard the hooves of a *pyroki* striking across the land. Perhaps the *pujerak* was returning to the horde, to tell the others.

It was such a long walk back to the Dead Mountain. A part of me just wanted to curl up on the ground right there and sleep. Because I knew it would be uninterrupted. I knew I would be safe right there.

But I had work to do, and so, on heavy legs, I slowly trudged my way back toward the others. I needed to figure out a way to get the key from Benn, and I thought I knew of a way where that would be possible.

I should have known not to pass by the horde king's cell when I returned from the outside. Only I didn't expect to see Benn standing out in the hallway, the door open behind him, speaking in a low tone with Jacques, that early in the morning.

I only saw Benn's back, and it was Jacques's widening gaze that alerted the other male to my presence. It was too late to dart back into the stairway. Even if I had the time, I didn't know if my legs would've cooperated.

Benn swung around, the horde king's sword absent from his grip for once. He'd been carrying it around like a trophy, reminding others that he alone had possession of it.

The look on his face told me he was in a foul mood, his temper running hot. I wondered if he'd been trying to get a rise out of the horde king again and was failing miserably. My stomach twisted, wondering what fresh wounds would greet me this night when I went to him.

"Where were you?" Benn demanded, glowering at me as I approached, resigned to the fact that I wouldn't be able to escape his notice today.

I didn't answer him, and I felt his irritation only rise. He grabbed my arm when I was near, his grip punishing enough that I knew it would leave a mark. But I didn't make a sound, and that seemed to frustrate him more.

"When I ask you a question, I expect you to answer," he hissed. He was in a foul mood this morning. Dread began to build in my belly.

Out of the corner of my eye, I saw Jacques take a step forward until Benn threw him a dark look.

"Up-Up..." I started. "Up-Upper levels."

"Why?" he growled.

"Couldn't sleep," I said in a rush, relieved when the words came out.

Benn turned his head toward the open door to the horde king's room when he heard the chain rattle. I recognized the gleam in Benn's eyes. The malice.

Jacques did, too, because he took my arm. "Let me take her back. She has work to do with the washing."

Benn tugged me forward, making my gut flip, wrenching me from Jacques's grip.

"I want to see something first" was all he said.

Before I knew it, Benn pulled me into the dark, familiar room, pushing me forward until I fell to my knees near the horde king, the skin scraping there. Our eyes connected briefly. Glowing red against a startled green. His eyes narrowed. I saw a fresh cut marring the side of his face, but then his long, dark hair fell forward, shielding it from my view.

The horde king's gaze cut to Benn then, just as he sealed us into the room, closing the door in Jacques's face.

"Do you recognize her, Dakkari?" came Benn's voice.

I spread my palms on the cold ground, beginning to push myself up to a kneeling position. My knees began to throb and sting, blood welling from the small scrapes, but I paid it no mind. The malice in Benn's eyes—dangerous and almost gleeful—told me I needed to be on my guard.

"Look at her closer," Benn said, his sudden, quick footsteps echoing around me. I made a startled sound in the back of my throat when he grabbed the back of my neck and pushed me forward, until my face was only an inch away from Rowin's.

In the darkness of his eyes, I could see myself. Reflected pitifully. My frightened features made determination lurch in my belly, and I told myself I would *not* be afraid. Not in front of him. A horde king of Dakkar was brave.

I could be brave too. If only for a few moments.

Out of the corner of my eye, I saw the horde king's tail slide. My lips parted. I looked deep into his eyes and placed my palm over it. It wiggled underneath my grip, warm and strong, but didn't he understand? Benn would rather cut his tail off him than bother chaining it.

Rowin's eyes narrowed.

"No?" Benn's voice sounded. In it, I could detect his growing frustration though he kept it carefully masked. I knew why I was here. It was in Benn's nature to pick and prod, to find all the places that *hurt*, those vulnerable places we kept close and guarded.

Why he thought the horde king would react to *me* was another question entirely. But this was a test. One of many. I was a pawn in a larger game. Nothing more.

Benn jerked me up. The back of my neck would be bruised too.

My fear returned to me in a rush when Benn dragged me against his body. There was a dagger in his other hand now, one he flashed in front of me as his other hand left my neck to wrap around my waist.

I felt the press of his cock against my back. He was hardening against me—and fast. My fear, my rapid breaths aroused him. The smell of him made me want to vomit. It wasn't that he smelled unpleasant, but I would forever associate the saltiness of his skin and his natural musk with pain and the feel of his hand striking my face. I would forever associate it with the smell of metallic blood and the way his hands had been coated in Song's blood after he murdered our former leader in his sleep.

"This is the female who led you to us," came his voice, purred into my ear. "She is the reason why you are here, why you are chained on the floor like an animal, why your sword cuts into your own flesh daily."

Benn pulled my hair back until my throat was exposed, but my eyes never left the horde king's. The dagger flashed. Rowin leaned forward.

I thought Benn might actually kill me. I thought he would do it because he would want to see how the horde king reacted.

Instead, he cut my dress. From the nape of the neck all the way to my waist, the rough slide of the material against the knife scratching at my ears in a grotesque way.

Cool, frigid, unyielding air rushed against my exposed chest. Benn pulled my dress away, leaving me naked in his arms, with his cock against my back, and he threw the ruined material into the corner.

"Do you recognize her now?" Benn asked, though there was an edge to his voice as he spoke the words. Benn walked me forward until I stood just before the horde king. If his arms were free, he'd only have to reach out and touch me.

Instead, it was Benn's hand that trailed over my flesh, and my belly roiled in revulsion and panic as he skimmed the undersides of my breasts.

"This is the body you followed like a beast in heat," came the words from behind me. "Look at her!"

The horde king growled when he saw me squirm, when he saw me try to avoid Benn's touch. The sound was ominous, dark and echoing in the cavernous room. The chain links shook behind him.

This only delighted Benn.

"I admit her face is not much to look at and she has the mind of a child," Benn spat out. "But her body. It's incredibly...

well, I don't need to tell you. You're only here because you thought of nothing else but fucking her, didn't you, Dakkari?"

"What is it that you want from me?" Rowin asked. I was surprised at his voice. It was calm. Even. Nothing like the dark growl that had slipped from him. Even Benn's touch stilled over my skin when he heard it. "Only a true coward tries to use a female as a shield. Let her go."

I felt Benn tense for a brief moment.

Spurred on by the words, however, Benn's touch lowered, skimming down my belly. My throat tightened, my mouth went dry. My heartbeat was a wild, caged thing, trying to pound its way free.

The horde king lunged forward against the chain, that dark growl rising again. Those eyes promised pain. His expression had morphed into barely leashed rage. That was when I saw his tail flick. Benn's leg was only a short distance away. He would—

Benn's touch registered between my legs, and a feral thing within me rose. Reacting on instinct, my belly churning in disgust, I lashed out, throwing my elbow back and reaching around to try to rake my nails against whatever skin I could find. A sound escaped me, one I'd never heard before.

"*Ahh!*" came Benn's startled cry. My nails scraped against his brow, and I went for his eye, but it closed quickly. Still, I gouged my nails deep, wanting to leave a mark, *needing* to. "*Fucking bitch!*"

The heat of his body retreated away from my back, and that was a reward in itself. The explosive crack of his hand against my cheekbone whipped my face to the side. Dizzy, disoriented, I fell to the floor.

I felt the pointed tip of his heavy boot connecting with my ribs, and I wheezed, curling myself into a ball on the icy ground.

Though my ears were ringing, I still heard the roar. The horde king's roar—because it shook the whole room.

When I lifted my head, I saw the horde king's tail had

wrapped around Benn's leg like a vise. Benn's gaze was panicked as Rowin pulled him away from me, as he fell against the stone, his head hitting the ground hard.

In that moment, Benn looked like a child in all his fear, panicked and out of control and flailing, as the horde king pulled him closer and closer, reeling him in. Benn lashed out with his booted feet, but neither connected.

"No," I whispered when I saw Benn's hand flash. The dagger shone in the low torchlight, and I saw him stab straight through the horde king's tail, right in the middle of it.

Rowin didn't make a sound, but his tail released Benn in an instant, going limp as blood began to bubble from the wound.

Benn scrambled to his feet, snagging his dagger back out from his tail in the process, as if afraid Rowin would be able to take it. He backed away from us both. I shivered on the ground, tears beginning to well up in my eyes. Benn would kill me for this. There was no way around it.

"Benn," came a ragged voice. "What's going on?"

I recognized Jacques's voice, but I didn't look at him. It took me a moment to realize he'd entered the room when he heard the horde king roar, that he'd witnessed everything afterward.

"Don't touch her," Benn grated, and I assumed that Jacques had tried to approach me, to help me up. "Let the horde king have his whore."

A deep sound reverberated in Rowin's throat. I felt it vibrate through even me.

"When I kill you, *vekkiri*, I will smile as you scream."

The words were soft—like a caress from a lover—but I heard how deadly they were, dripping from the horde king's lips like venom.

Rowin continued, "And after you are dead, I will forget you, as insignificant as you are to me. A thing in my way. You'll be just another body littering this tomb."

I heard Benn's rough breaths as he tried to regain his

composure. His ego was bruised. He'd be in a dangerous mood once he left.

"Mina," came Jacques's voice.

"I said leave her!" came Benn's shout. "If you lay a hand on her, then you will join her here."

Jacques made a sharp exhale through his nostrils.

"Go," came Benn's command. "*Now.*"

A tense silence came, but at the end of it, I heard Jacques's footsteps retreat. The splashing of water came next. I saw Benn standing at the workbench, where we'd found broken vials of glass and aged parchment—remnants of the Ghertun. There was a basin of water I hadn't noticed, and I saw Benn wash his hands in it, cleaning off the blood from his knuckles. The horde king's blood from when he'd struck him.

When he was done, I heard the basin scrape off the bench. A moment later, I gasped, the air stolen from my lungs, when the icy coldness of the water dumped over my body. It slid across my skin and soaked my hair.

The chain rattled again, as if the horde king was trying to break free from them. I shivered violently, curling deeper into myself, trying to save my warmth, though the water leeched it from me.

"There, Dakkari," Benn said. Gone was the mocking humor in his voice. In its place was disgust. He scooped down to snatch my torn dress from the floor, taking it with him. "I even cleaned her up for you."

A moment later, the light from the torch left and the sound of the creaking door sealed me inside with the horde king. Darkness was all I saw, save for a little sliver of light underneath the door, where I saw shadows of footsteps moving.

"Mina, come to me," came the horde king's voice, in a deep, husky tone that left no room for argument. "*Now.*"

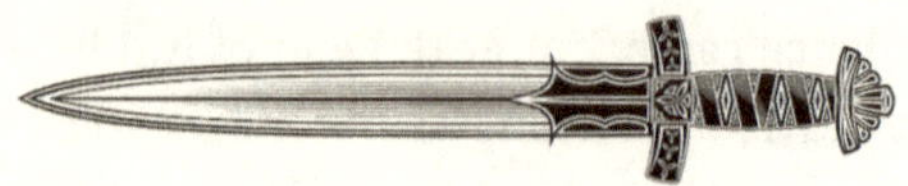

CHAPTER 18

When Mina made no move toward me, when she didn't move at *all*, I softened my voice. "Let me be certain you are unharmed, *kalles*."

I detected a deep exhale from her. Another violent shiver racked her body, and again, I felt my rage rise. Only it had never left, had it? It was always there, right under the surface.

What kind of a male—what kind of a *leader*, for that matter—treated his people like this? Treated a *female* like this?

Seeing Benn touch her...seeing Benn strike her...

It had undone something within me that I feared would never be restrained again. Feral and wild and *vengeful*.

I had never wanted to kill another as much as I wanted to kill that pitiful excuse for a male. My bloodlust was still running high. I wanted to gut him, remembering the frantic expression on Mina's face as she squirmed in his grip, trying to break free. I wanted to rip out his innards when I remembered the violation etched on her face. I wanted to *vokking bathe in his blood* when I remembered the desperate little sounds she'd made in her fear.

There was a special kind of hell for males like him, and I would *gladly* help shove him there.

My palms were bloodied and throbbing from where my

claws had imbedded themselves. Fresh blood drenched the cuffs where the skin was cut again. I'd nearly wrenched my shoulder from its socket trying to reach her.

Though I cursed her, though there was a bitter part of me that blamed her for her trickery, for exposing a weakness I never knew I possessed, I was inexplicably drawn to her in a way I'd never experienced before.

"Mina," I called to her. "Come to me. *Hanniva, kalles. Hanniva.*"

Please.

When was the last time I begged? I couldn't remember.

She shifted. An unknown ache built in my chest when she lifted her head toward me and I saw her eyes were glassy with tears. Dakkari could see better in the dark than humans, and my belly twisted when I saw the deep bloom across her cheekbone.

"Come," I murmured, the chain rattling as I moved, seeing her shiver and straighten. She wrapped her arms around her nakedness. Her wet hair stuck to her cheek, her neck, and dripped water down her breasts.

She had no protection against the cold. Thin skin, no fat or muscle to speak of, no clothing to keep her warm.

Mina moved toward me. Her hand grazed over her ribs, and she winced. She'd be lucky if none were broken. I growled, still hearing the sound of her pained wheeze when Benn had drawn back his foot to kick her. It echoed in my ears, taunting me with my inability to protect her.

She froze at the sound, backing up a few paces.

"*Nik, kalles,*" I murmured. "I won't hurt you. I only want to warm you."

Like a wary *privixi*, she resumed her approach, tentative and slow. Another shudder racked her body when she crouched near me. I widened my legs, shifting to move them around her, and she settled between them, though her movements were uncertain.

I grunted. Her skin was like ice.

"Lean against me," I ordered her.

Mina waited a breath. I heard the crack of her teeth as they chattered together. Then, slowly, she did as I said. If she were over my lap, she'd be cradled like a babe. The side of her right arm was pressed into my chest. Her hip bone was tucked against the furs of my loincloth. When I drew my knees up, the inner sides of my thighs bracketed her, bracing against the column of her spine and her shins when she drew them up against her.

My thighs tightened, keeping her in place, pressing warmth into her.

As the moments ticked by, I heard Mina let out a shuddered sigh. Her body relaxed into mine. Giving in? I tilted my head to regard her, and I was taken off guard when she straightened, when she pressed her cold, tear-stained face into my neck and huddled there. She spread her palms across my chest, not caring that half of my tunic was stained with my dried blood.

Though I stiffened in surprise, she didn't pull away. For such a timid little creature, she was certainly brave to touch a horde king like this.

Slowly, I felt my muscles begin to relax around her. My jaw unclenched as her icy flesh began to warm against me, though her soaked hair continued to run down my chest. She wouldn't be able to regulate her body temperature until it was fully dried. And in this damp place, I feared it would take much too long.

"Are you hurt?" I rumbled, and I heard her small intake of air at the words. Could she feel the way the words threaded up my throat? Could she hear them before they ever escaped my lips?

"Oh," she whispered, pulling back, frowning. "Yo-Your tail—"

"I'll be fine," I assured her, though truthfully, my tail

throbbed, sending hot pain zinging up my spine. Our tails possessed numerous nerve endings, which made them especially sensitive to pain and injury. It was why Dakkari battle armor included a sheath for the tail, plated in blackened steel. "Did he break your ribs?"

Carefully, Mina uncurled herself just enough to press her hand to her side. I swallowed, seeing her body bared to me. Her full breasts with tight pebbled nipples. Between her legs, the outline of her *melir* was concealed with soft curls.

Gritting my teeth, I told myself that only a monster would feel arousal at this moment. I told myself that the last thing she needed to feel was my cock thickening against her, tenting my loincloth, which was pressing into her hip.

She likely assumed I couldn't see her because of the darkness. Humans were strange about nudity, whereas Dakkari were not.

"No," she whispered, and I watched her palpitate the area, like she knew what to feel for, like this had happened before. "Just bruised."

I leaned my head back against the pillar. The fresh cut on my face pulled when I licked my dry lips, and I focused on that pain instead of the pain from my tail.

"He has hurt you like that before?" I growled out.

She stiffened a little. Then gently, she leaned her cheek against my chest, seeking warmth once more.

"Yes."

My claws curled into my palms again.

"He has touched you like that before?" I forced myself to ask, my voice going deeper.

The silence was long and tense.

"No," she said, sniffling, and I didn't know why I felt such *relief* at that. "He doesn't...doesn't like the way I speak. It angers him. Yet it spares me from him. From that."

"The way you speak," I repeated, not understanding. "You speak well."

"With you. With you, I speak well," she told me. My brow furrowed. Had I heard her speak around others? *Lysi*, I supposed I had, but I hadn't noticed anything strange. "With others, I stutter my words. I've done it ever since I could remember. It makes others think I'm...it makes them think something is wrong with me. That I was cursed."

That was why Benn referred to her as having a child's mind.

I scoffed. This female was more intelligent than most. Even I'd seen that from the very beginning. They scorned her because of her *words*?

"A blessing," she whispered. "Though I didn't always think so. But I see it now."

So the others treated her like an outcast. Something to be used and then ignored.

"How many of you are there?" I asked.

"Thirty-one of us," she said. "There were more before..."

"Before what?"

She swallowed. "Before Benn killed Song. And then Benn gave Jacob, Song's son, a choice. Death or exile. So Jacob left, and those that were loyal to Song went with him."

"You didn't go?" I asked, trying to understand why a group of humans were living under the Dead Mountain and how in Kakkari's name they were associated with the witches.

She sniffled again and pressed closer to my chest. Another shiver racked her, though her flesh was warming. Her icy hair was still dripping down her back, however.

"I stayed because of Tess," she answered, her teeth chattering together. "She's my friend. More like a sister actually."

Why did her voice sound so dejected then?

"She thought it was too risky to leave with Jacob, though she's always regretted that decision. Or at least, she did."

So she stayed out of loyalty to her friend?

"Now she seems to believe Benn and the witches," she told me. "Or at least, she believes that the fog is a curse and that the witches can break it."

"With my heart," I finished for her, a short huff escaping my nostrils.

"Yes," she said. "Do you know of them? The witches?"

The *sarkias*?

"*Lysi*. And they are dangerous. You should never have gotten caught up with them."

"Because of their magic?"

"Their *alleged* magic," I corrected. "I know the female that leads them possesses none, though I cannot attest for the others."

Her breath hitched. "But they said..."

"You believe that just because they are witches, they cannot *lie*?" I asked her. "There are very few on this planet who *actually* possess a fragment of Kakkari's powers. Like you. But believe me, *sarkia*, the head witch is not one of them."

She stiffened against me. "I...I-I don't..."

"Say what you wish. Deny what you wish. But I saw it," I told her. And for that reason alone, she was more powerful than the entire horde of witches. She was more powerful than any being under the Dead Mountain, for that matter. "They call her the *Setava Terun*. The First Elder. She once lived in *Dothik*, but she was banished from the city when she was discovered sacrificing firstborns, all in the name of the *Dothikkar* and for his glory. Or so she claimed at the time."

"Children?" she whispered, a shudder running through her.

"Blood magic," I told her. "Only there was no magic about it. Only blood and her own delusions. Others heard of her. Others came to seek her out in the wildlands, where she made a small horde all her own of only females. Only females who claim to possess Kakkari's powers. The *Vorakkar* track them whenever a horde is close to their territory, but they can disappear as easily as they are found."

In the darkness, I saw her arms were prickled with bumps, her hair rising on end.

"They want to take over Dakkar," she whispered. "They want to make the horde kings kneel before them. They want to take your king's throne."

My lips curled in a humorless smile. "And they promised the *vekkiri* glory alongside them, *lysi*?"

A shuddering sigh left her, measured and tense.

"Did you meet her?" I asked, curious about one thing. My eyes fastened on her in the dark, on her cheek pressed to my chest, and I swore I felt that familiar sensation of *rightness* at seeing her there.

"Yes."

"And did Kakkari tell you to run?" I asked.

She froze.

"If you have her magic, then you have her will," I told her, my voice grim, even to my own ears. "I am curious of what the goddess told you. So did she tell you to run?"

A human priestess.

And she isn't even the first, I thought, thinking of Rath Drokka's queen.

Mina lay perfectly still against me.

"Yes."

The word slid from her throat, lingering between us. She sounded frightened as she said it.

"Everything in me told me it was wrong," she continued. "And I felt it again. When we captured you."

I inclined my head, though I knew she couldn't see me.

Then she surprised me by saying, with fierce determination in her voice, "I will get you out of here, Rowin. I spoke to your *pujerak* this morning. Before Benn brought me here."

That made *me* stiffen. Just the fact that she called him *pujerak* told me she was telling the truth.

"What did you tell him?" I asked.

"To be ready in the night. One of these nights before the black moon. That is when we expect the witches to come, and you must be gone before then."

"*Lysi,* but *this* makes an escape all the more unlikely," I told her, referring to her being locked away with me.

"No," she whispered. "This will make it easier."

I furrowed my brows. "How so?"

"He will free me eventually. And then he will ignore me for a brief time, as if the mere sight of me will make his temper rise. And he can't have that. He already senses Jacques's hesitation. Benn knows he will need to tread carefully around the others, at least for a short time."

A huff rose from my throat. "And he thinks you have the mind of a child?" I asked.

"It has its advantages," she told me. "Being overlooked."

I regarded her in the dark, my eyes studying the lines of her face, at least the half that wasn't pressed into my chest.

Lysi, this female was powerful. I didn't think she knew how much. How much of an *advantage* she could be against the fog.

She was an advantage for my horde that I couldn't ignore.

Perhaps she was wrong. Perhaps Kakkari *had* meant for me to be here…because it brought me to her.

I need her, came the realization. Not only to escape this hellish place, but I needed her for my *horde.* We *all* needed her because she could do what no one could: control the limits of the fog.

That was when I realized that when I did escape the Dead Mountain, when I unshackled my wrists and took back my sword…I would need to take *her* too.

I am owed *her,* I thought, my fists clenching in the cuffs.

She was my prize. I'd felt it in the fog, hadn't I?

That she was *mine*. She'd vowed it to me in that beautiful, haunting voice I could still *feel*: *Lo rune tei'ri, Vorakkar.*

And though this *sarkia* would never get her claws deep enough into me to control me again, I realized that she was incredibly useful.

And when I took her to my horde, whether she was willing or not, I would show her just how useful she would become.

Lysi, I thought, *I will secure her for my horde's safety.*

No matter what it took.

CHAPTER 19

It was Tess that came to retrieve me from my newest prison.

I didn't know how long it had been, but one moment I was talking to the horde king and the next, my eyes were cracking open to the sound of the door.

Not long, I decided. I'd been here only long enough to sleep.

To have a good sleep, I mentally amended. Despite my aching side and the tenderness of my face, I felt surprisingly well rested. Despite the fact that my hair hadn't dried yet, the right side of my body felt meltingly warm.

I heard it then. His heartbeat. That had been what lulled me to sleep, I remembered. Strong and even and soothing.

"Mina," Tess called out for me. "Come away from him."

She sounded afraid. The idea made me want to laugh. She was afraid that I was plastered against the horde king, situated between his strong thighs, and sleeping against the male who'd only wanted to make sure I'd be warm? But she wasn't angry at the male who'd struck me, who'd ripped my dress off and touched me, who'd kicked me until I couldn't breathe and then thrown icy water over my body for good measure?

I could see now. Tess had brought in a torch, and it flickered over all the shadowy, dark places of the room. Lifting my gaze, I saw Rowin was watching me. There was a strange expression on his face as his eyes flickered back and forth between mine.

In the torchlight, I saw the wound on his face was already beginning to heal. I wondered about his shoulder, his tail. He hadn't made a sound as the blade penetrated. As for his shoulder, he'd told me he'd endured much worse.

What *had* he been through? What had he needed to endure in his lifetime to be where he was now?

For the first time, I wondered how the horde kings were selected. I'd always assumed it was through bloodlines, but perhaps not.

"Go, *kalles*," he murmured quietly.

A moment later, Tess threw a blanket into my lap and backed away quickly, eyeing the horde king's tail with trepidation. Now that there was light, I looked at his wound. It was toward the end of his tail, and it was *still* bleeding. A small pool of black blood had formed underneath it, and I watched the end twitch, sending a small spray of it to the left.

"Go," he said, his voice soft. "It will heal. Do not return this night, *lysi*?"

I knew he was right. Benn might be on thin ice with the others, but I would be watched as well. Closely. Especially by Tess, if her shrewd expression was anything to go by.

Still...the thought of him injured, alone in this room, in darkness, made my gut churn.

Soon, I thought.

He would be free soon.

He'd go back to his horde.

And it was very likely I'd never see him again.

I nodded and took a deep breath, though a dull ache in my ribs made me wince. I shifted, and he uncurled his thighs from around me. Cold air rushed against the warm places of my flesh, and I shivered as I wrapped the blanket around myself as quickly as I could, shielding my nakedness.

Rising on unsteady legs, I walked toward Tess, who held her hand out for me. I could feel the horde king's gaze on my back, and when I looked over my shoulder, those red eyes burned into mine.

There was something changed about him. Something… focused. It made awareness race up my spine and a familiar feeling tingle over my flesh.

I remembered him as I'd first seen him. Proud, grim, and strong. Even now, even chained, he was still all those things.

Jacques was lingering in the hallway, but he shied away from my gaze as Tess shut and latched the door.

All he said was "I'm sorry, Mina."

A knot lodged in my throat. I didn't say anything, and Tess took my arm, leading me away.

"Benn told me to come get you," Tess said. "He said you *hit* him, that you went *wild*. What were you thinking, Mina?"

A laugh bubbled up in my throat, making Tess pause and turn to face me. "Is that what he told you?"

Tess swallowed. Her gaze flickered to the end of the hallway.

"I have done everything to protect you," she whispered. "Things you don't even know about. But I can't protect you if you go against everything he wants."

"Did you know," I began, "that the Dakkari know how to defeat the fog? That priestesses are already on their way here?"

Tess paused, considering my words. But my stomach sank when she shook her head. "It's smart, I'll give him that."

My brows furrowed.

"I told you not to be a fool," Tess said.

She thought he was lying to me? To make me doubt?

I'd considered it. But in the end, I'd chosen to believe him. *Something* told me to believe him.

"He struck me," I told her, my voice trembling with my sudden anger. And by the way her gaze flashed, she knew I wasn't talking about the horde king. "He kicked me. He *touched* me. So maybe *you* shouldn't be the fool, Tess."

For a moment, she looked dumbstruck. My words hit her. Hard.

"He said he wouldn't touch you. That was our deal," she said.

I swallowed. Reaching out to take her hand, I knew that our relationship was developing larger cracks. The smaller ones that had arisen after our village burned were only deepening and widening. Fracturing.

And yet I still believed I could repair them. I *had* to.

She spoke of deals with Benn. Deals that she'd made to protect me.

"Don't deepen your ties with him, Tess," I said, the words, for once, strong and clear. "Not for me. I fear..."

Once I helped the horde king escape, once my part in it was discovered, Tess would suffer too. And I didn't want that. No matter what she believed, no matter what she turned a blind eye to, I still considered her my sister. And blood was blood.

I couldn't turn my back on her.

"And I beg you, Mina," she whispered, her gaze suddenly glassy and fierce, "don't do anything that would jeopardize their plans. For all our sakes."

This was just the same conversation we'd had earlier. Just framed in a different way. She still believed that the witches could dispel the fog. She believed sacrificing the horde king was the only way, as did the others, and they wouldn't consider that there might be other possibilities.

My shoulders sagged. Looking down, I told her, "I won't. I promise."

Her relief was palpable.

And it was perhaps the first time that I'd lied to her in my entire life.

Benn didn't look at me, though I certainly kept my eye on *him*. And though he was the only one that kept the majority of my attention, I felt the weight of the others' stares. The way the meal room went quiet as I walked in.

"Taylor," Benn called, "Emmi, Jos, Bray."

There was an inner circle among us. Everyone knew it.

At the last minute, Benn added, "Tess. Meeting in my quarters before we eat."

"What about Jacques?" Taylor asked. "Should I—"

"No," Benn said, his tone tinged with irritation. Jacques's questioning of him still pricked, I realized. "He's on guard duty. I'll inform him of the plans later."

The men stood and strode from the room with Benn, down the hallway that led past our sleeping room and up to Benn's private one. At the last moment, my gaze connected with Tess's. Part of my eyelid was swollen and it drooped slightly into my vision, but I didn't miss her worried expression. As if when she turned her back for a moment, I'd return to the horde king.

There was a reason she was being summoned. And though not long ago we had jested in secret over those in Benn's inner circle—I would giggle quietly as Tess did her best impression of them all—I couldn't help but wonder if a part of it thrilled her now. To be chosen. To be included.

Breaking my gaze, she walked from the meal room, and my belly soured. I huddled down in my usual place, immediately turning my thoughts to the key in Benn's pocket and trying to ignore the way I heard my name every so often, whispered among the others that remained.

But it wasn't long before someone hovered before me.

When I looked up, my lips parted in surprise as I saw it was Farah, Hassan's mother. In her hand was a flat stone. The smoothest I'd ever seen.

I stayed perfectly still as she pressed the stone to my swollen eyelid. Sucking in a sharp breath, I realized it felt like ice, though the stinging sensation slowly morphed into one of numbness.

"For the swelling," she told me quietly. "It was my mother's. She often got terrible aches in her legs, and she would use this. Keep it cold with water."

She took my hand and placed it over the stone, keeping it there as she pulled her own away. I remembered Farah's mother in our village. She'd claimed a reputation as an old, cranky woman who liked her quiet. Only I thought she'd taken a liking to my father, as she was always kind and welcoming to him.

"Thank you," I whispered quietly.

She nodded, peering down at my face closely before she turned, walking back toward her son, who sat watching the exchange.

The stone was cool on my hot flesh. It felt soothing. It helped numb the tenderness, though it was Farah's small kindness that had me closing my eyes, trying to hide the sudden glassiness that stung beneath my lids.

By the time Benn and the others emerged from his private quarters, the rest of us were restless with hunger. Tess caught my gaze but stayed at Benn's side when he approached. Most of us sat on stools carved up from the mountain rock, though there was a large table in the very center with a long bench on both sides. Like the other rooms, we could only speculate what this one was used for, but given its proximity to the "kitchens," where we'd discovered a large roasting pit, we assumed this hall was for eating.

And so we ate here too.

"The witches will arrive in two days," Benn told us all, his voice booming easily off the walls. No one made a sound. "I expect everyone to be amenable hosts to our guests, though their presence may make you uneasy."

Guests? Like we weren't guests ourselves in this stolen kingdom?

"I sent Patrick and Kyl ahead as scouts this afternoon, to help guide the witches to the northern tunnel. They will be sleeping in another room once they arrive, though they will take their meals with us. Shayma and Jess have been working hard preparing our dried rations, but there will be a small feast with the remaining fresh meat once the witches arrive. To *celebrate*."

Benn smiled when a small burst of excited chatter started up with the news. That smile made my fist clench over the stone at my brow. When Benn caught sight of me, that smile died. His jaw tightened, and I saw Tess shift closer to him, saw her reach out a hand to touch his forearm.

"With one or two exceptions, you have all worked hard. And despite what you may have heard today, I treat everyone here equally. And when a crime has been committed against us, I punish it in kind," Benn continued, and I focused on breathing through my nostrils. "It is time to eat, but let us first take a quiet moment to be grateful for our blessings. This is a special time. We are on the cusp of change. I only ask that you hold on for a little while longer. Endure this pain, this frustration, and you will all be rewarded tenfold."

There must have been whisperings about me throughout the day to elicit such a speech from Benn. He was really aiming for benevolence tonight. To distract from the rumors of my brief imprisonment?

It must have been Jacques who told someone. He'd been the only one there.

No one seemed to move as deafening silence spread throughout the room. I even saw a few close their eyes. Once Benn was satisfied, he went to the storage room just off the hall. He brought back the chest, full of the rest of our rations, pulled out his key from the pocket, and unlocked it.

There was a casualness about his movements that suddenly put me on edge. That and the fact that he'd brought the entire chest out in front of everyone.

Across the room, Kaila shuffled backward behind Emmi. But Emmi was looking at Benn without a hint of trepidation. Instead, his arms were crossed over his chest and there was even a hint of a smirk on his expression.

My heart began to pound. Because I could see it all unfolding before me. And I *knew*. I *knew* that this was not right.

Slowly, I stood, the rock hanging limply in my grip.

Then the words came from Benn. Soft and angry and somehow gleeful.

"There are rations missing," he said.

CHAPTER 20

No one gasped. No one spoke.

The room went dead silent.

I didn't think anyone even *breathed*.

It was Tess who finally said, "That can't be right. Only you have the key to the chest, Benn."

Benn shot her a look, his shoulders bunching. "Are you saying I'm lying?"

Tess immediately realized her mistake. She shrank back. "No. Of course not."

"I count the rations every two days. I *meticulously* plan out meals so that everyone can eat their fair share," Benn began, raising his voice. "And someone has taken more than their share. Someone has stolen food from us, from *all* of us, and I want to know who!"

Kaila's face was pale. A slim hand settled on the swell of her belly, and she looked down at her feet, though a moment later she shot a look up at Emmi.

"If *anyone* knows anything about this, step forward now and speak! This will not go unpunished. When you steal from one, you steal from us all," Benn said, his voice booming in the small hall. "So step forward! Look your sisters and brothers in the eyes and tell them that you stole food from their own bellies."

Kaila's eyes caught on me. And she flushed when she saw me watching her. I knew. Of course I knew. She was waiting to see if I would say anything.

Standing tall next to her, Emmi's gaze cut to mine. He glowered at me when he saw me looking at Kaila, and in that brief moment, I knew what he would do. My belly flipped in mild panic as he stepped forward, and somehow, the already silent room grew even more hushed.

Unconsciously, I took a step forward, as if to silence him myself before he said the ugly words.

"It was Mina," Emmi said, his voice ringing clear and sure. "It must have been. I saw her slipping the key back into your pocket, Benn."

There was a ripple through the room, and my face burned, even hotter than the throbbing from my wound, when I felt dozens of eyes round on me. My fist squeezed.

"And you just inform us now?" Tess asked, her voice rising. I recognized a tendril of desperation in her voice, and my belly soured when I realized that she was still trying to protect me. "That doesn't make sense. Mina wouldn't steal from us."

"I wasn't certain what I saw," Emmi defended, his arms tightening across his chest. "But now that Benn confirms food has been taken, I believe she's been feeding the horde king from our own rations. The door to his rooms was unlatched last night, and I noticed she was gone from her bed."

A chorus of murmurs erupted. Throughout it all, my eyes never left Kaila's. The pregnant woman bit her lip...and looked down to the floor, unable or unwilling to keep my gaze.

Then I looked to Benn. In my ears, my blood rushed. And instead of fear, I felt *rage*. Fury. It burned in my veins, sizzling underneath my skin.

Because when I looked at him, I didn't see the anger I

expected. Which told me two things. He'd known the food was gone. And it was Emmi's deception to throw blame off Kaila that led to this little show. They'd planned this. Together.

Emmi had likely told Benn today while I was locked away with Rowin. He'd known that Benn was already upset with me and had decided to tell him *I* was the one stealing the food. Benn was only too happy to accept the lie. And Emmi...well, he was protecting his lover *and* tossing me into the fire, payback for my threats.

Benn's footsteps were quick, booming across the floor as he strode toward me.

"What do you have to say for yourself, Mina?" he hissed when he grabbed my arm, right over the bruises that were already forming from his fingertips.

Out of the corner of my eye, I saw Farah and Hassan. Farah's brows were furrowed, but I hated the realization that was spreading across her face.

"I didn't steal anything!"

I didn't know if everyone was more surprised that the words weren't stuttered...or that I'd yelled them in my anger. My voice was clear, overpowering Benn's even.

"Lies," Benn hissed, shaking me hard, making my neck snap back. "She's lying!"

Tess stepped forward but then stopped when Benn cut her a sharp look. She bit her lip...and I didn't even feel disappointment when she stepped back. The hesitant look she was giving me, it was like she might actually think the lie was *true*.

My best friend, a woman I considered my own *sister*, thought that *I* was lying? I would never steal food from the others. She *knew* me. I had only given food to Rowin that was from my own rations.

"The real reason she was locked away today was that I discovered her plotting with the horde king!" Benn announced. "Isn't that right, Tess?"

My heart stopped then. Tess looked at Benn, her lips parted, a flash of panic crossing her expression.

She'd told him?

Benn had known all along?

She'd...betrayed me? There was something always unspoken between us. That we could trust each other. That we would look out for each other. After Song's death, after Jacob and the others left us, our once-strong village had slowly crumbled into mistrust and fear and hunger. All were a part of our daily lives and had been for quite some time.

But through it all, I'd always had Tess.

Only now I didn't think I did.

It cut. It cut *deep* until I felt like I couldn't breathe.

Benn shoved me to the ground, and I fell, smashing my knees and my knuckles against the floor, scraping back skin. Only I didn't feel a thing.

He tugged me up by my hair until I was on my knees.

"Benn, please don't," Tess pleaded, her voice shaking.

"Look at them all," Benn rasped in my ear, his hot breath making my flesh crawl.

I was strangely numb inside, though I did as he asked, meeting the eyes of the group. Dozens and dozens of pairs of eyes. All different colors and shapes and sizes. All looking at me with anger or pity or disappointment or discomfort.

"Tell them what you did," Benn said, shaking me, his fist curling tighter into my hair. "Tell them!"

When I looked at Kaila, I swore there were tears in her eyes. I saw her tug on Emmi's hand, and he cut a look toward her. He shook his head, his lips pressing together.

Then both of her hands moved to her belly, and I looked at that mound, covering and protecting her unborn child.

What did it matter if I lied? I'd already lost Tess's trust, and hers was the only one that had truly mattered to me.

Words meant nothing.

"I took it," I said softly. "I took the food."

Kaila froze. The whole room seemed to freeze. Tess's brows furrowed, a hand coming up to cover her lips.

Then I heard an exhale whistle from Benn's nostrils. I heard the startled cry that rippled through the room before I actually felt him strike me.

Power meant violence to Benn. Power equaled leadership. Which was why his temper always rose when his power was threatened.

I fell to the floor again, tasting blood. In my hand, my fingers curled around the smooth stone. And I felt my fury and frustration boil over. I'd had enough. A part of me was broken and would never be whole again.

"Benn, stop!" I heard Tess cry out. When I looked up, she was rushing toward Benn as he raised his arm to strike me again. "Stop this!"

He growled in frustration when she grabbed hold of his arm.

Then the sound of his hand connecting with her face came. That sound spurred me into motion. Tess fell to the floor, and I rose. My ears were ringing. My breaths came fast. With an animal cry all my own, one I'd never heard before, I rushed at Benn.

If he responded to violence, then I would be violent. A part of me might even *like* it.

I raised my own arm and swung. I brought the rock down across his temple. I heard a sickening thud. Then I heard it clatter to the ground.

"Fucking bitch!" he hissed, stumbling back before he tripped over the bench underneath the table. He fell to the floor hard, a tangle of limbs and flailing arms.

Something fell from his pocket, sliding across the floor.

A key.

The key.

With a small gasp, I grabbed for it before anyone could see, and I curled it into my palm tightly, the metal digging until I wondered if it would make me bleed.

For a moment, no one moved. My breaths were coming fast. In slow motion, I saw Benn raise a hand to his temple. I'd narrowly missed his eye, and I saw his fingers coated with blood as they came away.

That gaze was rapt on me. In the blink of an eye, he was lunging for something in the corner, leaning against the wall.

The horde king's sword.

Benn would kill me for this. I'd humiliated him. I'd struck him. I'd made him bleed.

Good, I thought, something feral rising in me.

"Grab her!" Benn roared, clamoring to his feet, the sword in his grip.

I didn't wait.

If anyone caught me, I was dead.

No one moved except me. Everyone was still in shock about the turn of events, and I used that to my advantage.

Without another look back, I darted from the room. With the key digging into my hand, I had a clear destination in mind. The *only* destination.

I had to free him. This would be my only chance. I would face the consequences of my actions later, but *right now*, I knew this was the only choice. The *only* way.

I took a shortcut—a small, narrow staircase that I didn't think Benn would even be able to squeeze through. But it dropped me down to the next level, giving me precious time to work on Rowin's cuffs before Benn caught us.

I sprinted down the pitch-black hallway, relying on memory and the feel of the wall underneath my fingertips to navigate it.

When the glow of Jacques's torch grew brighter, relief coiled into my belly. He was frowning at me, an incredulous expression on his face, when he saw me sprint toward him.

"Mina?" he asked. "What—what happened?"

I didn't think I'd even be able to respond. My tongue was glued to the roof of my mouth, and I was focused on one thing only. So instead of answering him, I snagged his torch from the wall, unlatched the door, and darted inside.

"Mina—"

I slammed the door closed.

Then I froze in shock. My eyes went wide.

The horde king was...*gone*.

CHAPTER 21

Sudden movement came from my left, and I gasped, whirling around, my torch tumbling to the floor in my surprise.

Rowin loomed in the corner behind the door, his expression darkening when he saw the newest cut on my face.

My breath left me. I'd forgotten how *massive* he was. How tall and broad he was.

He'd...he'd managed to escape from the pillar? Had he *cut* through the stone?

I shook my head. We didn't have time. Every second that passed, Benn was drawing closer and closer.

I darted toward him and fumbled for the key in my palm. His hands were still cuffed behind his back even though he'd broken free from the pillar. Had he been hiding behind the door to ambush whoever entered next?

"The key," he rasped. "You got it?"

"You have to le-leave *now*," I breathed, going behind him. "He's coming."

My hands were shaking, and it was pure luck when the key slid into the cuff's lock. I turned it, and a beautiful clicking sound filled the room. The cuffs clattered to the ground behind him.

His arms moved. Freed. The rope-like muscles underneath his flesh shifted and flexed, stretching. He wore gold cuffs around his wrists, and I saw the skin was bloodied around them.

The moment his arms were free, however, there was a calmness that came over him, completely at odds with my own panic.

Dropping to my knees, I fumbled with the lock chaining his feet.

"I'll guide you to the entrance," I told him, my voice puffing out of me. I felt out of breath. Uncontrolled. "And then guide you through the fog."

Just then, I heard a bang against the door.

"*Where is she?*" Benn roared to Jacques. But he didn't wait for an answer. Because a moment later, the door crashed inward so hard that it nearly splintered on the wall when it rebounded.

The key fumbled in my grip and dropped to the floor.

Shit.

Rowin didn't move. His stance was almost *relaxed.*

And when Benn charged into the room, the horde king's sword drawn out in front of him, though his arm sagged with the weight...it all happened so fast. So blindingly fast.

Though Rowin's ankles were still chained, his arm flashed out like lightning, the gold of his cuffs gleaming in the torch's light, which was sputtering on the ground where I'd abandoned it.

A bone snapped. Benn's wrist. And from it, the horde king's sword toppled from his grip as he screamed in pain. Rowin snagged it neatly by the hilt, so easily, like he'd been born with that sword in his hand.

A sigh escaped the horde king just as my hand closed

around the key. I scraped it against the lock at his ankles, trying to find the—

There.

The key slid inside, and I turned it.

The cuffs fell away from Rowin.

Freed.

Benn stumbled back against the workbench, cradling his wrist and making choking sounds as Rowin stalked forward. Slowly. Like a predator circling its prey. It was the first time that I felt a rush of fear skitter down my spine at the sight of the horde king. The first time I realized how dangerous he could be.

A ringing sound chimed from his sword when he slid the edge against his gold cuff in one quick motion, like he was wiping the blade clean. And I wouldn't lie—that sound scared the shit out of me.

It also made *awareness* of his strength curl low in my belly, hot and unwanted and unexpected.

My lips parted.

"We ne-need to go," I told him, shaken by the sudden, strange feeling that came over me.

It was like Rowin didn't hear me.

"I told you that you would die under the Dead Mountain," came his rough voice, but he was only addressing Benn, "and that I would *relish* your death."

"*Rowin*," I bit out, gasping for breath.

Benn held his hands out in front of him, stark fear shining in his eyes. The scent of piss suddenly filled the room, acrid and sour, and I heard the horde king make a sound of disgust as the front of Benn's trews suddenly darkened.

"No, d-don't," Benn pleaded, one wrist hanging limp.

Rowin's sword glinted and flashed. I lunged for his arm, and for a moment, he stilled. In the hallway outside the room, I saw Emmi and Bray, their dull daggers drawn, though no one dared to step into the room. I assumed there were others behind them too.

"No more death," I pleaded. "*Please.*"

I was so tired of death. I was so tired of *everything.* I would *not* be responsible for Benn's death. I didn't want that on my conscience, no matter how vile or reprehensible he was.

Rowin's jaw tightened. I heard his teeth grind together in between Benn's shuddering gasps.

"Very well, *sarkia,*" he said smoothly.

Then, quicker than I could blink, his sword came down.

I screamed as the blade cut cleanly through Benn's broken wrist. His hand fell to the floor with a disgusting, wet, heavy plop.

"A fitting punishment for one who raises a hand to females," came Rowin's growl, sounding unaffected by what he'd just done.

Benn's roar of shock and agony filled the room. He fell to the floor, holding the stump of his wrist, blood flowing profusely from the wound.

"You are no leader. They will figure that out soon enough," Rowin told him.

Then he turned from Benn, and I saw the cold flash over his features.

Like he's already forgotten him, I thought, my heart pounding at what I'd just witnessed. I was clutching a hand over my heart, willing it to slow.

Rowin took my arm, though his grip was shockingly... gentle. He pulled me from the room, leaving Benn crying out in pain on the floor, blood blooming quickly beneath him.

Most of the men had followed Benn. I saw Tess hovering behind them all, her eyes wide and stricken.

The horde king eyed them all, and I realized why his demeanor was so relaxed.

Because he knows he can kill them all, I knew. Now that he was free, he could handle them all. I thought he could even if he hadn't had possession of his sword.

But it gleamed from his grip, shining and strong and sharp, compared to the dull, black daggers made of mountain stone that hung from the men's grips.

"Would any of you like to challenge me?" Rowin growled to them all once we'd stepped into the hallway. Even half-starved and injured, the horde king looked ten times stronger than all of them.

I saw a dark grin curl over his lips when none moved. It was Emmi who finally took a step back, who lowered his dagger. Next to him, Bray followed his lead.

"I didn't think so," came Rowin's rasp. His hand tightened on me. "Lead me from this place, *sarkia*. I have been away from my horde too long."

With that, he turned. He turned his bare, unprotected back on a hallway full of armed men, and he didn't seemed concerned in the slightest when he did.

I had no choice but to follow. His grip, though gentler than Benn's, was unyielding, and I had to jog to keep up with his long strides.

We were journeying toward the eastern stairwell. My body functioned on instinct, and my legs climbed the seemingly endless stairs, my lungs tight as I huffed for breath.

Soon, we reached the ground level of that silent, eerie kingdom. I thought of Tess, and my gut churned when I knew that I couldn't leave her. I needed to return once I helped the horde king escape. I would not abandon her now. *Especially* now.

When we emerged from the entrance of the Dead Mountain, I spied the sliver of the moon through a break in the fog overhead. A burst of cool air filled my lungs, and an unseen wind ruffled through my hair.

"*Sarkia*," came his voice.

The fog was thickening.

The exhaustion of the evening—of the whole damn *week*—and the shock of what had happened was starting to catch up with me.

The fog was merciless to my plight, however. It began to swarm against us.

Pull it together, I told myself, stopping at the entrance, closing my eyes. Rowin wouldn't be able to last long in the fog. I wouldn't risk it. I only needed a small barrier of protection. It wouldn't take much of my remaining strength, would it?

Focusing, I drew in a solid breath, forgetting what had just happened. I needed to focus on one thing and one thing only.

The hum in the air started. I imagined my little bubble of protection. Where no one could hurt me. Where I was *safe*. I rolled it in my hands like it was clay, and then I expanded it, hurtling out from me until it was large enough to encase Rowin too.

I heard his sharp breath.

When I opened my eyes, I saw that I'd warded off the fog from us both.

And he was staring at me. With a furrowed brow and a determined look in his eyes that I recognized.

"Hurry," I told him, my voice coming out like a whisper though I hadn't intended it to.

Behind us, I heard a rush of footsteps and an echoing of voices at the mouth of the mountain, bouncing off stone and funneling toward us.

"Are we just going to let him *leave*?" came Mo's voice. "We *need* him! Or else we are all dead!"

They couldn't see us through the fog.

"He cannot go far. He will fall to it soon. We will just need to be ready when he does," came Emmi's voice. "Mina doesn't have the strength to drag him all the way to his horde."

Rowin pulled me forward, and we ventured farther and farther from the Dead Mountain, heading west, toward where I knew his *pujerak* and his hordesmen patrolled the fog's edge. My barrier of protection spasmed and lifted briefly when I felt a wave of dizziness overcome me, but I built it up once more.

Like a flame that needed tending, I realized. That needed *feeding*.

"There," I gasped out, seeing something begin to appear through the fog. A golden glow.

With a burst of adrenaline, I hurtled my barrier outward, making a clear path before us, like I'd done before.

And there, at the end of the pathway, was a small encampment. One that hadn't been there earlier that morning. In a golden basin, a fire was roaring, and Dakkari males milled around, talking and eating.

A chorus of cries lifted into the air—Dakkari words and shouts of alarm that I didn't know the meaning of—when a small group of hordesmen closest to the edge spotted their king.

"Rowin!" came a sharp yell, a voice I recognized. The *pujerak* rushed forward, not caring that he'd entered past the line of the fog. The tunnel was clear for him, however, and he ran toward his horde king.

I pulled my hand away from Rowin's grip, taking a step back, lingering on the edge of my barrier.

The *pujerak* gripped Rowin's shoulder, but at his horde king's grunt, he pulled his hand away, which glimmered with dark blood. His shoulder wound still hadn't healed over.

Rowin was looking at me, however. Not his *pujerak*. His expression was tight. Watchful. When his *pujerak* noticed his stare, he asked something in Dakkari. Low words that I didn't understand, but the inflection of them had me backing away. My heartbeat sped. My instincts were telling me to run.

I needed to return to Tess. I would do whatever I could to convince her to leave with me. After tonight, it was clear we couldn't remain at the Dead Mountain. We *had* to go north, follow in Jacob's footsteps, and perhaps we would find them. There was no other choice. Perhaps—

"*Take her.*"

The rough order barked from Rowin's throat.

Without a moment's hesitation, the *pujerak* lunged for me.

And with a startled cry, I dropped the barrier that held the fog at bay. It swarmed in, all around them.

And all I saw was red.

CHAPTER 22

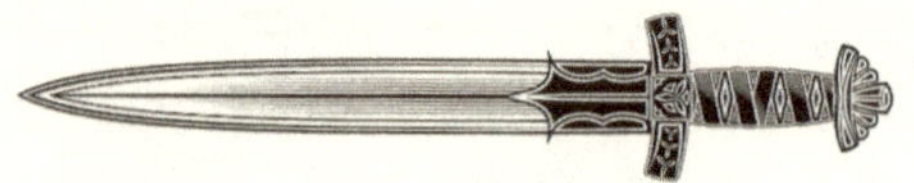

The *sarkia* thought she could hide from me in her fog?

I could smell her. I could hear her heart beating furiously in her chest. I heard her shallow gasps.

She cannot hide from me, I thought. I would find her wherever she was.

"Get to the edge," I ordered Valavik, my *pujerak.*

I only breathed in the fog when I needed to catch her scent.

She didn't get far. When I sensed her presence, I lunged. She would *not* escape me.

A fierce little cry rang from her lips, but I growled, wrapping my arm tight around her, fighting the urge to bite at her neck to subdue her—an ancient instinct. Why was I always reduced to my most primal form around her?

When she continued to struggle against me, I gave in to the urge. I leaned down and bit her neck, eliciting a strangled gasp from her, and she froze. I used just enough pressure to not break the skin but to keep her *still.*

"Never run from me, sarkia," I growled against her skin. I felt...unhinged. Out of control. I didn't like it. But I figured I just needed time to recalibrate myself after being imprisoned under

the Dead Mountain. That was all. A couple days in my horde would cure me of this madness.

Her gasps were ragged. I felt the sharp sting of the fog wind its way down my throat, and I knew I was running out of time.

I hauled her up...and over my shoulder. My uninjured one.

She struggled against me, making outraged sounds at my back.

"Stop, Rowin," she cried out. "I ha-have t-to get *back*!"

I would've scoffed had I not been trying to hold my breath. She wanted to go *back*? To what?

She weighed nothing to me, and I strode through the fog easily, though whatever was in the mist began to sting my eyes.

Valavik's relief was palpable when I emerged. His shoulders loosened, and he came to me.

"Are you all right?" he asked me, looking me over, though his eyes lingered on the wound in my tail and my blood-stained tunic.

"*Lysi*," I grunted, bucking Mina off my shoulder and placing her in front of me, dragging in lungfuls of clean air to clear the fog from my throat.

Surrounded by grown Dakkari males, Mina's weaknesses were even more striking. She was not a fighter. She didn't know how to defend herself. With bruises marring her flesh and a swollen lid over one eye, she looked like a frightened, helpless, little creature.

She froze up, surrounded by my *darukkars*, who approached me.

And...I couldn't help but notice that she took a step back toward me when they strode forward. Seeking my protection?

My nostrils flared. With a hand on her shoulder, I pushed her into Valavik's arms, ignoring a strange stinging sensation in my gut at the sight of her so close to another male.

"Take her to the council's *voliki*," I ordered him. "And tie her up so she doesn't escape."

An outraged gasp tore from her throat, breaking her from her frightened stupor.

"What?" she whispered, her eyes round, on me.

"I want guards posted outside at all times," I told him, watching his grip around her arm tighten, "until I decide what to do with her."

"*Lysi, Vorakkar,*" Valavik said, inclining his head.

"Rowin," she said in disbelief.

Hearing my line's name from her lips, the name of my horde, especially in front of my *darukkars*, in front of Valavik, made a little ember of anger burn in my chest. Anger I'd thought dead. She dared to address me so familiarly in front of *my* horde members?

"I told you I would make you regret it, *sarkia*. Do you remember?" I growled out. My words made the *darukkars* shift in their places, made one or two pass their hands over the hilts of their swords. "I swore it on Kakkari."

Her lips parted. Her face paled.

I approached her. Close enough that I could see the gold strands reflected in the firelight. Close enough that I could smell her—that earthy, tantalizing scent, though it was mingled with her fear and her blood. Close enough that she needed to crane her neck back to meet my eyes.

Her own were wide with realization.

"I thought..." she whispered, trailing off. "I thought that..."

"That I'd forgiven you?" I rasped. "That I'd *forgotten*?"

Her knees gave out from underneath her, and I saw her eyes close briefly. Valavik caught her around the waist before she tumbled to the ground.

When her eyes opened again, they were shimmering with tears and tiredness.

"I am *owed* you, *sarkia*," I told her softly, reaching out to run my bloodied claw down her cheek.

I ignored the voice inside that cautioned me to tread carefully. I ignored my concern for her. I ignored the bitter taste in my mouth when I saw her shoulders slumped in defeat and the way she looked...*lost.*

So incredibly lost.

My hand trailed underneath her chin until I tilted it up, until she met my eyes again.

The longer I looked into them, the more that familiar sensation pushed between us. Everything seemed to hush. All I could focus on was her. I felt myself softening toward her when I needed to remain *cold.*

"Please," she whispered. "Don't do this."

Stilling, I knew what was happening.

Weaving her spell over me again? Just as she'd done to lure me to the Dead Mountain in the first place.

I released her in disgust. Disgust mostly directed at myself, for allowing it to happen in the first place, for my own weakness.

Angrily, I told her, "You're *mine* now. Just as you vowed to me! And I will do *whatever* I wish with you."

I looked away from her when I saw her expression go slack. Like she was...disconnecting. From me. From everything.

When I met Valavik's eyes, I saw they were wary. He was studying me. *Carefully.* And I hated when he did that, like I was something to be picked apart and analyzed. Like I was a stranger to him.

"Get her out of my sight," I growled to him.

He inclined his head.

"*Lysi, Vorakkar.*"

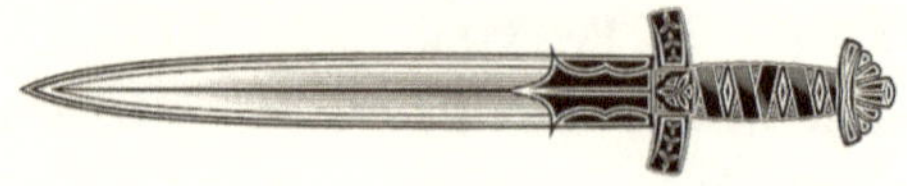

I was grateful it was dark when I slipped through my horde, keeping to the outskirts as I made my way to my *voliki*.

Grateful not only because I needed to recharge and recompose myself before addressing the members of my horde but also because I was in a foul mood. I didn't want to see anyone. I didn't want to speak to anyone.

What I needed now was to eat, bathe, and sleep.

In the morning, I thought.

In the morning, I would take care of everything that needed to be done. I would speak with Valavik, see to permanently securing the edge of the fog in case the humans came, send a new pack of hunters to the north, and form a new group of scouts to patrol our land.

Then I would deal with Mina.

But the horde came first. And always would. Which was why I'd taken her in the first place.

When I reached my *voliki*, I ducked underneath the flap and breathed in the familiar scent of my furs, of the rugs lining the floor. The sight of my daggers shining against the far wall and the wooden gleam of my chests.

A knot loosened in my throat.

Home, I thought, seeing the fire basin was already lit, banishing the chill that had crept in in my absence.

I saw that Valavik had already had a bath sent in, steam curling from its surface. A loaded tray of food sat at my table, piled high with braised meats, dried *hji* fruits, and creamy bone broth. A goblet of black wine sat next to it.

Ravenous, I ate first as I waited for the healer to arrive. As I drank the broth and plucked at the rich fruits, discomfort swam in my filling belly when I thought of Mina, when I thought of her tears when she'd dropped that lump of *wrissan* meat onto the floor of my cell. She'd offered it to me though she couldn't hide the hunger in her own gaze.

My nostrils flared. I steeled myself. I would not be swayed by her again. I could not be soft when it came to her. I'd seen how disastrous that had turned out to be. I remembered thinking that all my life's work had been destroyed in a single moment because of a *female.* Because of *mere moments* with her.

I would not feel that way again. *Ever.*

My father had often said that my mother had ruined him. Love, to him, had equaled ruin, however, and I was in no danger of loving that little witch.

But I would heed my father's warnings and keep her at a distance, regardless.

The healer entered my *voliki* just as I finished eating.

"*Vorakkar,*" Jrisanna murmured, inclining his head. "I am relieved to see you home."

"*Kakkira vor.* I have a shoulder wound that concerns me," I told him, watching his approach. "And a wound through my tail."

Jrisanna nodded, calm and collected as always.

At his beckoning, I shrugged off my tunic, and he inspected my wounds. The cuts on my face would heal. My tail would as well, eventually, but my shoulder needed treatment before infection took root.

Jrisanna worked quickly and quietly as I drank down the wine, feeling it work its way down my throat and burn in my belly. The thick, cool sensation of the green *uudun* salve touched my skin. Jrisanna packed it into the wound and did the same for my tail.

Once I was bandaged and Jrisanna rinsed his hands in the basin he'd brought with him—the sight of which only reminded me of Mina, *again*—the healer rose.

"Wash but try to keep the bandages dry," he told me. "I'll return in the morning to change them."

"*Kakkira vor, Mokkira,*" I murmured. *Thank you, Healer.*

Jrisanna left as quietly as he came, and I turned to my bath, stripping and settling underneath the water. I flipped my bandaged tail out over the tip of the bathing tub, heeding the *mokkira's* words. The hot water felt sublime as I washed and scrubbed at my flesh and hair.

Peering down at my chest, I touched the small, closed wound across my pectoral. A snap of anger went through me— a wound made with my own sword—and then my eyes fastened on that sword, which I'd laid across the table where I'd taken my meal.

My father had labored over that sword. For weeks. He'd once been a *darukkar* for the strong horde of Rath Rowin, the *Vorakkar* of which had eventually settled into the North Lands to make a *saruk*, an outpost, of his own name.

And my father had fallen in love with that *Vorakkar's* daughter. My mother. The princess of the horde, and later, the princess of the *saruk*.

Once he married her, though her father had not approved of the match, he'd given up his role as *darukkar* and taken his place as weapons master of the *saruk*. As the weapons master, he'd painstakingly crafted a sword for his unborn son, a sword fit for a *Vorakkar* to continue his wife's family's legacy.

And on the night I was born, on the night my mother died, he'd laid it next to me. A gift and my new purpose, my destiny, bundled in his own grief and my mother's blood.

It was her name I carried with me across the wildlands. Rowin. The name Mina had spoken tonight.

Underneath the water, my fists clenched. I rose from my bath and dried myself off with my furs. Then, uncaring that I was still nude, I took up that sword and went to my weapons chest, where I took out a blackened Dakkari-steel block.

I cleaned the blade first, wiping down the hilt, running my claw between the grooves on the hilt to flake out the dried blood. Then, with practiced motions that felt as natural as breathing, I sharpened the sword on the block, running it across the surface quickly, with even pressure. I flipped it and repeated the motion. I flipped it again. And again. And again.

The sound and the rhythm of it relaxed me in a way that not even a hot bath and a nourishing meal could. When I was finished, when the blade was sharp and clean and I'd erased all memory of another's grip on it, I felt more like myself. I felt *right*.

But when I slid into my bed and pulled the furs up around my hips, sleep would not come. Only thought of *her* would. Of her haunting, perfect voice. Of her wide, sad eyes and the dirtied hem of her dress. Her swollen cheekbone and cut lip. The softness of those lips...

I cursed myself.

Why would she want to return to the Dead Mountain? Nothing but pain would greet her there. She should be thanking me. I'd kept my promise to her. I'd taken her to my horde, hadn't I? Though, other than an order to have food and water brought to her, I hadn't given Valavik any other instructions. Only to keep her restrained.

"*Vok*," I ground out, sliding out of bed. I cursed her again as I reached for my trews and shoved my feet into my boots. The night was warm, so I didn't bother with my furs. And I was within the gates of my horde, so I didn't reach for my newly sharpened blade.

Stalking from my *voliki*, I made for the north side of the encampment, to my council's *voliki*, which lay next to the training grounds. It was one of the larger *volikis* and appointed comfortably. The horde was quiet, and luckily, I encountered no one until I neared the training grounds and saw Valavik approaching.

He had a basin of water in his arms, and when he saw me, he paused.

Talking quietly, I asked, "Does she have food?"

"*Lysi*, I brought it in earlier. Though I need to untie her so she can eat," he said. "Would you like a bath brought in for her?"

I needed time to think, and as such, I only wanted a select few to even know she was within my horde.

"*Nik*," I said, nodding to the basin. "I'll take that. Get some sleep. You look like hell."

His expression was wry, but he handed me the basin. "I do not envy you, Rowin. If you died in there, I would never have forgiven you for leaving me with your horde."

Huffing out a sharp breath, I said, "Bastard. You were supposed to thank me for that, not moan about it. You would have accomplished what some *pujeraks* only dream of."

Valavik grinned, though it was tired. But then he looked at the basin and then turned his attention to the *voliki* behind us. "Let me take that in. It is you that needs rest," he said.

"*Nik*," I responded, stepping away. "I'll go to her."

I'd barely told Valavik anything when I emerged from the fog earlier, and I read the questions lining his face. Questions about *her*.

I clapped a hand on his shoulder. "I'll tell you everything in the morning."

He inclined his head, seemingly content with that. I didn't wait for him to leave. Instead, I ventured toward the domed tent, nodding at the *darukkar* I'd posted on the night watch right outside it, and ducked underneath the flaps.

Her scent hit me like a wall, and my nostrils flared as I greedily dragged it into my lungs. When I sought her out, I found her against the stabilizing pole. Directly in the center of the *voliki*, next to an unlit fire basin, the pole ran vertically up and provided support for the domed structure.

Like I'd been, her hands were tied behind her back and around the pole. She saw sitting with her spine against it, and when she saw me enter, her knees drew up to her chest, huddling. *Protecting herself?* Because she thought I was a danger to her?

I ignored the way that bit at me, how the knowledge *cut* at me.

There was food on the large table near the center of the *voliki*, a high table more suited to battle plans and horde movements than eating. A tray was perched on the edge, and I saw it had the same fare as mine, though it had grown cold.

I put the water down next to her, and she turned her head away, staring at the unlit fire basin. The only sources of light were a small lantern next to the food tray and the sliver of moonlight pouring in from the venting hole at the top of the tent. Otherwise, she'd been in darkness.

She was doing her best not to comment on my sudden presence. I wondered if it was as strange to her as it was to me. That *I* was the one bringing her water and food now, and not the other way around. That *she* was the one restrained in my possession.

Her face was dirty. The tracks of her dried tears were highlighted against her skin. I dragged the tray of food off the table and crouched in front of her, the hide of my trews creaking behind my knees.

Her breath hitched when I touched her face, when I grasped her chin and turned it so she would meet my eyes.

When she did, she said, "Tess was right. I should not have trusted you."

Setting the tray down beside her, I scooped up the bowl of bone broth.

"Drink," I murmured.

She turned her head away, but I simply turned it back, pressing the bowl to her lips and slowly tipping it back before she could move again. She made a muffled sound in the back of her throat, a sound of protest.

And when I lowered the bowl, thinking that I had succeeded, she glared at me.

Then she spit the broth right at me.

Shock rushed through me. My nostrils flared as I wiped the liquid from my eyes. My chest was already damp from my wet, washed hair, and now I had bone broth streaking down it toward my trews.

The witch needed to be taught a lesson. And I needed to test my own restraint. The anger was rising, but so was something else. Frustration mingled with...*need*.

I grabbed her around the back of the neck, my hand flashing out so quickly that it was a blur.

She flinched. But if she was expecting me to strike her in retaliation, she was wrong.

I would do something worse.

I kissed her.

A startled, outraged sound drew up from her throat, and I bit at her lip to quiet it. The kiss was hard and rough, meant to punish, meant to remind her just *whom* she was dealing with.

Only...her scent dragged deeper into my lungs, her angry gasps threading down my throat. She was warm, though her lips were cold and dry. And I tasted salt on them. Tears from earlier.

The kiss had an unintended effect. It made me *desire* her. It made dizzying need swarm in my mind and thicken my cock, and I *hated* her for it. It reminded me of that pivotal moment in the fog, in that early morning light. When *she'd* kissed *me*. That treacherous kiss that had nearly cost me everything.

I'd meant to repay her for it...only it felt like *I* was the one losing something. Again.

She bit my lip, just as I'd bitten her neck earlier.

Hard enough to be a warning but not hard enough to make me bleed.

Her dull little teeth squeezed the flesh, and her green eyes *poured* into me, shooting daggers all her own.

I pulled back, huffing out short, quick breaths, and she released me. Her lips were wet and reddened. And her chest was heaving.

"Your claws return, *rei sarkia*," I murmured, wiping at my bottom lip with my thumb.

A part of me was glad to see them.

Perhaps she was a fighter. Perhaps I'd misjudged her.

"And I will continue to cut you with them if you do not let me go, Rowin," she warned.

Kakkari. Her voice. It was husky and soft, and I felt it prick the back of my neck and race down my spine. My family's name on her lips didn't fill me with anger this time. I wanted to hear it again. I wanted to hear my given name fall from her lips, the name only my father knew.

Mina made that vow bravely, but when I drew close to her again, her eyes widened in alarm. The hand I had at the back of her neck tightened, and then I dragged it through her hair, the strands tangling around my claws.

Her lids lowered briefly at my touch.

She felt it too. The...*need*. She'd felt it in the fog too, just as I had.

Maybe I wasn't the only one succumbing to this madness. Maybe she'd be right next to me as we both fell.

"I welcome it," I growled. "Cut me as deep as you want, *sarkia*. But I will never let you go."

CHAPTER 24

Disbelief went through me.

"*Why keep me here?*" I asked the infuriating horde king before me. "Just let me go if you hate me so much!"

He pulled away, his hand leaving my hair, and he rocked back on his heels next to me.

"There's no reason for me to be here beyond your own desire for revenge."

"Wrong," he murmured, his voice soft. "There is plenty of reason for you to be here beyond that."

I looked at him then. *Really* looked at him. He was in a strange mood tonight. Colder. Angrier. And yet...his touch had always been gentle on me.

He'd bathed, his wet hair mingling with the broth I'd spat at him. He didn't reach for a cloth to wipe himself with. Instead, he crouched low. And instead of the tunic he'd worn in the Dead Mountain upon his capture, tonight he was bare-chested like his warriors, only dressed in trews that clung to him like a second skin.

My mouth went dry at the sight of his golden flesh. Because without a tunic on, he seemed even larger. Muscles that human men didn't even possess braided underneath his flesh. Scars, which shimmered golden underneath the moonlight, criss-crossed over almost every inch of his body.

So many scars, I thought, my lips parting. And when he turned to pick up the spilled broth bowl from the ground and replace it on the tray?

I must have made a surprised sound because he turned to regard me, cutting off my view of the plethora of raised scar tissue that hardened his back.

Whipping marks, I knew.

Dozens, perhaps even *hundreds* of them.

"Wha-What happened to your back?" came the soft question, slipping from my lips before I could stop it.

"*Vorakkar* markings," he answered, surprising me. "The last test of the Trials."

The Trials?

Vorakkar markings?

"Do you not like the sight of them, *sarkia*?" he asked next, that voice gentling into a purr as he loomed closer. "Do they frighten you?"

I couldn't get a read on him again.

"What does *sarkia* mean?" I asked him again, avoiding his question.

He answered me this time, only his answer left my spine stiffening against the pole I was tied to.

"It means *witch*."

An incredulous, ragged breath escaped me. Then delicious anger, mingled with a sting of hurt, returned to me.

"You've been calling me a witch this entire time?" I asked.

"*Lysi*," he replied easily. "Because that is what you are. You wound your magic around me tightly in the fog, and you haven't let me go ever since."

"What are you talking about?" I asked, a wave of exhaustion creeping over my head. "You saw what I can do in the fog. *That* is the only thing I can do."

"And that is a power that I cannot ignore," he growled. "It is a power that I will claim for my horde."

For his horde? A power he couldn't ignore? But when the priestesses came, my power would be useless to him and his horde, didn't he realize that? Once the fog was gone...

An ugly realization came over me.

It made me freeze, made the blood drain from my face as an icy wash of despair crashed over my head.

"You were lying," I whispered, an invisible fist connecting with my lungs, whooshing out my air as I choked. "About the priestesses. About the fog happening before. You don't know how to stop it, do you?"

Fool, fool, fool.

I needed to understand. But everything was so jumbled in my mind. A part of me couldn't believe that just that morning, Benn had locked me inside the horde king's cell with him and I'd found warmth against his body. A part of me couldn't process Emmi and Kaila's betrayal, Benn's lies. The rock making a sickening sound as it crashed against Benn's head.

The whistling sound of a blade as it cut through tissue and bone.

And the *blood*. So much blood. Black and pooling, reflecting like a mirror.

And now, I thought, my fists squeezing behind me. *Now this.* The rope was tight around my wrists, though not tight enough to cut off my circulation. The *pujerak* had been gentle, at least, when he'd blindly followed Rowin's ridiculous order.

The horde king's gaze narrowed. "It is possible it's happened before, but only the priestesses would have record of it in their archives."

Which meant that *yes*...he had been lying to me.

I'd believed him, just like he'd known that I would.

"Tess said you would say anything to sow doubt. Tess said you would do anything to try to escape. Did that include trying to show me kindness? Talking with me because you knew how lonely I was? Acting like you cared that I'd been hurt and struck?"

Gods, I was such a goddamn fool.

His expression didn't change as he said, "I did whatever it took to return to my horde."

I laughed.

Rowin stiffened at the sound and watched as I leaned my head back against the pole, looking up at the venting hole above me. A cloud passed in front of the moon, but otherwise, the sky was clear. Empty of red.

I laughed again until the sound started to sound wretched and tears began to burn in my eyes once more.

"How you must love this," I whispered once my laugh finally died. "How you must have been laughing at me. I'm so pathetic."

Now I was stuck here. Tied to this pole. Did I want to be back at the Dead Mountain to witness the aftermath of the horde king's escape? To witness Benn's rage if he survived his injury?

No.

But I *needed* to be. Because Tess was still there. In the darkness. And the witches were coming. When they discovered our failure, how would they react? Rowin said they practiced blood magic. Sacrifices. What would they *do* to us lowly humans who hadn't kept up our end of the deal?

If the horde king can even be believed, I reminded myself.

Had he painted the witches as villains? Had he purposefully told me that they sacrificed children to make me feel repulsed and disgusted?

I didn't know what to believe anymore. The only thing I was certain of was that I was so goddamn *tired*.

"I'm so pathetic," I whispered, still looking up at the moon, with tears streaming down my face. "I was so starved for kindness that if anyone showed me the smallest hint of it, it made me want to do anything for them. And I think you knew that. I think you recognized that, and so you used me like everyone else, like Benn. Only it feels so much worse because I actually *believed* you."

When I leveled my gaze at the horde king, I saw him tense at my words. Those red eyes gleamed in the darkness, and I saw his mouth turn down into a scowl.

Was there a breaking point? Was there a point where I would just *give up*?

I thought I had nearly reached that breaking point after my father died. After our village burned. And I was family-less and without a home in the North Lands, on the cusp of the frost. Our prospects had been grim, our chances of survival low.

Yet Tess had been there for me. She'd built me back up. She'd been a true friend to me and had always been prior to that.

Without her, I wouldn't have survived. I would've lain down on my father's grave and wished to join him, wherever he was.

But what had I truly gained in continuing on, in staying alive?

Pain and hunger and aching hurt.

I thought of Tess's betrayal under the Dead Mountain. Despite her trying to protect me, she'd talked to *Benn*, of all people, behind my back and given him more ammunition to hurt me. She'd believed Emmi when he said I'd stolen food from the others. She'd believed the worst about me, when I thought her faith in me was unwavering. She *knew* me. Yet she'd betrayed me, swayed easily by mere lies. Too easily.

I'm lost, I thought. I didn't know where to go from here.

I had no home. After my father died, I never did. There was nowhere I felt safe. Nowhere I could run to when I was in trouble.

I was on my own.

Truly on my own.

And I was a prisoner in a Dakkari horde.

"What do you want from me, Horde King?" I asked him, my voice hardening.

I was hurt and pissed off and mortified and possibly at my lowest point ever. And I had two choices: give up or move on.

I thought that I was angry enough to...move on.

"I want you to eat," he rasped after a lengthy pause as he studied me. "Then I want you to sleep."

My jaw tightened. "Very well. That's hard to do, however, when my hands are tied."

"*Kalles.*"

"I think you mean *sarkia*," I corrected, my tone sounding bitter even to my own ears.

I didn't care. I was allowed bitterness and anger, if only for tonight.

Rowin blew out a rough, sharp breath through his nostrils. His hand slid out toward me again, and I tensed when he drew close.

His scent was clean and crisp. Like that first deep breath on the morning of the first frost in the North Lands. Fresh and new. Underneath it was another scent I couldn't place, only it reminded me of bundled warm furs and a crackling fire, smoky and musky. So at odds with the first scent.

And, of course, there was another. The scent of the bone broth I'd spit at him. But I couldn't bring myself to feel sorry for *that*.

"If you want to play a battle of wills and stubbornness," he began, "I think you will find I will win, *sarkia*."

He emphasized that last word, which ended in a purr, as he reached behind me. I felt the rope snap as his claws dragged through it with one clean swipe.

I stilled as my hands came free.

"*Ahh*, my little Mina, I can see your mind working," he rasped, that gaze rapt on me as he returned to his crouch before me. "But I advise against your plans. There is a guard posted out front. This *voliki* is positioned at the back of the encampment, and even if you weren't spotted running through the horde, you would still need to make it past the gates and my *darukkars* positioned there. Not to mention the ones I left at the edge of the fog."

I swallowed.

"Even still, you'd have to get past *me*," he growled.

I looked at him, his bulk somehow looking graceful even in a low crouch. I would never be able to overpower him or outrun him.

"But I dare you to try," he finished. "I like the hunt."

I thought of his kiss. How...*conquering* it had felt. And I thought that yes, this was a male who enjoyed a good hunt. So I wouldn't give him the satisfaction.

Though my cheeks flushed at the memory of the kiss, I dragged the food tray toward me, my mouth watering at the sight.

More food than I'd seen since my village. Perhaps more food than I'd seen at once in my entire life sat on that tray, each food type neatly organized in separate dishes. Juicy, fragrant, *fresh* meat, a dried preserve that was purple in color, and a small amount of bone broth remained in the bowl, the taste of which I knew was rich and creamy. There was even a heavy golden goblet of what I thought was *wine*, which I'd never tasted in my entire life. We'd only ever heard stories of it.

"I'll eat instead. I need my strength to escape you," I informed him, feeling determination flare to life inside me, welcome and contrasted brightly against my anger. "I can be patient. I'll eat your food and drink your wine. I'll listen to you when you speak to me. I'll be your servant, if that's what you wish, and I won't complain. But one day, I *will* leave. And when that day comes, I will never let *anyone* use me again."

Rowin stared at me, his brow furrowed. He watched as I tipped the rest of the broth up to my lips, swallowing the delicious, decadent liquid. Then I plucked meat from the dish, and it practically melted on my tongue. I'd never tasted anything better in my entire life. I could have *cried* at how good it tasted.

Finally, his voice came, dark and husky. I narrowly avoided shivering as it caressed its way down my spine, like a touch.

"I'm beginning to think I do not know you at all, *sarkia*."

"Good," I said, turning my face away from him, ignoring the way that voice made me feel, ignoring how pleasing I found it. "Let's keep it that way."

Only one goal was on my mind.

To get *stronger*.

And once I felt strong, body and mind, then *I* would decide the path for the rest of my life.

No one else.

In the light of day, much of my bravado from the night before faded.

I woke with a pounding headache because of the...of the *wine*, I remembered.

Drinking it had made me feel pleasantly light and dizzy. I could almost forget about the Dead Mountain, about the fog, about the witches, about *him*. For those brief moments, I could understand why stories of the Dakkari wine had circulated around the planet. For those brief moments, the wine had made me feel better.

And then it made me feel worse.

I gasped when a lightning-like streak sizzled behind my eye, and I groaned. Then I remembered the horde king.

He'd warned me about drinking too much of the wine, hadn't he? He'd tried to take the goblet from me when I began to sway, ordering me to rest instead. Only I hadn't listened. I'd drained the whole goblet as he watched in muted displeasure.

"Very well," he'd said in that gruff, rumbly voice. "You will learn when morning comes, *kalles*."

Damn him, I thought, pressing my cheek to the cushion that had been brought in for me. It was cool against me, as were the furs I was lying on. I was a prisoner, and yet to me, this was luxury. A full meal and a comfortable, quiet, warm place to sleep.

Though that meal was not settling well. I'd gone too long on too little. And last night, I'd stuffed myself with rich, decadent food I'd never eaten before. The cramping in my belly made my nausea all the worse.

But I would *not* throw it up. I needed the nutrients. I needed to nourish my body, make it stronger.

As I sat up, ignoring the wave of dizziness, I heard the clinking of *chain links*. And then I remembered.

Looking down at my left leg, I saw a blackened-steel cuff around my ankle, heavy but smooth. A chain connected it, leading to the pole, where it was linked around and wrapped tight.

The chain had a very long leash, though I would get nowhere near the entrance flap. Not even to the assortment of swords and daggers that lined the far wall. But I could reach the basin of water that sat on a circular, black wood table, and so I set my sights on that.

I supposed I should be thankful he hadn't kept my hands tied around the pole. Still...he obviously didn't trust me to not leave in the middle of the night if he left me unchained.

For good reason, I knew. I'd told him myself last night that I would escape eventually. Which, in hindsight, I probably shouldn't have done.

I sighed, pushing myself up on shaking legs, feeling my belly churn with the wine.

I need to make him trust me, I thought. And I hated myself for the thought because I could empathize now with what he'd done to *me*. He'd lied to me, yes. He'd manipulated me.

All to gain his freedom and return to his horde.

Yet I could understand why he'd done it. He'd spied a weakness in me, and he'd used that to his advantage.

Could I do the same to him?

Once I was stronger, I would leave. I would find Tess. And I would take her away from the Dead Mountain, no matter what it took. We would travel north, back toward our home—the one thing I didn't have—and we *would* find Jacob.

That was the only path I wanted to travel. The only path I saw for myself. I couldn't return to Benn and the others. And I certainly couldn't stay here.

The North Lands were the only option left.

And to get there, I would *need* to make the horde king trust me.

I nearly vomited up the contents of my stomach thinking about it, but I breathed in deeply when I reached the edge of the table. Leaning against it heavily, I dipped the clean goblet that had been left out for me and brought the water-laden cup to my lips.

It tasted like euphoria, soothing my parched throat and dry mouth, which felt like it'd been stuffed with fur. As I drank the water, I looked around the domed tent. The walls were rounded, but the black wood cabinets that lined them fit perfectly, the tops of them sloping to match the curve of the hide seamlessly. More weapons than I'd seen in my entire life lined one side of the tent. A large table sat closest to me and the pole I was chained to. A fire basin was immediately to my left.

The floors were lined with *rugs*. Colorful tapestries swirled with shimmering gold. Underneath my bare feet, they felt plush and soft. My toes curled into them. Toward the back of the tent, I saw tools, though I didn't know their purpose. And hanging above them was a map. It took me a long while to realize it was a map of *Dakkar*.

My lips parted, and I shuffled as close as the chain would allow. My gaze ran over the elegant, dark lines of the coastline and traced thinner lines that ran through the land, though I didn't understand their purpose. To map out different territories, perhaps, different regions? There was writing scrawled across the map at certain areas, though I couldn't read it.

Instead, my gaze was drawn to the blot of ink on the right side of the map, and I recognized the Dead Mountain depicted there. That blot of ink was the fog, and I realized that sections of it were darker than others, like that blot was constantly being added to.

They are tracking the spread of it, I thought. It encased the entire Dead Valley and was beginning to extend its reach *north*.

A burst of light flooded the tent, but I didn't tear my gaze away from the map. I was tracing my gaze north, trying to find the place I'd once called home, the place my father was buried.

I smelled him before I saw him—the crisp smell that reminded me of forest walks in the frost, of compacted snow crunching under boots and ice shards glittering from trees.

Out of the corner of my eye, I saw him still next to me. I could feel him looking at me, and with a deep breath, I turned to meet his gaze.

My neck craned up and up. I was tall for a human woman, and even still, the Dakkari towered over us. Those red eyes looked a little quieter this morning. Last night, the strands of black in them had swirled wildly.

Rowin looked...

I swallowed, hating that I found him as handsome as he was intimidating.

His long black hair shone with health, ending at his waist. The top half of it was tied back and braided away from his face, exposing the sharp cut of his cheekbones and the regality of his features. All hard edges and strong lines.

He was bare-chested again, and I noticed something in the morning light that I hadn't before, even in the Dead Mountain. Golden swirls of ink adorned his chest and pectorals. A shimmer of them wove around his shoulders and down his biceps as well, though they were fainter. *Tattoos?* I recognized the same scrawling script across the map of Dakkar. I wondered what they said.

He was clean and looked well rested. His shoulder was bandaged, and when his tail flicked behind him, I saw it was wrapped too.

Looking at him made my heart beat faster, so I turned my attention back to the map.

"I've never seen one before," I said quietly. "I've never seen Dakkar laid out like this. Like I can touch every place on it, like I can imagine being there."

"There are some places on Dakkar that you would not wish to be, *sarkia*," he said.

My belly twisted at the word. I had the strangest sensation that he'd said it purposefully...like he was trying to remind himself what I was.

His hesitation was palpable, but then he asked, "Would you like to see where your village was in the North?"

His question...surprised me. I shot a quick look up at him. He was scowling, like he didn't know why he'd asked.

"Yes," I whispered. "Please."

His shoulders were tight, but he walked closer to the map. Unconsciously, I moved to follow, but my ankle snapped tight and I remembered the taut stretch of the chain.

"Here," he murmured gruffly, brushing his fingers over a tiny place near the top of the map. Next to it, I saw the depiction of a mountain range. There were dozens of them, actually, that stretched all over the North Lands. I'd never realized there were that many. "Next to the bog."

Most wouldn't enjoy living so close to a bog. During the warm season, the smell had been potent, the smell of decaying plant life and still water. Yet thinking about that bog, I always felt comforted because I remembered my father. Walking with him there and making up songs and laughing because our voices echoed across the water.

My gaze fastened on that small place he touched. I memorized it. There was a circle drawn there with a horizontal slash just above it.

They'd always known where we were, I thought. For so long, since we'd never encountered a horde, I thought that maybe the Dakkari didn't know we existed at all. That all changed when *he'd* come to our gates, however.

I sucked in a small breath when another thought occurred to me, one that made the contents of my belly slosh.

"Were you…" I whispered before I cleared my throat. Steeling my voice, I asked, "Was it really you who came to our village? Or did you hear that story from another horde king and decide to use it?"

Was it another lie used against me? To soften me toward him?

Those red eyes flashed, and he walked away from the map, approaching me. I wasn't prepared to meet him head on this morning, not when my head was pounding, and I was a moment away from spilling bile all over his boots.

"It was me," he said.

And I *believed* him.

So he wasn't lying about everything, I thought, not entirely certain how that made me feel.

"Does that disappoint you?" he rasped, tilting his head to regard me. "To know that it really was me?"

"Disappoint me? Why would it?" I asked, feeling a sharp spark of pain bloom in my head. I blew out a breath and turned away, going back to my little pallet of furs on the floor. "I don't want to fight with you this morning."

"When you were so full of fight last night?" he questioned, watching as I sank down and leaned my back against the pole I was chained to.

I had been uncharacteristically temperamental last night. I'd even been surprised at myself, but I figured it was the stress and shock of the day...and my newfound reality as his prisoner. And the disappointment at knowing that he'd only been using me. That there had been a duality to his kindness.

"What do you plan to do with me?" I asked.

A part of me thought of faking my usual stutter, just to see how he'd react. Just to see if it would anger him like it had angered Benn. A part of me hated that with him, I spoke clearly. A part of me hated that I didn't know *why*.

"How do you control the fog?" he asked, ignoring my question.

Because I didn't see the point in lying, I told him, "I imagine a barrier, small at first, no bigger than my palm. And once it's tangible to me, once I *feel* the energy of it tingling in my hand, I expand it."

"How long have you been able to control it?" he asked next, crouching in front of me, studying me with a rapt expression.

"Not long," I murmured, swallowing. "Or maybe I've been able to do it all along. The ability came and went. I wasn't really able to control it until..."

Him.

I pressed my lips together. My mouth was dry again, but my muscles were weak and I didn't feel like standing again to get water.

"Until me? In the fog?" he guessed.

I shrugged.

"You will demonstrate it for me," he told me after a short pause. "Today."

Today? I went dizzy at the thought. Not in my state.

"I can't today," I said. "I feel sick."

He scowled. "I told you not to drink the wine."

I met his eyes but didn't say anything. What did he want me to do? Go back in time and *not* drink it? So that I would be well enough to perform for him today, his little human amusement?

"Fine," he clipped out. "Tomorrow. And you will practice strengthening your ability every day."

"So that's my purpose here?" I asked, my voice sounding hollow to my own ears.

"Until I say otherwise," he rasped, baring his teeth a little, "*lysi.*"

I really didn't like him, I decided. And he clearly didn't like me. I'd go so far as to say he detested the mere sight of me.

So why did he kiss me again last night? I couldn't help but wonder. Humans kissed when they desired one another or… loved one another.

Perhaps Dakkari used them as punishments.

We were staring at one another—or rather, he was glaring at me—when the tent flap opened, and I winced when the bright light made my eyes water and my temple throb.

When my eyes adjusted, I saw two Dakkari males hauling what looked like a massive water basin. *A bathing tub,* I realized, oval in shape and deep. Back at our village, we had a few we'd all shared, though they hadn't been as big as the one currently being hauled inside.

The horde king said, *"Jurak,"* to the males, and with a sharp point of his chin, he gestured to the open space next to the fire basin.

They heeded his order quickly and didn't even look in my direction. In fact, they seemed to make it a point *not* to look at me. They left but quickly returned, hauling in barrels of water that steamed when it met the inside of the tub.

They filled the entire bath in record time. I was filled with both longing and trepidation when I realized it was meant for *me.*

Once it was filled, the males left. When the tent flap opened a final time, I saw a Dakkari female lingering on the edges of the entrance.

She was beautiful, I noticed, with hair longer than the horde king's, plaited in an elegant line down her back. Her complexion was dark and golden from the sun, and her eyes were yellow. Even the long, jagged scar that tracked down her face, over her left eye, didn't detract from her beauty.

She was dressed in a simple shift dress spun from a light material that swayed as she moved. Its color was a cross between brown and orange, an earthy tone that complimented her skin.

I'd never seen a Dakkari female before.

"*Jiria,*" Rowin said, and the female approached immediately. In the universal language, he told the female, "You will help her bathe."

My breath hitched.

When I swung my gaze back to the horde king, he was watching me, his eyes narrowed in *challenge*.

"Undress, *sarkia*."

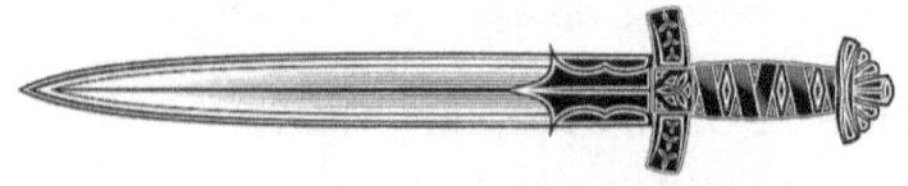

CHAPTER 26

"With y-you in here?" Mina stammered quietly, her already wide eyes rounding even more.

My nostrils flared.

"Shy now, *kalles*?" I rasped. "You came to me bared the first time I ever saw you. I assure you, I remember every moment."

A deep flush raced to her cheeks as she stared at me in shock. When I felt my cock twitch in response, at the *memory* of her body, I growled, rising from my crouch. I backed away toward the table, watching as Hukri approached the little witch.

Hukri helped Mina stand, though the *vekkiri kalles* did so begrudgingly. With a gritted jaw, I kept my eyes on her. Another one of my tests? Though I wasn't certain whom I was testing... her or me.

A test I was already failing, I realized, given the state of my thickening cock.

Hukri stripped Mina of her dirty gray dress. The human female was frozen in place, her eyes wide on me, not even seeming to recognize that she was now nude.

My lips pressed together, my fists clenching at the sight of her abdomen. A large, blackened bruise had bloomed there. From when Benn had kicked her, I knew.

That was just yesterday morning, I reminded myself. Was I pushing her too hard? Or was I justified in my treatment of her, keeping her chained like my prisoner? I wasn't certain.

Smaller bruises lined her upper arm. Bruises from fingers. The cut on her lip was healing, and while her lid was no longer so swollen over her eye, another bruise marred her flesh there, stretching over her cheekbone.

I did not want to feel anything for this female. So why did discomfort, mingled with rage, swarm my chest? Why did I feel the need to return to the Dead Mountain and slaughter that useless excuse for a human wherever he stood for daring to mark her flesh?

Hukri said something to Mina I didn't hear over the rushing in my ears, but a moment later, the Dakkari female was leading her into the washing tub.

A gentle, shuddered sigh left Mina's lips the moment she stepped into the water. For that brief moment, I watched her eyelids flutter shut as her lips parted in wonder. I was forgotten. It was only Mina and her simple pleasure as she sank down into the hot bath. I watched a tendril of steam curl around her neck and caress her flesh as she sighed.

If my cock hadn't been fully hard before, it was now. A harsh breath escaped me, feeling my control begin to slip. What was it about this maddening female that made me feel perilously close to my baser instincts? Baser instincts I'd long judged other males, other *Vorakkar*, for acting upon?

"*Vorakkar*," came Hukri's voice. My attention snapped toward the Dakkari female, feeling like I'd been pulled from a dream.

I blinked, swallowing. "*Neffar?*"

"Her dress is in disrepair," she said in Dakkari, keeping her gaze at the base of my throat, as was respectful of my horde members. "Should I retrieve a new one from the seamstress? Perhaps one of a smaller size to suit her? And I should go retrieve bath crystals."

She is my prisoner, I reminded myself. What did I care if she remained in her dirty dress or had no soap to wash herself with?

Then why did you order her a bath if you do not care? a small, taunting voice came. *Because even now, you know what she will become? What she will be to the horde?*

With a growl, I waved my hand and said, "*Lysi.* Go."

Hukri departed, striding past me with a small incline of her head. Leaving me alone with Mina. I crossed my arms over my chest as I regarded her. I didn't dare step toward her because I wasn't willing to see when my tentative control would officially snap.

She huddled underneath the water, the ends of her wavy hair bobbing on the surface before sinking below. With relief, I saw her hair covered the fullness of her breasts and she drew up her knees to shield her sex from my view.

Over the edge of the tub, her chain was pulled tight, stretched to its limit. I had a million things to do this morning, and yet the first thing I'd done was come here. To her.

Word had already gotten out that I'd returned. Many had greeted me on my walk here this morning, running their hands over my arms and my cuffs, as if in reassurance. So while my horde knew of my return, I still needed to brief my council and Valavik about what I'd learned under the Dead Mountain. About the humans, the witches, and Mina.

"Will you tell me one thing?" came her soft voice.

As if her voice pulled me by a string, I felt my feet moving.

With gritted teeth, I forced myself to still. "*Neffar?*"

Her lashes lowered briefly, her arms moving to hug her knees to her chest.

"You call me a witch. Is that what you want me to be for your horde?" she asked. "You want to keep me because I can control the fog? But I know your hordes move all across Dakkar. Places the fog does not reach. So what then? Will you set me free then?"

"Why do you want to go *back*?" I growled. "I thought you would want to be here, under my protection, with the swords of my horde behind you."

"And am I? Under your protection?" she whispered, eyeing me. Her foot moved, rattling the chain against the washing tub as if to prove her point.

"Every member of my horde is under my protection."

"But I'm not a member of your horde," she said, her voice quiet. "I'm your prisoner. I'm just a human you *took*."

I grinned, though it was humorless. "Only because you took me first, *sarkia*."

A small breath left her, though I sensed the seemingly endless stretch of her patience right then. "You didn't answer my question."

"Because I know you will not like my answer."

She stared, waiting.

Finally, I said, "The fog will stretch and grow and consume whatever it touches."

"You don't have to tell me that. I've seen firsthand what it can do," she said. "How it can kill."

So, had some of the humans lost their lives to it? They seemed more immune to it than the Dakkari, but it was gratifying to know they could still be *killed* by it if they weren't careful.

"Then you know my answer," I rasped. "The fog will come. If the priestesses cannot stop it, it always will. And you will be there to protect the horde when it does. You are too valuable to let go."

My words rang around the *voliki*, certain and unmatched in their truth.

I think Mina realized that too because her face paled. Her nostrils flared as she took in a deep, steadying breath.

She *was* immensely valuable. A prize for my horde that I would not disregard. The moment I'd captured her in the fog I'd known what I would do with her, though I'd thought that perhaps there was another way. I'd known what she would *become*—to me, to my horde—though I'd fought against it.

This morning, however, after a full night of rest and with a calm mind, it became clear to me.

There was only one option to secure her for my horde, in a way that they would accept. In a way that they would *support*. They would see her as a witch, a sorceress once they saw her power. Because of that, they would mistrust her. They would be wary of her. They would never accept her. Unless...

Unless she wore my markings on her flesh. The markings of my family, my bloodline. The markings of Rath Rowin. *Their* markings.

The horde would never accept her unless I made her my queen.

My *Morakkari*.

And *that* was what I intended to do.

Because of that decision, I would never let her go, no matter how much she wished it.

Chapter 27

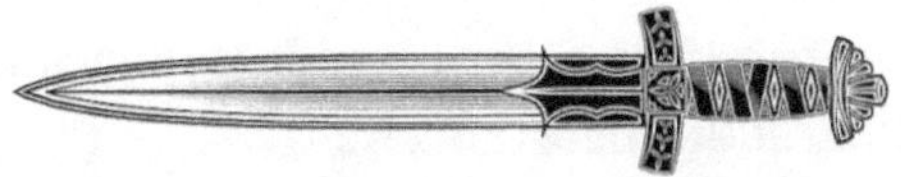

"You cannot be serious," Valavik murmured.

"I have made up my mind already. There is nothing you can say to sway me," I informed him.

And because Valavik *knew me*, he heard the unwavering truth in the words.

Valavik blew out a short breath, and he turned, looking out over the training grounds, at the *darukkars* that were sparring. The frost had ended, and once the season of life began, the *darukkars* trained hard. To shake off the cold season's effects. Like untamed *pyrokis* waking from their hibernation, jolting to life.

"You will see that it is the only way," I finished, watching Hukri's mate take down Arkoni with one perfectly timed strike. I'd left Hukri with Mina, to finish helping her bathe.

Briefly, in my mind's eye, I recalled Mina's bared flesh. The smooth, warm expanse of it. Her tight nipples, the soft curls between her thighs.

My nostrils flared, and I shifted, feeling the weight of my sword against my back.

"I will marry her."

The words sprang from Valavik, soft and completely unexpected. For a moment, I couldn't think about anything but the sudden wave of...*possessiveness*. For Mina.

"*Nik*," I snarled, still reeling from his suggestion. The *wrongness* of it. "You will not. I forbid it."

Valavik's eyes assessed me. They narrowed. "Why not? The horde will accept her if she marries your *pujerak*, will they not?"

He made a good point. Yet I couldn't understand why my belly was roiling at the mere thought.

You do though, came that taunting voice. *You do know why.*

My fists clenched so tight that I drew blood from my palm. If she had bewitched me or if Kakkari had shown her to me, had chosen her as *mine*, I wouldn't know.

But whatever *had* occurred in the fog was already seated deep within me. Its roots had grown, weaving through my body like veins. *She* had already wiggled herself inside me, binding herself to me in a way I knew I'd never be free of.

Whether it was by her own design or Kakkari's...*I wanted her*.

If Mina didn't have a lick of power, I thought that I might've still kept her. Perhaps as my lover or perhaps as an *alukkiri* during the cold season, to warm my bed and sate my lusts. At least until I chose a *Morakkari* for my own.

I'd always known that I would marry for the purpose of *strengthening* my horde. Not for ridiculous things like love or lust.

For *strength*. Always.

And Mina strengthened my horde.

No one would deny that once they saw what she could do.

Would the horde still accept her if she was Valavik's wife?

Lysi, they would.

However...

"With the female at my side, as my queen, the other

Vorakkar would have no choice but to yield. She would have *my* protection, the protection of a horde king, not that of a *pujerak*," I told him, feeling *relief* settle my mind at the realization. "You have no power against them. And if war came and I fell, your position would require you to yield to them. As such, she would as well."

Valavik asked, "You think the other *Vorakkar* would misuse her power?"

"I think there are those in *Dothik* that would misuse her power," I told him, emphasizing the name of our capital city. "A year ago, her power would have been meaningless. *Now,* however, it is the most important defense we have."

Valavik's gaze settled back out on the *darukkars.*

"You're right," he murmured.

"We keep the power for our horde," I decided, steeling my voice. "I will inform the other *Vorakkar* but only those I trust. And I will wed her under the black moon."

"That is in two nights," Valavik murmured, his eyes cutting to me as he frowned. "Should you not wait until the moon is bright again? It is a slight against her to marry in such darkness. The horde will think—"

"Rath Kitala wed his queen under a black moon," I pointed out.

"Because he could not wait any longer to possess her," Valavik growled out.

"Then let the horde think that," I said, my lips twisting bitterly. "That I am so undone for my bride, that I cannot wait to claim her."

"Rowin," Valavik said, shaking his head.

"The black moon," I repeated, my jaw tight. A humorless smile crossed my lips. "It is when she and her kin planned to have me killed, after all. It is only fitting."

Valavik held his tongue, though I saw he wanted to protest.

To soothe his thoughts, I told him, "We cannot wait to secure her. We cannot wait for a bright moon. The fog grows every day. It may surround us by that time. What then?"

Valavik blew out a sharp breath. He was a more superstitious male than I, though I knew others in my horde would see it as a bad omen too, taking a *Morakkari* under a black moon.

"And you have told her this?" he asked, raising a brow, his tail flicking wildly behind him in his discomfort. "She will help shield the horde if the fog does come?"

My lips pressed together.

"You capture her, chain her, force her to wed you, and you still expect her to help us? She has no loyalties to us, to *you*," Valavik argued softly.

And even though I'd seen Benn and the others mistreat her, she still had loyalties to *them*. She'd told me herself that she would run back to them, at the first opportunity she had.

Unless...

Unless I threatened the Dead Mountain and all those who were within it. Unless I threatened to have my vengeance against all who took part in my own capture.

"There are those she cares about in the Dead Mountain," I told Valavik, my spine straightening.

"Rowin," he growled warningly. "Be careful. This is your future *Morakkari*, after all."

"Who has no loyalties to my horde. But I can force those loyalties if need be. She *will* protect us when the fog comes. Or else we ride for the Dead Mountain."

Valavik said, "She will hate you for it."

I grunted. My gaze shifted to my council's *voliki*, at the guard I'd posted outside the entrance.

"She already does," I replied. "So what does it matter if she hates me a little more? The horde comes first. Always."

We needed to move quickly. The black moon would come soon. And preparations needed to be made.

"She will need to demonstrate her power," I said, changing my mind. Mina might be sick from the wine, but I realized I couldn't give her a reprieve. "Tonight. I want the horde there to witness it. Afterward, I'll announce her as my *Morakkari*."

"*Lysi*," Valavik said. "That will be best."

"Tell the horde. Tonight, we will all meet the fog."

CHAPTER 28

"Is-Is this for me?" I asked, my tone uncertain as I ran my fingers over the dress.

"*Lysi,*" the Dakkari female replied, just as the fire crackled loudly in the basin, sending sparks flying. "For tonight."

"What's tonight?" I asked, my heart giving a little stammer with nerves.

The Dakkari female had been with me for most of the day, though her presence had mostly been a silent one. When I'd asked what I should call her, she told me to call her *lirilla*. Which, to my understanding, wasn't exactly a name. Rather, it was a title. One meant for female acquaintances who were not yet friends.

Though she'd been quiet, my *lirilla* hadn't been unkind to me. She'd been patient, actually. Nothing seemed to rattle her, not even needing to assist a strange human throughout the day with mundane things. She hadn't blinked when she helped bathe me earlier. She'd given my hair a thorough scrubbing and had even washed between my toes. I didn't think I'd ever been cleaner in my life. When I'd needed to relieve my bladder, she left with the half-full chamber pot and returned with a clean one.

She'd also made sure I had plenty to eat. Though I was chained and the leash of it wasn't long, she brought me food and watched as I ate. I had the impression that she'd report every morsel of food I put into my mouth. And I ate *a lot*. I had never been so full—and for so *long*—in my entire life.

As the day dragged on, my nausea settled and my headache abated. The food helped, as did the water and the rest.

When darkness had begun to fall, the *lirilla* briefly left the tent—which she'd told me was called a *voliki*—only to return with the dress.

"*Lysi*," she said, taking it from my hands and gesturing that I stand up. With all the rest and the food, I stood easily, on strong legs that didn't shake underneath me. "The *Vorakkar* requests it."

The *Vorakkar*.

My lips pressed together.

"He will be here soon. So you need to dress," she informed me. The mere words sent my heart racing. I hadn't seen Rowin since this morning. Not since he'd stormed from the *voliki* as I bathed.

In the blink of an eye, the Dakkari female had me naked. The dress she'd given me earlier was thin and billowy. She unclasped the fastenings at the shoulders, and it slid from me, pooling at my feet. Then she was dressing me once more, sliding the material over my head like I was a child.

Only the dress was not something a child would ever wear. The white material was just as thin as my previous dress. And if not for the beautiful and intricate pattern of the gold threads that weaved across the bodice and down toward my sex, I would have felt exposed. Not as exposed as in the dress I'd worn before Rowin in the fog—that translucent thing had revealed my entire body to his molten eyes—but still vulnerable.

For such a revealing dress, the length was long, ending past my knees. It was only held up, however, by thin straps against my shoulders, so thin I could barely see them.

"This will do," she said with a self-satisfied nod as she inspected me. Her fingers brushed my face. "And your color is returning now that you have rested."

As I was still reeling from the dress—and wondering why Rowin wanted me dressed like *this*—the *lirilla* turned me and started brushing out my hair. I hadn't even seen a brush when she entered, but it slid through my wavy hair, pulling at my scalp in certain sections.

"The *Vorakkar* gave you this to wear," she informed me, flashing a golden thing in front of me. It took me a moment to realize that it was meant for my hair. It was some sort of decorative clasp. And *beautiful*. It was pure gold, shimmering in the firelight. At half the size of my palm, it had golden leaves adorning it. "Isn't it beautiful?"

A gift? I wondered, frowning. *From Rowin?*

No, that couldn't be right. The *lirilla* must be mistaken.

I reached out to touch it. The gold was warm to the touch, as if it had just left his own palm.

Snatching my hand back, I bit my lip, unsure of what to say. If the Dakkari female expected me to say anything, she would be disappointed, and a moment later, she pulled back the top half of my hair and secured it all with the gold clasp at the back of my head.

Not a moment later, I heard the entrance flap hit against the hide wall. When I turned, Rowin was entering. Those eyes were fastened on me, running from my hair to my bare feet and back. It was probably the first time he'd seen me so *clean*, I realized.

His nostrils flared. I felt my cheeks flush when his gaze heated. The sudden tension was thick. Thick enough that I even saw the *lirilla* back away, as if to escape the intensity of her horde king's eyes.

"Good," he rasped, his voice gruff and husky. "*Rothi kiv.*"

A moment later, the Dakkari female exited the tent, not looking back at me once. I felt panic rise in my throat as I watched her long hair disappear through the entrance.

Then Rowin was approaching me.

The firelight made his skin gleam gold. He was bare-chested again, though he was wearing a fur loincloth, mottled with beige and white, instead of the trews he'd been wearing this morning. It took me a moment to realize the bulge underneath the loincloth was *rising*.

My lips parted, and my gaze flashed up to his in surprise. Though I'd rested, I began to feel a little dizzy.

Rowin moved toward me, wearing that predatory look. One I recognized. Like I was his prey. I was reminded that he'd told me he liked to *hunt*.

And he seemed every bit the hunter tonight. All golden muscles and scarred flesh.

I froze when he circled me, stepping over my chain. At my back, I heard him inhale, like he was *smelling* me?

His fingers brushed through my hair, and I felt him lift the strands. With my scalp tingling, I bit my lip, my heart drumming in my chest. He rubbed my hair between his clawed fingers and then let it fall. I felt the brush of his hand at the base of my neck and then that hand was running down the length of my spine.

I gasped, his slow touch unexpected. My nipples pebbled even tighter, though it was warm in the *voliki*. Since the dress was thin, I felt his touch like it was on my bare flesh.

His fingers paused when they reached the cleft of my buttocks. I didn't even realize I was holding my breath until I released it as he moved again. He circled back around my front, his touch sliding across my hip until it rested on my pelvic bone, just above my sex.

What was most alarming wasn't that he was so incredibly close. It wasn't that he was looking at me like he'd looked at me in the fog. It wasn't that his gaze flicked to my lips like he would kiss me again.

What was most alarming was that my body was *responding* to him. Heat pooled low, tight and pleasurable and unexpected. His scent invaded my nostrils and wove down my throat. His warmth seeped into me.

And when he spoke, I nearly shivered at the velvety richness of that dark voice.

"You will meet the horde this night," he informed me.

My half-lidded eyes snapped fully open. I tried to move back, but his other hand wrapped around my waist. The hand that was pressed below my belly rose. And rose. And rose. Sliding between the valley of my breasts...to wrap around my throat.

To keep me in place, I realized. His touch was overbearing, dominant. Yet it didn't frighten me. I wasn't worried that he would squeeze. I was worried that his words weren't a jest.

"No," I whispered.

"*Lysi,*" he murmured, his thumb tracing the outline of my jaw. His eyes flicked back to my lips. He pressed closer, close enough that I felt his cock against my belly.

My eyes widened as I felt the outline of it, hard and impossibly thick even through his fur loincloth.

"You will show them your power. You will show them how you control the fog."

I stilled.

"Ahh, *lysi,*" he purred. "We go to the fog this night. But will you truly try to run from me, *rei sarkia*? Remember, I like the chase. And if I have to recover you again, you won't like what I will do in retaliation."

"You would strike me?" I whispered, fastening my eyes on his, feeling a surge of bravery as I did. "Hurt me?"

He smiled, that disarming, cold grin. "*Nik.* Never strike you. But I have other ways of making you yield to me."

I couldn't suppress my shiver that time, and seeing it made his smile widen.

"Do well tonight, and I might even leave you unchained as you sleep."

That made my spine snap. My voice hardened. "Am I your pet now? You take me out when you wish and then punish me when I don't behave?"

I gasped when he tugged me toward him, lightning fast. When his lips met mine, it was for a quick, hard, punishing kiss. One that left me reeling, especially when he sucked on my bottom lip before giving it a fast nip in warning.

"Don't tempt me, *sarkia*," he growled, glaring. "You wish to be my pet? See how you like it when I keep you chained to my bed."

I froze, my tongue darting out nervously, and I tasted him there.

Was that...was that a possibility?

"*Kakkari*, you drive me mad," he growled, releasing me, and I reached out behind me to steady myself on the pole. My knees were shaking now, though it wasn't from fear. I was actually *glad* to see that I got under his skin...though I knew that he got under *mine* too.

I watched as he procured a key from the belt of his loincloth. He dropped down to one knee and lifted my foot. He inserted the key into the locked cuff around my ankle. A moment later, the chain dropped from me, but he didn't release my foot. His hand slid up my dress, up my calf, behind my knee.

I was staring down at him in bewilderment, my heart still racing, trying to beat its way from my chest. If he was trying to unnerve me again...it was working.

"You are mine, Mina," he rasped. "Do you understand that?"

My lips parted. Why did hearing my name fall from his lips leave me feeling unbalanced?

"Your loyalties still remain underneath the Dead Mountain,

but soon, those loyalties will be tied to *me*. To the horde. Do you understand that?"

A sharp breath whistled down my throat, and I forced myself to look away from him. I didn't know what he was saying. Or why. He thought I would *stay*?

I heard his own sharp sigh, and then he was rising, his hand falling away from the back of my knee. I didn't know how *sensitive* I was there until he touched me. That small space felt branded by his hand.

"Come," he rasped, taking my arm and guiding me from the *voliki*. When we stepped outside, only the night and the tiny sliver of the moon greeted us. "We are late. And my horde waits for you."

CHAPTER 29

I'd been stared at before. Yet I wasn't comfortable with nearly a hundred—or more, I couldn't be certain—pairs of eyes on me. Especially since those eyes were yellow and red and they belonged to fearsome-looking warriors or tall, imposing females who looked like they could snap me in two.

My own physical weaknesses had never been more apparent to me than right then.

Rowin's voice was booming across the East Lands. Strings of Dakkari words that were roughened and yet smoothly elegant. Their language transfixed me, mesmerized me. Even though I was frozen in place, pinned by hundreds of eyes, I found myself picking out certain words, rolling them around silently on my tongue, wondering what they meant.

We were beyond the gates of the horde. Tall, black gates I hadn't even known existed, flanked by even higher walls. As if walls and gates could keep the fog at bay.

Behind us, that reddened mist lingered. I had the strangest thought that it was *listening*. That it was consuming Rowin's words as readily as his horde was, as *I* was.

I looked over my shoulder. Just as I sensed the fog, I sensed the Dead Mountain. It wasn't that far away, though far enough to keep the Dakkari away.

Tess, I thought, swallowing, before I faced forward again. I wondered about her. About Benn. Jacques. Hassan. Kaila. I thought about the flash of anger that appeared on Farah's face when Emmi accused me of stealing food. The ripple that went through them all, so eager to condemn me.

My fists clenched at my sides. Again, I felt that swelling in my breast. That swelling of determination.

Rowin wanted me to put on a good show?

I would.

I would do what he asked of me because I wasn't foolish enough to believe that I was in control of anything.

He was wrong about one thing though. My loyalties were not to *them.* My loyalties were only to Tess. And even then, only to the woman I'd known nearly all my life. My friend. Not the woman who slept beside Benn and whispered about me into his ear. That Tess was a stranger to me.

It was my friend I wanted to save. I still thought I could. But until that opportunity presented itself, I would wait. I would watch and listen. And wait.

Could my loyalties be tied to him? I wondered, frowning. He'd certainly seemed determined as he declared that in the *voliki.*

I didn't trust him though. I'd wronged him, yes. But he'd wronged me too. Would we ever see past that?

I didn't think so.

A rippling murmur started throughout the crowd before us. They'd created a half circle around us. Many carried torches, which brightened that dark night almost as much as the sun.

It took me a moment to realize that Rowin was looking at me. Drawn, my face tipped up toward him. Our eyes connected and held.

I felt it again. *Right then.*

His gaze wasn't angry or cold. Not like it'd been in the *voliki.*

It was something different. Something that made me shiver and...soften.

Looking at him, the world began to hush. I could hear my heart begin to slow and the rushing in my ears begin to calm.

His touch came next. His fingers dragged up my inner wrist. Even now, it always surprised me how gentle he was. For such a terrifying and intimidating male, he had never hurt me. Not like Benn.

The strands in his eyes began to swirl. Mesmerizing. Almost as mesmerizing as his voice. My lips parted.

"*Leika,*" he whispered, almost to himself, staring down at me. His brow furrowed. He looked *bewildered*.

Then he seemed to shake himself. I watched as he cast a gaze toward the crowd of his horde. Breath returned to me, and I was shaken to realize that I'd all but forgotten them...in that single, brief moment.

His touch left me. Cool air rushed in where his warmth had been.

"Show them," he murmured gruffly, gesturing with a sharp nod toward the fog, that wall between us returning. "Show them they have nothing to fear now."

Now that he's claimed me, I realized, finishing the sentence for him silently in my mind.

All at once, my heart tripled its speed. I swallowed hard, casting the horde another look. That feeling of exposure—especially in this damn dress—returned to me. I was vulnerable. What if I failed? What if—

It didn't matter. What did it matter? Maybe if I failed, Rowin would let me go. If I embarrassed him in front of his horde, maybe...

I caught sight of a young Dakkari child. A girl. Though she looked half the age of Hassan, her black hair was long, brushing her waist. All silk and smoothness, surrounding her dark, beautiful face. Chubby cheeks and wide eyes, she didn't look much different than how I remembered Hassan at that age. *Innocent.* Her eyes were yellow, and she peered at me in curious hesitation.

My eyes lifted to the female whose legs she was peering out from behind...only to be greeted by the sight of the *lirilla,* that endlessly patient female who'd spent the better part of the day with me. She was standing beside a bare-chested warrior, a glint of a sword at his hip, and his six-fingered hand was wrapped around his female's waist, holding her close.

For a moment, I couldn't breathe. I didn't know why the sight of the family formed a knot in my throat, but one thing was certain. I *longed* for that. Their eyes were not desperate with hunger. They were only desperate with trepidation whenever they looked toward the fog. It took me a long moment to realize that the Dakkari child wasn't hiding behind her mother but rather the *lirilla* was keeping her there. As if the fog would swarm toward them at any moment.

I wanted to assure them that it wouldn't. That wasn't how it acted, how it behaved. But they wouldn't believe me until I showed them.

"Mina," came his voice.

I licked my lips, tearing my gaze from the small family to regard the horde king, standing tall next to me.

His jaw was set. A strand of hair fell into his eyes. That little tendril seemed to soften the severity of his face until he raked it back with annoyance.

"Show them that you can protect them."

Protect.

Such a simple word.

I might not be a fighter, but that word seemed to seep into my skin and infuse my very blood. *That* was what I wanted to be. A protector. I didn't want to hurt anyone. I only wanted to help.

I stepped toward the fog, breaking his gaze before he saw

the tears that had pooled there. Out of the corner of my eye, I saw warrior guards shift forward, their hands flashing to their swords. They were wary I would run. But with a subtle slash of his hand, Rowin had them backing away.

He seemed confident I wouldn't run, at least.

This was my chance. Tess was so close. I could reach her tonight. I could sneak into the Dead Mountain and take her from there before Benn even woke.

I only needed to outrun the Dakkari, outrun *him*, for a brief while. They wouldn't be able to follow me beyond a certain point, or else they wouldn't be able to turn back.

So why was I building that little circle between my palms?

Why was I imagining it, constructing it like pieces of a puzzle, stacking and crafting and forming and building? Building and building...

I sensed Rowin stepping toward me. Could he feel it too? Could he feel the energy that was trapped in my palms? It tingled up my arms and prickled down my spine. And when he stepped toward me again, I swore I felt another jolt of that energy rush at me, adding to the jittering bundle in my palms until it *almost* broke free.

Behind me, I heard the crowd hush.

The hair on the back of my neck rose, and my eyes lifted to the fog. It hovered there. Lingering.

Leave, I thought. *If only for a little while.*

Then with gritted teeth, I hurtled that little ball of energy forward. Outward. Expanding it exponentially. I wanted to see the Dead Mountain. I wanted to see how far I could stretch myself. I wanted to see what my limits were, if there were any.

A prick behind my eye had me gasping, but I was determined. I wouldn't stop until I saw it.

The barrier I'd created was like a wave. A rippling wave. And I heard, rather than saw, the barrier hitting the fog because behind me, I heard the sharp, bewildered cries of the Dakkari horde. I heard their shocked gasps and the murmuring that rose, the shuffle of their feet as they drew closer, or perhaps drew away.

The wave crashed against the fog almost violently. Immediately, it pushed it back. The fog was thrown out of the way, so thick and red against the barrier that it appeared like a solid thing, trying to beat its way back in.

My head throbbed. My temple *pounded,* but I didn't stop. I wanted to see the Dead Mountain. As if I would be able to see Tess there. I pushed and pushed and pushed as the chatter behind me grew even louder. The land was revealed quickly. Land I'd never seen clearly before. The earth was dark. The fog looked like a shadow under the sliver of the moon.

"Mina," came Rowin's rough voice. "Enough."

But I couldn't stop. I was *so* close! The Dead Mountain was only just there. *Right there.*

It wasn't until I saw it—until I *actually* saw that dark mountain kingdom—that I realized what I'd done.

Before us, the entirety of the Dead Valley was presented, offered up. Cleared of all traces of the fog. Though it wasn't entirely gone. It was furious, banging at the barrier angrily, *needing* to get back in.

I was crying, my breath ragged. When I felt a sharp jolt—like a dagger stabbing at the base of my neck—I cried out, and I saw the barrier ripple.

I can't hold it, I realized. *Too much, too much.*

"Mina," Rowin growled. Then I felt his hand on my arm. I felt that energy spark into him, and I felt him flinch. I figured it would hurt, but his grip only tightened, as if he was fighting through the pain. Or as if he was no stranger to pain, as if he could endure it. "Let go, *kalles.* You have done so well already. Just let go."

Fear infused me for the first time. Potent fear that made tears stream down my cheeks.

"I can't," I gritted out. *"Rowin!"*

I couldn't drop the barrier. Before, it had given way so easily. With a wave of my hand.

Now, I'd played with something I didn't truly understand. And I was going to pay the price.

I felt something running from my nostrils. Blood?

"Vok," he cursed, seeing it too. My vision wavered. I swayed underneath the press of the pain, but he held me. He came up behind me, wrapping his arms around my front. Those hands slid to my palms, which were open, my fingers spread. The little bones there felt like they were pulled *tight.* Stretched.

He closed my palms, wrapping his fingers between mine and pressing hard. His scent drifted to my nostrils. I focused on that scent, following it. I thought of the forests of the North. I thought of the frost.

"Kalles," came his ragged voice, though it sounded distant. Distorted and hushed, like I was hearing it under water, the tones of it shifting and changing. "That's it. It's closing."

It was?

It was!

I closed my eyes, squeezing them shut. I inhaled, breathing through the pain. Pain so fierce it felt like I'd been kicked in the head a hundred times over.

Forests, I thought, urging myself to focus, to control the panic. *Cold, icy forests.*

He smelled like a comforting fire burning in that forest. Keeping me warm.

"There," he murmured in my ear. His voice sounded louder, stronger. "You're controlling it, *leika.* A little more. A little bit more."

With one last desperate attempt, I slashed my hand, which was still entwined with his.

The barrier dropped.

And when it dropped, it *dropped.*

I felt the earth tremble. I felt a ripple of energy blow my hair back and freeze my bones as it rushed toward us. The pain left me, and I dragged in lungfuls of air, so relieved that I wanted to sob. So relieved I wanted to curl up in a ball and cry.

Then it was still.

So still. *So* quiet.

When I opened my eyes, I saw the barrier was gone. The Dead Valley was gone. The Dead Mountain was shrouded once more. The fog had returned, though it swirled wildly when before it had been calm. Was it angry? Was it closer? I couldn't tell.

"Rowin," I croaked, feeling the world tilt. I gripped his hand tighter with the last of my strength, fearing I would fall.

Then behind us, as sudden as the quiet had come, I heard it broken by the *cheers*.

Behind us, the horde was celebrating, exuberant and exhilarated cries filling the air. They shocked me. Their excitement was contrasted with my own feeling of fear, of exhaustion and the memory of the pain...and it made me feel *wretched*.

Rowin turned me in his arms. One hand slid around my back, keeping me upright, and I let my weight sag into his hold. I trusted him enough to keep me from falling.

His expression was tense as his horde cheered. Watchful. That red gaze flickered back and forth between my pupils, and I felt his hand drag underneath my nose, wiping the blood away, though it coated his fingers.

I couldn't see the horde beyond his broad shoulders. I couldn't see anyone but him.

"Take me back," I whispered.

I'd meant the *voliki*—to sleep and recover away from the hundreds of eyes—but his mouth pressed at the words, and I realized he thought I meant the Dead Mountain.

Before I could say another word, he swept me up into his strong arms, cradling me against his chest. My cheek met his warm, bare flesh, and I heard the strong thud of his heartbeat. A familiar position. One I'd been in before, hadn't I?

Yes. Under the Dead Mountain. When he'd tried to keep me warm when I'd been so, so cold.

"Rowin," I huffed, feeling my vision go hazy. I thought I blacked out for a second. "I'm going to—"

My exhaustion won. I gave in.

Everything fell away.

Though...I swore I heard Rowin's booming voice. Like a dream. I swore I heard a familiar word as it tumbled around my quiet mind, mingled with raucous cheers.

Morakkari.

I didn't have the strength to remember why that word sounded so familiar.

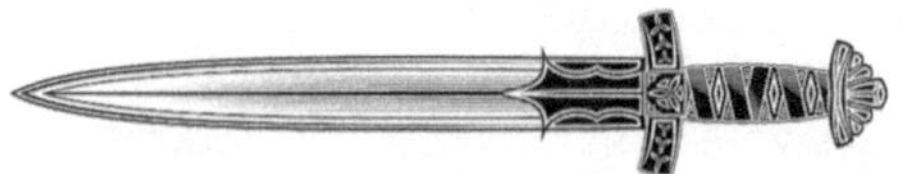

"Have you ever seen anything like it?" Valavik asked quietly, his eyes pinned on the slumbering female.

Laying Mina down onto the fur roll, I was careful to be gentle. Valavik's presence, so near to her in such a vulnerable state, was making discomfort prowl in my chest, and I covered her body with the other fur blanket. It didn't make sense. I trusted Valavik more than I trusted anyone. Why did I feel this potent jealousy, then?

"*Nik,*" I said. "I've never seen anything like it."

That was the truth. What she'd done...it was like going back in time. Seeing the Dead Valley uncovered once more, seeing the Dead Mountain loom, made me remember the battles waged there against the Ghertun stronghold. Made me remember how the land had once been lush and brimming with life.

She'd cleared the valley of the fog entirely, if only for a brief moment of time. Then it had flooded back in, and I, for one, was glad of it.

Valavik hadn't seen her. Only I had. She'd been...

Vok. Even I'd felt the extent of her pain. The moment I touched her, it had flowed into me like a current. And I had felt her panic. I had felt her immense fear. Like the thing she'd wielded and coaxed to life was now in control of her and she knew that what she'd done was a terrible thing.

Her eyes had been bloodshot. Vessels broken in the whites of them. Red had poured from her nose. Her skin had been leached of color, and her hair had floated out around her head, like the air was charged with electricity. Like a violent storm was approaching.

It made me wonder, for the first time, if she'd felt similar pain leading me through the fog. If she'd sacrificed anything seeking out Valavik while I was still under the Dead Mountain.

Or had she pushed herself too far this time?

"We need to show the other *Vorakkar* what she can do," Valavik said quietly.

"*Nik*," I growled. When I met his eyes, I saw he was incredulous about my protest. "Tonight cost her. A lot. I do not want her doing that again unless absolutely necessary. And only to save the horde if need be."

"It cost her?" Valavik asked. "How?"

Smoothing back a strand that had drifted onto her cheek, I rose from my crouched position and faced my *pujerak*. He was still lingering near the entrance, as if he knew his presence might stir unease.

"She was in pain," I informed her. "I...I felt it."

His brow furrowed, but he said nothing. He was merely observing me, processing the words. And I was thankful he didn't ask *how* because I didn't know if I could give him an answer. Even I didn't know *how*.

"Have you told her yet?" Valavik wanted to know, gesturing his head toward the sleeping female.

Already I'd made the announcement to my horde. And after what they had just witnessed, though they had not witnessed the price Mina had paid for the performance, they had been joyous. Just as I'd wanted.

Some were wary, however. I'd spied wariness just as I'd spied relief.

With time, I thought. *With time, they will accept her whole-heartedly. They must.*

"*Nik,*" I said, feeling a ripple of unease go through me at the confession. I had not asked her to be my queen. I would demand it of her. There was no choice anymore. Not for either of us. "She will know soon enough."

Valavik's displeasure was evident, but he knew better than to voice it. After a short silence, he inclined his head and left the *voliki.* Leaving me alone with her.

I went to her again. Her bare foot stuck out from underneath the fur blanket I'd draped over her. Reaching out, I touched the side of her ankle, noticing a red scratch there. No doubt from the cuffs.

Frowning, I tucked her foot back underneath the furs, discomfort swelling in my chest at the sight of the small wound. Leaning back against the pole she'd been chained to, right next to her sleeping pallet, I examined her face. Warm skin and small, pursed lips. A smattering of dark freckles across her nose and cheekbones. A too-small nose and soft cheeks.

Calm. I felt so damn *calm* looking at her. She wasn't awake to weave her magic around me. For the first time, I forced myself to recall those fleeting moments when I'd first met her.

I forced myself to consider that perhaps it hadn't been *magic* that had drawn me to her. My first instinct—though I hadn't wanted to believe it—was that Kakkari had brought us together for a reason. That she was my gift, my purpose. My *kassikari.* A mate, taken in the old tradition. One based on instinct and knowing.

That fated morning, I'd felt Kakkari's guiding light deep within me, and it had shaken me ever since.

I brought a hand down the length of my face.

Everything had begun to feel...fated. The humans, the Ghertun, the heartstone, the fog. Now humans and Dakkari alike were given Kakkari's gifts, gifts they'd most likely had since birth. As if Kakkari was preparing us all for what was to come.

Or giving us the weapons needed to fight it.

Reaching forward, I traced Mina's cheek. Her lips were parted, and even breaths made her chest rise and fall.

She's not a weapon, I thought. No one in their right mind could ever think that this soft little creature was a weapon.

She might have to be, I thought next, the realization making dread swim in my belly.

A moment later, she stirred under my touch, and I realized my fingers had brushed her lips.

When her eyes opened, they were heavy at first, closing immediately. When she tried again, her gaze fastened on me.

She's not afraid of me, I realized, watching her carefully as she roused. I'd pushed her too hard this night, and her exhaustion was evident.

"What happened?" she whispered, her voice soft and slow and languid.

"You dropped the barrier," I told her, though I didn't know how. I'd felt the strength of it. Strength no one should be able to endure. "But then you passed out from the force of it."

Her eyes closed. She swallowed. For a moment, I thought she'd dropped back into sleep. And I thought that I should leave. Before I was tempted to stay with her all night.

"Did you feel it?" she asked.

I knew what she spoke of.

"*Lysi,*" I said, seeing no point in lying to her.

"Did it frighten you too?"

My heart twisted at the question, and I frowned, rubbing the spot on my chest where it lay.

When I didn't answer her immediately, a breathy sigh left her lips. "I suppose a horde king doesn't feel fear."

In the basin, the fire flickered.

"I feel fear every day," I told her, my voice gruff. She blinked up at me, her legs shifting underneath the furs. "Fear for my horde. Just because I am a *Vorakkar* does not make me immune to it. It just means I need to handle it differently than others."

"And show them that you have none," she guessed softly. After a long moment, I inclined my head. "You care for your horde."

"The horde comes first. Everything I do is in service to them," I said, willing her to understand.

She swallowed. "Why?"

I exhaled a sharp breath, thinking back to *Dothik*. Thinking back to when I began selections for my horde, shortly after the Trials. Thinking back to that first year on the wildlands.

"Because they had faith in me when I did not have faith in myself," I rasped. The words surprised me. Words I had never voiced to a single soul. I was not allowed to be weak. I was not allowed to have doubts. My father had ingrained that in me since I was old enough to wield the sword he'd made me. "I work to repay them."

Mina's green eyes seemed otherworldly as they regarded me. She was still tired. I could see that as plainly as I could see she was surprised by my admission.

"Why are you telling me this?" she whispered.

Intelligent creature, I thought, pleased.

"Because soon, they will be your horde too," I murmured, our eyes locked together. "And you need to be strong for them. And if you are strong for them, you will have their loyalties forever. *Kor anir ji vorak.* The way of the horde," I translated.

Mina heard something in my voice that made her struggle to sit up. She swayed a bit, even half lying down, and she pressed two of her fingertips to her temple.

"Why would I need their loyalties? I am a prisoner here. *Your* prisoner," she whispered.

"*Nik.* I didn't bring you here to be my prisoner, *sarkia*," I said. Once, I had spat that word out like a curse. Now it softened on my tongue, as gentle as a caress.

She went quiet, but her eyes burned into me.

"That word," she whispered, though I had the impression she was speaking to herself. Her eyes widened. Her spine straightened. "That *word.*"

"*Sarkia?*"

"No," she said, shaking her head. Her eyes lifted, stricken. "*Morakkari.*"

Ah.

"I remember now," she said, her eyes flitting back and forth with panic. "Why it was familiar. But tell me I'm *wrong.* Tell me you don't mean it. That you *can't* mean it."

She must've heard the words I'd bellowed to my horde, announcing her as my queen. I thought she'd been sleeping. She must've come awake without my knowing, albeit briefly.

Reaching out, I cradled her face in my palm, tilting her chin up so she was forced to meet my gaze.

"I meant every word."

She shook her head, fear swimming in her eyes, mingled with the lingerings of her pain. "I won't," she vowed softly.

"You will," I told her. "You will be my *Morakkari*, Mina. In two nights, under the black moon, we will perform the *tassimara,* and it will be done."

Her lips parted. "The *tassimara?*"

"The joining ceremony."

Her nostrils flared. "And if I-I refuse?" she asked, licking her bottom lip.

Didn't she understand? There was no refusing *this.*

My jaw tightened. Valavik did not think it wise to threaten my future queen.

I disregarded his warning when I said, "Then I will lay siege to the Dead Mountain and all those that reside underneath it."

The words drummed between us, loud and harsh.

She stared at me in shock, all comfort between us gone, however brief. I wondered if she feared me *now*. I swore I spied a tendril of it dancing in her eyes when she heard my unyielding tone.

"You're threatening me?" she whispered.

Why did her voice sound so solemn? So sad?

I growled, ignoring the warning in my mind. She needed to understand the severity of this. "If that is what it takes, *lysi*."

"You can't reach them," she said. "The fog would—"

"You think we do not know about the tunnels the Ghertun made?" I asked. "All under Dakkar?"

I knew my bluff hit home when she paled further.

"If I don't join myself to you, you would kill them all?" she asked, her voice hardening. "Just because you can?"

I kept her gaze. "Like I said, the horde comes first. I will do anything necessary to keep you for them."

"To use me," she amended. "To use me when the time is right, you mean. There are innocent people under that mountain! Children too. Mothers. But you don't care about them, do you?"

"And *you* care about them?" I growled. "After the way they treated you? I saw more than you think, Mina. They treated you like you were dirt underneath their feet. Here, at my side, you would be a *vokking queen*. No one would hurt you ever again."

"Only you! And that doesn't make it okay," she hissed. A moment later, she closed her eyes, a flash of pain crossing her expression.

Concern made my retort die on my lips. "Mina."

She pushed my hand away, turning. She was quiet as she took deep, steadying breaths.

After a long while, she said, "Say you don't mean it. And I can still forgive you for it."

Forgive me? That wasn't what I had expected her to say.

Was she trying to call the bluff?

"I won't," I said. I'd already told her in a battle of wills and stubbornness, I would win. "Because I do mean it."

A huff left her throat. Humorless and dry. I was backing her into a corner. Trapping her there until her choices were taken away. Even I hated me. I could see I was the villain in this and I would always be.

This will be easier, I thought.

It would be easier if she hated me. That way we would never be in any danger of other emotions entering into our marriage. Emotions made us weak, after all.

"Do you agree to the joining or not?" I prompted, leveling her a cold gaze. When I recounted this to Valavik in the morning, he would shake his head at me. He would tell me how ill-advised it was to make my future queen hate me before we'd even performed the *tassimara.*

What was it about Mina that made everything I did so *difficult?* Was it because I still harbored bitterness about my capture? Was it because I realized my weaknesses and vulnerabilities with her?

A laugh sounded from her throat.

I offered her marriage to a horde king of Dakkar, a marriage where she would never want for anything, a marriage where she would have the protection of a horde, and she laughed in my face.

"Why ask me?" she wondered when her laugh died, as suddenly as it had appeared. "You've already ensured that I have no choice."

CHAPTER 31

"**C**ome dry your hair by the fire, *missiki*," the Dakkari female said.

She'd taken to calling me that.

Missiki.

When I'd asked her what it meant, she told me it meant *mistress*. And that only *pikis* were allowed to call me that...which had only led to more questions.

The female's given name was Hukri.

She'd told me that the morning after Rowin announced his intentions to take me as his queen. His *Morakkari*. Hukri had entered the *voliki* that morning, bowed her head, and told me in a soft, hushed voice that it would give her great honor if I knew her name.

In the past couple days, I'd learned a lot about the Dakkari. Hukri was a patient teacher and seemed more than happy to answer my endless questions. And so I knew all about *pikis*—a valued position among the horde as they were seen as confidants to the *Morakkari*—and daily horde life and where the horde had come from and where they were planning to go.

I knew much about moon cycles, about how the fullness of the moon dictated certain celebrations but only during certain seasons, and whether they were allowed to eat a certain kind of meat that month. Hukri had painstakingly helped me memorize the map of Dakkar which hung against the wall. Since Rowin had left me unchained, I could brush my fingers over the lines, and I repeated the Dakkari words, committing the swirling letters to memory. I learned about the different territories. I learned about the borders that made up the East, West, North, and South and all the places in between.

I learned about *Dothik*, and since Hukri was born there—and studied there—she'd told me much. And in so much detail that I could almost envision the cobbled streets, the *Dothikkar's* soaring, golden palace, and the bustle of the market stalls that sold oils and perfumes and jeweled baubles and cloth so silky it felt like water running through your hands.

I learned about Hukri too. About the *ungira* encounter she'd had when she first ventured out onto the wildlands, which left her with the deep scar down her face. How it had been a warrior that had come to her aid, that had helped see her well. She told me they'd fallen in love, that their daughter had been born under bright, blessed stars, and that she was carrying again. She felt it was another daughter, which she said delighted her warrior husband.

Hearing the female talk emptied a little of my loneliness that had been bottled up for years. She'd been my constant companion for the last two days. And though I knew she was here in duty—duty to her *Vorakkar*—I also thought that we were building a friendship, little by little. A *piki's* duty was to serve a *Morakkari*, but she'd also told me that with time, they became trusted companions as well.

"*Missiki*," Hukri said again, waving me over to the fire, her lips pursed as she studied me. I heard drums in the distance, and every beat of them made me want to drag this out even longer. "Your hair."

I blew out a breath and approached. Once she got me situated in front of the basin, I could feel the waves of heat at my back, sinking into the strands, making my neck tingle. Hukri went to the table, snagging a goblet made of white bone from the tray that had been delivered.

"Here," she said, handing it to me. If she noticed the way my hands shook, she didn't say anything. "Drink a little to help ease your nerves."

With relief, I brought the dark wine to my lips. The strong fermented drink burned a path down my throat, settling comforting heat in my belly. I hadn't said a word this night.

"You have nothing to fear, *missiki*," Hukri whispered. I could see the concern etched into her face. "The *Vorakkar* is an honorable male. He will treat you well in marriage. And you will be queen to the horde."

I would've laughed had I not had the sudden urge to cry. An honorable male? She didn't know that I had only agreed to this because he'd threatened to kill what remained of my village.

And this night, I was expected to *lie* with him. To take him and his seed deep into my body. I wasn't a fool—I knew what happened between males and females. Hukri herself had told me to slick *uudun* salve between my thighs the morning after once I confessed to her I'd never been with a male.

I took another sip of the wine. And one more for good measure before Hukri pulled the goblet away.

Once my hair was dry, I felt lighter. Some of the tension in my shoulders released, and my tongue was just loose enough to ask, "Why hasn't he taken a *Morakkari* yet?"

Hukri began brushing out my hair. The last step before I would have to face the horde. And in the outfit I was wearing... or rather, the lack of outfit. I'd felt more covered in the translucent dress the witches had given me.

"He was expected to. Everyone believed it would be Junira."

Another thing I'd noticed was that I was now privy to anyone's given name.

"She is the daughter of one of Rath Rowin's best *darukkars*," Hukri informed me. "The *Vorakkar* drank from her goblet two feasts ago when she presented it to him. She spent that night in his bed. We had expected an announcement soon. I don't think anyone expected you."

I didn't think Rowin expected me either, I thought, pressing my lips together, wondering why I felt a prick of hot *jealousy* lash at me at the thought of this Junira. Some of my nerves were leaving me. Anger was rising again only it felt different. It was *baffling*. I didn't care for him. So why did I care if another female had been in his bed not long ago?

"Is she upset?" I asked. "I stole her place."

"You didn't steal anything," Hukri said, pausing in brushing my hair. I heard the frown in her voice. "The *Vorakkar* chose you. We all saw your strength. Even Junira cannot fault him for choosing you over her."

Though it had been two nights ago, I still felt the lingerings of exhaustion from my overexertion.

I didn't want to speak of Rowin anymore—or his almost queen.

"Will I get to meet your daughter tonight at the feast?" I asked instead. "And your mate?"

The smile in Hukri's voice was evident though she said, "*Nik,* likely not. You will be up on the dais all night with the *Vorakkar*. Though it is the *tassimara*, there is no actual cere-mony. It is more of a celebration for the horde, and you will be expected to be with him all night."

"Oh, I see," I whispered, disappointment flooding me.

Hukri worked on my hair in silence after that, brushing it until it was soft and supple down my back. She'd told me she liked my hair, had often sighed over it as she brushed through the waves.

Once she was done, she pulled the top half of it back and secured it with the same golden clasp I'd worn a couple nights ago. A gift from Rowin, apparently. Then she added in little gold beads and small cuffs to my hair, securing them around the wavy tendrils.

"One last thing," she said, rising. She'd brought many things this night, which were all laid out on the table. "And I fear you will not like it."

She procured a tiny, clear pot of what looked like gold paint, holding it out before me. She opened the lid and was just about to dab her fingers into it when she hesitated. She peered at me and said, "This gold is meant for the *Vorakkar*."

My brow furrowed.

"When he kisses you here tonight," she finished, reaching out to touch my bared breast, making me jump.

Realization made my cheeks flush hot.

The gold...was meant to cover my nipples?

Tonight couldn't be more discomforting or mortifying already. I was already half-naked. Though the skirt was long, the material was nearly translucent and a long slit went from my ankle to my hip bone. When I walked, the slit shifted, and if I wasn't careful, it flashed my bare sex for all to see.

As for my top...it was nonexistent. Only my hair would cover my back. A gold necklace was the only covering for my front. Large and heavy, it was encrusted with red jewels and shimmering opals, dipping just low enough to hide my nipples from view. Nipples that would be painted with gold, so that Rowin could lick them clean later...

A shuddering breath left me.

"I'll do it," I whispered, taking the pot of gold paint from her hand. With my cheeks burning, I dabbed the paint onto myself, my nipples pebbling tight underneath my fingers.

When I was done, Hukri handed me a small yet ornate mirror. With hesitation, I took it from her and lifted it.

I'd only ever caught sight of myself in water reflections, so to see myself clearly for the first time was jarring. A strange sensation. With disappointment, I saw that I was no great beauty. Not like Tess or Kaila or Shayna.

However, the gold powder that dusted my cheekbones and nose made my skin look luminous and glowing. The dark powder that lined my eyes deepened their color and made them appear almost...sultry. My cheeks were flushed with nerves. Tendrils of my hair framed my face, softening my appearance.

Hukri was waiting for my approval, and I gave her a shaky smile, returning the mirror to her.

"Thank you. *Kakkira vor,*" I added, since she'd taught me the words in Dakkari. And I figured if I would be living among a Dakkari horde, I should begin to learn their language. Not everyone spoke in the universal tongue. Very few did, actually.

At the very least, I didn't stammer in their language. Only in my own.

Though I'd realized in the last two days, I hadn't stammered *once.* Not since the fog. Not since that damn *pain.*

It was as if the pain had reset something inside me. Or unleashed something inside me. I couldn't be certain which.

"Remember," she whispered, touching my cheek, "you have nothing to fear from him."

I fear everything from him, I thought silently.

Rustling came at the entrance—the sound of hide hitting hide—and I sensed his dominating presence before I ever saw him. Hukri's eyes darted toward the entrance, and then her head was bowing and she was stepping away from me.

Before he said a word, Hukri departed, and I turned to watch her go, catching sight of Rowin standing tall at the entrance.

The fire in the basin sparked loudly when I met his eyes. Suddenly, it felt as if all the air in the *voliki* was sucked out, especially when his gaze dropped, when his nostrils flared and his feet brought him closer toward me as if he couldn't help himself.

Seeing him made my mouth go dry. And I cursed the way my belly flipped and my heart skipped a beat.

But there was no denying that he was the most handsome male I'd ever seen in my lifetime. Harsh and cold, the severe lines of his face should have been terrifying, and yet they made him seem all the more powerful. He stood bare-chested and in a fur loincloth, this one black in color. The golden tattoos that traced and swirled across his chest seemed to glow. His dark nipples were wide and tight. His shoulder was no longer bandaged, and except for a raised scar, I would have thought that the sword wound had never been.

His black hair swayed down his back as he approached. Clasped in his palm, there was a solid gold cuff, glittering and ominous, though not unlike the ones he wore around his wrists. Like mine, his eyes were lined with dark powder, making the red appear devilish and dangerous.

When he drew close, so close that his wide, solid chest brushed the metal of my necklace that draped over my breasts, his hand lifted.

"*Leika,*" he rasped. Hunger burned in his gaze. I gasped softly, not expecting to see it, and I mentally made a note to ask Hukri about that word. *Leika.* He'd said it to me before. "*Rei leika Morakkari.*"

I knew *rei* meant "*my.*"

My Morakkari.

"Not yours yet," I corrected him.

"Are you still angry with me?" he murmured in that deep, spine-tingling voice. He drew even closer. My eyelids closed briefly when he stroked his fingers through my hair.

"Yes," I whispered in answer.

I hated that he affected me like this. I didn't like him one bit. I thought he was overbearing and unkind. He'd lied to me. Threatened me. Manipulated me.

So why did my body respond to his touch?

Why did my body respond to him like it had *known* him before, like it *remembered* him?

His head dipped. When his kiss came, I didn't fight it. He would be my husband after this night, and I would be his wife. When the heat of his tongue stroked mine, I made a small sound in the back of my throat. A sharp sigh huffed through his nostrils, and I thought that maybe I'd had too much of the wine again because the world swayed beneath my eyelids.

Rowin pulled back quickly, and he had to snag my waist to keep me steady, to keep me from stumbling. Belatedly, I realized I'd placed my hands on the wide berth of his chest, and I snatched them back swiftly. When I tried to step away, his grip tightened.

He held up the gold cuff. My eyes flicked to it, swallowing.

"Are you going to chain me again?" I asked, raising a brow.

"Not chain you," he corrected. "*Claim* you."

With that, he clasped the cuff around my *neck*. I heard it snap tight.

"What...what is this?" I asked, suddenly nervous, bringing my fingers up to touch the warm metal.

"A *Vorakkar's* claim. *Your Vorakkar's* claim," he told me. "You only need to wear it this night. And whenever I wish."

A gasp of outrage whistled through my nostrils. The Ghertun had cuffed their slaves like this. Or so I had heard.

Did...did *Morakkari* wear this too?

"Will I feel your claws tonight, *rei sarkia*?" he murmured. "Will I feel them raking down my back when I am seated deep inside you this night?"

My head swam again. Stunned, I felt my sex throb between my legs, and I was mortified by the response his words wrang from me.

In my shock, I whispered, "You think I will let you?"

The curl of his grin was like smoke. There one moment, and gone the next.

"*Lysi*," he said easily. He leaned down, his fingers brushing the gold at my neck. Against my lips, after a lazy kiss, he whispered, "You will beg for me by the night's end."

I stiffened in disbelief.

Rowin straightened. I felt his cock, hard and thick, pressing into my belly. As if the mere thought had aroused him too.

That was when I felt the first tendril of fear. Perhaps I was out of my element with him. I'd never known a male in that way. And he was a Dakkari horde king. He would've had his pick of females. Any of them. *All* of them. If he'd wished it.

What did I even know about sex? About pleasure? About seduction?

What was apparent to me was that I could hate him and desire him at the same time. He was proving that to me even now.

"It's time."

CHAPTER 32

"Are you frightened?" I murmured, unable to keep my hands off the human female in front of me.

Situated on Okan, Mina was rigid in front of me. Her back was pressed to my chest. My thighs encased her own. I had one hand draped across her lap, dangerously close to the high slit of her skirt. When I brushed the backs of my fingers up and down her exposed thigh, I heard her small gasp and felt her straighten further. My other hand held Okan's reins as I guided us through the horde.

"Of your *pyroki*?" she asked, reaching out a hand to spread across Okan's neck. It surprised me. For a skittish little thing, she was awfully brave with a horde king's beast. "Should I be?"

"He will not hurt you," I assured her. Another brush of my fingers against her leg. Though this time, my touch was bolder. For two days and nights, I'd avoided her. Now that she was back within my grasp, I couldn't stop touching her.

The pad of one finger brushed the curls shielding her cunt. In a flash, her hand wrapped around my wrist—well, half of it—right over my *Vorakkar* cuff. She squeezed.

"This will be mine soon enough," I growled in her ear.

Her voice sounded breathless, but her hand never left my wrist. "Are you trying to frighten me?"

I stilled, pondering the words and the way they made discomfort churn inside me.

"*Nik*, I am not, Mina."

"I don't understand you," she said, her eyes forward as we both swayed together, propelled forward by Okan's rocking gait. She no doubt saw the glow that encased the encampment. Soon she would see the pathway that led to the feast. She would see the pathway lined with the members of the horde, waiting to pay their respects. My horde.

And now hers.

"How can you even want me? Considering everything you think I've done to you?" she asked. "I'm a witch, remember? The same one who bewitched you, who captured you, who tricked you. A witch no better than Benn in your eyes."

Did she believe that? Worse yet, had I made her believe that?

"I know you are nothing like him," I told her.

"Well, thank you. Thank you so much for clearing that up."

"You are still angry with me," I murmured. "No matter. You can take your aggressions out on me tonight after the *tassimara*."

She was bewildered by my words. "How can you even talk about that right now?"

"You'll find, *rei sarkia*," I rasped, my fingers brushing her curls once more, "that fucking lends itself very well to frustration and anger."

Her breath hitched.

She was saved from answering when the first members of my horde became visible on the pathway, the nearer we rode toward the feast. They lined the road on both sides, awaiting our arrival. In their palms were little papery orbs of golden light.

"What...what are they holding?" she asked instead, distracted from the thread of our conversation. Her voice was soft, awed.

"Lanterns," I told her, shifting, pressing her more fully into me as Okan treaded forward. "*Tassimaras* are about change. About new life." My palm spread across her belly, and she stilled. "The lanterns are filled with seeds. They are an offering to Kakkari and her earth. Our home."

"Seeds?" she asked, not understanding. But in a moment, she would.

When we came into view, the lanterns began to lift. Bright little orbs that gently began to drift upward, higher and higher. One after another, the horde released more and more lanterns as we approached.

Mina's head tilted back, and I could see the brightness in her eyes as she watched the lanterns. Her lips were parted in wonder. The light of them cast us all in gold, as if it were sunset and not a black moon this night.

Seeing the innocent delight on her features, at such a small thing, made something twist inside my chest. Affection? *Nik*, that couldn't be right. Whatever it was, however, it was a soft thing. And I didn't like the feeling of it.

Hands drifted over our legs as we began to ride down the lit pathway. Mina softly inhaled and looked down in surprise, watching as the first female lining the pathway blessed us. Then another. Then another. Palms, dusted in gold powder, brushed over our legs and down Okan's sides. The light from the lanterns reflected the golden dust, luminous and beautiful.

Slowly, I led Okan down the pathway, presenting my *Morakkari* to the horde. About halfway down the road, I caught sight of Junira, standing beside her father, Besik, one of my best *darukkars.*

Junira kept her gaze averted as she ran her hands over us. I knew what the horde believed. I knew the rumors that had circulated. While I had not been ready to make a final decision regarding my *Morakkari*, Junira was one of the females I had been considering. In all likelihood, she *would* have been queen of this horde. She came from a strong line of warriors. She would have given me an even stronger son.

Then Mina had appeared to me in the fog.

She had come to me and vowed herself to me in that beautiful, haunting voice. Her eyes had held me captive. She came to me and made me want her. Then she made me *need* her, for the sake of the horde.

But it was the *wanting*—and not the *needing*—that frightened me the most.

In the last two days, Besik had made his disapproval of my decision evident, though I had been too preoccupied to deal with the disrespect accordingly.

Now, as my *Morakkari* sat before me on my *pyroki*, as his daughter gave us her blessing, I watched as *he* refused to. He had not made his offering to Kakkari. He had not pressed his hands to us in acceptance. He considered my decision a slight against him, against his daughter and, by extension, his line. Even though he had seen Mina's powers. Even though he had seen her strength.

Others didn't even dare to look the human female in the eyes. That was the extent of *their* respect, *their* awe at what they'd witnessed.

I would deal with him later. Tonight was about the *tassimara*. Tonight was about the strength of the horde, not the displeasure of a single *darukkar*.

But I would not forget it.

Urging Okan forward, we soon reached the end of the pathway. Valavik stood there, hands behind his back. Behind him was the celebration feast. Long tables, laden with food, ran in rows. An area had been cleared for dancing, and the drums had been placed. A raised dais at the front of the feasting area had been erected, a single throne on top. Fire basins roared with life. The smell of smoky meat filled the air.

The horde had been busy in seeing to the preparations for the *tassimara*.

When we reached the front of the line, I wheeled Okan around to face the horde.

In Dakkari, I bellowed out, loud enough for all of them to hear, "I present my chosen *Morakkari* for Rath Rowin to see, under Kakkari's night sky and with the goddess' blessing. A *Morakkari* that came to me under Kakkari's guiding light." I heard the murmurs of surprise that broke out at the words. "And when I saw her, I felt the knowing within me. I knew then that this female would change the course of my destiny. I knew then that Kakkari had revealed her to me for a purpose. That purpose has never been more clear to me than it is now."

Mina had stiffened briefly when I began addressing my horde, but I had the sense that she was listening carefully. Picking out words she would memorize, words she would whisper in the dark later. Hukri had reported to me that Mina was interested in the Dakkari language, that she often asked the meanings of words.

"You all witnessed her power. The *Morakkari* of Rath Rowin is meant to be a protector. *Our* protector. She makes the horde stronger." A chorus of agreement, of cheers rose to the sky. "On this night, we bind ourselves together. She will give me strong sons and daughters for the horde. She will serve this horde as I serve this horde. And together, as one, we will enter the uncertainty of these times with power and courage. The darkness that blankets the land is not something to be feared from this night forward. The *Morakkari* of Rath Rowin will never let this horde fall."

The cries were deafening, rising into the night sky as if they were the lanterns overhead. Exuberant cries to Kakkari. Cries of relief. Of grief, for since the fog had come, our lives had been changed. But mostly, I heard battle cries. War cries. For the horde believed that we now had a great weapon at our side to defeat whatever evil plagued this land.

When I tilted my head to regard Mina, I saw her lips were parted and she was looking at me, not at the horde before her.

Seeing her this night, in Dakkari ceremonial dress, with her long, wavy hair wild and soft, with her green eyes glittering...it unleashed the desire I'd tried desperately to keep locked away. Emotions got one killed. Lust had almost ruined my life's work once before with her. I'd wanted to ensure it never happened again.

Yet I lusted after my *Morakkari* now.

It was expected that she bear my heirs. Many, many heirs.

And so I told myself I was duty bound to bed her. Only that excuse was laughable to me now.

I wanted her. Desperately. I had since the first moment I'd seen her. This small, frightened creature, who held the future of my horde in her hands.

"What did you tell them?" she whispered to me now.

Drums started behind us, the beat primal. If she felt my thickened cock at her back, she didn't comment on it.

"I told them the truth," I rasped, swinging off Okan, the *mrikro*—the *pyroki* master—approaching to lead my loyal beast away. Reaching for her, I heard her gasp when my hands settled around her slim waist and pulled her down. Her hands scrambled for the tops of my shoulders, steadying herself on them, as if she was afraid I'd let her fall.

I let her slide down my body. A ragged gasp flew from her throat when the heavy necklace covering her breasts slid up too. I felt the pebbled tips of her nipples drag down my chest, and I barely hid my muffled groan.

The night would be long, I decided, watching as her face flamed and she hurriedly righted the necklace.

As my horde began to walk toward the feasting area, down the lined pathway we'd just traveled, I, too, led Mina forward.

Instead of going to the tables, however, I led us toward the dais.

"Am...am I expected to stand?" she asked, as I pulled her up the steps.

"*Nik,*" I murmured, taking my seat at the single throne made of *ungira* bone, one of the most dangerous beasts on Dakkar. Pulling her down onto my lap, I felt her freeze.

"I-I can't sit like this all night," she said quietly. Though her voice sounded frightened, her eyes were steady as they met my own.

"You have been in my lap before. Wearing much less, remember?" I growled in her ear.

"With your hands tied behind your back," she responded. "You were no danger to me then."

My grin was slow. Her lips parted when my hand slid up her bare spine, and when I reached the bones of her shoulder blades, I slid my touch around her front.

Her heavy breasts heaved when I brushed the undersides with the back of my fingers. The jewels on her necklace flashed as she moved.

"Afraid of this, *rei Morakkari?*"

Her heat seeped into me, licking at me like flames from a fire.

Licking her lips, she said, "I am not your *Morakkari* yet."

"You are," I replied.

She blinked. "What? I thought there was a ceremony. Or..."

"I announced you to the horde. We rode the path. My horde made their offerings to Kakkari and gave us their blessings. It is done."

"*That's it?*" she asked, surprised.

Amusement bloomed within me.

"Well, all that's left to appease Kakkari will take place

tonight," I informed her. "Though there will be no audience for that."

Her cheeks burned a tantalizing red. Her chin lifted, and I watched her throat bob as she swallowed.

A *bikku* approached the dais, and Mina tried to turn her attention toward her, as if desperate for any distraction. I wouldn't let her though. I tilted her chin back toward me as I beckoned the *bikku* forward with a curl of my claws.

Those green eyes were rapt on me as the *bikku* deposited a heavy tray on the wide arm of the throne.

I watched Mina's expression shift the longer we looked at one another. For a moment, I remembered the girl who'd come to me in the nights while everyone else slept. I remembered the risks she took, even as I cursed her very name.

When the *bikku* slid away, as silently as she'd come, I didn't even notice.

"You'll hurt me," Mina whispered.

She was speaking of what would come tonight.

"Only for a little while," I murmured, brushing my fingers over her lips. "And then you will come to crave it."

Her throat bobbed again. Her tongue wet her lips, and I growled, acting on impulse for once, leaning forward to steal a kiss. She held perfectly still as I brushed my lips against hers. A chaste kiss. Almost sweet.

"Rowin," she whispered, turning her head away, not meeting my eyes. "Your horde."

I grunted, pulling away. My *Morakkari* was shy. I would have to keep that in mind.

Turning to inspect the tray the *bikku* had brought, I lifted a goblet of wine first. Made of white bone inlaid with gold, it was filled to the brim with dark, fragrant liquid.

I offered it to Mina first. We would drink from the same goblet and feed one another from the same plate. Though she'd already fed me before, I remembered.

She kept my eyes as I tilted the goblet to her lips. The intensity of my gaze seemed to make her shy too because her lashes swept down as she swallowed the wine. Once she was done, I took a healthy swallow of it before replacing it on the tray.

There was still a mottling of bruises across her cheekbone, and I brushed my fingers over them.

"Humans heal slowly," I commented.

Her eyes flickered to my shoulder, which had been without a bandage for the last two days.

"Did you expect them to be gone? Since you haven't come to me for two days?" she asked.

"My apologies, *Morakkari*. I did not think you noticed my absence, considering the last conversation we had," I pointed out.

Her lips pressed together at the reminder—the reminder that I'd threatened her and that that was the only reason she was sitting on my lap right now, dressed the way she was, as our horde celebrated before us.

"I didn't," she protested softly. "I mean, I didn't care."

"Mmm."

Her skin was soft and warm as I slid my palm to wrap around her waist.

"I don't care for you, you know," she informed me, sounding surprisingly miserable about that fact. "I don't even like you."

"That's a lie," I replied.

She gaped at me. "How so? You've been nothing but terrible to me since we left the Dead Mountain. After all I did to help you—"

"Including plotting to capture me in the first place," I murmured easily, my hand tightening on her waist. "Let us not forget that very important fact, *rei sarkia*."

"You know I had no choice in that," she said. "*You know that.*"

My jaw tightened, but my touch on her gentled.

"You cared for me under the Dead Mountain," I said. "You liked me then."

Her eyes flickered down my chest, though her gaze was unseeing.

"I liked the male who talked with me," she said quietly. I stilled at the softness in her voice, feeling discomfort swim in my chest. "I liked the male who spoke of the frozen North Lands. Who comforted me when I needed it." Her eyes lifted and met mine. "Who warmed me when I was cold. Who made me feel a little less lonely."

Swallowing hard, my brow drew down. "*Kalles...*"

"I liked that male," she said. "But then I realized that he never truly existed. That it was all just a farce. A manipulation to make me trust him, to make me care for him. And the worst part is that I cannot even blame him for it. Because I would try to do the same thing."

How could I tell her that there had been no plotting on my part for most of those instances? How could I tell her that I'd wanted to warm her because I needed to? How could I tell her that I'd wanted to comfort her because I needed to?

"The only thing I ever lied to you about, Mina," I told her instead, "was that the priestesses knew how to defeat the fog. Everything else was the truth."

"And how can I believe that?" she asked me. She didn't seem angry. Or upset. In fact, she was quite calm. She met my eyes steadily.

And in that moment, I knew, without a doubt, that I'd made the right decision. I knew right then that she would make the horde of Rath Rowin proud to have her as its queen. I knew right then that we were where Kakkari had meant for us to be.

"You said it so convincingly that I believed it immediately. You are talented in lying. And that makes me nervous."

I sighed. Looking out over the horde, I broke her gaze briefly. But I couldn't stay away from her eyes for long.

"In time, you will see I speak the truth," I said. "In time, you will find your husband prides himself on loyalty and honor."

Mina's gaze was unwavering, but she blinked at the word *husband*. As if right then was the first instant when she realized everything I would become to *her*, not everything she would become to *me*.

Her swallow was audible.

"Ask me for something," I told her, sliding my hand up her back again to delve into her hair. The feast fell away from us. It was only the two of us. Like fog swirled around us and no one else existed. "Ask me for anything you'd like on our *tassimara*, and I will give it to you."

"Don't attack the Dead Mountain," she said immediately.

I huffed out a short breath. "That deal was already made between us, Mina. And as long as you are at my side, you know their safety is guaranteed. Ask me for something that I can give you."

Her gaze was cool. Assessing.

Even still, the request she made of me caught me off guard. It surprised me because it was entirely unexpected.

I had expected her to ask for jewels or silk or the whitest of furs to keep her warm, as most females would have. Then again, Mina was not like most of the females I'd encountered in my life. At the very least, I had expected a rueful request for me to let her go.

Instead, she said softly, "Then give me your name, husband."

I stiffened underneath her. My spine and my cock. Hearing her refer to me as "husband" was jarring, and yet it filled me with a purpose I hadn't even known I possessed. A *longing*. It filled me with...pride.

However, there was no denying the discomfort I felt brewing in my gut.

Names are important. Names can be used against you, my

father had often said. *And so, never give them the opportunity to use it against you.*

No one on this planet knew my given name anymore. It had died with my father, and that knowledge lay buried with him in the North Lands beside the mother I had never known.

Yet the person I trusted least in my horde was now asking me for it. The person I trusted least was now my wife. She would be the mother to my children and the salvation for my horde if it was ever threatened.

I had not forgiven her for her betrayal, though I knew she'd truly had no choice. And I didn't think she had forgiven me for my own betrayal either or for the way I'd callously threatened those she still cared about under the Dead Mountain.

"That is what I want," she told me. "I want your name. Your true name. Not the one they all call you."

If she was testing me, she would find that I was true to my word. I said I'd give her anything this night. A gift on our *tassi-mara*, to go with the others that lay within her *deviri*, the chests of trinkets and riches I'd collected over my lifetime, a gift for my future bride.

I dragged her close, making her breath hitch. My hand curled around the nape of her neck and my nose brushed the shell of her tiny, cold ear as I leaned close.

"Wrune," I told her. I caught the subtle shiver that raced down her spine and heard her small gasp, as if she was surprised I'd actually given it to her. "My name is Wrune of Rath Rowin, *rei sarkia*. Now you know the true name of your husband."

CHAPTER 33

Wrune.

"It sounds like ruin," I whispered, meeting his eyes when he pulled back.

His jaw clenched at the comment. A comment I hadn't meant to voice out loud.

"In Dakkari, it has a similar meaning," he informed me. His lips twisted briefly before he dragged the goblet toward him again. "My father thought it fitting."

His father named him? The father he'd told me was buried in the North Lands, like my own?

"Why?" I whispered.

He took a healthy swallow from the goblet, pondering my question. Once he was done, he brought it to my own lips again.

The heady, full wine burst on my tongue as he said, "Because my mother died bringing me into this world. Because for her, I *was* ruin. For him too."

My heart froze in my chest at the unexpected confession.

"I—" I licked my lips, feeling a flooding of sympathy at the words. "I'm sorry."

I'd never known my own mother either. Not truly. She hadn't died giving me life, but she had died in the year after I was born. She'd always been sick, or so my father had told me. But he'd always told me that I was her ultimate joy. That she'd been blessed to be able to care for me, to love me, if only for a short time.

Which was why I found it so tragic what Rowin—*Wrune*—had just told me. Because with a *name*, his father had marked him to always remember her death.

"Let's not speak of it," came his gruff voice. "Not this night."

I swallowed, unsure of how to respond to that. All I could do was nod.

But the simple confession made me realize that I truly knew nothing about the male I now called *husband*.

I knew nothing of his life. How he'd come to be *Vorakkar*. His family. His purpose.

Conflicting emotions warred within me, making my head throb. I realized I could dislike him and like him at the same time. I could hate him for threatening me, and in the next moment, my heart could twist for him. He could make me breathless with a single touch, could make me desire him. Though he could also make me want to scream in frustration.

I'd shocked him with my request for his name.

I knew that. I'd felt it.

And yet he'd been true to his word. He'd given it to me.

Wrune of Rath Rowin.

Just the name could strike fear in the hearts of his enemies, of which I was certain he had many.

His gaze had tilted away from me, but I watched him silently. His eyes tracked the members of his horde. His posture was relaxed, but I had the distinct impression that he was still aware of everything happening around him. Always alert, always on guard.

I wondered if that was tiring. I wondered if he ever loathed being a horde king of Dakkar. Because I would. I thought I would hate it, having to shoulder the responsibility for a hundred or more beings. Did he ever lose sleep over it?

I will find out, I realized, my lips parting. Tonight, I would be in his bed. And though I wanted to run, though I wanted to find Tess and just *leave* this land...I knew that I wouldn't.

He was right. We had made a deal. And I would keep up my end, if he kept up his. There was no running from this anymore. It was much too late for that.

Another *bikku* approached the dais and ascended with the permission of her *Vorakkar*. This time, the tray was laden with food. Neatly arranged and decorated with white blooms, as if the presentation of the food was just as important as eating it. A strange concept, but one I'd noticed the last two days whenever my meals were delivered.

"*Kakkira vor,*" Wrune said, and the *bikku* bowed her head before leaving us.

I didn't have the courage to face his horde yet, especially when I was sprawled across Wrune's lap and the slit on my skirt was dangerously close to revealing my sex to all that looked on.

But I chanced a peek then. Their voices were loud and jovial, carrying over the slight breeze of that darkened night. Laughter was plenty, and it was so incredibly strange to hear—and so *often*. No one had laughed under the Dead Mountain. No one had laughed in our makeshift camp, deep in the woods, before we'd come to the Dead Mountain. Solemn faces and hungry bellies were what I was used to.

But not here. There was food aplenty. Smiling, round faces. A group of humans were even present, though I had purposefully avoided looking at them. I'd been aware of their presence. Wrune had told me himself, when he was chained in his cell, that humans lived in his horde.

He'd been telling the truth about that at least.

The group was small, however, and clearly kept to themselves, though their shoulders were relaxed. One man was even talking with a Dakkari female, his hand perched on her hip, though she was taller than him.

"Here, *rei Morakkari*," Wrune said, drawing my attention away from the humans. "Eat."

When I reached forward to take some braised meat from the tray, he snagged my hand gently.

"I feed you tonight," he murmured. My eyes widened. "And you will feed me as well."

Another custom of this *tassimara*? Or was it...for always?

With that, Wrune took some braised meat from the dish and raised it to my lips. The flavor of it exploded on my tongue. Rich and slightly smoky. The fat was like silk, and the meat practically melted, it was so tender.

I swore I caught a hint of a smile on Wrune's face as he pulled his fingers away, briefly sucking the juice that ran down his thumb. My breath hitched at the sight. Swallowing hard, I watched as he selected another dish, something green and hard.

"Open for me, Mina," he murmured, bringing it to my lips. His words made another shiver race down my back, one I couldn't hide from him, and this time, I was certain of his smile.

I opened my mouth, and he fed me the small morsel, keeping my eyes all the while. Why was something like this so incredibly intimate? I felt the panic rising, just as surely as the flush that was threatening to flood over my cheeks.

"Only a *Morakkari* is allowed to feed a *Vorakkar*," came his voice, surprisingly soft. "And only a *Vorakkar* is allowed to feed his *Morakkari*."

Given the intimacy of this, I understood why that was.

The green thing he'd just fed me was tart and sharp, though the next moment, it dissolved into sweetness. It made my mouth water as I pondered his words, and then I noted quietly, "I fed you before."

"*Lysi*, you did."

"I—I should not have done that then," I remarked next.

"Given that you became my *Morakkari*," he commented, his eyes fixed on my lips, "there was no harm in it."

"The humans," I murmured quickly when I saw him lean toward me, as if he would steal another kiss. My hand was shaking slightly when I reached out for the food tray, to snag a piece of the meat. "How did they come to be here in your horde?"

Wrune knew exactly what I was doing, but he allowed it. He relaxed into his throne. The muscles of his thighs released underneath me, though his cock was still pressing hard against my hip. His arousal was nearly impossible to ignore, especially in his loincloth.

"Remember when I spoke to you about heartstones?" he said. Tentatively, I nodded, and then before I lost my nerve, I offered him the meat.

He leaned forward to take it, his eyes flashing as his lips brushed my fingers. Transfixed, I watched the way his jaw worked as he ate. This *was* familiar. As if we'd done it a thousand times before, and that was almost as frightening as the thing between his thighs, aching and needful.

"The human queen of Rath Drokka used the heartstone underneath the Dead Mountain, and in the panicked aftermath, the Dakkari that accompanied her helped free the Ghertun's slaves," Wrune told me. He nodded his head toward the humans on the far end of the feasting tables. "They were among them."

Sympathy went through me. For everything I'd endured in this life, from loss and grief to derision and abuse, I'd at least never been a slave of the Ghertun. I'd heard horrible, horrible things.

"You will meet them soon enough," Wrune said after a brief moment of quiet.

"Since you mean to release me from my prison," I murmured, "and let your pet roam freely around your horde?"

Wrune made an impatient huff. I was only half jesting, the wine slowly loosening my tongue. There was a gentle rush in my ears. My body was beginning to warm.

All my bravado faded, however, when his thick, hot palm landed on my knee and slowly slid its way up my thigh. The back of my neck pricked and my heart pounded in its cage.

"You are a queen now," he murmured in my ear. "You are free to do as you please. However, you always have to submit to me when I wish it, though you know how much I enjoy your claws, *rei sarkia.*"

Oh, this maddening male, I thought, my spine straightening even as my flesh tingled from his bold touch.

"And in private, I will take them gladly."

My eyes connected with his and held. I understood what he was telling me. I understood what he was trying to make me realize.

That I might be his queen but this was *his* horde. And if I did anything to undermine his authority among his horde, he would not be happy about it.

I was, however, free to argue with him in private. Without the eyes and the ears of his horde watching.

Appearance was important, it seemed. It had been that way with Benn too.

It discomforted me to realize that. However, I knew, even just from tonight, that Wrune's horde actually respected him. They might fear him as well, but it was easy to see that his people were cared for. That they were healthy. And, with the exception of the lingering fog not that far away, *safe.*

Wrune wanted us to create a strong front, as *Vorakkar* and *Morakkari,* for the sake of his horde. That was what he was telling me, what he was willing me to understand.

And in return, I would receive everything his horde did. I would be cared for. Safe.

"*Lysi?*" he rasped, tilting my chin up with the hand that wasn't slowly sliding to the junction of my thighs.

And I will be in his bed, I added silently. I would have a powerful male seated deep between my legs each night. And why did that knowledge make me feel more powerful, though I didn't quite know what to expect?

I swallowed. I looked out over his horde, focusing on the laughter and the taste of sweetness on my tongue.

He was offering me everything I'd ever wanted. All I had to do was *take it.*

"*Lysi,*" I whispered to him, saying the word in Dakkari.

And if I had power, I would have power to help Tess. To help those underneath the Dead Mountain that wanted it.

As *Morakkari*, I had the power of an entire horde at my back.

Would I be able to wield it? If the time was right?

His fingers traced the crease where my upper thigh met my hip.

"Good," he grunted.

And I wondered if this was what Tess felt when she slept beside Benn each night. I wondered if he made her feel powerful and that was why she'd done everything she'd done.

"Now watch, *rei Morakkari,*" he murmured, nodding his head toward the celebration. "The dancing will begin soon."

CHAPTER 34

My heart was throbbing alongside the drums.

I was full and sated.

I was warm and surprisingly relaxed, though I assumed that was partly due to the wine.

And sometime after Wrune fed me the last morsel I could possibly eat and when the dancing was well underway, I had begun to feel a different kind of heat entirely.

A heat that had something to do with the primal, gyrating, erotic dancing I witnessed...and everything to do with the male that was stoking it with his maddening touches.

"I can smell you, *sarkia*," Wrune growled. "If I touched you now, would I find how wet you are for me?"

Well, that was mortifying if that was the case, I couldn't help but think. But my cheeks didn't flush, and the embarrassment was short lived. My eyes were glued to the dancing spread out before us. My gaze flitted from couple to couple, each performing dances of their own, as mesmerizingly beautiful as they were breathlessly erotic. Graceful limbs twisted expertly, passionate kisses were stolen. The more brazen of the couples had the female's legs wrapped around the male's hips. Their dancing looked more like a desperate coupling as moans lifted toward the night sky.

Throughout it all, however, Wrune's eyes had only been on me. I'd felt them, hot and observant, as if he found *me* more arousing than the dancers.

His lips brushed the back of my shoulder again. He'd swept my hair to one side long before to stroke the column of my neck with his claws. It made me shiver though it wasn't unpleasant. The opposite, in fact. And I was beginning to fear that maybe he was right.

I was beginning to fear that maybe he *could* make me beg for him tonight.

Sexual pleasure was not something I was very familiar with. I'd never coupled with a male in my lifetime. And with the exception of Benn's unwanted gropings, I had never been touched by a male either.

Back in my village, when life had been much easier than it was now, I still remembered the first time Tess had told me about an orgasm. She'd told me that she'd touched herself—and wasn't shy about leaving out the details either—and that she'd felt the most *sublime* sensation. Those things were whispered and giggled about often, especially among the younger generation, though I had never been privy to other conversations about it, considering I'd been somewhat of an outcast even then.

The first time I ever touched myself, I'd understood what Tess meant. I'd done what she said she did. Touched that little pearl between my legs, the thing she'd learned was called a clit. Heat had built. My legs had shaken and squeezed. Though I'd had no idea what I was doing back then, my body had seemed to catapult me effortlessly toward the pleasure I was unknowingly seeking.

After that first time, however, the opportunities to be alone had been far and few in between. My father, aunt, and I had all slept within the same room. And once the village burned and my life had been upturned, nothing had been the same. Though I was the loneliest I had ever been, I'd never been *alone*.

And so sexual pleasure had slowly faded from my mind. Desperation, hunger, fear, and anger had taken its place.

Only...right then...Wrune was reminding me of that first time I'd touched myself in secret. That exhilarating rush, that tingling that seemed to spread to all parts of my body, that ball of heat that was growing and growing between my thighs.

I was leaning into him more fully, softening for him, as if my body knew what he could provide for me. I'd had just enough wine to loosen the tension between my shoulders without making me dizzy and sick like that first night.

My lips parted, my back arching slightly when Wrune slid his hand up my thigh again.

"*Ahh, vok, kalles,*" he murmured gruffly just as the edge of his knuckle brushed my curls once more. That knuckle pressed, and a jolt raced up my spine when it nudged against that *perfect* spot. "That's it."

Gasping, I acted on instinct by crossing my legs. I didn't realize it, but I'd effectively trapped his hand while also shielding what he was doing from the view of his horde.

Which...only made him more brazen.

My thighs squeezed when my sex throbbed. His fingers curled further, and his knuckles ran down and up over my slick folds, as if coaxing them to open for him. He pressed, and then a ragged sound rose out of my throat when those knuckles thrummed my clit back and forth. That little, hardened bud that made me pant.

"*Don't,*" I whispered, meeting his eyes, frightened that he would give me pleasure like *this*. In front of his horde. And I'd always been taught that pleasure was something that was hidden, something that was done in private. "Not here."

Those red, half-lidded eyes lowered to my lips.

"Ask me," he growled.

"W-What?" I whispered, not understanding.

"Ask me to take you from here. Ask me to bring you to our furs, and I'll give you *everything* you need there, *rei Morakkari*."

The confidence in his voice was almost as intoxicating as his touch.

"Maybe you should ask *me*," I replied, realizing what he was doing. He wanted me to submit to him. He wanted me to beg, which was what he'd vowed would happen this night.

Another growl rose from him. I leaned back when he moved forward to kiss me. I couldn't think straight if he kissed me. Not that I could really think straight right now with his hand between my legs, stroking me with the backs of his fingers.

If he kissed me, however, I'd be lost.

Looking down between us, I felt a jolt when I saw the head of his cock peeking out from his fur loincloth. The tip was rounded, tapering down to a thick, pulsing shaft. Liquid glimmered at the head, and as I watched, I saw his cock bob.

"We...we won't," I breathed, meeting his eyes in bewilderment. "We won't fit."

A low, deep sound rose from his throat. "We will, *sarkia*," he grated.

I didn't see how that was a possibility.

Tingling pleasure bloomed in my belly when he pressed his fingers into me, trapping my clit gently between two of his knuckles.

For a moment, I had a flash of bewilderment. I wondered how I could be sitting here now, on the verge of an orgasm, with a horde king of Dakkar. A horde king who'd made it very clear he didn't trust me, who'd purred to me that fucking went hand in hand with frustration and anger.

And I was beginning to see what he'd meant.

Because I was frustrated and angry. But I also felt deep, pinching lust building inside me for *him*.

My eyes flickered out to the dancers. To the feast that still took place beyond them. And beyond that, from the raised dais, I could see over the top of the gate. Into the night.

But I didn't see the fog. I didn't see anything. Only the stars overhead, that seemed twice as bright given it was the black moon.

A black moon when he was supposed to die, I thought.

And despite everything, despite his betrayal and his threats, I knew.

"I would still do it again, you know," I told him, meeting his eyes as I felt pleasure prick and press into me. "I would still help free you from the Dead Mountain. Even knowing what would happen next. I wouldn't change anything."

His fingers stilled between my legs.

Horror. I felt *horror* at the thought of the witches sacrificing this male. Of tying him down, of drawing his blood to keep him weak. Of taking a blade and...

I couldn't avoid his kiss this time, and I made a sound in surprise when he rose from the dais, his lips still attached to mine.

The drums didn't falter. The dancers didn't stop. The celebration continued even as he broke the kiss and descended the stairs, his steps heavy. He still carried me in his arms as he wove through the crowd. Hands of his horde pressed against us, Dakkari words I didn't understand being lifted into the air.

Suddenly, his *pyroki* was there, led to us by the older male who'd took him earlier that night. Wrune placed me easily on his beast and swung up behind me. He didn't spare the celebration another look as he urged his *pyroki* into a gallop.

My heart was in my throat. We were riding fast and hard. Wind slapped at my cheeks and blew back my hair, and I'd never felt anything like it before. For a moment, it felt like I was *flying*. Like I was *free*.

Then we were approaching a large *voliki* at the back of the encampment. One I knew was *his*.

Wrune had me off his *pyroki* before we even stopped, and then he was striding toward the *voliki*. Smoke was drifting from the venting hole at the top.

Once inside, I was hit by the warmth and the dim, golden light. A small fire was flickering in the basin, but that was all I saw, all I registered before my back met soft furs.

I was on a bed. An actual bed, made high with supports underneath and furs as cushioning.

It smelled like him. Suddenly he was everywhere, all around me. That wonderful masculine scent that reminded me of *home*.

Swallowing, I looked up at him from my position on his bed. He loomed at the foot of it and was shedding the strap of his sword, which was always positioned down his back. He leaned his sword against the bed, never taking his eyes off me.

The heavy plate of the gold necklace heaved with my breaths.

I wasn't prepared when he reached down and unclasped it from around my neck, tossing it onto the floor like it was expendable. Next went my skirt. His claw ran through the waistband of it, cutting through the material with ease.

I didn't make a sound when I suddenly found myself lying naked before him. Like a sacrifice on an altar.

Save for the golden collar around my neck, a collar I guessed he *liked* seeing, I was completely exposed to him.

And it wasn't fear I felt.

I wasn't afraid of this. Of *him*.

I felt determination. Like I needed to prove to myself that I could master him too. As easily as he mastered me. This was just another battle between us. One of many that would come.

Those red eyes flashed as they roved over my body. His nostrils flared. His knee hit the bed.

"Frightened, *rei sarkia*?" he rasped.

Since when had *sarkia* started to sound like a purr instead of a curse on his lips?

"Not of you," I told him.

His lips quirked, a dark little smile that sent my heart racing.

"You always surprise me," he murmured. "Just when I think I have you figured out, you change everything."

My lips parted, and then I gasped when his head lowered. He crawled over me, planting his hands on either side of my waist. His lips pressed to my belly, dragging upward. Goose bumps broke out over my flesh, and I barely suppressed my violent shiver. He pressed kisses across my abdomen before moving to my breasts.

"And these," he growled, one hand reaching forward to cup the weight of my left breast. "*Vok*, how my mouth has watered for these. Since I first saw you."

A ragged cry burst from my lips when his head ducked again. That hot mouth found my breast, sucking and rolling my hardened nipple with a strong, seeking tongue. Licking at the gold I'd painted onto them earlier that evening. Wrune gently thrummed my other with his fingers, being mindful of his claws, and my back arched off the furs, pressing further into his mouth and touch.

I wanted to hold him there forever. I wanted his kiss there, hot and demanding, forever.

"*Lysi*," he groaned. "But there is something else I need more right now."

Suddenly, he flipped us. One moment I was on my back. The next thing I knew, he'd taken my place, rolling us until he was underneath me.

His speed and strength should have frightened me, but I'd always known that humans were the weaker of the two species. It shouldn't have surprised me.

"Wrune," I whispered.

His expression changed as soon as I said his name. I wasn't certain if he was displeased or if he was *relieved*. But as I was trying to discover the sudden shift, his hands wrapped around my waist and he brought me up until I was straddling his face.

Looking down at him in shock, I barely registered that the glistening folds of my sex were parted almost obscenely for him. I didn't register the plushness of the furs underneath my knees or the way it should have embarrassed me to have him so *close* to that private place of mine.

To steady myself, I dug my hands into his hair, eliciting his growl. His hands came up to wrap around my hips, effectively keeping me in place.

"What are you—" A ragged gasp tore from my throat. "*Ohh!*"

With those eyes burning into mine, his chin dipped beneath me.

The heat of his dark tongue sizzled between my folds as he licked my very center. Soft yet violent pleasure assaulted me as my startled cry mingled with his groan.

His grip on my hips tightened, so tight that I wondered if there would be bruises in the morning. But I hardly cared. My jaw had dropped, and all I wanted to see was that tongue.

"*Divine,*" he rasped. A rough growl threaded up his throat, and my hands curled in his hair as he licked me again. And again. And again. "*Lysi.*"

Teasing me at first, I thought. That tongue curled around my clit briefly before it retreated, and my hips began to rock to find that pleasure again. He lapped and laved between my legs, those eyes watching it all. Then his head would dip and I'd feel that *long* hot tongue wiggling deep inside me, stroking against my sensitive inner walls until I was whimpering.

And he was doing it on purpose, I realized. He wanted to make me come undone. He wanted to see me *fall.*

He wanted to hear me beg.

And I was too far lost in the pleasure to care.

"*Wrune,*" I groaned, meeting his eyes. "*Please.*"

"Mmmm" was the only sound that left him, but I swore I felt his mouth quirk into a self-satisfied smile.

His hands pulled me until there was no space left between us. His mouth pressed tight, and he began to suckle on my clit.

And I saw *stars.* A desperate cry burst from my throat. My eyelids drifted shut and my head tilted back. The tightness of the collar around my neck was the only thing that stopped my head from lolling around my shoulders as sublime heat exploded between my legs all at once.

"Already, *rei Morakkari?*" he rasped. "Sensitive *kalles.*"

My hips rocked against him as my orgasm continued. I perceived his tongue lapping at the juices that ran from me. That long tongue flicked upward to my sensitive clit, making me twitch and moan.

When it became too much, I tried to lift off his mouth, but his hands held me captive.

"No," I moaned. "It—it's too much."

"*Nik,*" he growled, clamping me tighter. The kiss he placed on my throbbing clit was gentle, so at odds with his rough tone. Then came the wet slide of his tongue, and I jerked. "You'll come again on my tongue. I'm not done with you yet."

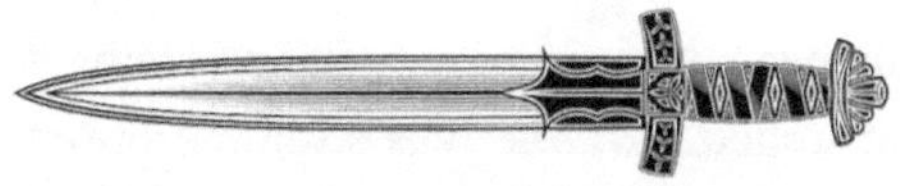

"Please," came Mina's hitched words, followed by a small moan. "*Please, Rowin!*"

Ahh, so now I was Rowin?

She watched with disbelief as I suckled on her clit again, as punishment. She moaned, her hips rocking up from the bed.

Yet I knew I was being cruel. I had told her I wanted another of her orgasms. And now she was on the heels of her third and I still hadn't risen from between her thighs, though I'd changed our positions.

I licked my bottom lip, tasting her there. Raising my head, I knew that my eyes were flooded with black. My pupils were dilated. The taste of her cunt lingered on my tongue, and already I was hungry for more.

After her second orgasm, I'd maneuvered her onto her back and slipped between her thighs. Now I finally moved off her, standing, admiring the way her skin was flushed and her eyes were bright. Her nipples were a mixture of pink and brown, with the remnants of shimmering gold from her paint, but the tops of her breasts were flushed red.

I undid my loincloth, letting it fall to the floor as my gaze zeroed in between her thighs. There...she was a mess. A delightful, slick mess that was my own handiwork.

Madness, I thought. This was certainly the madness my father had always warned me about. He'd always called it a beast. A beast within all males that rose up, banishing all reasonable and logical thought, usually stoked forward at the hands of a female.

I shook my head, gripping my cock and giving it a few rough strokes as I watched her. She was slumped onto the bed. Her legs splayed wide. Her chest was heaving. Her lips were red because she'd bitten them as she orgasmed.

"*Leika,*" I rasped.

Beautiful.

And she was mine. Finally.

But I wanted to hear her say it. I wanted to hear her acknowledge it. Because I needed to know that this madness was a shared madness. That it wasn't only mine.

"Give me your vow again, *rei Morakkari,*" I said, though I hardly recognized my own voice.

She shivered, as if she felt my voice like a touch, trailing up her sensitive thighs, encircling the little bud between them.

Grabbing her ankles, I pulled her to the edge of the bed. Her breath hitched, as if the furs underneath her were too much for her overly sensitive flesh.

"W-What vow?" she asked. Her voice was hoarse and husky already from her cries. I had the impression that she'd surprised even herself with her enthusiasm.

"You know the one I seek," I told her, widening her legs and bringing them up until they wound around my hips. They tightened, and I felt the way they trembled against me.

Her eyes flickered down to my cock, which I stroked for her gaze. Her lips parted, her eyes widening when she saw a drop of liquid drip from the wide head before landing on her belly. The beginnings of my seed. The front of my loincloth was already a soaked mess.

"Give it to me," I purred. "I need to hear it. I need to remember it."

A soft, maddening moan left her when I pressed the head of my cock to her slick folds. I rocked my hips, dipping the tip inside her briefly.

"It—it's so hot," she remarked in disbelief.

I'd guessed that she was untried. Or if a male had claimed her before, he hadn't given her much pleasure during it. As I'd brought her to orgasm after orgasm, she'd seemed almost *shocked* by the fierceness of it.

Yet her innocent observation only solidified my musings.

"*Lysi,*" I murmured. "For you. All for you, *leika.*"

She would be the only female to ever lie in this bed again. The only female *I* would ever lie with again.

"You only have to tell me, and you'll have it all," I told her, shifting my hips, letting my cock run up her tight seam before the heat of it pressed to her clit.

Our eyes connected and held.

Then she gave me what I so desperately sought.

"*Lo rune tei'ri, Vorakkar,*" Mina said.

My eyes slid shut as I felt those word bind themselves to my very bones. My hands *vokking* shook as I reached down to clasp her hips.

When I opened my eyes, she was staring at me, those red lips parted. I took it as an invitation and didn't hesitate when I lowered my head to kiss her.

Unlike the other times, she met my kiss immediately. Her lips moved and brushed. Her tongue stroked my own with eagerness, as if she was as lost in the pleasure as I was.

My hips shifted forward in one quick thrust, and I groaned out a rough breath against her lips. She tightened, however, stiffening from the sudden invasion.

"It's all right, *rei Morakkari,*" I soothed raggedly, pressing my lips to her jaw, her cheeks, her closed eyelids. "I'll wait for you, *lysi?*"

My jaw was tight with the temptation. *Vok,* she was hot and she rippled around me perfectly. But she was tight. *Too* tight, and I did not wish her pain, though it was inevitable.

Ducking my head, I kissed the tops of her breasts. I suckled on her nipples until they were tight and puckered and her breath began to hitch. And even then, I continued until she was making little sounds underneath me and her hips were shifting restlessly.

Only after that did I retreat from her body, her cunt gripping my cock tight, and then I pushed forward again, thrusting into her waiting sheath.

When that elicited a breathless moan, I felt strength fill me. I released her breast and rose, bracketing my hands on both sides of her head.

Her gaze was filled with awe and pleasure and trepidation and curiosity. I wondered what other emotions I could wring from her, and I intended to discover them all.

I began to fuck her in a steady rhythm at first. Stretching and exploring the limits of her body as her jaw dropped and her back arched. She was a sensual thing, surprisingly so, exploring this new pleasure with me when I knew that most of her life had been filled with turmoil and fear.

I can give her this, I thought. *If nothing else, I can give her this part of me.*

All too soon, I felt the pinching at the base of my spine. My *dakke*—that bump at the base of my shaft—began to harden and heat. It thrummed with my heartbeat, with the rushing of my blood.

Mina felt it then too. Her head tilted down to look between us, and she saw the raised flesh when I retreated from her body. Then she moaned, feeling that bump press into her clit when I slid fully forward, hilting inside her, stretching her to the brim.

"You like that?" I growled to her. "Does it feel good on your clit, *sarkia?*"

She nodded wordlessly, her lips still parted in disbelief.

"You want more?" I asked.

She nodded, my greedy little female. I thrust harder into her, making her teeth chatter together and her eyes roll back in her head. I held there, letting her feel my *dakke*, before I retreated again.

"Mmm," I groaned, feeling her flesh ripple around my cock. "Are you going to come for me again?"

"It—it's very likely," she breathed, somehow sounding entirely too *proper.*

A strangled, short bark of a laugh tumbled from my throat.

"*Nik*, you *will*," I told her, my hand wrapping around the golden collar at her throat, holding her still as I fucked her steadily. A purely Dakkari instinct, keeping one's mate at their mercy.

My own *Vorakkar* cuffs flashed in the low light. Tomorrow, she would get the markings of Rath Rowin encircled around her own wrists, but for tonight, I enjoyed my gold around her neck. Perhaps I would keep her in it. I grinned, thinking about how she'd cut me with her claws if I tried to demand it.

"I'll make you come on my cock, Mina," I purred, punching my hips forward quickly, making her gasp and groan. "I'll wring it from you. And when you come, I want to hear my name on your lips."

Her eyes were wide, but her brows were beginning to furrow. I recognized the expression. I'd been watching her carefully, studying her. She was about to fall into the arms of that divine pleasure again, and with gritted teeth, I realized I would be at her heels.

I couldn't last much longer. Not like this. Not when I'd been hard and aching for the better part of the night. Not when she'd pushed me to the edge of my limits and made me *crazed* with her scent and her sounds and her taste.

Maddening witch, I thought.

Then again, I'd always known it would be like this, hadn't I? With her, I'd been doomed from the very beginning.

With pleasure, however, I saw it in her eyes that *she* hadn't expected it to be like this.

She'd never expected me.

"Give it to me," I growled to her, leaning down to capture her lips again, quickening my pace between her thighs, hearing our flesh slap together, the obscene sound filling my *voliki.* "Come on my cock, Mina. *Now!*"

A ragged cry burst from her lips. I had control over her just like she had control over me.

Her cunt squeezed and fluttered around me. Then she clamped down on me, tight but expected, and I felt the purest, primal satisfaction when I heard my name leave her lips.

"*Wrune!*"

"*Lysi,*" I rasped, lunging into her, feeling my *deva* begin to tighten underneath me, heavy with hot, thick seed. Seed for her. Seed that would fill her cunt and mark her as my own. "*Vok,* that's what I want."

My eyes slid shut as my body jerked, as her cries of ecstasy filled my ears and her dull little claws dug into my forearms, where she clung to me. Pleasure rippled up my spine, and I bellowed to the domed ceiling as the first of my seed burst from my cock.

Mindlessly thrusting, I filled her to the brim as her cunt gripped me greedily.

"*Voook,*" I groaned, never feeling pleasure quite like this. Pleasure that bordered on pain it was so intense.

When it was done, I collapsed forward, though I was careful

not to crush her under my weight. The motion thrust me inside her deeper, and I held there as my cock twitched.

I shuddered, grunting as she squeezed the very last of my seed from me.

Mina was warm. My head was pressed between her breasts, and as if she couldn't help herself, her hand drifted to my hair. Stroking through the strands as we both came down from that dizzying high.

Her skin was slick with sweat, as was my own. Her chest heaved as I reclaimed my own breath and got my thundering heart under control.

"Is it..." She breathed before huffing out a small sigh. "Is it always like that?"

Her voice was husky and soft and damn near the most erotic thing I'd ever heard. But what really struck me was the innocent curiosity I heard in her tone too. The disbelief.

"*Nik*," I murmured into her flesh, her tight nipple pebbled right before my eyes. I brushed the tip of it with the backs of my fingers, and she jerked, oversensitive. "It's not."

And already I felt my cock stirring within her.

Madness, I thought, closing my eyes.

As the pleasure was slowly fading from my orgasm, as my lust began to prick again, I realized that she had too much power over me. Because after *that*, I thought I'd do anything for her, if only to be able to slip between her thighs again.

How often had I heard *darukkars* joke and jest about the all-consuming power of females? Even in *Dothik*, the war general during our training had always forbid us from mating.

You'll only find destruction between a female's thighs, he'd often chided, *when you need to be focused*.

And, of course, I'd had many females in my bed. In the *saruk* where I'd grown up, in *Dothik* despite the war general's warning, and here, in my own horde. I'd enjoyed them all, enjoyed the pleasure with them because it helped release the tension I'd always felt *building*, and yet...

Yet I'd never felt this *panic* rising within me when I'd lain with them.

I'd never felt this deep, all-consuming satisfaction and fear and bewilderment and need.

And I only wanted her again. With her soft, gentle hands in my hair and her legs still wrapped around my waist, I only wanted her *again*. And *again*. And *again*.

I wanted her until I lost myself with her.

And I realized that that couldn't happen.

It had happened before with her.

I'd vowed it wouldn't happen again.

That single moment where desire and need had overshadowed everything. This was another of those moments, and I needed to be on guard.

Lifting my head off her chest, where I'd felt the gentle thundering of her heart, I pulled away.

Mina's eyes were half-lidded. The wine had relaxed her, but now she was drunk off pleasure and the aftermath of mating.

Her eyes widened when I stood, however, and tracked me as I strode to the water basin to splash my face. The cool droplets ran down my face, focusing my mind, helping me remember my duty. She was my *Morakkari* now, but I still felt the sharp prick of wariness when it came to her. Not that I believed she weaved her magic over me. Not anymore. But because I *knew* I was vulnerable when I was with her.

If she sensed the sudden change in my demeanor, she didn't voice it. However, when I turned to regard her, with my cock still half-hard and covered in her essence, those eyes were observant and she knew that something had changed.

I could still hear the drums pounding from the *tassimara* celebration. When I walked to my chests, I pulled out a fresh pair of hide trews and I dragged them up my legs, tucking my cock within their confines, though it tented the thick material.

Mina watched it all. She'd sat up in the middle of my bed—*our* bed now, I realized. She'd hunched forward, sliding her arms around her knees to shield her nudity.

"Are you leaving?" she asked quietly, watching me dress, though I left my sword next to the bed.

I inclined my head, my throat bobbing with my swallow. When I licked my bottom lip, I tasted her there, and my nostrils flared with the memory of her whimpers and her moans.

"*Lysi*," I told her. I needed to clear my head. I needed to put distance between us before I decided to risk everything again. "I still have some things that need to be done this night."

I kept my voice soft and quiet. Even so, she jumped a little when the fire crackled in the basin.

"Tonight?" she asked, incredulous.

"I'll post a guard outside the door," I informed her.

Those words made her lips press together. A little softness on her features hardened, but she nodded.

"*Veekor, kalles*," I told her. "Sleep."

I didn't wait for her response. The air was getting tight in the *voliki*, a place that had always been my quiet sanctuary.

Turning, I left without another word.

And I strode away like a coward from the only thing that had scared me in a long, long time.

<h1 style="text-align:center">CHAPTER 36</h1>

Hissing quietly, I felt the sting of pain as I lowered myself into the warm bathing tub.

Hukri's lips pressed together, and she said, "Once you dry off, apply the *uudun, lysi*? It will help with the discomfort, I promise."

I was sore this morning. So incredibly sore, but I sighed as I began to relax in the bathing tub, leaning back against the edge. It was made with a Dakkari's bulk in mind, and so the water covered my neck, stopping just below my chin. And though I had my knees up and pressed to my chest, the surface of the water was unbroken.

"Did you bleed, *missiki*?" Hukri asked next, going over to the furs of Wrune's bed and inspecting them in such a way that made me uncomfortable. She made a clicking sound in the back of her throat when she did see the blood, and she bundled them up, snatching them from the bed. "I'll have these cleaned."

"Thank you," I said. Underneath the water, I saw the bruises Wrune had left behind. The ones between my thighs, the ones around my hips and waist.

Sighing, I found that I didn't mind them. This morning, I

felt strangely calm. Last night had been a whirlwind of different and new emotions and sensations. Truthfully, I was *glad* for the calm. Otherwise I would probably be melancholy or irate or embarrassed.

I hadn't even cried last night. I was proud of that. After Wrune left, after those dizzying and sublime and wonderful sensations he'd pulled from me, I'd felt incredibly vulnerable. More vulnerable, perhaps, than I'd ever felt, with the exception of the loss of my father.

But I hadn't cried. I'd waited—for quite some time, truthfully—for Wrune to return. This was his *voliki*, after all. He had to sleep sometime.

Yet he hadn't come back.

And it made me wonder where he *had* slept.

"Is it not normal for Dakkari to share beds?"

The question slipped from me before I thought better of it.

Biting my lip, I remembered I was a queen now. The *Morakkari* of a horde. Wrune might not appreciate me asking such questions of my *piki*, though I knew she was duty bound in her loyalties to me.

I had a strange realization at that. That someone was solely on *my* side. That it was their duty to see to my comfort and well-being.

Hukri came close and kneeled next to the bathing tub. She must have sensed that something was wrong this morning. I'd been quieter than usual. Typically, I'd have asked her many, many questions by now. I suspected that she'd thought I'd have plenty after the *tassimara* celebration last night.

"Humans typically sleep close to their lovers or partners," I finished quietly. "I just wondered if it was the same for the Dakkari."

"*Lysi*," Hukri said, and my belly twisted at the word. "We do share beds. Of course we do."

I nodded, and I blew out a slow breath. I'd figured as much. Reaching forward for the cloth that was draped over the side of the tub, I held it open as Hukri sprinkled the soap granules into it.

"Here, let me, *missiki*," she offered, taking the cloth. I'd had a restless, nearly sleepless night, and so I let her take it without protest.

I closed my eyes as she washed and scrubbed through my hair. As she gently washed my limbs. I handled the cleaning between my legs, however, biting my lip when the soft cloth was almost too much. I was sensitive, especially there.

"Give him time, *missiki*," came Hukri's gentle, whispered voice, as if she was aware of the guard out front listening in. "Marriage is change. For a *Vorakkar*, especially *our Vorakkar*, I suspect that it is especially jarring."

My brow furrowed, and I frowned a little. I didn't know what she meant by that exactly, but I nodded nonetheless.

"Regardless," I said, making up my mind, "I think I'll sleep in the other *voliki* tonight. The one with the map."

Hukri frowned. "I don't think that's wise, *missiki*. He will not allow that."

I shook my head. "This is his *voliki*. I won't drive him from it. And it will be good to have my own space, won't it?"

I'd fallen asleep with the scent of him filling my nostrils, and I'd dreamed of his touch, of sex. When I woke, I'd bemoaned that I was ruined now. That he'd ruined me because how could I go back to a life without such pleasure and heat and *need*?

I was getting spoiled. I needed to remember what it was like in this world before him. Only that would keep me grounded. But he'd been right. I could dislike him, with his high-handed and cold arrogance, but still *crave* him.

"And can you take this off me?" I asked, touching the golden necklace around my throat that reminded me more of a cuff. "I can't figure out where the clasp is."

"Here," Hukri said, reaching underneath my wet hair, her sharp claw fiddling with something at the back of the collar. I took a deep breath when it popped off and Hukri pulled it away.

I rubbed at my throat. "Thank you."

"Such a fine thing," she admired, rubbing the solid gold. I noticed etchings within the metal that I hadn't noticed last night. I didn't think they were words, however. They were more decorative, like a swirling, intricate pattern. "It's probably from your *deviri*."

"My *deviri*?" I asked.

"Your wedding gift," Hukri translated. "But I am sure the *Vorakkar* will present it to you later today. After you get the markings."

Markings?

My head throbbed a bit. I felt a wave of tiredness wash over me, and suddenly, I felt the overwhelming realization that I had so much to *learn*.

Underneath the water, my hands shifted. On instinct, I cupped my palms. What would it be like to make everything just...*pause*? What would it be like to make my own little home, safe from others, where I could just *think*?

I smiled a little. My own little home. It would be deep within a forest, wouldn't it? In the North Lands, though the cold would require more fire fuel. I could make a hide tent like the *volikis*, couldn't I? Or build a little wooden home and insulate it much better than our home in the village had been.

I could forage and hunt. In the mornings, I could walk through the forest and remember singing with my father. In the evenings, I could warm myself by the fire and remember the overwhelming touches of a horde king.

Slowly, my smile died. The image of a perfect little home for me was overshadowed by loneliness. Because that was what I'd be, tucked deep in a forest. I'd go mad from the quiet.

"*Missiki*," came Hukri's whisper. Only it sounded frightened.

Blinking, I looked down underneath the water and saw that I'd created that familiar sphere of energy. The surface of the bath was rippling as the energy forced it away. Water zipped and thrashed around, forced away, and it sloshed over the sides of the tub, wetting the carpets.

My lips parted. Momentarily, I was stunned, frozen.

"*Rothi kiv*," came a sharp bark from behind me. My breath hitched. His voice. Of course he'd come back to his *voliki* at this precise moment.

Immediately, Hukri rose. Panicked, I envisioned the sphere bursting and I waved my hand through it, breaking whatever surface it had, interrupting whatever energy flowed there.

Like a river, I thought. To stop the flow of a river, one had to block it up.

All at once, the water calmed and I sagged back, breathing hard. Underneath the water, my fists squeezed to keep from trembling too much.

"*Rothi kiv*," came Wrune's order once again, though it held an edge of impatience this time. Hukri immediately scuttled away, and I heard the entrance flap open and close behind her.

Swallowing, I heard his heavy footsteps tread across the carpets, and then he came into my view. My eyes rose to him, feeling something sharp twinge in my chest when I saw he was bathed and dressed in different clothes than he'd left in last night.

So where had he bathed? Where had he slept?

I thought of what Hukri revealed to me last night. About a female named Junira. How everyone had believed she would become *Morakkari* of the horde because Wrune had drunk from her goblet—whatever that meant—and spent nights in his bed.

The bed I'd slept in last night. The bed Wrune had thrown me onto before he'd wrenched orgasm after orgasm from me.

I hadn't cared last night about Junira. At least, that was what I'd told myself.

Now, however, I felt a sharp ache of jealousy, wondering if perhaps he still cared for her. If perhaps he would still slip into *her* bed now that I lay in his. Was that where he'd been?

I knew nothing about the mating customs of Dakkari. I knew they took wives, obviously. But beyond that, I knew little, though Hukri had told me they certainly shared beds with their partners.

Wrune just didn't want to share a bed with me.

"You will never use your gift within the horde. Or without me there," he growled at me, looming over the bathing tub. "Do you understand that?"

My voice sounded hollow and wooden when I said, "Good morning to you too, husband."

I looked away from him, dragging my knees back up to my chest to at least shield part of my nudity from him. Not that it mattered. He'd seen parts of me *I* hadn't even seen properly.

A whispered curse came under his breath. He was in a foul mood this morning, so perhaps he hadn't spent the night with another female.

It was quiet for a long moment, and then I was surprised when he dropped to his knees next to the bathing tub until he was eye level with me.

"It's dangerous," he said, seeming to make an effort to soften his tone. I blinked when he reached out to clasp my chin, turning me to face him. His hands were warm. Rough. And so, so familiar to me now. I couldn't help it when my heart skipped a beat. "What happened last time—I do not want that happening again. I know how much pain it caused you. I know it *hurt* you, Mina."

That...wasn't what I'd expected him to say.

"I didn't know I was doing it," I told him softly, defensively.

His frown only deepened. "Which makes it even more dangerous. It's unpredictable because you don't know how to control it. The only time I ever want you to use it is when the horde is threatened. *Lysi?*"

Right.

Because that was why he'd even joined himself to me in the first place.

Because I'd be useful to him and his horde if the fog ever encroached too closely. Like a beast led to its sacrifice.

Turning my face away, I sighed.

We didn't speak, the silence stretching awkwardly as I decided how best to get out of the bath without him seeing too much.

"Did you sleep well?" he asked.

No. I'd woken what seemed like every hour to see if he'd returned. I hated how *needy* that made me seem.

"Yes," I replied. "And you?"

He rose from his place on the soggy carpet, where wet patches from the water now soaked into his hide trews around his knees.

"I didn't sleep," he informed me. I didn't know what to do with that bit of information, if it should make me more jealous or less. "We need to leave soon. To get your markings. We are expected by a *terun*."

Again with the markings.

"What is a *terun*?" I asked, watching him snag a fur pelt that Hukri had laid out for me.

"It means *elder* in your language," he said.

"And what are markings?"

He jerked his chin up, motioning for me to stand. Instead, I held my hand out for the furs, which he gave me with a frown. I opened the furs and did my best to stand while also shielding my body from him. Water sluiced off me, and I wrapped the furs around me quickly. A twinge made me suck in a breath when I stepped over the tub, ignoring his outstretched hand.

"What is it?" he asked, barely concealing the quick scowl that came over his expression. "Do you hurt from last night?"

"No," I said. "It's like it never even happened."

I didn't know why I added that. Perhaps it was the hurt rising inside me. Hurt I hadn't wanted to acknowledge, hurt that confused me. And maybe I wanted to see if I could hurt him too with my flippant words.

Wrune's scowl deepened.

"What are the markings?" I prompted again.

He was studying me. Perhaps he was trying to read my strange mood. I'd been calm, hadn't I? Now I was a mixture of unpleasant things, and I hid it behind indifference. Or at least, I tried to.

He tapped his *Vorakkar* cuffs. The wide bands of gold metal that Hukri told me all *Vorakkar* received after they passed the Trials in *Dothik*. That was how *Vorakkar* were selected. By passing grueling tests, meant to challenge their mental and physical and spiritual strength. And their tolerance for pain.

Hukri had told me the last test of the Trials was always the whippings. A *Vorakkar* had to endure at least a hundred and among a full audience in *Dothik*.

It sounded barbaric to me. And when she told me that a couple days ago, it had brought nausea rising because I remembered being shocked by the scars that adorned Wrune's back.

"You will get your markings around your wrists," he informed me. He pressed a finger to his chest, where the golden tattoos glimmered in the light shooting down from the venting hole. "Markings of Rath Rowin. Markings of the horde and of my line."

My mouth went dry.

"And how are such things done?" I asked, my wet hair dripping down over my shoulders, slipping underneath the furs and weaving down my back.

"I will receive new markings too," he told me, stepping closer. "There is nothing to fear."

I was no stranger to pain, so I realized that he was right. I could handle anything after I'd handled the pain under the Dead Mountain, the pain I felt when my power had become too wild.

I nodded, and I spied a flare of satisfaction in his gaze. As if he was pleased with me.

"Very well," I murmured. "I'll meet you outside after I dress."

A huff of what I thought was amusement came from him. "You think to dismiss me from my own *voliki*? I'd rather stay and watch my *Morakkari* dress."

I was too tired for games this morning. I wanted him gone so I could apply the *uudun* salve between my thighs like Hukri had suggested, but it seemed like that would have to wait if Wrune was being stubborn again.

Hukri had laid out a simple shift dress for me this morning at my request. She'd brought it with a plethora of other dresses, which she'd tucked into one of the spare chests lining the wall. The material was light and flowing. A little thin for my tastes, but it was more conservative than the lot. The color was a slate blue, reminding me of the frost.

Ignoring Wrune's taunt, I dried off as best as I could and, knowing it couldn't be helped, I dropped the fur pelt to the floor. My backside was to Wrune, and quickly, I reached for the dress, which was smoothed out on the bare bed.

I felt his approach. The back of my neck tingled as I sensed him drawing near.

His touch came, unexpected and yet expected, first at my hips. Those calloused, warm palms lingering and sliding.

"I'm sorry, Mina," came the words, and I stiffened in

surprise at them, thinking he was apologizing for leaving so suddenly last night. A little ball of hope rose in my breast. "I did not want to leave marks on you. But I forgot myself, my strength."

Oh. He was apologizing for the bruises. His touch was making me entirely too jittery, however, so I stepped forward, and his hand dropped.

"It's all right," I told him. "It couldn't be helped. Just forget it, and I will too."

Then quickly, I pulled the dress over my head, slipping my arms through the thin straps that would loop around my shoulders. I felt relief when I was no longer bared to him, though when I looked down and saw my nipples poking through the thin material, I bit my lip. But, like many things, it couldn't be helped. I just prayed to Kakkari—and all the other gods and goddesses in the universe—that it would be a warm day.

"Where are the furs for the bed?" he grunted from behind me, as if now realizing that it was stripped.

"Hukri took them to be washed."

"Why?"

I turned, smoothing down the dress as best as I could. Something warned me that he wouldn't like my answer, and I didn't want to talk about it, frankly.

"Mina," came his growl.

Why couldn't he just leave it alone?

When he caught my wrist, keeping me from moving toward the door, though my hair was still dripping down my back, I felt a small spark of irritation.

"Because they had blood on them," I finally told him. "I figured you wouldn't want to sleep on it tonight."

Wrune stiffened, his expression darkening.

"You were bleeding?" he asked.

It was mortifying, and I felt my face flame.

"Yes," I said because I knew he wouldn't leave it alone. "Let's—let's just go. Please. I don't want to talk about it."

This time, when I turned away and walked to the entrance, he actually let me. I pushed through the flap, not needing to duck underneath it like Wrune had to, and saw the bright morning sun overhead, though the sky appeared red. It always did these days.

Wrune must have sent the guard away when he'd entered because I found myself alone. At least until the hide parted behind me and my husband joined me. His expression was cold. Unreadable. As usual.

The *voliki* was positioned toward the back of the camp, abutted against a short mountain. A small incline led up to the *voliki,* and I wondered if he'd chosen this location because it gave him a perfect view of his entire encampment...and the fog beyond.

Because from here, I could see it. Just a hint of it, lingering in the Dead Valley. It was still so far away and yet it was clear enough to see in daylight. An ever-present threat to his horde.

Within the gates of the horde, however, I saw *voliki* after *voliki*. Most were smaller in size, but toward the front of the camp, I saw larger ones and I wondered about their purpose. To the right, I saw a massive enclosure. Hundreds of *pyrokis*, which looked like little lumps from this distance, roamed or slept beside one another or ate. To the left of the horde, I saw another enclosure, very close to where I'd been kept chained upon first arriving. I thought I recognized the *voliki* I'd stayed in. Hukri told me it was the *voliki* in which Wrune's council met.

Smoke rose from many of the structures, though one in particular seemed to have a steady bloom of it. The smell of cooked meat and spice filled the air, even that early in the morning, and I figured that was where the *bikkus* worked their days.

Seeing the horde like this, for the first time, was overwhelming. Hundreds of *volikis*, hundreds of lives, of purposes, of fears, of wants, greeted me on that morning when I was feeling particularly vulnerable.

And there I was. Queen of it all. Which was laughable. I'd practically been a slave before this. I'd been treated like an unwanted animal most of the time.

Now I was dressed in the finest of silks, and it just made me want to cry.

CHAPTER 37

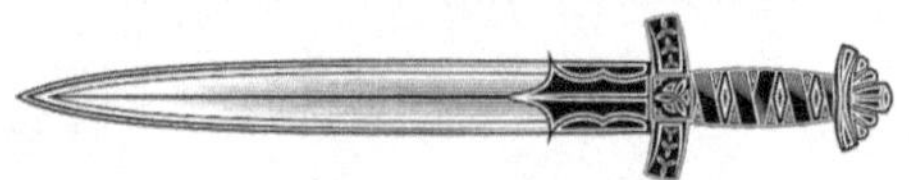

Valavik's breaths were coming fast when I knocked him back again. He stumbled but managed to right himself. When he didn't fall, I gritted my teeth and my sword shot forward. I threw most of my strength into the blow, and the steel rang and clashed. I wondered if it could be heard throughout the entire encampment.

"*Vok*, I yield, Rowin!" Valavik grunted when my sword sliced a thin line across his chest. A killing blow. "I yield!"

He was panting, drawing in ragged lungfuls of air. We both were. Sweat dripped into my eyes, and I went to one of the water basins the *bikku* kept stocked and I splashed my face with water.

I'd sullied the new bandages around my wrists, and I was lucky they stopped the sweat that rolled down my arms.

The newest of my markings. Binding myself to Mina, who wore matching ones around her own wrists now.

A jolt of awareness ran down my spine, and I looked up, ignoring Valavik's whispered curses as he continued to pant against the training enclosure.

My wife.

She was standing with Hukri near the *mitri's voliki*. Straightening, I continued to watch her, wondering how much of that small battle she'd witnessed.

Judging by the wary expression on her face, I'd say she'd seen quite a lot of it.

My gaze ran over her. The icy blue dress made her skin glow, and instead of dimming her green eyes, it only made them brighten. Her limbs were all willowy grace, and she stood tall next to Hukri, though I saw many speculative looks cast her way.

Many of the horde came to watch the sparring sessions. Especially children. Especially unmated females, who were hoping to catch the eye of a *darukkar*.

There was a healthy sized group now, made even larger by the unexpected presence of the new *Morakkari*. But Mina held herself apart, sticking with Hukri, as she looked on with a mixture of wary curiosity and...discomfort.

I expected the raw brutality of such things might remind her of Benn. His violence. It might remind her of the flash of my sword as I'd sliced through the bones of his wrist.

"What in Kakkari's name got into you, Rowin?" Valavik ground out, keeping his voice low, always aware that we were watched. Constantly. He sucked in another lungful of air. "I'd think a night between your pretty *Morakkari's* thighs would have cured you of your tension."

Pretty.

Did he think so?

Why did that thought make me want to punch him right across the jaw?

I wasn't used to jealousy. I didn't think I'd ever been jealous over a female in my entire life.

What I was really angry at, however, was that my *pujerak* had hit the nail on the head, only not in the way he'd expected. A night between her thighs had *caused* this turmoil within me.

I'd been furious at myself for most of the morning, plagued

with unfamiliar emotions when I was forced to realize that my own *Morakkari* might view my actions last night as unforgivable.

I'd marked her.

I'd made her *bleed*.

And then I'd left her.

Three offenses against me.

And this morning, when I returned to our *voliki*, the first thing I'd done was snap at her. Yet I couldn't help the fear sizzling through me at the sight of her power, bubbling just under the surface of the water, threatening to break free.

She thought me a villain now, no doubt. She'd been soft with her words and her touches last night, except when her nails had scratched down my forearms in her pleasure. For a moment, she'd looked at me in awe, like she couldn't believe what we had been building together. She'd kissed me with enthusiasm. And she might not have realized it but she'd *smiled* as she'd come for me, and I swore I'd never seen anything more beautiful.

This morning, however, she'd barely met my eyes. I'd seen the bruises across her flesh, and though she'd tried to hide it from me, I'd caught her winces as we walked through the encampment.

Even now, I was scorning her. *I* should be the one showing her around the horde. Not Hukri. *I* should be walking beside her, the first day after the *tassimara,* as was custom, showing off my *Morakkari* proudly to all.

Yet after we received our markings, I'd left her with her *piki*, feeling shame and restless guilt build under my flesh, buzzing and irritating, and I knew I needed to scrape it free. And I'd taken it out on Valavik.

Mina turned, said something to Hukri, and the pair left the training grounds, weaving east to take the pathway that led to the *bikkus'* kitchens. The moment my *Morakkari* turned her back, I saw the whispering begin. I hadn't greeted her. She hadn't greeted me. She walked with her *piki* this day, and though I'd tried to hide it, I knew that some horde members had seen me early this morning, bathing in the commons and retreating to my council's *voliki* before the sun rose.

There would be rumors I hadn't stayed the night in our bed.

"*Vok*," I rasped, turning from the onlookers and drawing my sword up. "Again," I told Valavik, wiping the sweat from my eyes.

The day was long. Oftentimes, as *Vorakkar*, I felt like a rope being pulled in different directions. The *bikkus* reported the horde's food stock to me after my training session. Our root supply was lower than usual for this time of year, and so I ordered more to be planted.

The ground was hard, however. In the East Lands, the soil was like compacted clay. And so I'd had the plots broken up and tilled. I'd sent a group of hunters to a forest that lay in the South Lands to retrieve satchels of tree pulp and rot and anything that would bring new life to the soil. But they wouldn't return for two days, so the planting of the roots would have to wait, and I knew that we would run out of our rations completely before new crops grew.

Then the *mitri* reported that after crafting new blades and arrows for the *darukkars*, the Dakkari-steel supply was depleted. We'd used much of it on the construction of the gates surrounding our horde. And so I'd sent off our last *thesper* to *Dothik*, requesting more to be brought to us.

Midway through the day, I rode out to the encampment I kept near the edge of the fog. The *darukkars* traveled the path often enough that there was a subtle road etched into the land. They'd reported a sighting of a human, climbing up one of the mountains that lay to the north of the horde. Though the *vekkiri* male had scuttled away when he spotted the *darukkars* in pursuit.

The humans were still watching the horde. By Mina's account, the Dakkari witches would have arrived under the Dead Mountain already. Were they still trying to claim the heart of a horde king? For their blood magic?

It was worrying. If they were desperate enough, would they twist their words and say that *any* Dakkari heart could make a heartstone? Would they try to take one of the *darukkars*? Or one of the *bikkus* that traveled the pathway to bring meals out to them?

With that in mind, I'd ordered that no male would go off alone and that anyone leaving the gates needed to be accompanied by an armed *darukkar*.

My council met as the sun dipped low. I had another sparring session afterward with Valavik, testing the new weapons that the *mitri* crafted, strong and durable blades. Then I checked on the *darukkars* stationed at the fog once more, though they had nothing to report.

The day was long. As were the days of a *Vorakkar*.

Finally, when I could avoid her no longer, as the smallest sliver of a moon guided my path, I began the short trek back to my *voliki*.

My temper was short this night, but I vowed to myself that I would not take it out on her. She did not deserve it. And I had much to be sorry for already.

Only, when my *voliki* came into view, I could see from that short distance that it was dark. No smoke floated out from the venting hole. No glow from within illuminated it. And no guard was stationed outside it.

Worry and fear pricked my insides, but I told myself not to be alarmed. I strode up the short incline and ripped back the flaps.

Darkness. The bed had been remade with fresh furs, but no bath had been drawn. There *was* a small fire in the basin, but it smoldered pitifully. A tray of food sat on the table—how long had I been away?—but it was cold and untouched.

Mina was nowhere to be seen.

CHAPTER 38

I was woken suddenly, and I gasped, my heart thundering in my chest. Pulled straight from a dream. *No, a memory.* I swore I could still smell the lingerings of smoke as my village burned, but I realized it was only the fire still roaring in the basin.

"What the *vok* are you doing in here?" came Rowin's voice. Because he was Rowin to me right then, cold and angry, as he crouched low beside my sleeping pallet. He'd shaken me awake, though I hadn't heard him enter the *voliki.*

For a moment, I was bewildered. The dream had been so real that I felt I should have woken in the North Lands. That I should have woken to darkness and the sound of sobbing and the bitter softness of ash on my tongue.

"W-What?" I whispered, blinking.

"What are you doing in here?" he asked again, his voice low but clipped.

Then I remembered. Hukri had tried to convince me not to sleep in the council's *voliki.* She'd worried her lip even as I ate my meal at a table filled with more maps and notes scribbled in words I couldn't read. She'd refused to translate the words for me, however, saying it was the council's business and no one else's.

"You're angry?" I asked, struggling to sit up, feeling a dull throbbing coming from my wrists, which I remembered were now marked in swirling golden lines that Hukri *had* translated for me.

They were names. Ancestral names of Rowin's family. Some of them were even *Vorakkar* and *Morakkari.* He came from a line of horde kings, though that hadn't surprised me.

And my own name had been added beside his.

On my left wrist was a vow. *His* vow. A vow to protect me and honor me. A promise that together, we would lead the horde of Rath Rowin to prosperity and longevity. Though Hukri had explained that the Dakkari word for *longevity* also had a dual meaning for *fertility.*

I'd been dumbstruck for a brief moment. Because for the first time, I'd given thought to *children.* I'd been surprised by the longing, how sudden and intense it was, but then I thought of Wrune's coldness. I tried to imagine him as a father, a *loving* father, as mine had been...and I couldn't. Despite the heat and passion of the night before, Wrune was driven only by duty to his horde. I couldn't imagine loving him, or what that might even feel like.

But would he love his own children?

Especially if they were also mine?

He still called me a witch, after all.

Looking at him now, all those feelings came bursting back to life. He *was* angry. His expression was icy and his eyes were narrowed on me.

"I thought you would want this," I told him, still clearing the blurry remnants of my dream from my mind.

"And why would I want the *Morakkari* of my horde sleeping on the floor in a *voliki* that is not my own?" he asked.

"You left last night," I told him. "You should be able to sleep in your own bed. I don't want to intrude."

A low laugh escaped him. The sound would have been beautiful, soft and husky, had it not been filled with a subtle darkness.

"Or perhaps you do not want to sleep in my bed because you fear my attentions now," he said. "It is a *Morakkari's* duty. To satisfy her *Vorakkar*."

My lips parted. Hot anger rose. Now he was just trying to get a rise out of me because even I knew he had no such expectations of me.

"We shouldn't pretend that this is something it isn't," I said, scooting away from him, drawing the furs up over my shoulders when I shivered. "If—if I need to give you a child eventually, then that is something we can discuss. In the future. But there is no reason for me to be in your bed every night."

"Perhaps I desire you," he growled. "Have you ever thought of that, *rei sarkia?*"

"Because of last night?" I asked, though my voice shook a little. "That was expected, was it not? Because of the *tassimara?*"

He looked away from me, and a whispered curse fell from his lips.

Just the memory of last night, of his hot, seeking tongue between my thighs, of his soft kisses at my breasts made me breathless. He'd shown me pleasure so intense that it *still* scrambled my mind just thinking about it.

And then there were the moments when I'd felt my belly flutter and my heart sing. Soft moments. When he'd stroked my hair and murmured that he'd wait for me to get used to his size. He'd been patient. He'd stroked me until I was rocking against him. And after we'd come together, in a dizzying rush, he'd placed his head right over my heart and seemed to melt into me when I touched his hair.

My heart gave a dull thud. He'd been...surprisingly vulnerable with me last night. Sex had shown me a different side of him. An erotic, maddening, wonderful side of him. In those moments, I'd felt cherished. I'd felt wanted and needed. He'd even made me feel *beautiful*. As if I were the only female in the entire universe, as if I were the only female he desired above all others.

Then reality had returned. He'd pulled out from my body, risen from me, and I'd felt the cold shift of him, just as tangible as the cold air drifting across my flesh, filling all the places where his warmth had been.

I told myself it was for the best. If he'd been that way with me *always*...I might actually be in danger of loving him. Of caring about him with everything I had in me.

I wasn't sure I could survive that, and so I told myself it was best to keep my distance, especially when he'd made it clear he felt the same.

"If you wish for me to sleep elsewhere, I will," he said. The words shocked me. Was...was that a *threat*? Did he mean that he'd take other females, that he would warm their beds since he was not in my own? "But you will not sleep in here. I forbid it."

I...didn't want that either. I didn't know why the thought of him with other females bothered me so much, but the hot jealousy threatened to choke me.

Looking at him, it occurred to me that he looked tired. So very tired. He'd told me he hadn't slept last night, after all.

What would arguing accomplish? Nothing. The male was stubborn. I'd known that even under the Dead Mountain when I tried to clean his wounds and give him fresh well water.

"What's the word for *stubborn male* in Dakkari?" I whispered, repeating words to him I'd once asked, though we'd been in an entirely different situation then.

His eyes flashed. His brows furrowed, and for a moment, he looked surprised. As if he was remembering that moment too, remembering those words, remembering *me*. It had been the first time he said I had claws of my own. Those words had filled me with...*pride.*

"*Sailon,*" he answered, his eyes narrowing. I was surprised he actually gave me the word.

"Now I know what to call you when you call me *sarkia,*" I informed him.

I *swore* I saw his lips quirk. Just briefly. But it was gone in the next moment, replaced by that unreadable, hardened expression.

"Come," he murmured. "I'll guide you back to the *voliki.*"

I asked, "Where did you go last night?"

Wrune stood. He reached down and gripped my waist, hauling me up until I was before him.

Our eyes locked. For a breathless moment, I remembered the soft stroke of his tongue and the way he'd kissed me. His hands tightened on my waist and I felt a dull pang where he'd left his bruises, but I didn't move a muscle.

Unconsciously, my hand reached out to touch his forearm. It was as hard as a boulder, unyielding and strong. Yet I spied scratches down it. From my own nails?

Our bandaged wrists touched and pressed, and I felt tension rise between us, though it didn't feel unpleasant. Just...charged.

"Does it matter where I went?" he asked quietly, his voice tired. His answer disappointed me. I thought of Junira. Hukri had pointed her out to me in the horde this morning, and I'd seen she was beautiful, tall and dark, with wide hips that attracted the gazes of many males.

Wrune had been attracted to her, I knew. It was her place I'd stolen, after all.

He took the furs that were bundled up on the sleeping pallet and draped them over my shoulders. Then, without another word, he led me from the *voliki,* our hands falling away from one another.

In the morning, I'd ask Hukri if it was common for Dakkari

to stray to other beds, even in marriage. I might not like her answer, but I needed to know. If I knew there would be other females, it would make it easier to detach.

We walked in the silence of his horde, and once we reached his *voliki*, we ducked inside. I wondered if he would stay this night. A part of me...hoped he did.

Wrune moved through the *voliki* with familiarity, further showing me that *I* was the intruder here. He stoked the fire back to life in the basin. He shed his sword and placed it on hooks on the wall. When he shed his trews, my heart leapt. Scarred, golden flesh greeted me. The sight of his firm buttocks giving way to thick, muscled thighs made me swallow hard. He pushed back the furs on the bed, his half-hardened cock swinging, and climbed inside them.

With his red eyes pinned on me, he motioned me forward. We *were* sleeping together this night, it seemed. Hesitantly, I moved to the bed. I crawled underneath the furs, noticing they no longer smelled like him since they'd been washed this morning.

I lay on my side and he lay on his side. We were facing one another, wary but curious. His eyes trailed over me, and for a moment, I wanted him to touch me. I wanted him to uncover that desire within me as effortlessly as he'd done last night.

Underneath my shift dress, my nipples pebbled though I was warm under the furs. I was watching him, waiting to see what he would do as the tension wrapped around us, tight and thick.

His jaw tightened, that long muscle just above the bone jumping.

Soft disappointment came when he gruffly said, "*Veekor, rei sarkia.*"

The word meant *sleep*. I remembered that from last night.

I rolled over until I was on my back, staring up at the

venting hole at the top of the *voliki*. Clouds shielded the stars this night. All I saw was darkness.

"*Veekor, sailon,*" I replied.

A rough sound emerged from his throat. I closed my eyes, though I was still aware of his gaze, and I focused on my breathing. I wasn't tired anymore. I didn't think I'd get a wink of sleep now that he was beside me, delicious heat rolling off him like the forge in the weapons master's workshop.

I'd seen Wrune fight today, I remembered, thinking of his brute strength and the surprising grace to his movements, lightning quick for someone so large. It reminded me that if a battle between humans and Dakkari ever came...the humans truly had no fighting chance. We'd always known that the Dakkari were a strong species, but I hadn't realized how *powerful* they were, how frighteningly focused they were when they battled, until this morning.

Next to me, I heard Wrune roll over.

I couldn't sleep, but I kept still. And for a long time, I heard Wrune fight to sleep as well. I focused on my breathing, keeping it even.

Eventually, I heard his soft curse, his sharp exhale. My stomach sank when I felt him move from the bed, though he was careful to keep his movements quiet. He thought I was sleeping. And he was leaving the bed.

I heard the gentle rustle of his trews as he slid them up his legs. Cracking open my eyes, I saw him add another clump of fire fuel into the basin. He looked over at me, a tight expression on his face, and I closed my eyes quickly, hoping he hadn't seen.

When I heard the *voliki* flaps open and close, my nostrils stung. A lump rose in my throat, physical reactions to something I didn't quite understand.

Opening my eyes, I was greeted with emptiness, though the fire roared.

Wrune couldn't stand to sleep next to me. He would find another bed this night.

Closing my eyes again, I felt tears sting them. Because I didn't know why I was crying, it only made me cry more, as frustration and turmoil roved inside me.

Was this to be my life now?

Though I was now queen of a Dakkari horde...I'd never felt lonelier.

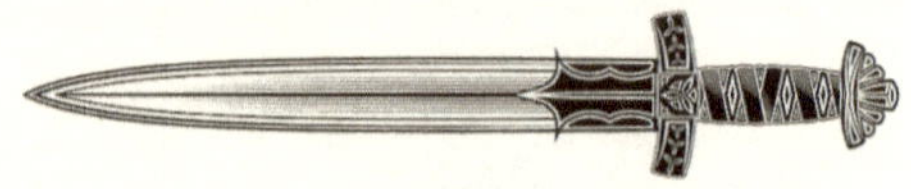

CHAPTER 39

"I knew I'd find you up here."

My *pujerak's* voice came from behind me.

I grunted. "The *darukkars* told you, did they not?"

It was a week later. I'd visited the *darukkar* encampment to see if they had anything more to report for the night. Then I'd gone off on my own, weaving away from the camp and climbing up the mountain path that overlooked the expanse of the Dead Valley. It was a steep climb, but on that dark night, it was exactly where I wanted to be.

Valavik walked to the cliff's edge before eyeing me. I had my back to the mountain wall, a knee drawn up, my arm slung over it. Since it was colder that night, especially on the mountain, I'd brought my pelt with me and wrapped it tight around my shoulders.

"What are you doing out here, Rowin?" my *pujerak* asked. "Should you not be asleep, in your own bed?"

A pointed, dangerous question. One I'd felt him skirting around for a full week now.

I grunted. I'd been in a foul mood lately. Due to lack of sleep and this biting frustration that I just *couldn't* shake. It was unlike me. It made me vulnerable.

"Don't you think it's time you told me about her?" Valavik asked, raising a brow. "About what this is really about?"

I barked out a short laugh. "I told you everything already."

"*Nik*, you didn't. Because one thing I never understood about your account was how you *allowed* yourself to be captured in the first place. By humans, nonetheless. I know you, Rowin. You're intelligent. You think situations through meticulously, painstakingly before you act on them. You knew the risks of the fog, but I never thought you'd be foolish enough to actually get *lost* in it."

That's because I was too busy getting lost in her, I couldn't help but think.

He was waiting for my explanation. He was my *pujerak*, and I knew that I owed him one. An explanation that was long overdue.

"What I said at the *tassimara* was true," I said gruffly after a long silence had passed. "When I first saw her, I experienced the *knowing*. I experienced Kakkari's guiding light in that dark, dense, consuming fog."

"Truly?" he asked quietly, his gaze rapt on me.

I inclined my head. "She vowed herself to me in the old language. *Lo rune tei'ri,*" I said softly. "No one speaks like that anymore. And I felt this *ancient* thing rise up in me at those words. That is why I call her a witch—because underneath the Dead Mountain, I believed that she *had* cast some sort of magic over me. It was the only logical explanation. In my arrogance I believed she'd taken my free will...as if it hadn't been *my* decision all along. A decision I made, to follow her wherever she went, no matter the price."

The words poured from me. Effortlessly. Like they'd been waiting to be set free.

"*Vok,*" Valavik said, the shock evident in his voice. "That was why...that was why you reacted so strangely when I offered to marry her instead."

I ran a hand down my face. "I lost my mind in that fog, Val. My damn *mind*. But it wasn't the fog that took it from me. It was *her*."

Quietly, he said, "And a part of you has not forgiven her for it since."

No truer words had been spoken.

I blew out a rough breath, leaning the back of my head against the mountain.

"*Nik*, I have not. And I know that she does not deserve my ire. I know that she does not deserve any of it. I *know* she was just a tool. A tool used by the true makers of that plot to capture me. A tool used against me, though I don't think they understood just how effective she was. She'd had no choice in it either. *Vok*, you should have seen how they treated her."

Yet I have not treated her much better, I thought, nostrils flaring.

"I cannot seem to move past this...this *bitterness*. This mistrust," I finished quietly.

"Yet you must," Valavik said simply. As if that would solve all my problems. "Already there are rumors within the horde this last week."

"What rumors?"

"That you are regretting your choice of *Morakkari*. That she is perhaps not as strong as they think she is."

I scowled. "They all witnessed her power. How could they deny her?"

"You tell me, Rowin. They see their *Vorakkar* hardly able to look at her. You never go near her. You do not touch her, speak to her, you do not sleep in her bed. It is unnatural behavior for a mated couple, especially for a horde king and his queen. In their eyes, you don't respect her. And if *you* don't respect her, how can you expect your horde to?"

It felt like a punch in the gut. The words wove down my throat, roving and merciless. They ate at my insides.

I'd thought all this myself, but to hear my *pujerak* repeat them, unafraid to say them out loud…it felt much, much worse.

"You are right," I rasped, my fists clenching. "I know you are right."

"*So you must get past this,*" Valavik said, emphasizing his words. "Or else Besik will get more smug as the days pass. He tells everyone who will listen how *you* regret not choosing his daughter as your *Morakkari*. Speaking for you as if it's the truth! Especially after the entire horde saw you walking with Junira two days ago."

Vok.

"She was asking me if she could tend to the planting of the new crops," I said. "I gave her my permission, and that was all. The whole encounter lasted a few moments."

"Yet the entirety of the horde knows about it now! Did you know that the *bikkus* haven't delivered your *Morakkari's* meals since yesterday? Her own *piki* must retrieve them from the kitchens. I am told that your wife went to the seamstress this morning to see about getting one of your furs mended and she was turned away. Wherever she walks, your horde meets her eyes. They do not look away in respect anymore."

I closed my eyes, swallowing hard.

"And where were you during all of this?" Valavik asked. "Taking out your frustrations on *darukkars* on the training grounds. Or calling meeting after meeting with the council, if only to avoid your own bed. *Vok*, Rowin. Maybe it would have been better if I *had* married her. At least I would *care* about her. At least I would—"

I was up in an instant. His furs were clenched in my fists until I swung him around and threw him back against the mountain wall, his furious gaze meeting my own.

"Be very careful with your next words, *Pujerak*," I snarled. "My temper has been short as of late."

"A long night seated between your wife's thighs might help

with that," Valavik growled back, bringing his hands up to my wrists and flinging them away.

"She doesn't want me!" I roared, my frustration finally boiling over. "I *vokking* hurt her. I made her bleed! I left her that first night. And if she doesn't already, then she *should* hate me for it!"

Cursing, I turned from him, walking to the cliff's edge to look out over the Dead Valley, in its dark vastness. I blew out a rough breath, trying to quiet the self-hatred I'd felt since I first realized I'd hurt her during the *tassimara*. Trying to quiet the sudden jealousy that flowed hot in my veins at the thought of Mina with my *pujerak*.

Long moments passed between us.

Finally, Valavik said, his voice noticeably quieter, "You do care about her. I know you do, Rowin."

"When we were under the Dead Mountain," I said, my eyes fastening on that wretched place, though it was shrouded in fog, "she came to me every night. I had fresh wounds for her to clean, wounds made by my own sword. She brought me water. She brought light. She even gave me portions of her own food, though I knew she was starving. And she did all this at great risk to herself, that brave *kalles*. At first, I thought she was sent to me purposefully. To gain my trust, to seek information about my horde. But it quickly became apparent to me that that wasn't the case. She was mistreated by her own people. *Abused* right in front of me when I could do nothing to stop it."

Those words fell from my lips like a harsh curse.

"She came to me because she *wanted* to help me. And even then, when she helped set me free, she begged me not to kill those that had wronged her. She said that she couldn't stand any more death," I said, swallowing. "I knew, even before she helped free me, that I would take her for the horde. I told myself it was because of my duty. But truthfully...I wanted her. I wanted her for myself."

"Then take her," Valavik said, coming to my side. Even in *Dothik*, he'd been my friend. My advisor. He was wise well beyond his years. He would have made a good *Vorakkar*, but he didn't have the stomach for battle, for death—not like I did. The old saying was that *Vorakkar* needed to be cruel to lead best.

And Valavik wasn't cruel.

"She is your *Morakkari* now. You are mated to her for life. Though some males stray from their wives' beds, I know you are not that male, Rowin," Valavik said. "As such, it is in your best interest to make this work with her."

"I threatened those she cares about under the Dead Mountain," I said. "That was the only reason she agreed to be my queen."

Valavik went quiet.

"And would you have seen those threats through?" he asked.

I scoffed. "I don't know. She told me there are females and children down there. But I think I would have said anything to make her agree."

"Then give her a reason to *choose* you instead of keeping her chained."

"How?" I asked quietly, discomfort swimming in my chest.

For all my experiences with females, they had mostly been confined to my furs. I knew nothing about *wooing* a female, courting one. Especially a human female who had become my *Morakkari*.

"I saw the shell that my father was as I grew up," I told Valavik quietly. "I always knew something was wrong, but it wasn't until I learned of how deep my parents' love was that I began to understand. He taught me to be wary of females. He taught me to be wary of partnership, of love. All my life. My father only ever said, in his bitterness, in his hatred of me, that females *ruined* males." My lips twisted bitterly. "In the fog, in those first moments with her and all the ones that came afterward, I understood what he meant. And now I have a female of my own. And I have no *vokking* idea how to treat her, and so I push her away. Because it is what I know. It is what I know how to do best."

"*Vok,* Rowin," Valavik said, his voice low. Sympathetic. Carefully, he said, "With all due respect to your *pattar*, he *was* half-mad by the time he passed into the next world. He was an angry, grief-ridden male. We all heard the stories. Of how he trained you in secret before you could even lift a sword. You were scarred before you could even walk."

I blew out a sharp breath. "I know the failings of my father better than most. Believe me."

"Then recognize that he was *wrong*," Valavik said. "Or else you and your queen will both suffer for it."

I looked up at the night sky. Clear and endless. The stars were bright. Constellations that depicted Drukkar's great battle greeted me, though I couldn't help but feel it was an omen of what would come.

"I know what I have to do," I told Valavik, turning to face him, reaching out to clasp his shoulder. "It is long overdue."

"Begging for forgiveness was never your strength," he said wryly, though a part of him looked delighted at the prospect. "I almost wish I could witness it for myself."

His small laugh echoed as I turned from him, heading back down the slope that led to the ledge.

I needed to find my *Morakkari*.

I needed to make things right between us.

CHAPTER 40

"Such beautiful hair," Hukri murmured.

"Hay...*hay-air*," Rakoni murmured from her spot on the floor, her mouth forming the word in a language I knew she did not yet know. Hukri's daughter was watching us both from her place next to the fire basin, watching as her mother brushed through my strands. Then she asked a question of her mother.

Hukri's reply was sharp, and Rakoni pouted.

"What did she ask?" I wondered.

Hukri blew out a sigh. "She wanted to brush your hair."

I smiled at the young girl. Though she'd been around quite a lot in the last week, she was still shy, wary of me.

"It's all right," I told Hukri gently. "She can brush it."

My *piki's* hand stilled. "It's...it's not proper, *missiki*."

"It's just hair," I told her, beckoning the young girl forward with a wave of my hand. I was sitting on Wrune's bed—where I'd slept, alone, for the last week. Tonight I expected the same. Already the moon had risen, and there was no sign of my husband. "*Jiria*," I said to Rakoni. *Come* in Dakkari.

Hukri sighed again, but her daughter's excited smile swayed her and she relinquished the brush. Hukri's own brush since I didn't have one of my own.

Small, tentative fingers ran through my waves. A hushed whisper came next, one laced with awe. I'd learned that my hair was strange to the Dakkari. I'd only ever seen Dakkari with silky, straight locks, and so mine, wild with waves and more coarse, must make an odd sight.

My scalp tingled as Rakoni began to brush through it. It was wet from my bath, freshly washed. Such a simple pleasure, having one's hair brushed.

When Rakoni hit a knot, my head pulled to the side sharply, and I laughed when her mother immediately broke into rapid apologies.

"It's all right, Hukri," I said, grinning when I heard even Rakoni's small giggle, so at odds with her mother's panic. "It's—"

I spied a figure, lingering near the entrance of the *voliki*, and my smile died, my spine straightening.

He'd entered so quietly I hadn't even noticed. And I wondered how long he'd been watching us.

"*Vorakkar*," Hukri gasped out, as surprised to see him as I was. She looked at Rakoni and then back to Wrune. She said something rapidly in Dakkari, words too quick for me to understand.

I imagined my *piki* was apologizing for her daughter's presence, especially in his own *voliki*. Though it was at my request that the small girl join us. I knew how much Hukri missed her daughter throughout the long days she spent with me. There was no reason for Rakoni not to be with her.

Wrune listened to Hukri's words, but his reddened gaze was only on me. I felt a knot rising in my throat, wondering what version of him I would get this night. In the last week, I'd hardly seen him. I went to sleep alone and I woke up alone, no sign of him ever having lain beside me during the night. Occasionally I saw him walking through the horde, speaking with different members, *darukkars* or *bikkus* or his *pujerak* or elders or the *mrikro*. Occasionally I spied him training, but I didn't stay to watch for long.

This was the closest we'd been since the night he retrieved me from his council's *voliki*. I'd like to say that his presence made me feel indifferent. I'd like to say that his presence didn't affect me in the slightest.

Unfortunately, it did. My heartbeat sped. My breath came faster. To try to mitigate these things, I avoided his eyes, keeping them pinned to the bathing tub, which still had steam rising from its surface.

Wrune waved his hand once Hukri stopped talking.

"*Kakkira vor,*" he said. My brow furrowed. "You are dismissed for the night."

"*Lysi, Vorakkar,*" Hukri murmured, dropping her gaze to the ground and chastising Rakoni when she looked up at Wrune with wide eyes, as big as a *pyroki's*.

Something swam in my belly when I saw Wrune place his large palm on the young girl's head as she passed him. For a brief moment, Rakoni seemed to forget her fear because she grinned up at him. A strange expression passed over my husband's face, but then Hukri shuffled her daughter from the *voliki,* and with a murmured goodnight to me, my *piki* disappeared.

Leaving me alone with Wrune.

Strangled silence descended between us, but I refused to be the first one to speak. If he wanted to play another one of his games, I would let him. If he wanted—

"I've been a fool, Mina."

I blinked. The guttural words fell from him, as soft as a confession.

Those words made me freeze in place, especially when he began to approach me. I straightened even further, wondering what the hell he was doing, and nerves erupted in my belly when he dropped before me, his knees digging into the carpets that lined the *voliki*.

He was still taller than me, even though he kneeled. My knees brushed his hip when I shifted, and his familiar scent swarmed me. I purposefully tried *not* to breathe him in because the smell of him always made me feel so incredibly aware of him.

"What are you doing, Rowin?" I asked quietly, meeting his eyes in bewilderment. Because surely a horde king was not on his knees. A horde king would never be caught in such a position.

His expression was still as unreadable as ever as he let out a sharp exhale through his nostrils.

Then his hands found mine. I watched, incredulous, as he brought my palm up, brushing his lips over the very center of it. A shiver raced up my spine, never realizing how *sensitive* I was there.

"I have mistreated you, *rei Morakkari*," he murmured. "I have disrespected you. I have hurt you. I have no excuses for any of it. Only that I held onto bitterness and anger and used it against you, when you deserved none of it."

Shock made my lips part. For the first time in over a week, I stuttered, "Wha-What?"

"I saw you for who you were even under the Dead Mountain. I knew your spirit was pure and giving. Yet I scorned you for it. I blamed you for events that I knew were completely outside of your own control. I *used* you, callously and mercilessly. And still, you wanted to help me. In return, I chained you. I leveled threats against you to make you bend to my will. I let my horde think you were weak when, really, it was my own weakness that they needed to witness. For all this, I need to make amends."

"What are you doing?" I whispered again because it was the only thing I could think to say. A knot was rising in my throat.

Because yes, he *had* done all those things to me. He was wrong for it.

But to hear him admit it...it loosened a tightness in my chest.

His eyes dropped to the golden markings that wound around my wrist. I was sensitive there too, I realized, when his thumb brushed over the words there. The skin was still healing, but I no longer needed to wear the bandages.

"Already I have broken these vows," he said. There was a gruffness in his voice that made my nose sting. I heard...*regret.* "I told you once that your husband was an honorable male, and yet I have not shown you him once—nor given you reason to believe it."

My eyes dropped to the markings he was stroking. Vows of protection, of respect, of loyalty, of...fidelity.

Did he mean he'd broken that one too?

I'd seen him with Junira with my own eyes. Walking together through the horde, something *I* hadn't even done with him. In that moment, I couldn't help but think that they made a handsome couple. She was more suited to him than I ever would be. Her head had been held high, and she'd smiled at him, beautiful and wide and adoring.

Instead of skirting around the question, I decided I needed to know. Once and for all.

"If I ask you something, will you be honest with me?"

His brow furrowed, and his thumb never rose from my wrist. "*Lysi.*"

"Where have you been sleeping?"

His eyes flashed. He seemed perplexed by the question—a question I saw he hadn't expected. "Where have I been sleeping?"

"Have you..." I took a deep breath, bracing myself for his answer. "Have you been in others' beds? In Junira's?"

Wrune stared at me. I heard the rough sound that rose in his throat. "Junira?"

"I know about her. I saw you with her," I told him, feeling a rush of heat flare up my neck. He wasn't answering me. Or was he stalling for time? "I know that she was meant to be your queen. That I took her place and—"

"*Nik,*" he said, his tone low and even. His eyes held mine as he gave his answer. "You wish to know where I have been? I have been sleeping in my council's *voliki*. I have been sleeping on your own pallet because I find that your scent helps me sleep at night."

I reeled back slightly. "W-What?"

I'd been so *certain* he'd been with others, especially after seeing him with Junira. They'd seemed so comfortable in one another's company, nothing like how *our* interactions were.

And yet...I heard the truth in his voice.

"Believe me when I say that my fidelity to you is the last thing you need to worry about, *rei Morakkari*," he said. "*That* is one vow to you I have not and will not ever break."

A soft exhale, perhaps one of disbelief, of shock, left me.

Shock because...I actually *believed* him.

"Why?" I asked. "Why is that so important to you when the other vows aren't?"

I caught his subtle flinch. His hand tightened on my own.

"It's not that they aren't important to me, Mina," came his ragged voice. "It's that I've been so foolishly blinded by my own pride, by my own weakness when it comes to you that I have disregarded them." He tilted my chin up so I met his eyes. "For all of this, I am sorry. So very sorry, Mina."

He was *apologizing*?

The only time I'd ever received an apology in my life was from my father. Right before he died. He'd apologized to me because he knew that he would no longer be able to protect me, to be with me. He'd been too sick, and he'd known that his time was limited.

The memory—and Wrune's apology—flooded my eyes with unexpected tears.

His expression shifted. His brows furrowed, his mouth pulled down. "*Nik,* don't do that, *rei Morakkari,*" he said softly. "Don't do that."

I wiped at my cheeks, embarrassed that I was crying in front of him. And yet it felt good. Like a release. A release of all the tension that had been building between us.

"I will not break these vows to you again," he murmured. In that same solemn, honest voice. "That I promise you, Mina."

"You can't promise that," I whispered, trying to blink back the tears that continued to fill my eyes.

"I can," he said easily, a hint of the arrogant, confident male I'd come to know shining through with those simple words. "I know that I do not deserve your forgiveness, but I ask that you let me try to be worthy of it. I ask that you let me try to prove that I can be a good husband to you."

I was beginning to feel a little overwhelmed. Just a few moments ago, Rakoni had been brushing through my hair...and now a horde king was on his knees before me, begging for my forgiveness.

Swallowing, I asked, "What brought this on? Why are you doing this *now*?"

"Because I no longer have the strength to stay away from you," he rasped. My eyes widened at the words. "Since I first saw you, I've always been torn in two completely opposite directions. And I've come to realize that I've been following the wrong one."

"What are you talking about?"

"You are my *kassikari,*" he told me.

"*Kassikari*?" I whispered. "What does that mean?"

"My mate. A mate of the old way," he explained. "Of the old tradition. A mating pair chosen by Kakkari herself."

I stilled.

He was telling me that he believed the goddess had chosen me for him? And that she had chosen him for me?

"I have known since you first appeared to me in the fog," he confessed.

"I don't understand," I told him. "I don't understand what that means."

"It means that you were always going to be my *Morakkari*. You did not steal that place from anyone because you were meant for it since your very birth," he growled softly. "It means that a part of my soul attached itself to you even then, marking you as mine. You felt it, didn't you? I called it a madness, a small madness, but I knew what it really was. It was *knowing*."

A sharp exhale left me. I felt a prickling at the back of my neck. His words were impossible, and yet they felt *familiar*. So incredibly and achingly familiar.

"And I know that you felt it too," he added gruffly. "So you see, you were always meant to be mine. I recognized that from the very beginning, but I fought against it with everything I had in me. Even after our *tassimara*, I fought against that path, the path that Kakkari had revealed to both of us. I couldn't let go of how *easily* I fell to you. I blamed you for something that was *fated*, that neither one of us could have controlled. Or foreseen."

"That was why you always called me *sarkia*," I whispered, realization going through me.

"In my pride, I believed that only magic could have made me want you so much. A want and a need so powerful that in that moment, I gave up everything. Because in that moment, I forgot my horde. Myself. For *you*. You wish to know how you led me through that fog so easily? Because I would have followed you *anywhere*."

I brought a hand up to my mouth.

For a male like Wrune, for a *horde king* who had fought for his position, who had endured endless pain and hardship to be where he was, who had the weighted responsibility of hundreds of lives on his shoulders, for him to disregard all of that for a female he had only just met...I could *finally* understand his hatred of me. It must've been an incredibly frightening thing for him.

Now I understood *why*.

"Oh, Wrune," I murmured, biting my lip. "I didn't...I didn't mean to—"

"I know, Mina," he rasped. "Believe me, I *vokking* know. But I punished you for it regardless...because *I* was afraid. I was afraid of the power you had over me."

My shoulders slumped.

This...this had cost him. For such a proud male, this had cost him much to come to me on his knees, to ask for my forgiveness, to tell me that I was his weakness and that it had frightened him.

"What do we do now?" I whispered.

A deep breath filled him. Gently, his hand cupped my face, and I felt the warmth of his palm sink into my cheek. We were so close that we shared the same breath. We were so close that I saw the strands of black in his red eyes and saw a tiny nick of a scar I'd never noticed before across his wide nose.

"I wish for us to start anew."

My breath hitched, and my eyes flickered between his own.

"And I will not deny my instincts any longer when I am with you," he told me.

Instincts? I wondered. What instincts was he talking about?

"You are my *Morakkari*, my *kassikari*. I will treat you as such because I have neglected you for much too long," he continued. My belly fluttered, hearing something in his voice that made me aware just how close he was to me. "I will touch you because I need to. I will take care of you because I need to. I will sleep beside you each night because I *vokking need* to, Mina."

I swallowed hard.

"I have given you no reason to take me at my word, but soon, I will prove to you all that I promise. Please let me," he murmured. "And from this night forward, I will show you everything a husband should be to his wife. I will show you everything a horde king should be to his queen."

It sounded too good to be true. And I asked myself if I could *allow* myself to give him a second chance.

"I don't know if I trust you," I told him honestly. "I haven't forgotten, you know. I haven't forgotten your threat. You got me as your queen because of that threat. You have everything to bargain with, and I have *nothing*."

"No more bargaining between us," Wrune said. I spied regret and guilt in his gaze, heard it in the gruffness of his words, and my eyes widened in realization. "And I cannot take it back. I think we both know that."

"There is a lot we cannot take back," I agreed quietly. On my end as well. I hadn't forgotten my role in his capture. I could never forget it. The pain he'd endured. His injuries.

"But I know about Tess, I know how much you care for her. Like she is your blood," Wrune said.

Hearing Tess's name leave his lips ushered more tears forward. I hadn't thought he remembered. I hadn't thought he cared enough to remember a faceless *vekkiri's* name.

"So let me bring her to you."

Those words made me gasp.

"What?" I whispered, meeting his eyes in disbelief.

I didn't miss the way his expression softened the longer he looked at me. He brought his lips to the center of my palm again.

"I will bring her to you. I will offer her a place among our horde. And any that wish to follow me from the Dead Mountain, I will offer them a home too. Or at least help them build a new one if they do not wish to remain in the horde."

He'd once promised death. Now he promised *hope. Life.*

The tears rolled down my cheeks, and I couldn't stop them. Everything I wanted...he was freely offering it to me.

"You would do that?" I whispered.

"I would do it for you," he answered.

"But...but how would you get past the fog?" I asked. "I can help and—"

"*Nik,*" he rasped. Smoothing his hand against my cheek, wiping away the steady stream of tears. "I will not risk using that power again. It is too dangerous for you."

For me? Was he worried about my safety now?

"We will need time to plan," he told me. "But we know of the tunnels that run north. The same ones that the witches used to reach the Dead Mountain, *lysi*?"

The reminder of the witches made my mouth dry. I remembered the head witch's rasping tongue as she licked the line of my hot blood. The very memory made me go cold.

"You cannot," I whispered, realization making my shoulders sag. "You would be walking right to them. You would give them exactly what they want. *You.*"

A deep exhale left him. His hand slid upward until his fingers gently threaded through my damp hair. A shiver built up at the base of my spine, pleasurable and warm.

"Have more faith in your husband, *rei Morakkari*," he told me. My lips parted. "I *am* a Vorakkar, after all. I have known too many battles in my lifetime, and my *darukkars* are trained well."

"I don't want it turning into a battle," I reminded him softly. "I don't want any more death. I've seen you fight. I've seen your *darukkars* train. It would only be too easy for it to end in bloodshed."

His head lowered in agreement, but his eyes never left mine.

"Will you at least trust me to get you your Tess?" he

murmured. "And I swear to you, I will not spill anyone's blood unless my *darukkars'* own lives are in danger."

A soft, choppy sigh left my lips.

"I regret ever having made that threat to you, Mina," he told me. And I heard it. I heard the truth in his voice. "Let me make amends for it. I will give you what you want because I do not want you feeling like you have *nothing*. Truthfully, you have more power than I think you realize. Especially when it comes to me."

That last part felt like a confession. Vulnerable and deep.

"I do?" I whispered, feeling the hard lump in my throat begin to soften.

Those red eyes flared, his pupils dilating. That tension was beginning to rise between us. Thick and electric.

"*Lysi,*" he said. "You most certainly do."

Tentatively, I moved my hand. I moved it to rest on the back of his own, touching his warm skin, running my thumb across the raised scar there.

I didn't need to say anything.

Wrune didn't need any words from me.

Could I move forward with him?

Could I give him another chance?

Time will tell, I thought to myself.

Whatever he did next would tell me.

But I'd never been one to hold on to hatred. Hatred was rotten. It ate at you from the inside out.

Moving forward was what I did best. It was one of my biggest *strengths*.

And if he kept the promises he'd made to me tonight... then yes.

I thought I *would* be able to see where this path with him led.

"Words mean nothing," I told him. However pretty they

were. "Show me who you truly are. Show me you mean it. And I will be open to it. Open to *you*."

Those eyes burned with sudden determination, fierce and hot.

That look made my belly quiver with memory and made a flush rise up my neck.

I had the strangest thought that I might regret those words.

"I will show you everything, *rei Morakkari*. This I promise you."

CHAPTER 41

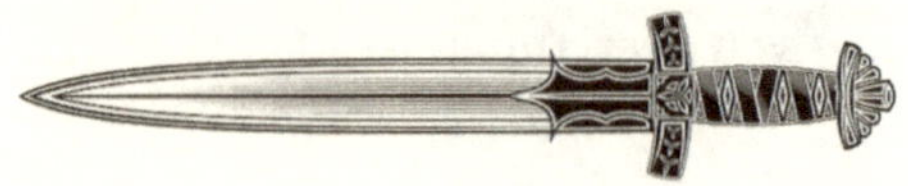

When I woke, it was in the early hours of morning, when the sun had yet to rise.

Mina was curled in my arms, the waves of her hair tickling my nose. I'd pressed my face to the curve of her neck in sleep. As if I needed her scent, as if I was addicted to it.

I'd slept solidly through the night. The first restful sleep in perhaps a long, long time.

I'd told her I would not deny my instincts any longer, and I thought she'd been surprised when I actually meant it. Last night, I'd pulled her into bed and wrapped her close for sleep, close enough that I knew she heard the steady rhythm of my heart. And that was how she'd fallen asleep, slowly relaxing in my arms, tentative at first, but then her limbs loosened completely. I'd followed her shortly, the short, restless nights of sleep having finally caught up with me.

Relief bloomed in my chest. She hadn't said she would forgive me, but she hadn't turned me away either. I was determined to win her. I was determined to make this right between us. I only needed the chance to. And Mina seemed willing to give me that.

Waking to her scent and warmth, however, had me aching.

Aching like I'd been since the night of our *tassimara*. Since even before our *tassimara*.

Nuzzling my head deeper into her neck, I brushed my lips over the slim, delicate column. Her back was to my chest. Her hips shifted underneath the furs, and I nearly groaned when her backside rubbed my hardened cock. The only thing separating us was the small fur covering across my groin and her dress. I could so easily lift up her shift and nudge my way inside her heat.

Nik, I thought, remembering that I'd made her bleed. That I'd hurt her. *Nik,* I could not do that again. I wouldn't be able to stomach causing her pain again.

But I could still give her pleasure...something I should have been doing *every* night since our *tassimara*.

One of my hands slid to the hem of her shift, dragging it up slowly. I palmed her warm hip, pleased that the bone didn't feel as prominent. There was a fullness there that hadn't been there before, now that she was actually giving her body the nourishment it needed.

Mina moved again, a small sound rising from her throat. My lips quirked against her neck as I brushed another kiss there, slowly trailing my mouth to her ear. I nipped at the soft lobe there before sucking it. I pushed her shift up until it uncovered her tantalizing, full breasts. Her nipples tightened underneath my fingers when I stroked them softly, thrumming them to stiff peaks.

A small gasp left Mina, and she stilled.

"*Rei Morakkari,*" I rasped in her ear. "Are you awake now?"

"Y-Yes," she whispered, the word slightly strangled. "What are you...*oh*..."

A breathy sigh left her when my other hand drifted between her thighs.

"Let me give you pleasure," I murmured to her and then kissed her ear again. A strong shiver raced up her body, making me smile. "Let me make you feel good, *rei sarkia*. So very good."

She didn't answer me. Not with words, at least. And she didn't stop me when I softly ran a finger over her folds, when I stroked the curls that shielded them.

She was curious, I knew. Curious about *this*.

I continued to pet her between her thighs, light and gentle. Teasing her there as I continued to suck and lick and kiss and nibble along her neck and behind her ear. As I continued to lazily thrum her nipples, switching between them. When I pinched one, a shuddering gasp left her. When I pinched the other, a moan tumbled from her even though I saw she was biting her lip and her hips rocked.

She was getting hot. So very *hot*.

My cock throbbed and ached and pressed. It was jutting out from my loincloth, bobbing against her bare buttocks. It was growing too warm underneath the furs, but I didn't want to stop touching her to throw them off us.

I moved my knee between her legs, parting them. With her inner thigh resting on my outer one, I moved my own up so she would be exposed to me. Hurriedly, I brought my hand up to my mouth and I bit off the pointed edges of two of my claws so I wouldn't hurt her, dulling and blunting them. I touched her again, and I growled, desire making me feel dizzy, when I discovered her wet and slick.

Pressing a kiss to her neck, I murmured, "So hot for me, *rei sarkia*. You want me to touch you here?"

"Yes," she said, the word immediate and breathless. I grinned, gently pinching her nipple again in praise. "*Oh*."

"You remember when I licked you here?" I growled, finding the hidden little bud between her folds and pressing there. Another moan, louder this time, fell from her lips as her hips bucked up to meet my touch.

She was panting now as I rolled her clit, though I kept the

pressure gentle. Just enough to keep her on edge, just enough to drive her mad.

"*Yes,*" she answered me.

"Remember how you came so sweetly for me?" I murmured, bringing my hand up from her breast so I could turn her head. I wanted her eyes on me, *needed* them. Her gaze was half-lidded when it met mine, dazed with sleepy pleasure, as if she was in a world that was between dreams and reality.

So *vokking* beautiful, I thought, unable to resist taking her lips.

Mina turned a little in my arms, and I felt my seed begin to climb in my cock when she kissed me back. Bravely meeting my tongue when I slipped it between her lips. The kiss had a life of its own, suddenly turning into something more, something neither of us expected. I sucked and nibbled at her mouth, so *vokking* hungry for her, as two of my fingers slipped into her warm cunt, making her breath hitch.

My little witch might not trust me. She might not even *like* me.

But she *loved* this. She loved the sensations I dragged from her body, the way I made her shiver with my kiss.

She was a sensual, curious creature who had long neglected all pleasure.

I will show her everything, I vowed silently, her moan meeting my ears when I pressed my fingers deeper, when my thumb continued to stroke her clit.

At the very least, I owed her *this*. I wanted to make her feel good. I wanted to make her feel so good that she would crave me. That she would never choose to leave me.

Mina was rocking against me steadily now, and I gritted my teeth, my self-control tested to its very limits as I fought to keep myself from spilling my seed over her backside like a young male with his first female. Pleasure sizzled up from my *deva*, the sacs heavy with seed, so full I thought they might burst.

Against her lips, I rasped, "I want you to come for me, *leika*. *Hanniva, hanniva.*"

Please.

Vok, I had never begged so much in my life. Especially for a female. But for my queen I would. A thousand times over.

Her cunt was tightening up even now, and my fingers pressed deeper inside her, fucking her steadily, imagining they were my cock. The pace and pressure of my thumb increased until her cries were a continuous sound in the *voliki*. My hand returned to her breast, rolling her nipples, tugging and stroking.

All the while, I thrust against her backside, rocking my cock against the cleft of her ass. The soft flesh was slippery with the beginnings of my seed. I was making a mess of her, but I was too mindless in her pleasure, in my own, to pull away.

My spine tingled. My balls pulsed.

"*Come for me, Mina,*" I growled, my voice unrecognizable. The huskiest, the darkest it had ever been.

Her eyes rolled back, her lips parted in a silent cry. As her back arched, her cunt began to pulse and tighten. My fingers curled, and a strangled, hitched cry fell from her lips as she jerked and moaned.

"*Uhhh,*" she cried out, breasts heaving, moving her hips wildly against me as she surrendered herself to her pleasure completely.

I'd never seen anything more erotic in my life. In stunned disbelief, I watched her, memorizing every detail of her. My fingers left her tight sheath as I continued to roll her clit. Then I felt the head of my cock as it slipped through her legs with her frenzied movements. The slick tip of it slid up her folds as I mindlessly thrust. I nearly entered her pulsing cunt, but I pushed myself away, continuing to move against her.

The slippery head slid over her clit, and she jerked, another unabashed moan falling from her lips.

"*Vok,* I'm going to come all over you," I gritted out, and a moment later, I groaned, deep and loud, and then I felt the sizzle of my seed as it shot from my cock almost violently. "*Lysi!*"

Mina was shivering and panting as I continued to punch my hips forward, chasing that teasing, soft friction between her thighs. The glide of her slick curls. The heat and arousal that coated her folds.

I pumped my seed until I had none left.

Then I fell limp, drained, back onto the furs, though my arms were still tight around her. I brought her with me until she was half lying across me, still on her back. My breath heaved, and her own shallow breaths mingled with mine.

For a long moment, we said nothing as we recovered. And when I moved her so that her back was fully on the furs once more, when I loomed over her, I saw that her cheeks were flushed a tantalizing red and that she couldn't quite meet my eyes.

I huffed out a small breath. Shy? After what we had just done?

Slipping the furs off her, I looked down at her body. Her breasts were still heaving, and she bit her lip when I brushed my fingers over the flushed, jutting nipples. Sensitive?

And between her thighs...

Vok.

I really had made a mess of her.

The long lashes of my release had made it up to her belly. Thick seed mingled in her curls and dripped down her pink slit.

Just the sight made my cock stir to life once more. Reaching out my fingers, I touched her there, brushing my thumb through the folds.

Her body jerked, her small gasp made my gaze dart up to her. She was looking down at herself too, her lips parted in surprise, as if she couldn't believe *this* was the state of her own body.

"*Leika*," I rumbled. *Beautiful.* Those wide green eyes came to me, and another deep flush made its way up her neck. I grinned briefly, and she blinked, her eyes lowering to my mouth.

Before she could say anything, I pushed off the bed, padding to the filled water basin, dunking a fresh cloth inside and wringing out the excess.

When I returned to her, I kneeled between her splayed thighs. Though I was tempted to leave my seed marking her sex, I didn't want Mina feeling discomfort from it. So, gently, I began to wash her. Her breath hitched and her legs squirmed. But she never closed them to my touch.

When she was cleaned there, I wiped away the seed on her belly. And then I ran the cloth underneath her buttocks, remembering how slippery I'd made her there too.

I took my time.

Then I moved the cloth back between her thighs *just* to make sure I'd cleaned her there thoroughly. A small sound rose in her throat, caught between a whimper and a moan, when I let the cloth linger against her clit. When the soft, wet drag of it teased her.

My nostrils flared. She was staring at me, her once widened gaze going half-lidded once more. Between us, my cock was thick and hard, my *deva* hanging heavy beneath me.

I tossed the cloth off the bed. It landed somewhere near the fire basin, but I forgot it a moment later as I crawled between her thighs, going to my front on the furs.

I need her again, I thought, my mouth watering with anticipation.

My hands slid underneath her, tilting her hips up. I heard her suck in a breath and hold it. Waiting for me too?

When my tongue met her clit, her breathy cry rang out, loud and beautiful. A release.

"Until the sun rises," I murmured to her, my lips brushing against the little bud with the words, "you're mine. *Lysi?*"

I will keep her pinned to these furs until then, I vowed silently.

Her gaze burned into me. Her shyness had faded with her desire, with her curiosity as quickly as it had come on.

Her legs widened even farther, and I rumbled my approval, pressing a kiss to her inner thigh in satisfaction.

"*Lysi,*" she breathed.

CHAPTER 42

"*O*h," came Hukri's quiet exclamation when she stepped into the *voliki* that morning. "*Vorakkar*, forgive me."

Wrune was crouched next to the bathing tub that I was currently steaming in. His fingers were trailing a line in the water, and he seemed content to watch me bathe. We hadn't been speaking, but the air felt charged, vibrant.

The space between my thighs was still tingling from all of Wrune's thorough attentions. For hours, since I'd woken to darkness and his touch at my breasts, he'd demanded a plethora of exquisite orgasms, wringing them from me expertly and without mercy.

Truth be told, I was still astonished by everything that had transpired between us in such a short amount of time. The change in him was night and day. I couldn't understand it.

And yet...I liked it. He'd slept the night at my side. It was the first time in my life I'd lain beside a male, felt his arms around me as I drifted off. I'd felt safe. Warm. Protected. My sleep had been dreamless and energizing. Despite the early hour I'd woken, I felt like I could accomplish anything.

Flushing, I also knew I *really* liked everything we'd done that morning too. Though Wrune had never entered me. He'd only touched and licked and kissed. He'd come again on the furs, thrusting into them as he lapped between my thighs.

But he'd never once attempted to push into me.

Hukri was standing at the entrance of the *voliki*. Rakoni wasn't with her today, which was probably for the best. The last few days, she'd entered the *voliki* without warning, since Wrune hadn't been sleeping there. This morning, however, everything was different.

"I am expected at the training grounds this morning," Wrune murmured to me, those red eyes never leaving me. "And then I will meet with my council, to discuss the Dead Mountain, *lysi?*"

Out of the corner of my eye, I saw Hukri shift, but she kept her gaze straight forward, like she was a statue, though one that was trying to disappear.

"All right," I said quietly, feeling that same hope I felt last night rise, overwhelming and wonderful.

"I'll come find you later," he murmured.

He would?

Wrune stood, the hide of his trews creaking behind his knees. He was wearing a tunic today as well, which stretched across the wide expanse of his chest. He'd already bathed. After my fourth orgasm, I must've dozed because I'd woken to the sight of him in a hot bath—an unexpectedly tantalizing view.

To Hukri, he inclined his head. "*Piki.*"

Hukri dropped her gaze in respect.

Wrune passed her, but just before he ducked underneath the entrance, he told her, "Have the furs cleaned today, *lysi?*"

My face flamed, but I didn't sink underneath the water like I wanted to.

"Of course, *Vorakkar*," Hukri said. I swore I heard a note of *relief* in her tone.

"I'll clean them myself," I called out, not wanting anyone to see the mess we'd made of them.

"You will do no such thing," Wrune announced, casting a look over his shoulder at me. His expression was all satisfied arrogance, the maddening male. "*Lysi?*"

Then he disappeared from view, ducking under the flaps, and I heard his heavy footsteps begin to descend the slope from the *voliki*.

I huffed out a breath.

"*Sailon,*" I muttered, though I knew he'd be able to hear me.

A sharp, short bark of a laugh told me he did, but then it died as he strode away. I ignored the way that laugh made me feel and fought the smile that threatened to rise.

Still standing near the entrance, I saw Hukri glance my way, her eyes knowing and wide.

"Don't say a word," I groaned softly, sinking farther into the bath as she approached. "Please."

"I was very surprised to see him here this morning," she noted, her tone reserved. Then she smiled, the scar down her face pulling with the expression. "But *delighted*. I knew it would happen eventually."

"And what exactly did happen?" I asked quietly, though it was more to myself. "Because I'm still not sure *I* know."

"And you do not have to, *missiki*. Kakkari has a way with these things," she told me. "Sometimes we must be patient to see the right path."

I stilled. "Kakkari?"

"*Lysi*. The *Vorakkar* announced at your *tassimara*, to the entire horde, that he felt Kakkari's guiding light within him when he first saw you," Hukri said, a gentle, dreamy quality to her tone. "Considering the nature of our *Vorakkar*, I knew it was the truth."

I looked down at the surface of the bath water, biting my lip.

He'd told the entire horde that he felt our meeting was

fated? *Before* the *tassimara*? Why did that send a fluttering feeling straight to my belly?

"His nature?" I asked, meeting her gaze once more.

Hukri kneeled next to the bathing tub. "Our *Vorakkar* is always so serious. He takes the responsibility as our protector, as our leader with great consideration—as do many of the horde kings that roam our wildlands. It was partly why he was chosen to become one," Hukri told me, and I lapped up her words, processing them quickly. "He is always honest with us. Some *Vorakkar* lie to their hordes, especially when it comes to mounting danger. Some *Vorakkar* think it's best to hide the truth to keep panic from rising. But ours has always been open about the danger of the fog. He knows that it is greater than any of us, and he wants us to be prepared, should it come."

"But why set up the encampment so close to it?" I wondered.

"He saw it as our duty. It was our turn, you see," Hukri said. "The *Vorakkar* decided among themselves that one horde should always remain close, to report to the others if something should happen. It was Rath Rowin's turn, and truthfully, I have never seen him so tense during a season. He worries for us. I know he does."

Hukri sighed and fished out the cloth I'd used to wash myself. She wrung it out and draped it over the edge of the bathing tub.

"So you see, I knew he was telling the truth about you," Hukri said. She smiled. "And it brings me great relief to see things changing between you. You are even calling him a soft name."

My brow furrowed. "A...soft name?"

"*Lysi,*" Hukri said. "You called him *sailon.*"

I blinked. "That means *stubborn male*. Because he is always so—"

Hukri's laugh cut off my words, and I began to realize that I'd been tricked.

"*Sailon* means something like..." Hukri began, grinning as she thought of a suitable translation. "*Darling*. But the masculine form of it. For a female, you would say *saila*."

My lips parted in disbelief.

My so-called honorable husband had purposefully had me calling him *darling* this entire time?

No wonder he'd given me the translation for *stubborn male* so easily, I thought.

I shook my head but then felt a bloom of softened amusement.

"What *is* the word for *stubborn male*, then?" I asked.

Hukri grinned. "*Setovan* would be the best translation."

"*Setovan*," I murmured. Then I thought of something else. "And what does *leika* mean?"

He'd called me that often. The first time had been when I demonstrated the way I could bend the fog before his entire horde, in those brief moments when our gazes connected and it felt like the world had...softened around us.

Hukri's smile died, but her expression took on a pleased look in its place. "It means *beautiful*."

My breath hitched. I quickly looked away from my *piki*, feeling my belly begin to flutter anew as I bit my lip to keep from smiling.

He'd been calling me *beautiful*? Even when we hadn't been... *together*?

I couldn't figure him out.

A part of me wondered if I'd ever be able to.

"Right," I whispered, pushing up from the bath. I was no longer shy about my nudity in front of Hukri. She'd seen me naked more times than Wrune had at this point. "Shall I get dressed?"

Hukri retrieved the furs Wrune had draped close to the fire

basin. When she handed me them, they felt like a cocoon of warmth, and I smiled as I wrapped myself in them.

"As you dress, *missiki*," Hukri said, going toward the bed, not blinking an eye when she saw the mess on it, "I will take these to—"

"*No*," I said quickly. "I meant what I said. I'd be embarrassed if anyone had to clean these when it—"

"The *Vorakkar* knows what he's doing, *missiki*," Hukri said quietly, a strange tone in her voice that had me stilling. I stepped from the bathing tub and wrapped the furs around me, approaching.

"What do you mean?" I asked.

Hukri sighed. "It is no secret among the horde that the *Vorakkar* has not been sharing your bed. It is no secret among the horde that you two have had a difficult time adjusting to one another after your *tassimara*."

I closed my eyes briefly and blew out a breath. "The horde has been talking about us?"

"Of course."

Something from last night rose in my mind. Wrune had apologized for...letting the horde think I was weak. It hadn't made sense to me at the time, but was this what Hukri was saying? That his horde hadn't accepted me as their queen because of the obvious divide between their *Vorakkar* and me?

"Hordes gossip. It is natural. And you both have given them plenty to say this past week—though if the *Vorakkar* ever heard them, he'd probably send the offenders immediately back to *Dothik* for disrespecting you."

"And so," I murmured, my eyes going to the bed in realization, "the furs..."

"Exactly," Hukri said. "It is a message to the entire horde. Word will spread from the seamstresses and the washers. Like I said, the *Vorakkar* knows exactly what he is doing."

I blinked. Did that mean...was that the reason he'd spent his seed over the furs instead of *inside* me? Had he planned this, calculated it out since before he even woke me this morning?

The thought that that might be a possibility dimmed a little of the warm glow inside me. But then I remembered that the horde was like a village. Perception was everything. Perception was power. Wrune was more experienced in these things than I was. It was his horde whose gossip and rumors he wanted to silence, though in his own subtle way.

And so I nodded. Truthfully, now that I knew there had been talk about us, I felt a little flame of *purpose* building inside my breast. If this horde was to be my home, if I would accept Wrune as my husband, I didn't want to show weakness. Not as a queen to a Dakkari horde.

I needed to show strength.

So, after I dressed, I gathered up the furs myself, my lips pressed together with determination.

Turning to Hukri, I saw a flicker of approval in her gaze.

"Let's go deliver these together," I told her.

CHAPTER 43

Later that night, I was surprised to see a glow emanating from Wrune's *voliki*—and, I supposed, *my voliki* now—with smoke rising from the venting hole at the top.

The guard that constantly seemed to trail me slowly fell away, watching from a distance as I trekked up the incline leading to the domed home. When I walked through the entrance, I was greeted by the sight of Wrune in the bathing tub, and my belly flipped and flopped. My breath went a little shallow with anticipation and nerves—until I saw the long gash running down his arm.

"What happened?" I gasped softly, approaching the tub quickly, though I was flicking my gaze around for clean cloth to bandage it.

"It's nothing," he murmured, his eyes fastening on me. "A shallow cut from the training grounds. A young *darukkar* swinging his sword a little too enthusiastically. A mistake he will never make again."

My shoulders sank. Seeing the black blood from the wound —which I saw was actually dried blood—made memories of the Dead Mountain come flooding back. I swallowed, remembering the dread I'd felt whenever I walked down that long hallway, wondering what new wound the horde king would sport that night.

"What are you thinking of?" he asked quietly, water trickling as he lifted his arm from the water so he could touch the bunched spot between my brows.

"Nothing," I whispered, shaking myself. "Are you sure you shouldn't bandage that?"

"Worried I'll bleed on you when I take you to our bed this night, *rei Morakkari*?"

Surprisingly, I didn't flush at his obvious teasing. I looked at him steadily and said, "No, I'm not worried about that."

His gaze was warm and intense. The way he was looking at me made me feel feverish.

I'd seen him two times that day. He'd seen me walking the path I usually took with Hukri—a long walk I started taking every day because I enjoyed the warm sun and the fresh air— and he'd approached me, stealing a long kiss in front of the entirety of his horde, one that left me breathless and clinging to him. Another pointed message to his horde, I assumed. Though a small part of me hoped it had something to do with his vow the previous night. That he would no longer deny his instincts with me.

The next time I saw him had been just as the sun started to descend along the horizon. I'd wanted to see how the tanning process worked with the hides the hunters brought back and went to visit that section of the horde with Hukri, Rakoni trailing along behind us. It was toward the back of the horde, separated off from the rest of the encampment because of the smell, especially during the warmer days, but I'd found it fascinating. The process was smooth and efficient. I'd learned that the excess hides were sent to the outposts or *Dothik*, traded for other supplies that the horde might need.

To my surprise, Wrune had been there, speaking with one of the males in charge of the tannery. Though they'd still been deep in discussion, Wrune's red gaze had fastened on me and never left. When he finished his business with the male, he'd come to me and we'd spoken briefly. As we did, his hands had clasped my waist and held me still against him, as if he *needed* to touch me. Behind him, I'd caught the curious gazes of those around us, saw one or two heads bend together as they whispered.

He hadn't had the long gash then, so he must've returned to the training grounds shortly after.

"Where were you?" he wondered.

"With Hukri," I told him. "I didn't realize you'd be back so early."

"Have you eaten?" he asked. When I shook my head, he nodded to the heaping platters of food on the low table. "The *bikkus* delivered it a little while ago. For you."

"For me?" I asked, my eyes going wide. "I can't eat all that."

"And for me," he added. "Go eat, *rei sarkia*. I'll be there shortly."

I found it didn't bother me when he called me *sarkia* anymore. Strangely, I could hear the way his voice lowered as he said it, as if it were...a soft name now.

Which reminded me about what I'd learned that morning.

"All right, *setovan*," I murmured, rising from my place beside the bath. I heard a sharp huff leave his nostrils as I strode away, sinking down at the low table, on the cushions that lined the carpet.

A moment later, I heard the *whoosh* of water as he stood. I couldn't help but look over at him as I dragged a bowl of broth to my lips. He was looking at me, his cock swaying, as he stepped from the tub and snagged furs to dry off with. Water droplets slid down his wide chest, and I traced one until it dipped underneath the furs, disappearing from view.

"*Setovan?*" he growled softly. I sipped more broth from the bowl, my spine straightening when he hung the furs on the rack that attached to the fire basin, leaving him very, very nude. I swallowed when he approached, my eyes dipping to his rapidly rising cock.

"*Sailon?*" I asked him when I thought my tongue would work again. "Hukri told me what it meant. You didn't think you'd get away with that for long, did you?"

When his mouth curled in a brief grin, my mind temporarily went blank. I'd never actually seen a *proper* smile from him, and the sight was...dizzying. It made my heart speed to an alarming rate.

"I got away with it for a little while," he informed me, then dropped next to me on the cushion, his naked, warm thigh pressing into my own. "I think it was worth it, even though I risked your ire. Are you angry with me for it?"

"No," I said truthfully. When I spied his cock bob out of the corner of my eye, my cheeks went hot, and I sipped more broth. Then asked, "Aren't you going to dress?"

"Why bother?" he rasped, leaning close to me as he reached for the heaping plate of smoky, fragrant, herby meat. His hand met the small of my back, his touch unexpected and oddly comforting. "I expect no interruptions this night from my horde. And you will soon be undressed and lying across our freshly cleaned furs as I drink from between your thighs."

I gasped, heat pooling so suddenly with his words because I could picture it so easily. And I *wanted* it so much.

His touch on the small of my back rose, tracing my spine through my thin dress. "I've been a very patient male all day, and I think I deserve my treat."

When our gazes locked, I felt his hand curl around the back of my neck. He brought me forward, his head ducking and—

My stomach growled.

Wrune paused. His eyes flashed, and instead of the deep, scalp-tingling kiss I'd expected, he brushed a chaste one across my lips and leaned back.

"Eat, *rei Morakkari*," he murmured, his expression unreadable. "You'll need your strength."

That sounded like both a threat and a promise.

In response, I found anticipation curling in my belly, wicked and hot and needful.

But I ignored it for now, plucking off a piece of tender meat from the plate Wrune offered to me. The taste reminded me of something I'd had before, and I instantly knew what it was.

"Is this...is this meat from the same beast you gave my village?" I asked softly. It had an earthy taste to it, one that was so familiar to me.

"Well, not the *same* beast," he murmured. I huffed out a small breath, shaking my head. It seemed my husband could be playful when he wished to be. "But *lysi*. It is *bveri*. A large pack animal. It grazes during the warm season toward the South Lands, but when the frost comes, it heads north."

"Where it's colder during the frost?" I asked, curious.

"The one I sent to your village was already skinned and processed, but a *bveri* typically has thick, long, dense fur. We use their fur during the cold season because it insulates best. It is too hot for this season, but you will see it eventually."

I hadn't thought much about the future. *Our* future. I couldn't think past the Dead Mountain or the fog for now because nothing seemed certain. But Wrune didn't seem to have those same hesitations.

"For the frost, we may be in the North Lands," he added. My breath hitched, my eyes going wide at the prospect of returning *home*. "What would you think of that, *rei Morakkari*? If I claimed that territory for the frost?"

He was asking *me*?

Swallowing, I told him honestly, "I have no idea what goes into decisions like that. You're the horde king. You know your horde. And Hukri has told me many times that you will always do what is right for them. If you think the North Lands will be best, then what is to stop you from making that choice?"

"With time, *Morakkari*, you will be making choices that affect the horde too."

"And that frightens me," I told him, the words falling from my lips before I could stop them. "I feel...I feel like an imposter sometimes. Like I don't belong. Sometimes I don't think I belong anywhere except..."

Except in the North Lands, I thought. With my father. My aunt.

But I couldn't tell him that. I didn't want to sway his decision, after all.

I blew out a breath but then stilled when I felt Wrune's fingers tighten around my hand.

"I felt that way too," he murmured to me. "My first season in the wildlands."

I licked my lips and quietly asked, "Truly?"

"*Lysi,*" he murmured. "All hordes typically have a rough first season. It's to be expected. I doubted myself every day. I agonized over decisions until they almost paralyzed me into inaction. But then I realized that I was *chosen* for a reason, that I had *endured* the Trials for a reason. I realized I needed to trust my instincts or else my horde would suffer for it. Hordes fail, you know. All the time."

"They do?" I asked, surprise threading up my throat. I hadn't known that.

He inclined his head, dragging his goblet over and taking a long sip of his wine.

"There was a *Vorakkar* who passed the Trials only two years ago whose horde crumbled after a few moon cycles. It happens. I was determined not to be one of them. And I *learned*. You will do the same."

"You say that so easily," I said. I was reminded how easy I

found talking to him, at least when we weren't fighting. Under the Dead Mountain, I'd found talking to him as easy as breathing. Only, I supposed, he'd had a single-minded interest in capturing my attention then. To make me like him, to make me free him.

"Because I know it's true," he said, his voice so low and without hesitation that I wanted to blindly believe him. But that had gotten me into trouble before, and I didn't plan on making that mistake again. "You like to learn. You soak up our language frighteningly fast. You watch the horde and study its movements…and I know because I've watched you too. Today, you went to the tannery because you wanted to see it and explore it for yourself, though even seasoned horde members avoid that area like a plague. And you memorized the map of Dakkar, didn't you? You know all the territories, all the rivers and lakes and seas, all the mountain ranges. Hukri told me you even memorized the Dakkari words written across it."

I stared at him in surprise. He'd…been watching me this whole time? Keeping an eye out for me, even when I wasn't aware of it?

"Maybe I'm trying to learn as much as I can to make it easier to leave this place. Maybe I study the maps so I know which direction to run. Maybe I try to learn Dakkari so I can communicate with any hordes that come across my path."

I didn't know why I said those things to him. Things that I knew were lost to me now. No, not lost exactly. Just…willingly forgotten.

I'd made an agreement with Wrune, regardless of how that agreement had come to pass. I would honor my word, just as I expected him to honor his. And if last night was anything to go by, he would not only keep his word, he would give me exactly what I wanted. Tess, free and safe.

To give him credit, my husband didn't even blink at the

words that tumbled from my lips. Instead, a gruff sound emerged from his throat and he brought me closer to him. The kiss he gave me this time *was* the spine-tingling kind. Passionate and deep, and before I knew it, I was clutching onto his forearm because I was afraid I'd topple over.

Against my lips, he murmured, "If that is all true, *rei sarkia*, then you only make me more determined to give you a reason to *choose* me." My heart gave a pitiful little thud. "To stay willingly because you want to."

"And how would you do that?" I asked, curious.

"I have yet to present you your *deviri*," he told me. I remembered that word. The bride gift. The wedding gift. "Shall we do that this night to help sway you? Or should I take you right to bed and exhaust you so much you won't be able to run away?"

"Both are tempting," I managed to choke out, leaning away from him, trying to calm the thundering of my heart. "But for now, I think I simply wish to finish my meal."

His low chuckle spread goose bumps over my arms. *That sound.* I had the strangest urge to see if I could bottle it, to keep it with me forever, to pull the stopper off the vial whenever I wanted just so I could hear it at my leisure.

"I like your laugh," I found myself telling him. Though the next moment, I ducked my head in embarrassment, quickly picking up the dish of spiced, boiled nuts.

His hand slid from my neck, back down my spine. If I didn't know any better, I would think *I'd* dumbfounded *him* by the way I caught him staring at me. At a loss for words, for once in his life?

If all nights were like this one, Wrune wouldn't have to tempt me to stay, I mused. He wouldn't need to entice me with silks or jewels or golden trinkets. He wouldn't need to keep me limp and dazed and satisfied on his furs until I couldn't move a muscle.

"Maybe it's your laugh that will make me want to stay," I confessed quietly, darting a quick look over at him.

"Then you will hear it more often, *rei Morakkari*," he promised.

CHAPTER 44

"Ask it," Hukri ordered me.

For my *piki*, I was discovering that she was actually quite bossy. Not that I minded.

"Hmm?"

"Ask whatever you wish to ask me, *missiki*," she said, sending me a pointed look as we walked through the horde. Our daily walks, one of many. It was evening, however, and the red color from the sunset was making everyone uneasy. It wasn't often there was a red sunset. As such, many of the horde had retreated to their *volikis* for the night.

As we passed domed tents, I heard dozens of different voices, of laughter. A moan or two, which only spiked my curiosity. It made me realize, however, that *volikis* were not as soundproof as I thought. It made me flush, wondering if Wrune's entire horde had heard my own moans and cries this last week, echoing through the quiet camp. Then I thought it was probably best our *voliki* was situated apart from the others, if only to allow more privacy.

The last week had been...conflicting. And truthfully, I found it a little worrisome how *easy* life felt within Wrune's horde. I'd been so used to struggle and hardship the majority of my life that living here was...*strange.*

And life with Wrune?

Even more so.

My belly fluttered whenever I spied him throughout the horde. Pinching anticipation built inside me once night fell because I knew that I'd have him to myself soon. He had me addicted to his taste, his scent, his touch, his voice. He had me craving the pleasure only he could give me, pleasure he wrang from me every moment he got.

At night, we took our meals together. He'd spoken to me briefly about the outpost—the *saruk* of Rath Rowin, he called it, his grandfather's own—where he'd grown up. A cold fortress on the border of the North Lands, though it lay to the west, where the temperatures weren't as frigid.

I got the impression it hadn't been a *happy* childhood, not quite. He rarely spoke of his father, though I'd asked about him. He'd never known his mother, though he'd often heard tales of her from his grandparents.

In turn, I told him about my own village. About my father. About my aunt. Though I said nothing about what happened after the village burned, about Song's murder, about Benn's leadership, about the Dead Mountain. It went unspoken between us. And I preferred it that way.

And at night, after he'd wrung pleasure from me and taken his own release, I slept against him. When he fell asleep before me, I'd press my face to his chest and listen to his even breaths. I'd trace the scars across his abdomen that I didn't have the courage to ask him about. In those moments, I wondered what it would be like to have him as my own. In those moments, I pretended that he was.

And what I felt building within me those nights was a frightening thing because I realized that I was beginning to care for Wrune. Care for him in a way I knew I shouldn't.

In those darkened nights, I wondered if that was what happiness felt like. Or at least a deep, comforting contentedness.

And that made me feel conflicted. Because I felt like I was turning my back on the silent promise I'd made to Tess. I felt like I shouldn't *feel* this happy when there were others that were suffering, especially when I knew what that suffering felt like.

"You've been holding your tongue all day," Hukri added, shaking me from my thoughts. During the day, when we walked through the horde, she tended to trail behind me, as a gesture of respect for my position. Now that there weren't many Dakkari lingering around the encampment as witnesses, she strode at my side. Like a friend. A confidant.

That was exactly what she'd become to me.

The words prompted me to remember another issue I'd been mulling. One that made me embarrassed but which bothered me.

I stopped on the pathway, a natural road that had been made by the daily steps and strides of over a hundred Dakkari and a handful of humans.

Lowering my voice, I told her, "The *Vorakkar*...he hasn't... he..."

My tongue felt tied in a different way than what I'd experienced the majority of my life. After that excruciating power, mingled with that sharp, uncontrolled pain I'd felt on the plains, I rarely stammered over my words. I didn't understand it. Whether it was a gift from Kakkari or whether that pain had been a payment, the cost of giving me my words back...I didn't know.

"He pleasures me," I told her, feeling my face flame at the whispered admission. "And he takes his own release, but...since the night of the *tassimara*, he's never attempted to *join* with me."

Wrune usually spent his seed over the furs, rolling his hips to the rhythm of my moans, or he stroked himself to release, the long arcs of his seed landing on my belly or breasts, which seemed to please him immensely.

He'd even let me touch *him* a few times. I'd taken his cock in my hand, curious even as I squeezed my thighs against the throbbing sensation that pounded there. I'd loved watching the expressions that came over his face as I stroked him, almost as much as hearing his deep, endless groan and the thick heat of his seed as it rolled down the back of my hand.

Yet he'd never nudged that cock against me and thrust into me. I'd been aching to feel him inside me again. I'd been aching to feel that primal, dizzying sensation as his thick cock rubbed and teased places I never knew could feel that *good*.

"Oh," Hukri whispered. To her credit, she hid her surprise well. I was used to the expression she commonly wore whenever I asked her these kinds of things. One of patience and understanding.

"Is that strange?" I asked, frowning.

"Well..." She trailed off, and my shoulders sagged. "I'm not... certain."

"I knew it was strange," I said, sighing, and resumed my steps. After a moment, Hukri followed until she caught up with me. "I ask myself why that is, why he won't. And all I can think is that he wants the horde to know we...well, the washers have been busy with our furs, haven't they? And the seamstresses mended a couple when Wr—when the *Vorakkar* dug his claws into them."

"*Lysi*," Hukri said carefully. "There has been no gossip within the horde that the *Vorakkar* has not been in your bed— that I can assure you."

And I'd started to notice that no one met my eyes anymore. If I asked anything of anyone, they immediately jumped to procure me whatever I needed. The *bikkus*, the seamstresses. Even the *mrikro*, the *pyroki* master, had taken time to entertain my questions about the fascinating creatures.

"I need to ask him, don't I?" I murmured, thinking about how uncomfortable that conversation might be. I had no experience in these situations. None. Just the thought of confronting Wrune about it made me flush.

"Or just demand it," Hukri said, shrugging her shoulder. "Dakkari males are simple, *missiki*. Get him on his back, tell him what you want, and he will not deny you."

The image of that, of Wrune on his back underneath me, was oddly tantalizing. Just the thought made me swallow. *Hard.* All golden flesh and hard muscles that I could dig my nails into.

"You think that would really work?" I asked softly, biting my lip.

Hukri's lyrical laugh rose between us, gentle and lovely. "It works on my mate."

My laugh joined hers as we rounded a curve in the road, heading toward the training grounds, where we usually turned around to loop back.

"Or ask him," Hukri said when her laugh settled. "He is honest with you, is he not?"

"Yes," I said softly. *Lately,* I amended silently. "He has been."

He kept me updated on the plans for the Dead Mountain at least. Almost nightly, he told me what was discussed at the daily council meetings, though he was receiving pushback from the elders. When he told me the journey would take time to plan, he hadn't been lying. The elders were currently arguing among themselves on how many *darukkars* could be spared for such an endeavor.

"Then ask him," Hukri said simply.

Before the training grounds even came into view, I heard the deep timbre of Wrune's voice. Just the sound of it made my steps speed...until I realized he sounded angry. Low and cold and even. I recognized that tone.

When we rounded the last corner, I saw he was talking with a male I'd seen around the encampment. An older *darukkar*, though his age had done nothing to diminish the obvious strength of him, the sheer *breadth* of him.

The *darukkar* was staring Wrune straight in the eyes, which made me straighten in disbelief now that I knew the disrespect of it. The two males were alone, standing outside the council's *voliki* as if the *darukkar* had approached Wrune as he'd exited it. And with darkness falling, their hushed tones only made their conversation seem more tense. Even from a distance, their body language was tight. I watched Wrune take a quick step toward the *darukkar*, heard him utter a string of clipped words.

They stared at one another for a long moment. Then I watched as the *darukkar finally* lowered his gaze.

His head inclined. He stepped away. I released a breath I hadn't known I'd been holding.

"That is Besik," Hukri whispered to me, close to my ear. Neither male had spotted us or heard our approach. "That is Junira's *pattar*."

I recognized that word. It meant *father*.

And, of course, I knew about Junira.

Wrune said something else, but even for Hukri, I knew it was too quiet and too far away to hear it.

Besik stormed away, coming straight toward us. When he saw us, lingering close to the nearest *voliki*, his expression tightened, his eyes flickering to me briefly before they snapped away.

"*Darukkar*," Hukri greeted, nodding her head.

Besik didn't pause in his quiet, angry strides. He said nothing, pushing past us, heading back up the road. When I looked back to Wrune, I saw the dark glare he had pinned to Besik's back.

When those red eyes found mine, that expression signifi-cantly softened, but I still saw the tightness in his shoulders. When he reached us, he pulled me to his side, his hand curving around my hip.

"*Piki,*" he murmured in greeting, his voice still roughened with his mood, though he was trying to hide it. Then he said, "Go home to your mate and your child. I'll see to my wife this night."

"*Lysi, Vorakkar,*" she murmured, ducking her head. She met my gaze briefly before it flickered away. "Good night, *missiki.*"

"Good night," I told her, giving her hand a brief squeeze before she turned and made her way back up the path that led to her own family.

When I tilted my head back to regard Wrune, I saw he was already watching me. His hand came up to my cheek, and he took advantage of the position to kiss me, soft yet rough. I never cared *how* he kissed me. I craved anything he gave me, and this kiss was no different. By the time he pulled away, I was clinging to the thin tunic he wore and already tingling between my thighs.

"Ravenous, *rei Morakkari,*" he purred, his voice significantly softer. "*Jiria.* Let's go home, *lysi?*"

Home. Such a wonderful, tiny word. And yet it meant so much.

I nodded, and we turned down the pathway. We didn't speak a single word as we wound our way back to the *voliki,* both content to remain quiet until we were alone. But his warm palm never left my hip, and I found the tight grip comforting.

Once we were back inside the *voliki,* I saw our evening meal had been delivered, but for once, I wasn't all that hungry. I'd eaten a large afternoon meal, but I would happily graze as I watched Wrune eat the majority of it.

A bath had been filled too, though the water looked cool. I watched Wrune go to the fire basin and take one of the heated rocks there. He dropped it into the bath, along with a few others, until steam curled and danced across the water.

Then he came to me, and my lips parted when he began to unclasp the dress I wore at the shoulders. The slip slid down me like silk, pooling at my feet, leaving me naked before him.

"You want to bathe before you eat?" I asked.

"*Lysi*," he murmured, his eyes running over me as he got undressed himself. His movements were slow and methodical, and my gaze was rapt on every bit of skin he uncovered, making a low chuckle rise from his throat. "*Ravenous.*"

When he was nude, he led me over to the bathing tub and helped me climb inside. I sighed in contentment as I kneeled, the hot water making me want to moan in delight. Wrune slid behind me, but then he turned me so that I straddled his hips.

"I want to look at you," he explained to me when I cast him a speculative look, and then he smoothed hot water over the tops of my shoulders. My spine tingled at his touch. Whenever we bathed together, it always ended with water soaking the carpets. Usually from me frantically rocking against him as his fingers lazily rolled and pressed against my clit.

When I looked at him, I could see the tension in the lines of his expression, in the stiffness of his shoulders. I wondered if it had been his encounter with Besik, but even before tonight, I'd begun to notice it.

My hands came to rest on his chest, but he caught my wrist and pressed his lips to my *Morakkari* markings. Warmth bloomed in my chest, sudden and fierce. It was one thing when he kissed and touched me in front of his horde because a part of me assumed it was for...performance. I assumed it was another of Wrune's "messages."

It was another thing entirely when we were alone.

To distract myself from that feeling, I asked, breathless, "What were you speaking to the *darukkar* about?"

He continued to press kisses to my wrist, his lips lingering over the vein on the inside of it. However, I felt the way the muscles in his chest tightened underneath my other palm despite his apparent nonchalance.

I knew he would tell me. Every question I'd asked of him in the past week, he'd given me his answer freely.

"I know he's Junira's *pattar*," I told him. "Yes?"

"*Lysi,*" Wrune replied. "He said a lot of things throughout the horde after our *tassimara*. I simply found the time to make my feelings about it known."

"What things?" I asked, though I feared I knew.

"About me. About you," he said.

"He didn't look happy with the conversation," I noted, thinking about the tension that had thrummed through the both of them.

"He is one of my best *darukkars*. He knows this. And he uses it to his advantage, thinking he has more free will than the others. This evening, I told him that he would be one of the warriors I took to the Dead Mountain and he refused."

I straightened in his lap. "He refused you?" I repeated quietly.

"*Lysi,*" Wrune said, his hands sliding down my arms, his gaze flickering to my breasts which just sat on the surface of the water, ripples of it lapping at my nipples. "And so I accepted his refusal but told him that after this season, I expected him to return to *Dothik.*"

"W-What?" I whispered, wide eyed, even as Wrune cupped my breasts, lifting them. They were heavy in his palms.

He leaned forward and suckled lazily at one of my nipples, making my breath hitch.

"Wrune," I murmured, pushing him back a little so I could meet his eyes. "I don't want to be the reason any of your horde members are sent away."

His eyes narrowed. His hands fell away from my breasts, and he settled more deeply against the back of the bathing tub, his arms resting on the edges. The ends of his dark hair dipped underneath the water. His chest was wet and shimmering, and just the sight of him like this was making it hard to think.

"It is *your* horde too," he commented.

"What?" I asked, blinking.

"Are you not *Morakkari* of this horde? Do you not have more power and influence now than even my own *pujerak*?"

Oh.

"As such, any slight against you is a slight against me. Besik made his choice. He knew what he was doing in refusing my order, and I called him on his bluff. I don't tolerate games like that. Not in my own horde. Not when lives are at stake. He has served me well since the beginning days, but in the last weeks, he has shown me I cannot trust him. If I cannot trust him, I cannot rely on him. He is not loyal to Rath Rowin, to the horde. He is only loyal to his own interests. He will find *Dothik* a fitting place to live, if he does not choose to return to the outpost where he was born."

"And if he apologizes?" I asked.

Wrune blew out a long breath, and I leaned into him. Everything he said made sense. I'd come to realize that Wrune valued loyalty above all things, which was why we'd had such a rough start together.

However, he'd said himself that Besik had been a part of the horde since the beginning.

"Surely one mistake should not cost him his place in the horde," I murmured.

I pressed harder against him. Wrune's eyes flickered, shifting between mine before sliding between us. I could feel his hard cock against my belly. And when I moved down slightly, I felt the heat of him against my lower lips, the curls of my sex brushing against him.

"Always one for mercy, *rei sarkia*," he rasped, his voice significantly rougher than it was a moment ago. His pupils were dilating, so black that I could see myself in them. "When some do not deserve it."

"Let him cool down," I urged. "Let him make amends if he wishes. Everyone deserves a second chance, don't you think?"

A low sound built up in his throat. "You gave me one," he murmured quietly, his hand lifting from the tub's edge to run through my hair. Pleasure zinged up my spine as he brought me forward for a kiss. The taste and heat of him was so familiar. I found kissing him as comforting as sleeping beside him.

"And you gave me one," I added, against his lips.

He grunted, pulling away, desire in his eyes when he realized I'd begun to rock against him. "You think to sway my decision like this?" he growled softly.

"I can try, *setovan*," I told him, leaning forward. *Stubborn male.* Slowly, I kissed his neck, and I smiled when I felt the bob of his throat against my skin. "Or I can call you *sailon* tonight. Your choice."

"Enough talk of Besik," he ordered, leaning his head to the side as I brushed my lips along his jawline. "And you will call me *sailon*."

I grinned though my smile slowly died when his hands wrapped around my buttocks, cupping them and squeezing. Wrune kept his claws shorn now, if only so he wouldn't cut my flesh when he got a little too...*enthusiastic* with me.

"*Sailon*?" I whispered. *Darling.*

He grunted in approval.

There was another thing I wanted to speak with him about this night. About sex with him. Though thinking of bringing it up right now made my tongue feel a little tight. And so I thought of what Hukri told me to do. Pin him down and demand it from him. Well, Wrune *was* underneath me. All it would take was to tilt my hips, and I could lower down onto him.

Hukri had told me Dakkari males were simple when it came to sex.

Did the same apply to Dakkari *Vorakkar*?

"Wrune," I whispered, rocking my hips against his cock. Just a little to the left and he would nudge my clit and... "*Ahh,*" I moaned before biting my lip.

"*Vok,*" he huffed, that familiar tightness coming over his expression when he looked between us. That gaze flickered to where I was using his cock underneath the water. Then I watched as it trailed up my body, to the way my breasts swayed as I moved. "You make me so *vokking* hard looking at you. Look at the way you move over me, *rei sarkia. Leika.* Perfection."

His praise almost felt as good as the sensations that were building inside me.

I lifted higher and dragged my sex over his cock. His hands tightened on my buttocks as he groaned, and he used his strength to help me grind down harder.

I felt myself entering that state of mind where nothing mattered but *him,* but *pleasure.* I'd found Wrune could easily drive me to madness. I'd found...that I could do the same to him. Only not enough madness to make him thrust that thick, hot cock inside me.

I lifted higher, feeling determination thread through me.

Tonight, I thought.

Tonight it would happen. It *needed* to. Because I couldn't take this uncertainty anymore.

I lifted my hips high enough, pressing my knees into the bottom of the tub so I felt the head of his rounded cock nudge at my entrance.

A rough huff fell from him. His eyes closed, as if he was *savoring* the sensation. So *why* wouldn't he give me what I wanted? What I craved?

With his cock just underneath me, I snapped my hips down in a smooth, quick motion. His cock slid *deep.* I'd forgotten how big he was inside me, but I only felt a brief pinching sensation before it gave way to a feeling of *fullness* and *heat*.

Wrune's eyes flew open.

His hands gripped my buttocks tighter, but a moment later, he used that grip as leverage to pull me off him.

His cock slipped from my body, and I felt the loss of it. Frustration rose inside me.

"*What are you doing?*" my husband growled.

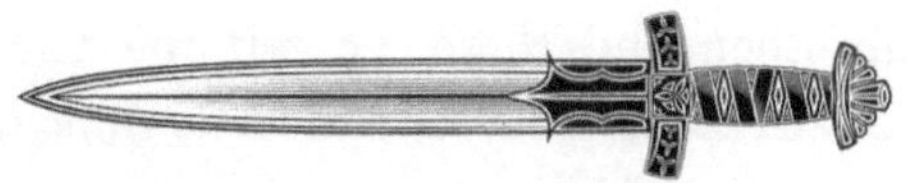

CHAPTER 45

*V*okking hell, I thought.

Didn't she know how little control I already had when it came to her?

"And I would ask you the same thing," she rasped, still trying to rock her hips over me.

"*Neffar?*"

I couldn't think. She'd pulled all reasonable thought from my mind.

"Mina, stop," I groaned when I felt the heat of her cunt find the head of my cock once more. "*Kakkari*, I'm *trying* to be good, and you do *this*."

She let out a little cry of frustration.

"Are you denying us both because you still want to send a message to the horde?" she growled. The first time I'd possibly ever heard that tone from her, and *vok* if it didn't make me even harder.

Until I registered the words coming out of her mouth.

I frowned, bewildered. "*Neffar?* What are you talking about?"

"The furs!" she exclaimed, as if that would clear up any confusion in my mind instead of adding to it.

"Wife," I growled. "When you have your mate underneath you with a cock so hard it feels like a *vokking* boulder, do not speak in riddles. I can't *vokking* think right now!"

Her lips parted in surprise.

Our breath heaved as we stared at each other, and my *deva* were still throbbing from that brief memory of sliding deep into her cunt. *Vok* if it didn't take every bit of my self-control *not* to fuck her right then and there. I'd felt the tension slowly building with each passing day, and the only thing that cured it was remembering that I'd hurt her the first time. That I'd made her *bleed*.

Then she said, "You've been spending your seed all over the furs each night instead of *inside me*. Ever since that first morning. So that when our furs were washed, the rumors circulating through the horde would be silenced. So that everyone would know we shared our bed again, that we'd mended the tear between us."

I blinked, disbelief running through me.

"Is it true?" Mina asked. "Because I think the horde got the message. They don't need any more."

"You think that I've been fucking the damn furs each morning and night because I need to send a message to the horde?" I asked, my tone low and dark.

"Well...*yes*," my wife said, her expression bewildered. "Hukri said—"

"*Vokking* hell," I cursed, only imagining what her *piki* had to say about this. "That first morning you made me so crazed I would've come anywhere. I wasn't thinking of sending a message to the horde when I was too busy eating out your cunt —believe me, *sarkia*."

Mina blinked. A look of pleasure crossed her face, briefly, but it gave way to confusion as she asked, "Really?"

"Sending a message to the horde was an afterthought. A

convenient one, but that was the only time it was intentionally done. *That* morning," I said, running a hand down my face.

"Then *why* haven't you been..." She trailed off, her cheeks reddening.

"Fucking you?" I growled, eyeing her.

"Yes," she whispered. "Do you not want to?"

I would have laughed in disbelief at the sheer ridiculousness of her question...but her tone was vulnerable. Embarrassed.

Like it was *her* that had been doing something wrong. Like it was *her* that had done something to make me *not* want that.

"Of course I do," I murmured, wishing my voice wasn't so rough and dark. Wishing it was softer for her. "I want you so bad it *vokking* aches."

Mina exhaled softly. Then her brows furrowed. "Then why haven't we been...?"

Wasn't it obvious?

It was my turn to be confused. Didn't she know?

"Because I don't want to hurt you again," I said gruffly.

"Hurt me?" she asked, shaking her head. "You didn't—"

"*Tysi*, I did," I growled. "You said I made you *bleed*. The morning after the *tassimara*, I could hear you wincing as we walked to get our markings completed, and it *vokking* ate at me, knowing I did that to you! I was too rough with you. Maybe you were right. Maybe we don't fit. You're so small, and I don't want to hurt you again or I'd never forgive myself for it."

"What?" she whispered, her eyes going round in astonishment.

Then she did something I didn't expect.

She began to laugh.

A beautiful sound, light and husky, it sounded almost like a song.

Affection slid deep into my chest—warring with my own

frustration—and I closed my eyes briefly, listening to that laugh, though I didn't feel like laughing myself at that moment.

It slowly died away as she regarded me, and then her expression softened. It softened in a way that made my *vokking* heart flip, something I didn't know if it had ever done before. I rubbed at it, scowling, when she leaned forward.

Her gentle kiss made a rough groan rise in my throat. She tilted her head as I murmured, "I'm glad you find this situation amusing, wife."

"Oh, you *setovan*," she exclaimed, biting gently at my bottom lip before she soothed it with her tongue. My cock bobbed against my abdomen as she did. "I find it incredibly funny and a little bit ridiculous now. Because we could have had this sorted a week ago."

I pulled back. "What do you mean?"

"You made me bleed because I'd never been with a male before you," she told me. With a dazed expression on her face, she added, "I think you knew that though. Because you were as gentle as you could be. But you *are* very, very big."

"And you are quite small," I said gruffly.

"*Lysi*," she said in Dakkari, teasing me with that whispered word. "But I liked it."

My nostrils flared. "*Neffar?*"

"I mean, it was really, *really* good, wasn't it?" she continued.

"*Lysi*," I growled. "It was."

"I didn't feel any pain after those first few moments. The soreness came later, but it was the first time—I would adapt to it. The only thing I didn't like that night was that you left so abruptly. I thought that maybe I'd done something wrong. Or that maybe you didn't like what we did..."

Vok.

And I realized that there was so much I needed to explain to her. So much I needed to make her understand about me. About how I was raised. About my father. About the aspirations

I had for the horde and the decisions I'd made to help me reach them.

I'd kept her in the dark about a lot of things. I'd told her of my outpost, though briefly. I'd told her about my mother's parents. I'd told her about the horde's travels throughout Dakkar.

But I hadn't really told her anything of importance. About why I was the way I was.

For now, however...

I wanted to be in the right state of mind for that conversation, and right now, with her naked in my lap, with my cock jutting between us as she whispered to me that she'd liked the way I'd fucked her...

I was *definitely* not in the right state of mind to even broach any of those topics, much less my father.

"That had nothing to do with you," I told her.

I spied a little relief in her eyes. "Really?"

Vok, I felt like a monster for making her think so.

And I groaned, understanding why she'd laughed because it *was* quite ridiculous.

Then I shook myself. I realized I had my wife, my queen, my mate naked and aching in my lap. She'd *liked* what we'd done. And remembering the way she'd rocked against me mere moments ago, I realized she wanted more. Much, much more.

I was such a fool.

Then again, this female scrambled my *vokking* mind, so I didn't beat myself up too much about it. Even from the beginning, she'd had that effect on me.

My hands slid around her backside again, making her straighten. Underneath the water, I reached below her until the backs of my fingers stroked her folds. Her eyes sparked, her gaze going half-lidded, which I always loved to see.

She was so beautiful, and I took my time as I ran my gaze over her. Always so eager and curious to explore this with me.

"Wrune," she murmured, a plea, squirming in my lap as she began to rock her hips against me again. Coming from her, the sound of my given name didn't fill me with dread. Coming from her, she transformed it into something intimate and something soft. I wanted to hear it falling from her lips all night long.

"You want me to fuck you, *leika*?" I purred to her, capturing her lips when she inched toward me.

"*Yes.*"

"You want me deep inside you?" I murmured against her lips. "You want to feel my seed shooting into you as you come around my cock?"

She gasped. When I pulled back, her eyes were determined. I could see her desire for me, and I felt her shift upward again.

"Yes," she told me. "I want all of that."

When her folds met the head of my cock, I felt a warning sizzle in my *deva*. *Vok*, I didn't need to come the *moment* she got me inside of her. But she made so *crazed*.

"I will not last long," I warned her, gritting my teeth. "*Oh, vok! Mina.*"

My head tilted back against the tub's edge, eyes rolling back, my abdomen and legs tightening underneath her as she slowly fed my cock into her tight sheath.

Unlike the first time, she took her time. This was for her, I knew. Letting her body get used to me again, and I held as still as I possibly could. She lowered down onto my cock, rolling her hips only until a couple inches of it were inside her. Then she lifted off. Then lowered. Then lifted.

"*Voook*," I breathed, focusing on my breath as she used my cock. The head was the most sensitive part—as was my *dakke*, the bump of flesh above the base, but luckily she was nowhere near that. Or else I would've exploded already.

I'd needed this for too long. Every morning and night with her only provided a new, excruciating test of my own self-control and discipline.

Now she was giving me everything I'd wanted since our *tassimara*.

A constant rumbling purr was threading up from my throat. When I looked at her face, I almost came right then and there. Pure pleasure and delight were spread across her expression. Her cheeks and lips were flushed. Her eyes were glassy.

I realized what she was doing.

"You're teasing me," I growled.

A dazed smile stole over her face.

"I think you deserve some punishment for being so stubborn," she replied, making my nostrils flare. When she sank deeper onto my cock, making us both moan, she added, though her voice was shaky now, "I think we both do."

Another lift, another snap of her hips down, which made her breasts bob.

Each thrust was getting harder. Each thrust, she took me deeper and deeper.

And soon her lips parted in disbelief when she took all of me.

My cock throbbed inside the tight heat of her cunt.

"*Lysi*," I hissed. "*Vok*, you feel so good, *rei kassikari*."

My fated mate.

"You do too," she whispered, huffing as she rolled her hips. She threw me a victorious smile, though it was accompanied by a low gasp. "No pain. And we fit. *So well.* See?"

A pleased growl rose from deep in my chest. Her eyes widened at it because she knew what it meant. That I was on the verge of losing my control.

Grabbing her waist, I thrust my hips up, and she huffed, a loud moan tumbling from her throat as her head lolled back.

"*Yes*," she whispered. "Again, Wrune."

I did as she ordered, only too happy to give my *Morakkari* what she desired, what we both did.

A small wave of water crashed over the edge of the bathing

tub as I began to fuck her. Her arms looped around my neck though her nails dug into the backs of my shoulders. As I thrust my hips up, she snapped hers down, and it made my *deva* throb. My *dakke* thrummed over her clit every time she did that, and my greedy little female wanted *more*.

"Faster," she pleaded, breathless.

My jaw tightened. I knew her command would be the end of me. I was already too close to the edge, and every time her clit met my *dakke*, it made the base of my tail tingle.

We were making a mess. The rugs were soaked, and soon there would be no more water left in the washing tub.

Mina gasped when I stood, unannounced and swift. Yet she moaned in frustration when I pulled her off my cock and scooped her from the bath.

We didn't make it far. Next to the fire basin, I brought us down, pushing her onto her front on the plush, dry rugs.

"Hands and knees, *Morakkari*," I rasped, using the brief reprieve from her body as a way to get myself back under control. "*Now.*"

Mina bit her lip but did as I ordered, positioning her body as I watched. I squeezed the base of my cock.

"Like this?" she whispered, looking at me over her shoulder.

"Perfect," I growled, swallowing hard. Perhaps this position had been a mistake. Already I felt my seed climbing up my shaft at the mere erotic sight of her. "So *vokking* perfect."

She flushed, pleased, and then her eyes dropped to my cock. I didn't leave her aching for long, and I kneeled behind her. Readying.

"*Ohhh*," she cried out when I pushed into her. Deep. Her tone told me she only felt pleasure, however, not pain. Relief mingled with the fierce ache I felt for her.

I gripped her hips harder. After slowly withdrawing, I thrust forward as I brought her hips back. Our flesh made a satisfying slap together as I went as deep as I could possibly go.

Mina's back arched, and she huffed and groaned.

"Good?" I grunted.

"So good," she said. "*Wrune!*"

With that final confirmation, I felt my fear leave me. With my name on her lips, I began to fuck her the way I'd always craved.

Driving into her body, fast and hard. My vision dimmed. My breath went ragged. My only focus was on the feel of her clenching around my cock and the little, beautiful moans that echoed around our *voliki*.

"*Rei Morakkari,*" I growled. "*Mine.*"

Vok, *this feels so right,* I thought. Like we'd always been meant for this.

"Tell me!"

"Yours," she choked out, meeting my eyes, her gaze half-lidded, her arms beginning to shake as she fought to hold herself up.

"Tell me," I ordered her, my voice changed. That deep, primal instinct was rising. She wore my markings around her wrists, but I wanted to mark every inch of her flesh. Because she was *mine.* She was always meant to be.

She knew what I wanted, my perfect, perfect female.

"*Lo rune tei'ri, rei Vorakkar,*" she vowed. *I am yours.*

Rei Vorakkar.

My horde king, she'd said.

Those words triggered my release, sudden and shocking, catching me by surprise. My shuddering bellow lifted to the domed ceiling as I thrust into her, my rhythm going choppy and short. When I felt her clench around me, when I heard her moans and saw her hands digging into the rug, I felt her orgasm only lengthen my own.

"*Lysi,*" I groaned. "So good. You feel so good, my Mina."

I'd spoken in Dakkari, I realized belatedly.

Her arms finally gave out from underneath her when her

pleasure reached its end. I caught her quickly before she fell, bringing her up so her back was to my chest. Inside her, my cock continued to pulse.

Tilting her head, I leaned down and kissed her, lazy yet needful. She gasped into me as she caught her breath.

"Need you again, *rei kassi*," I murmured against her lips. "And I intend to have you."

Always, I added silently.

The fire popped gently, and the light flickered, casting deep shadows around the *voliki*. Wrune usually added another chunk of fire fuel when it got this low, but my husband was relaxed beneath me and I didn't think I could move off him. My bones felt like jelly, and his heartbeat under my cheek brought a comforting sense of safety, of peace.

I want to lie here forever, I thought, feeling that troubling pang of guilt that arrived with it.

His dulled claws ran over my shoulder and down my arm. I didn't know what time of the night it was. Whether it wasn't yet midnight or if it was the early hours of morning. All I knew was that we'd been ravenous for one another and after the third or fourth or fifth coupling, we'd finally fallen into a sated heap.

We were still on the floor. We'd never made it to the bed, but since we were close to the basin, I was warm. The chill of night would never dare to reach me when I was tucked so closely to my husband, in the safety of his arms.

I want to lie here forever, I thought again. I felt a warmth building inside me at the thought. I held on to it, letting it grow. I fed it, nourished it, and in my hazy dreamlike state, I asked it to protect us because I knew that it would. I didn't want anything to touch us again. I wanted to keep him safe. Always.

"Mina," came his gruff voice, an urgent, quiet tinge in his tone.

I blinked and then realized what I'd done. Wrune's sword had been to his right, alongside our clothes. I heard the ring of the sword as it made contact with something unseen. The clothing was sprawled clear across the room, and his sword hit the side of the bathing tub with a dull chime. It held there, floating, rippling against something invisible.

I knew what I'd done, though I knew it had caused no harm. Luckily I hadn't cast the barrier far. Only a little more and I would've toppled over the fire basin and sent ash and sparks flying.

"Sorry," I whispered, staring at his sword, feeling the sudden tension within Wrune. I closed my eyes, breathing, focusing on that ball of solid warmth inside me, and then I twisted it, severing it in two, and then I dragged in a deep lungful of air.

The humming—something I hadn't noticed before now—ceased. The sword clattered to the wet rugs. Wrune relaxed, ever so slightly.

I sat up, feeling Wrune's large, hot palm slide from my arm to curve around the expanse of my back. His touch kept me grounded, and I focused on it as my mind reeled. I...I was beginning to realize that I'd always had this thing inside me. It was familiar. I just hadn't realized what it could do. Even when I was a child.

"You are not alone in this, *rei Morakkari*," Wrune's voice sounded from behind me as I stared at his sword next to the tub. He was still lying on the floor, staring up at me as he stroked my back, as if he sensed that I needed his comfort. "Those with Kakkari's gifts have been recorded throughout our history. In the past century, however, there have not been many."

My brow furrowed. "Why do you think that is?"

"Kakkari's power is seated in *balance*," he told me. "In all things. In the earth, in the forests, in the seas, in her creatures, and in her *people*. One thing is a certainty on Dakkar at present."

Balance?

"That there is an *imbalance*," I finished for him, looking over my shoulder at him, seeing his red eyes gleam with satisfaction at my answer. "The fog."

"Even before then," he told me, shaking his head. "Though some might not have seen it."

"The Ghertun?"

He inclined his head. "And the *Dothikkar* himself."

I stilled, not expecting him to say such a thing about his own king. Then again, we'd always heard the whispers of unrest between the *Dothikkar* and his horde kings.

"His greed stretches far, whereas his own strength does not," Wrune told me. "Imbalance in power. A king of the Dakkari that has never once stepped foot in the wildlands, where Kakkari herself lives in all things."

"Are you saying that the fog is a...a punishment? An act of rebalancing the power on Dakkar?"

"Perhaps," Wrune said. "Roth Drokka's queen used the heartstone under the Dead Mountain. That type of power is *immense*. It draws on *everything* to use it. If there was already an imbalance on Dakkar, the heartstone would have been the last drop that tipped the scales."

"And me?" I whispered. "And the others?"

Wrune's expression softened. "Kakkari's warriors."

My brow furrowed. My lips parted.

His expression darkened. "But your gift comes at a price. They always seem to."

"What do you mean?"

"Rath Drokka and his queen both possess gifts of Kakkari," he said. Yes, he'd mentioned it before. "Drokka can speak to the dead. He has since he was a child apparently." My lips parted. "His *Morakkari* can influence the will of others."

"And what is the price that Kakkari demands of them?" I asked, feeling a chill down my spine.

Wrune blew out a long breath. "Drokka was—and *is*—called the Mad Horde King. Many thought him out of his mind. Screaming into the night. Speaking to things that were not there."

My lips pressed together.

"And his queen...she experienced great pain whenever she used her own gift, sometimes leaving her bedridden for days."

Our eyes connected and held.

"I know what you felt out on the plains, Mina," he murmured. "I felt that pain, and I don't want you to feel it again."

"That was the only time," I told him, shaking my head. "The only time that it ever happened, and only because I pushed my limits. Usually, I would just feel drained of my strength, of my energy."

He took in a deep breath. "Still, I will not risk you using it."

"I don't feel tired now," I whispered to him, shifting until I turned to face him, kneeling next to his side. Between my legs, I felt a tight twinge, but I ignored it, knowing that it would take time to get used to him again. I pressed my hand to his chest, warming it on his skin. "Just the opposite."

"What were you thinking of?" he wanted to know. "Just now?"

My cheeks heated a little, and a sound of interest rose from his throat at the sight of it.

"Tell me," he murmured, leaning up. His hand slid into my

hair, and I practically *melted* at the sensation of his touch. "Tell me, *rei Morakkari*."

"I was just thinking that I wanted to be like we were forever," I whispered, feeling a little silly saying it out loud. His gaze flooded black at the words, his hand tightening in my hair. I touched his forearm, the heat of his gold cuffs warming my thumb. "That I wanted nothing to touch us, that I wanted to keep us safe."

"You enclosed me inside with you," he noted.

I swallowed and nodded. "Yes."

Biting my lip, I thought about telling him. And then decided that I wanted to.

"I've felt it before. I mean, I've done it before. Even before the fog. Even when I was a child. But I don't think I realized what it was or what was happening."

His brows shifted down. "Tell me," he murmured again, his voice soft.

"It's almost like a feeling at first," I said. "An emotion. A want or a need. Then I think about it longer. Harder. I build it up until it's a solid thing within me. I can feel it."

I touched the place at the center of my torso, below my breasts but above my belly.

"Here. And then I feel a release. *Relief.* Because I suddenly know that I can make it happen. That it will be okay. That I can protect myself."

"And even your father never knew?" he asked, frowning.

"I'm not sure," I said, shaking my head, trying to think back. "I—I think my aunt may have though. One time in the village, I remember *this* feeling. She'd been yelling at me. Berating me because I forgot to wash our clothes when it was our turn at the well. And I felt it building, this need to make it go away, to make it...*quiet.* To make the feeling of shame disappear. And I remember crying, and then...I remember her *falling*. Falling so suddenly, like something had hit her. And I remember the look on her face when she stared up at me. Her nose had been broken. The blood...*so* much blood."

"Mina," Wrune's voice came quietly. "It's all right, *rei kassiri.*"

I shook myself, licking my lips, looking back at Wrune. "I did that. I hurt her. I made her bleed. I think I *knew* I'd done it. Even then. But I didn't want to believe it. We never spoke of it again, though she never came close to me after that. She stared at me like I was..."

Wrune's hand came to my cheek.

"You were young," he murmured. "You could not have known what you were doing."

"Not until the fog," I told him. "I didn't know for sure until that moment, when I saw it so clearly for myself for the first time. And then you..."

"What about me?" he asked.

"That morning," I whispered. I swallowed, knowing it was a sensitive subject for us. We never talked about it. "The others don't know what I can do. Not even Tess. I was supposed to lead you through the fog quickly to the others, as quickly as possible. But then I saw you, and I just wanted to look at you. And that morning, I felt *control* over the fog, control like I'd never had before. I could maneuver it so easily. I felt strong in my power, stronger than ever before. And I think it was *you.*"

I didn't know how to explain it to him. I didn't even know how to explain these things to *myself.*

"I felt connected to you, and I think you helped with my control."

His breath blew out, and he ducked his head, pressing his lips to mine like he couldn't resist the small, wonderful little contact.

"I told you," he murmured. "I know you felt it because I did too."

I savored his warmth and his scent and his taste.

Then I pulled back. And I felt shame build inside me as I confessed, "I like the fog, Wrune."

His shoulders tensed briefly, but his gaze was open, warm even, as he regarded me.

"I know it's a terrible thing," I continued. "It *does* terrible things. Things I've seen, things I've witnessed for myself. And yet...I can withstand something that very few can. It made me feel powerful, and for an otherwise powerless being, that was an addicting feeling. In the fog, I was *safe*."

"Mina," he murmured, and I saw the understanding flash through his gaze.

"I was safe. No one could touch me. No one could reach me. Sometimes I would just pretend that I could make a home inside it. Because that way, I would be safe forever."

Wrune didn't say anything after my ugly confession. He didn't pull away, however. He didn't look at me with disgust.

Instead, he lay back down on the rugs, only he pulled me down on top of him this time. I blinked, finding myself straddling my husband's hips, my hands braced on his wide, scarred chest. A position I'd been in an hour or so ago, though it had been a moment filled with very different feelings and emotions than guilt and shame.

His hands settled on my waist as he noted, "That would have been a very lonely existence, *rei Morakkari*. Don't you think?"

"Yes," I whispered. "I know."

"How would I have found you that deep in the fog if you'd done that?" he asked next, catching me by surprise.

His hair was spread out beneath him, and his body was warm beneath me.

"You wouldn't have looked for me," I noted softly. "You didn't know I existed on this planet."

"Kakkari knew," Wrune said. "So *lysi*, I still would've found you. No matter where you thought you could hide."

To anyone else, it would have sounded like a threat. So why did it fill me with a familiar bloom of warmth? A feeling I could grow into something solid?

"I need to be careful when I'm with you," I told him. "Or else my gift might be uncontrollable."

By the way his expression softened—ever so slightly, in a way that made my belly flip and flutter—I knew he understood what I meant by the words.

His grip on my waist tightened. Quiet grew between us as he stared up at me.

"I know your feelings all too well, *rei Morakkari*," he finally said. "The need to escape. To hide. To run."

"What?" I whispered, frowning. "Even now?"

He shook his head. "Not so much now, *nik*. When I was younger."

I stilled on top of him, staring down into his red eyes. In the last week, it had become clear to me that conversation about *that* particular subject was off limits. He'd spoken of where he'd grown up, of course. But they'd been superficial remarks, like how cold the frost season got there or the layout of the *saruk* and how it differed from a horde's. He'd even spoken of his grandparents, though it had mostly been a history of the family's long line on the wildlands, a history of *Vorakkar*.

"Why?" I asked softly, spreading my hands across his chest.

"I know you've realized by now that I don't like to speak of my father," he murmured.

"Yes," I whispered. All I knew about the Dakkari male was that he was buried in the North Lands and that he'd purposefully named his son a word that meant *ruin*, letting him carry that burden his entire life. "I know."

"It is not because I did not love my father," he told me. "I loved him greatly. My *pattar* loved me, very much. His deep capacity for love is arguably the reason why he died. Not many know that."

My brow furrowed. I felt a knot rising in my throat at whatever I heard in my husband's voice.

"I don't understand," I whispered. "But I really want to. I want to understand everything when it comes to you."

Wrune's chest rose with his deep breath.

"And you will, *rei kassiri*," he told me. "I'll tell you everything you wish to know."

CHAPTER 47

"My father loved my mother," Wrune told me. "My grandmother told me it was a love that not many experience. Or even witness. But they were deeply, deeply in love and had been since they were young. My mother's *pattar*, the *Vorakkar* of Rath Rowin at the time, did not approve of it, however. My father was a bastard child, you see. His mother never told him who his father was, and as such, he had no valid claim to anything within the horde—most of all its princess."

"Your mother," I whispered.

He inclined his head. "And so my father worked his way up through the *darukkar* ranks. Being of no line, he knew the only way to win my mother's hand was through his honor as a great warrior of the horde. He would prove to my grandfather that he was worthy of his daughter. And so he did. With time, he became the greatest *darukkar* of Rath Rowin. No one could defeat him, not even the *Vorakkar* himself."

I heard the pride in Wrune's voice, and I gave him a soft smile. I shifted on him, my legs tightening around his hips. "And so they married," I guessed.

"*Lysi*," he rasped. "They did. And only a short while later, my *lomma* became pregnant."

"With you," I murmured, though I was surprised when he shook his head.

"*Nik*, with my sister," he told me. "Though Kakkari took back her breath in my mother's womb and she was born still."

I bit my lip, my throat tightening with realization.

"It was another year until my mother grew heavy again. With me," he murmured. His lips twisted. "You know what happened next."

His mother had died giving birth to him. He'd told me that the night of our *tassimara*. The night he'd given me his name.

"My *pattar* was...*mikira'ta*," he said. "That was the word my grandmother used when she told me this. It means *devastation*. Complete and utter devastation. My grandmother took care of me until my *pattar* could even bring himself to look at me."

The space between my brows pinched, feeling the gruffness in Wrune's voice wiggle its way into my chest.

"I'm sorry," I whispered, stroking his chest, feeling his solid heartbeat underneath my thumb. "I'm sorry, *sailon*."

The affectionate name made his eyes flare. One of his hands slid up from the curve of my waist, glancing over my outer breast. Being with him like this felt natural. Letting him touch me like this, feeling his eyes on me felt as natural as breathing.

"It was long after my *lomma's* burial when he finally could," he said. "My grandmother said she watched him fall in love with me in that single moment, where before there had been hatred in his eyes. But not hatred for me. Hatred for himself."

"But he named you Wrune," I murmured, trying to understand.

"*Lysi*," he said. "But you see, in Dakkari the word has another meaning. Ruin can lead to rebirth. It can lead to hope and beginnings."

My nose stung with realization. "He saw you as his new beginning. After your mother."

"*Lysi*," Wrune rasped, his voice sounding tight. Something

in his gaze shifted, however, a moment later. "Though I was his new beginning, he never forgot the past. He carried it with him. Every moment of every day. He held on to his guilt, his shame, his love, his torment. Because if he had never loved my mother, if he had never risen through the ranks of the *darukkars*, if he had never married her, if he had never lain with her...then in his mind she would still be alive. He thought that *he* was her true ruin, her true death. And nothing could sway him from that belief. He thought that Kakkari had warned him with my sister's birth. That he deserved punishment for planting the seed within my mother again."

"But they loved each other," I murmured. "Didn't he remember that?"

"He did." He took in a deep breath, and my hands rose on his chest with it. "His mind, however, began to warp after her death. As the years dragged on, he made me his new purpose in life. Because if I had been the price of her life, then it had to *mean* something. I had to be something great."

"Wrune," I whispered, hearing a bitterness in his tone that made my belly sink with dread.

His hand came to cup my own. He dragged it down, pressing my fingers deliberately to small, golden scars that decorated his flesh. One by his abdomen, long and slim. Another across his pectoral, deeper and ragged. Another few by his shoulders, his neck, down his side, over his arms, over his hard belly, on his hip, then the other hip.

He had me trace so many scars that I lost count. Tears filled my eyes, but I didn't let them fall. I understood what he was telling me without him needing to speak a single word.

"That many?" I asked, looking down at him, trying to keep my chin from quivering and my voice from shaking.

Wrune relaxed underneath me.

"He took me out to the frost forests every morning before the sun rose and every evening after our meals, when the rest of the *saruk* slept," he said. "He trained me hard. Without mercy. Without reprieve. This scar," he said, tracing the first I'd touched, the one across his abdomen, "was my first."

"How old were you?" I asked, not sure I wanted to know.

"Two, I suppose," he murmured, and his answer stole my breath. I remembered when Hassan was that age. With plump cheeks and wide, innocent eyes. Clumsy with his movements too, since he'd just begun to walk.

I couldn't stop the tears from falling then. I couldn't imagine it. I couldn't imagine a father, no matter how grief stricken, mercilessly training and *scarring* his young son.

"After they married," Wrune said, "my father no longer wanted to battle. Instead, he became the *mitri*, the weapons master." He gestured to the sword which I'd pushed up against the bathing tub with my barrier. "He made me that sword. And I have wielded it since I was young because he believed that it would make me the strongest *Vorakkar* our world had ever seen."

I stared at the blade. I knew how much Wrune cared for it. Sharpening it, cleaning it, polishing and oiling the steel of the hilt.

My husband's lips lifted into a humorless smile. "It was around this time I began to understand that my father was not...all right. When my grandmother discovered the scars, she was horrified. And yet my grandfather was swayed by my father."

"He let him continue?" I asked, wide eyed in disbelief.

"*Lysi,*" he murmured. "I was the last of his line. My grandfather's line, which had long boasted of great horde kings, was coming to an end. The name of Rath Rowin would die with him unless I made the name great again. That was my father's dream, keeping my mother's line alive. And after the death of his daughter, his only heir, it was my grandfather's dream as well. So, the training continued. Though it was now even more regimented than before. And that was my childhood, Mina. That was how I grew up. With a father that was half-mad with grief and a grandfather who would stop at nothing for me to continue on with his name."

I could think of nothing else to do but lean down. My hair fell around us, curtaining us against the outside world. Our eyes connected, and a fierce expression came over Wrune's face as I kissed him gently. He didn't like talking about this. I saw that. I *felt* it. It hurt him. It made him ache. And I wanted to take it from him. I wanted to take it all.

"My *pattar* always warned me," Wrune said, a soft whisper against my lips when I pulled away. Smoothing my hand over his cheek, I stilled when he said, "He always warned me that females would be the end of males. That I should never let a female too close or else I would lose myself the way he had lost himself."

Sobering, I lifted from his lips, straightening. Realization was spreading inside me, hot and *rapid*. A rush of sudden understanding.

"That I would be ruined the way he had been ruined," Wrune finished. "I never wanted to be like him. If I allowed myself to love a female, that would be my fate. It had been drilled into my mind even before I knew what my father meant. And so I vowed that I would not take a *Morakkari* for love. I vowed that I would only take a *Morakkari* to strengthen my horde. A *Morakkari* who would give me strong sons that would carry on the name of Rowin long after I was gone. My father and my grandfather made me into a *Vorakkar,* and they'd done so mercilessly. The least I could do was repay them with a strong line and a strong horde."

Such a heavy burden to bear, I thought silently, my vision blurring further with tears. When they rolled down my cheeks, Wrune reached up to brush them away.

And I *understood* now. I understood what he was willing me

to understand. About why he was the way he was. Why he'd been so cold and detached once he took me to his horde. Why he'd pushed me away after the *tassimara*, hardly able to look at me.

Because he'd been afraid *I* would be his ruin, just like his father had always warned him about.

It was like the last piece of the puzzle slotting into place.

It all made sense.

"Instead, you got me," I whispered. A weak, half-starved human with an unpredictable gift.

Wrune went quiet.

Then he said, "Never before had I understood what my father meant. With other females, I had never felt in danger. I had never felt in danger of losing myself."

A prick of jealousy pierced me, but I knew that it had no place in this conversation. Thinking about him with other females—especially with Junira, since I could put her face to a name—made my cheeks grow hot and nausea rise.

"But with you..." he started gruffly, a sharp exhale whistling from his nostrils. "With you, I lost myself."

I swallowed, feeling that confession wind its way into my chest. But it wasn't a happy feeling. It was one of understanding. Because I knew that Wrune had viewed that as a terrible, terrible thing.

"You know that already, Mina," he said, reaching up to stroke my cheek, cupping it in the large width of his palm. "And when I saw you, I had the strangest feeling that I'd follow in my father's footsteps. That you would be mine. That I would love you the way he loved my mother. And with that love, deep loss would also follow."

That made my heart race.

Love?

"But you don't," I whispered quickly, feeling those words

fall from my lips like stones. Heavy and unwanted. "You...you don't love me. We..."

I trailed off, uncertain what I would even say. *We what? We know that our marriage isn't like that?*

Thinking *that* while straddling him naked felt like a small mockery.

Wrune regarded me carefully, those observant red eyes flickering back and forth between mine. Did he see the way his words had made me flush? Could he *hear* how my heartbeat throbbed?

The words hit too close to home. They made me realize, in that single moment, that I *was* in danger of loving him. He'd made it only too easy.

Wrune didn't say anything. His hand left my cheek and settled back on my hip.

The tension between us was thick as I grasped for something to change the subject. But I knew what I wanted to know, and so I settled on asking, "How did your father die? What happened to him?"

Wrune's gaze slid past me, and he stared up at the ceiling of the *voliki*.

"After I completed the Trials, after I became a *Vorakkar*, I returned home one last time before I would take to the wildlands," Wrune said. "I saw my father. It was everything he'd ever wanted, everything he'd worked for, trained me for, and yet...he seemed so tired. I asked him to join my horde, but he said he did not want to leave my mother. He wanted to stay at the *saruk*, where she was buried. I understood. I left shortly after."

Wrune's eyes flickered back to me as unease built in my belly.

"After a moon cycle out on the wildlands with my horde, I received a message from my grandfather. Telling me that my father willingly joined my mother in death, that he would be buried beside her."

I bit my lip, feeling those words eat at me. More tears dripped down my face, ones that Wrune brushed away again.

"I'm sorry, Wrune," I whispered, though the words felt so inadequate. "I'm so sorry."

"It was what he wanted. To be with my *lomma*," Wrune said, though his voice was gruff and dark. "Truthfully, it was a small relief for me too."

I pressed a small kiss to his palm, holding it in my hand.

"I'd always known he suffered. All my life," Wrune continued. "Now he no longer does. And I think he was just waiting until I became what I was always meant to be before he joined her. His last promise to her fulfilled."

A small, shuddering sigh released from me.

Such tragic circumstances. Such a tragic life.

I thought of words I'd said to him under the Dead Mountain, which seemed like a lifetime ago. How I wished for a world with no suffering, only peace.

How silly and naive he must've thought my words. Knowing what I did now, how ridiculous they must've seemed to him.

Then again, we had all suffered.

"Thank you for telling me," I told him gently.

Wrune replied, "You needed to know, *rei Morakkari*."

The fire flickered out in the basin, and darkness took its place. When Wrune shifted underneath me, intent on adding more fire fuel to it, I kept him in place on his back.

I didn't know how to comfort him after such a tale. I didn't know how to make it all right. And I realized that I probably never could.

But we were with one another now. And I could comfort him in another way.

So, I leaned down to kiss him, pouring my unspoken feelings—my fear, my sadness, my understanding, my affection, my need—into him. A deep huff burst from his chest, and then he was meeting my kiss head on, as ravenous and consuming and eager as my own.

His tail wrapped around my ankle. His hands trapped my hips. And I kept him pressed down, my hands threading through his hair as my nipples dragged against his strong chest.

He was hardening underneath me. Quick and fast. Gasping, I sought him out, and he groaned when I found him.

And as our cries resumed in the quiet, dark *voliki*, as our pleasure mingled together and our breaths became one, I thought that it might not be such a frightening thing to love him.

What frightened me most was something else entirely.

It was losing him.

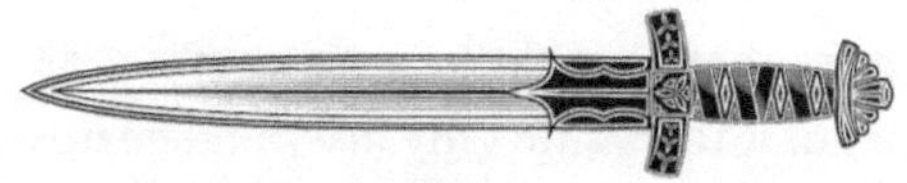

CHAPTER 48

"*Hanniva, Vorakkar,*" Junira pleaded with me, briefly flickering her gaze up at me before dropping it once more. Her yellow eyes were wide and solemn, though there was a hint of a smile on her lips, as if her smile would sway me.

"And why is your *pattar* not before me now?" I asked gruffly, crossing my arms over my chest. "Instead he sends his daughter to make his apologies? And over a week later?"

"My father has…" Junira trailed off, catching sight of lingering horde members as they pretended not to listen to the conversation she'd chosen to have in broad daylight. "Can we speak in private, *Vorakkar?*"

"*Nik,*" I told her. "If you wish to speak another time, then—"

"*Nik,*" she said, forgetting herself when she interrupted me. She bowed her head. "My apologies. I did not mean to…"

Out of the corner of my eye, I caught sight of Mina. Hukri was walking to her left and slightly behind her. My wife was wearing a thin sheath dress the color of a soft purple sunrise, though it did nothing to shield the heavy weight of her breasts and her pebbled nipples that stiffened in the slight breeze.

Desire tightened my trews, my nostrils flaring. Junira

reached out a hand to touch my forearm, and my gaze broke away from my *Morakkari* to regard the female standing before me.

Her hand fell away at my pointed look, but she said, "You must understand how difficult this has been for us, *Vorakkar*. He comes from a great line of *darukkars*. *Darukkars* that served your grandfather, even. He is used to the old way. He thought that…he thought that I would be your choice. Can you not see that? Can you not understand why he would be upset?"

Her cheeks bloomed darker under her bold words. Her tone sounded slightly exasperated and even a little bewildered.

"I know what you believe, Junira," I murmured. "But the fog was looming. The last thing I was thinking of was taking a queen for the horde. You knew what it was between us. You accepted it for what it was. And when I ended it, I told you, in no uncertain terms, that I would not be taking a *Morakkari* until after the fog. Did you not tell your father that?"

Her lips pressed together.

"But you lied," she said, and even I heard the hurt in her voice when she said it. Discomfort built in my chest. "You took a *Morakkari,* and last time I checked, the fog still lingers."

Mina stilled when she spotted us, watching the exchange with a careful expression on her face, an exchange which had drawn quite a crowd.

I told Junira, "*Lysi,* I did. And I will not apologize for it. I decided to take a *Morakkari* because she strengthens the horde. Because it was my duty to the horde."

"And I wouldn't strengthen the horde?" she dared to ask, meeting my eyes, a vulnerable expression on her face. "And the whole horde knows how much you've *enjoyed* your duty, taking her as your *Morakkari*. The whole horde hears it nearly every night!"

The silence was deafening between us. Then a warning, rough growl rose from my throat.

To her credit, Junira's face paled, and she stumbled back a step, immediately dropping her gaze, going to one knee before me in supplication. "I—I'm sorry. *Hanniva.* I'm so sorry, *Vorakkar.* That was not my place."

"It was not your place," I agreed with her, my voice dark, the warning in my tone palpable. "It is not your place to question my decisions. It is not your place, or your father's, to spread rumors throughout the horde that I had made promises to you. You know I did no such thing. I was nothing but honest with you, Junira."

"I-I know," she said quietly. I knew that her outburst had come from a place of jealousy. I had liked Junira. I had enjoyed her company, but that time was long past between us. I had never returned her feelings, though I knew that hers lingered. And perhaps that was my fault.

"My *Morakkari* implored me to give your father another chance in this horde," I told her. "As such, I will give you another as well. But if I hear anything throughout the horde about this again, I will not tolerate it a second time. You will not disrespect my queen a second time. Do you understand?"

"*Lysi,*" she burst out. "*Lysi,* I understand. *Kakkira vor.*"

Junira didn't wait another moment. She rose and wove her way through the horde, keeping her head down against the onlookers that watched her leave.

When the crowd saw me giving them a pointed look, they dispersed quickly, scattering to their respective duties, and I bit out a sharp sigh.

Mina approached me, and I straightened.

"Good afternoon, *Vorakkar,*" she murmured, meeting my eyes.

A tight knot in my chest loosened at the sound of her voice. Her cheeks were pink, and her lips were pressed together, as if Hukri had been translating the entire conversation between Junira and myself.

My hand slid into her hair, and my palm wrapped around the base of her neck, pulling her close. When her hands came to my chest, I leaned down to steal a kiss.

Mina kept it short, however, and she was a little tense in my arms.

I blew out a sigh, my gaze flickering to Hukri, who was lingering a good distance away to give us privacy.

"You heard that?"

"Hukri has very good hearing," Mina told me, meeting my gaze. "And she's an excellent translator."

"Mmm."

I slid my hand to her back, pressing her closer to me.

"She still desires you," Mina noted.

"Hukri?" I murmured softly, trying to soften some of the tension that I felt rising between us.

She slapped her palm across my bare chest. "Junira."

"I made her no promises, *rei Morakkari*," I told her, my voice steeling. "And I will not have her spreading rumors that contradict that."

"It's not about that," Mina said. "I can understand why she's upset, that's all. I can understand..."

"*Neffar?*" I asked, my brow furrowing, though I was fascinated by the flush that was slowly working its way up her neck.

"I can understand having you and then not having you," she said quietly.

I sobered, though I said, "You know that you have me always, *rei Morakkari*. I am yours. No one else's." Her bright green eyes softened at the words. But I recognized something else in her gaze, something that filled me with *relief*. "You are jealous?"

She bit her lip.

"There is no need," I assured her, dragging her closer, "though I like to see it on occasion."

Her eyes narrowed. "What?"

It had been a handful of nights since I'd told her about my father. As such, it had been a handful of nights since I'd felt disappointed by her reaction, when she'd quickly rejected the possibility of love between us. She hadn't even given it a spare thought.

To see her jealous, it soothed some of the uncertainty I'd felt building inside me since that moment.

"It reminds me that you are perhaps as possessive of me as I am of you," I told her gruffly, brushing my lips against hers for a brief moment before pulling away.

"You...you get jealous too?" she asked, the question innocent and bewildered.

I gave her a small grin. Leaning down to whisper in her ear, I told her, "Valavik offered to marry you, to keep you for the horde, instead of me." Her outraged gasp met my ears. "I nearly bloodied him right there for merely suggesting it."

Her gaze was slightly dazed when she leaned back. Her brow furrowed. "But...but that was before...the *tassimara*."

I grunted, lifting a shoulder in a shrug.

"My council is meeting," I murmured, swiftly changing the subject. "I've kept them too long already."

She sighed, shaking her head a bit. "About the Dead Mountain?" she asked.

"*Lysi*," I told her, running my thumb across her bottom lip. "Final preparations. We leave in two days."

Her gasp met my back when I turned. My council's *voliki* was not far, but I heard her running after me.

"Wait, Rowin," she called. She used that name whenever we were within the horde. When we were alone, however, it was always Wrune or *sailon*...or *setovan*, which always brought a grin to my face. *Stubborn male.* She enjoyed calling me that.

I let her catch up, though a few horde members we passed gave her peculiar looks when they saw her chasing after me.

The road wound toward the training grounds, but she grabbed my arm.

"So soon?" she asked, her eyes wide as she looked up at me.

"At first light, *lysi*," I replied, frowning as I took in her expression. "I thought you'd be pleased. I was planning to tell you tonight."

"I...I *am*," she said, though her face didn't reveal that to me. "It's just..."

"*Neffar?*" I murmured, bringing her closer when I saw concern flash in her eyes. "Tell me."

"What happens if something goes wrong?" she asked, looking up at me. "What happens if one of your *darukkars* gets injured or if *you* get hurt? Or...worse?"

Realization dawned, and it was followed swiftly by a sudden sensation of warmth and affection.

Mina was worried for me. For the *darukkars*.

"I don't want anyone to get hurt," she whispered. "Not for me."

"You are their queen. They will do whatever you ask of them," I reminded her. "It is their honor to."

"I know," she said. "And I'm sorry. I know you've been planning this. I guess it just took me by surprise to know that you will be leaving so soon. How long will you be gone?"

"It will take a few days to travel to the northern tunnels," I informed her. "Possibly more if we need to take alternate routes. We do not know how much the fog has grown up north. *Thesper* messages from the horde that was close to there have ceased as of late."

Though that fact wasn't entirely alarming. It was the *Vorakkar* of Rath Okkili that had been near there. And he'd been tasked with attempting to make contact with the priestesses of the North. If *thespers* from him had ceased, I assumed it was because he had moved forward with that plan.

Mina reached out to take my hand, and I knew what she would say before she even said it.

"It will take a handful of moments, Wrune," she whispered quietly, knowing no one would hear us. "Let me do it. Let me clear the way. That way I can ensure that—"

"*Nik,*" I said, my jaw tightening. "I told you already. I forbid it. Not unless absolutely necessary, and even then..."

My nostrils flared as I trailed off.

Softly, she said, "You made me your queen because I could help protect your horde."

"*Our* horde," I corrected gruffly, raising my brow, pressing my lips together tight.

And that was only one of the reasons I took you as my queen, despite what I tell others, I thought silently.

"Our horde," she amended quietly, those green eyes pinned to me, watching me carefully. "And what better way can I be of service than to help you, my husband, and the *darukkars* that serve you, that serve *us*? I've done it before. Multiple times— you've seen it. I won't let it get out of hand. Not like last time. You just need to trust me."

"Mina," I growled warningly, catching sight of Valavik step- ping out of the council's *voliki*. We had stopped a stone's throw away from it, and I knew the elders and the warriors I had assigned to the journey were inside as well. Waiting for me.

Mina glanced at Valavik too before she looked back at me.

"Let me do this," she implored, squeezing my hand. "Lead me inside that *voliki*, and I can save you and your *darukkars days* of travel. Days that they can spend with their wives and fami- lies instead of wandering around the North, looking for some- thing that might not even be there! Days that *you* can spend in the horde because this is where you need to be. Days with me. *Nights* with me," she added softly.

"You're doing it again, *rei sarkia,*" I growled to her,

squeezing her hip when I drew her closer. "And I am not going to be blinded by it again."

"Doing what?" she asked, innocently enough that I almost believed she didn't know.

"Can you not see why I believed you were a *sarkia* at first?" I rasped. "Because everything in me wants to give you what you want! And I cannot risk your safety for that."

"I will stay back, then," she said. "I will stay with the *darukkars* at the encampment and clear the way. I won't step toward the Dead Mountain. I won't go anywhere near it."

"Then you risk overexerting yourself again. You risk that *pain* again," I said, shaking my head.

"I don't care!" she exclaimed. "What's a little bit of pain if it means that you'll be *safer*?"

I stilled, regarding her as her words echoed between us.

She worried for *my* safety? That was why she was so upset?

She licked her lips, and I saw her concern *brightly* right then, reflected in her eyes.

"Pain is fleeting," she said quietly, aware that Valavik's eyes were on us. "If I can help you, if I can make the path for you safer, then I will do it. I know my limits now. I felt them out on the plains. I know how far I can go. I'm just asking you to trust me, Wrune."

Dread settled in my belly. A heavy thing. Because anything that risked her safety would never sit well with me.

Even so, I recognized that she made a reasonable argument. If she cleared the path for us, it would save days, possibly even weeks of travel, depending on the state of the North. It would save us the uncertainty of planning. We could focus solely on executing the plan underneath the Dead Mountain instead of spending time on the journey.

It would be safer for the *darukkars*.

It meant we would not be away from the horde for long, at such a precarious time.

"Please," she whispered. Then she went high on her toes and pressed a kiss to the corner of my mouth, then to my jaw, then to my neck. "*Hanniva*," she murmured in my ear.

I growled.

Then my shoulders sagged. I caught Valavik's questioning gaze before I looked back to Mina.

"Very well," I said, my voice deep and husky and so *vokking* hesitant it sounded like I was agreeing to my own torture. "But you will do exactly as I say. And you will have guards with you as well as the healer close by, in case anything happens."

My wife seemed to know better than to smile in victory when I was in such a begrudging, irritated mood.

"That sounds very fair, *Vorakkar*," she said, her tone practically prim and sullen.

"Get in the *voliki*," I growled, "before I change my mind."

"*Lysi, sailon*," she murmured, using that affectionate name for me as if she knew I would be softened by it.

As I watched her sway past me, I knew that it had worked.

Chapter 49

My nails dug into his chest. His palms were gripping my hips hard enough to bruise, but I didn't care.

That pinching, consuming need was making me mindless as I rocked over Wrune. I didn't recognize the woman I was with him. Not when we were like this. I was demanding and needful. Selfish, even. I ground over his cock, snapping my hips down in a way that had him groaning. I was selfish, focused on the heat building between my thighs, but I wanted to make him feel good too. Because he made *me* feel so, so good.

My orgasm was coming hot and quick. My legs tightened around his body, pinning him down to the furs of our bed. I knew he liked me in this position, on top of him. He could see everything. His eyes flickered constantly, going from my face to my lips to my bobbing breasts before trailing down to where we were joined. His gaze always heated when it landed there, when he saw the hot thickness of his cock plunging into my body, making slick, wet sounds that filled the *voliki*.

"Come for me, wife," he ordered, his voice dark and husky. His grin nearly stole my breath. "I can feel your cunt tightening on me. I know how close you are."

I closed my eyes, a gasp threading up my throat when his *dakke*—that hard bump at the base of his cock that throbbed with his own arousal—brushed my clit.

"*Nik*," he growled, beginning to take control. "Look at me, *rei sarkia*."

His hand reached up, wrapping around the back of my neck. He pulled me down until my breasts were pressed to his wide, strong chest. The change in position made him slide deeper, and we both groaned. My sex fluttered as my eyes connected with his because this position placed my clit right over his hot and thrumming *dakke*...and he held me there.

"Oh gods," I whispered, the words sounding strained and tight. "*Wrune!*"

His lips crashed against mine, and as my orgasm exploded between my thighs, I perceived his hips moving, quick and demanding with his thrusts, as his grip kept me still for him. He fucked me through my pleasure, elongating it, *strengthening* it.

When he finally broke our kiss, he roared with the intensity of his own release. I felt the heat lash against my inner walls, familiar and so *right*. As we huffed and panted, he continued to thrust lazily until the last drop of his seed was spent. Then he shuddered, his muscles loosening as he relaxed, boneless and sated, onto our furs.

I felt energized instead of tired, though it had been our second coupling of the night. Perhaps it was nerves or adrenaline, considering that in the morning, Wrune and his *darukkars* would journey to the Dead Mountain. And I would clear a path for them, as we'd agreed on.

My cheek was pressed to his chest, right over his thundering heart. I sensed his low chuckle before it ever rose from his throat. Just the sound brought a flutter of warmth swarming into my belly, and when I peered up at him, his grin only strengthened that feeling.

His hand threaded through my hair, raking through the thick waves.

"What is it?" I asked, my own voice husky from my moans and my cries.

"Come here, wife," he purred.

I knew what he wanted, and so I leaned up, feeling his cock slide out of me as I kissed him. A shuddering sigh drifted from my lips when his tongue stroked mine. It was a deep, passionate yet patient kiss. One with no urgency, only sensation. It sent a tingle down my spine and threatened to make me smile.

"I am undone for you," came his words.

My breath hitched. I pulled away from his kiss, only to see him watching me. His red eyes were soft but watchful. Always observant.

A deep sigh escaped him as he cupped my jaw, rubbing his thumb across my reddened, swollen lips.

"How easy it was," he murmured next, his tone softly bewildered.

My heart thundered. What was he saying?

I licked my lips, and my tongue met his thumb briefly.

"But just look at you," he said, his brows furrowing. "*Leika.*" *Beautiful.*

I bit my lip, hearing the softness of that word, the *awe* of it. Before Wrune, I remembered wondering what it would be like to be *chosen* by someone. Chosen above all things.

In that moment, I had an inkling of what that would feel like. I saw it laid before me, open and vast.

"There was a time when you wondered why you ever desired me," I whispered to him, pushing up so I could look down at his face. My hands stroked the golden tattoos that wove across his chest and traced the raised scars that ran underneath them. "There was a time when you couldn't stand the sight of me."

Wrune blinked. His hands came to rest on my hips before trailing softly down my outer thighs, keeping me in place.

"*Lysi,*" he murmured. "But I never *really* saw you. Well, *nik,* that is not entirely true."

"What do you mean?"

"I saw you in your entirety in the fog. At first sight. And the sight of you nearly brought me to my knees," he murmured. "But then my *kassikari* retreated from me, leaving another creature in her place."

I knew *kassikari* meant *fated mate.* Just hearing that word from his lips brought a burst of warmth to my chest, heating my cheeks.

As for his other words...I thought I understood what he meant.

"You think I hid myself? Under the Dead Mountain?" I asked.

"*Lysi,*" he told me, those red eyes glowing in the dim light. "I think you had to. I think you were afraid. Trapped. And only when you were not afraid anymore could you be free." His small smile was wry. "Though I caught glimpses of you. With your claws. And even then, my *sarkia* made my cock hard, even though I was bloodied and chained. Even then, I wanted her."

I didn't blush with the words. I simply stared down at him, memorizing the lines of his strong features—as if I didn't have him committed to memory already.

I feared...I feared I was undone for this male too.

Undone.

That word was fitting. Because I felt like a spool of thread, tangled and wild. Nothing made sense anymore. I felt vulnerable, like my heart was outside my body, exposed. And it was him that had possession of it. It was him that protected it.

He must've seen the strange expression on my face because he asked, "What is it, *rei Morakkari?*"

"I fear for tomorrow," I told him softly. "I fear for you."

His features softened. "Mina…"

"I cannot shake this feeling," I said, feeling my throat tighten, feeling it bubble up once more. I'd felt it earlier tonight, though I hadn't told Wrune. "That something is going wrong. Or will. I—I've lost many I've cared for in my life. I *cannot* lose you too."

Wrune's hands slid to cup behind my knees before he moved them back up my thighs, stroking me as if in comfort. As if his touch could soothe me. And it helped. Somewhat. I focused on him, on his heat and his scent and his touch, and I reminded myself that he was *here*. He was right *here*. With me.

"You care for me, *rei sarkia*?"

I slapped at his chest. The words came out gruff, but I recognized the teasing lilt of his tone. I could read him well now. All his moods and expressions.

His half grin made my stomach flip and flop.

"You know I do," I told him.

"There was a time when you could not stand the sight of me," he said, repeating the words I'd told him only moments before.

I huffed out a breath. "*Setovan.*"

But I understood now, with my words thrown back at me, how they must've seemed to Wrune. It made me realize that…

"Even when I felt that way," I began, "I still *watched* for you."

Those red eyes gleamed and glittered. I recognized that look. It told me I was about to be kissed. It told me I was about to be pinned to the furs of our bed. It told me—

Wrune's head snapped up, his muscles suddenly tensing, his gaze going to the entrance flap of our *voliki*. His nostrils flared, and he went deathly still.

I froze, my breath going shallow, though I remained as quiet as possible. Dakkari could hear better than humans. He could hear something that I couldn't.

Carefully, I slid off him, and he rose from the bed with a speed that shouldn't have surprised me but continually did.

That was when I heard it.

The shouts. The yells of alarm.

Rippling toward us as they broke through the stillness and quietness of that night.

"*Vok*," Wrune cursed, and he lunged for his trews, pulling them on with lightning quickness.

"W-What is it?" I asked, breathless as I began to shiver, despite the warmth from the fire basin.

"Stay here, Mina," my husband growled.

Like hell, I thought silently, watching as he ran from the *voliki* after he snagged the hilt of his sword on the way out. Gone in the blink of an eye, as more shouts reached the edge of our home.

Quickly, I jumped up from the bed and pulled my discarded dress over my head, though I was certain it was backward. I didn't care. I just needed to see what was wrong. What was happening.

Mere moments after Wrune left, I was darting from the *voliki* after him.

From here, we had a whole view of the encampment, the walls, the gates, and beyond. Nearly every *voliki* was glowing with light. Horde members were crowding, uncertain, and I spied Wrune racing through the camp, making a straight path for the gates.

I followed after him, dread churning in my belly. A *darukkar* intercepted me, however, just as I reached the first of the *volikis* that sat a good distance away from our own.

"What's happened?" I demanded from him, even when he tried to grab my wrist to keep me from following Wrune.

"The *Vorakkar* told me to keep you inside, *Morakkari*," the *darukkar* said, though his discomfort was clear.

"Tell me right now," I ordered him, steeling my tone and

meeting his eyes, as I stepped away from his grip. "Tell me what's wrong."

His jaw tightened.

Then he said, "There was an attack on the edge of the fog."

My breath left me.

"The *darukkars* were taken."

Chapter 50

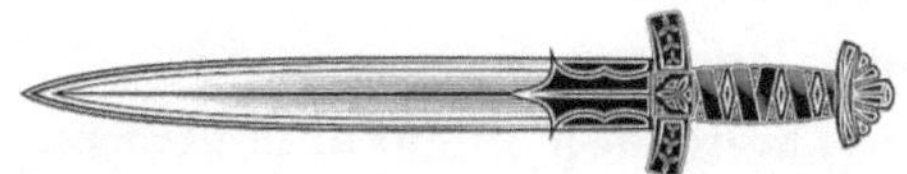

"What happened?" I growled, my voice booming ahead of me when I spied the small group huddled on the edge of the fog.

Valavik was there, his breath still heaving from the run over. As were other *darukkars*, ones I'd assigned the night watch at the gates. They were standing in a half circle around Olin, who sat next to the roaring fire basin, his face leached of color.

I crouched in front of him when I reached them. He kept his eyes on my throat as I asked, "Where are the others?"

"Gone," he rasped, raising his eyes to mine briefly.

"Where?" I pressed.

"*The fog.*"

I rose, my jaw tightening, and I met Valavik's eyes.

"There were females," Olin said, his voice finally finding some strength. "One moment, the night seemed to go still. The next, they were *there*. I remember seeing them. *Right there.*" He pointed to the edge of the red fog, which billowed and swayed, as if beckoning us closer. "Then I do not remember anything. My memory is blackened. I do not know how long it has been since they were taken. I woke and then immediately called for the guards at the gates."

"You were lucky," Valavik growled, meeting my eyes once he looked away from the *darukkar*. "Human females?"

"*Nik*," Olin said, shaking his head. "Not like our *Morakkari*. They were our own."

"Dakkari?" I asked, lips turning down. But I feared I knew what that meant. I cast my gaze to the ground before taking a nearby torch and lighting it within the fire basin. It roared to life, and I walked toward the fog.

Behind me, I heard the murmurs of *darukkars*.

"*Sarkias*," I heard one of them say.

The witches.

"*Setava Terun*," I heard another say.

The First Elder.

But how had they made it through the fog?

Had they used blood magic?

I nearly shuddered at the thought.

As I cast my torch toward the ground, I sensed rather than saw her approach. Mina was huffing, dodging the grip of the *darukkar* I had assigned to watch over her as she raced into the clearing.

When I turned to regard my *Morakkari*, I scowled at her but waved the helpless and lost *darukkar* away, and he faded back among the others. I didn't blame him. I knew how determined my wife could be, after all. And she had already disobeyed my own order to stay in the *voliki*.

"They were taken?" Mina demanded immediately, coming toward me. Her face was pinched into a solemn, worried expression.

"*Lysi*."

"Humans?" she asked next, a thread of discomfort entering her tone.

"*Sarkias*."

She took a step back at the word. I had bit it out harshly, so unlike the soft, teasing tone I used when I called her *rei sarkia*.

Once it had been a curse. Now I used it like a soft name for her. One filled with reverence and quiet warmth.

"Though it is very likely the humans helped," I added, turning from her, casting my torch to the ground once more.

Valavik approached. "You are looking for a blood mark?"

"*Lysi.*"

"A blood mark?" Mina asked.

"You think they used blood magic to enter the fog?" Valavik called out, stepping up to the wall of billowing, thick mist and walking along its perimeter, searching for the same thing I was.

"How else?" I bit out. "Unless one of their *sarkias* can do what our *Morakkari* can."

Four *darukkars* were taken. I had stationed five out here to guard the plains. Makeshift *volikis* now sat empty. A subdued quiet had begun to descend.

"*Vorakkar?*" came an alarmed voice. "What's happened? Where are they?"

I blew out a quiet breath, steeling myself. Then I turned, only to see three females and my *mrikro*, the *pyroki* master. They were all breathing heavily, as if they'd run here once they heard the terrible news.

Hukri was among the females, her hand pressed to her mouth when she saw Olin's head hung. I had placed her mate on the night watch for this week. He had been one of the *darukkars* taken.

As had my *mrikro's* son, Ujaki. As had Natevik's brother, Bevir. As had Riva's mate, Muniv.

Mina immediately went to Hukri—her friend, her *piki*.

"What has happened?" I heard Hukri ask her. "Where is my husband?"

My jaw tightened.

"The *sarkias* took them," I told the small, gathering group, my voice gruff and hard. "Back to the Dead Mountain. But we will return them to you. I swear it on Kakkari."

Riva's sobbing cry echoed out into the still plain, and I listened to it hard as my *mrikro* met my eyes, willing me to get his son back. But I saw in the grim expression of his face that he feared what I did. A fear that had plagued me since I left the Dead Mountain.

That in their desperation, the *sarkias* would try to use blood magic to banish the fog, since they could no longer use my own heart. And they would need a lot of blood.

The fact that they had survived within the fog told me that at least one of the witches possessed a gift. The *Setava Terun* had already been dismissed as powerless in *Dothik,* though she was driven by her own delusions of importance. But one of her followers, one of her coven, might actually possess a fragment of Kakkari's powers, just like Drokka and his queen, just like my own.

And what would the *sarkias* do with such an untamed power?

"Rowin," came Valavik's sudden call. "Over here."

I looked away from the group of females and my *mrikro,* seeing Mina reach out her hand to take Riva's as she wailed, trying to comfort her in whatever way she could.

Valavik was standing over something, and when I strode over to him, I saw what I feared. A blood mark. The blood was still fresh and glimmering. The pattern it depicted was intricate, confined within a circle, all branching lines and deep swirls. Words written in the *sarkias'* language, a language only they knew, shone black with blood. Their own? Or one of my *darukkars*?

"We don't have much time," I said, keeping my voice quiet so the others would not hear. "They may already be gone."

Vavalik inclined his head in agreement. "How many *darukkars* should we take?"

"As many as we can afford."

And we couldn't waste a single moment.

Spinning around, I bellowed out to the guards that had come from the gates, "Gather thirty *darukkars*. Ready the *pyrokis*. We ride for the Dead Mountain immediately!"

The *mrikro* didn't waste a moment, even in his fear. He ran with the guards back toward the horde, no doubt heading for the *pyroki* enclosure.

My gaze went to Mina, my expression grim. Her eyes met my own, but I knew she understood. She would have to guide our way sooner than expected.

"The plan is still the same," I told Valavik when he came up to my side, though my eyes never left my wife's. "We just ride with more *darukkars*. And we must find the *sarkias* quickly."

"*Lysi.*"

Walking to the fire basin, I deposited my torch, my sword still hanging heavy in my other hand.

Just when I started to stride toward Mina, I felt a prickling at the back of my neck.

I froze, though my palm clenched the hilt of my sword harder, as if on instinct.

The *air*...the plains...

Everything went silent.

Even Riva's cries ceased. All breath ceased. No one dared *move*.

And when my eyes met Mina's, I saw hers were wide. Her lips were parted and her face had paled.

Dread churned in my belly. The tip of my sword dragged on the ground when I turned to regard the fog, the scrape of the metal jarring and impossibly loud. The creaking of my trews, the whisper of my hair as I turned seemed amplified.

For a moment nothing happened.

Then I heard a roaring sound. It came from deep within the fog. But it wasn't a Dakkari sound. It wasn't a human sound. Or one made by a wretched beast.

It was the earth. It was the *mountain*.

The roaring grew and grew, and then it was coming straight toward us. Hurtling right toward us!

No one had time to move. No one had time to *act*.

A violent gust of wind pushed from the fog and threw itself at us, knocking us back. The roar had been wind. Wind unlike I'd ever heard or felt before.

It went quiet once more.

"Rowin!" came Mina's cry. "Get back!"

Her voice tunneled toward me, but it sounded thick and muted. Not a moment after her words pierced the air, the ground began to tremble. I heard the cries of alarm rise up from my horde, carrying over the congealed air.

"Get back to the gates!" I bellowed. "Get back to the gates now!"

But it was too late. A massive ripple of energy *boomed*—energy I remembered feeling once before. An energy similar to Mina's own power.

The red fog actually retreated toward the Dead Mountain—as if the mountain were breathing and it was *inhaling* the fog—revealing stretches of land that Mina had once revealed to us all. For a moment I thought she was using her powers. For a moment I thought the *sarkias* might have actually been *right* and—

The land shook, and then the mountain roared again.

The fog raced toward us, gathering speed and energy as it sped across the Dead Valley. The mountain disappeared from view once more, swallowed up. The merciless, roving wall of red would consume us all in mere *moments*.

"*Rowin!*" came my wife's cry again.

When the fog hit us, I was blinded by it.

All I saw was red.

"*Rowin!*"

Then came the screams of my horde, horrible and gut wrenching, filling the night sky as the fog consumed it too. And even as my horde suffered, even as I began to feel my strength leave me, all I wanted to see was Mina. To make sure she was safe.

I felt a buzzing. I *heard* it crawl across my skin, sliding up my arms, and trailing through my hair.

A blue glow came from within the red fog, small at first and then growing in intensity.

And just like what had come from the Dead Mountain, I felt that ripple of energy as it *burst*.

That blue orb grew and grew until the blue was stretched so thin that it became colorless.

And then Mina's barrier crashed against the fog.

It was violent and sudden, but my mate's power was merciless. The barrier grew and grew, more rapidly and quickly than it had done on the plains when she'd demonstrated her power for the horde.

And I knew the cost of it.

The fog lifted from my eyes.

The fog lifted from the clearing, from the Dead Valley, from the Dead Mountain, from the *horde*.

But when my eyes immediately snapped to my *Morakkari*, I saw what I feared. Her hair was whipping wildly, her dress a tangle around her legs, billowed by an unseen force.

Red blood was already beginning to drip from both of her nostrils, and her expression was contorted into one of extreme pain, though she didn't make a single sound.

"*Nik,*" I breathed before sprinting toward her.

When I reached out to touch her, she bit out, "*No.* D-Don't try to take it from me."

She meant the pain. I had channeled a portion of it into me before, giving her a small relief.

Vok, I *needed* to spare her from this! Didn't she understand that?

"*Go!*" she breathed. "Go quickly. I'll hold it!"

"*Nik*," I growled.

"*You must, Vorakkar!*" she cried out. I flinched at the title. She was reminding me of what was at stake. My eyes flicked toward the horde, then to Hukri and Riva and Natevik, who were all close to their *Morakkari's* side. "*Trust me.* Trust in me. And go save them!"

The pain was right there in her eyes. Blood dripped over her lips.

Torment speared through me, and I nearly roared with the fury that was building in my chest.

Tears began to pour down her cheeks. She was giving this to the horde. She was making a sacrifice for the horde, for me. I would not squander it. I would not keep her in pain longer than was necessary.

A rumble of *pyrokis* shook the earth, and I saw my *darukkars* racing toward us. Swords in hand. *Ready.*

Before I thought better of it, I kissed Mina, and some of her pain funneled into me. I tasted her metallic blood as the pain nearly brought me to my knees, as it roved and swarmed and *ate*, however briefly. And yet she was standing strong. My brave *Morakkari*.

When I pulled away, I vowed, "I will return quickly, *rei kassiri.*"

My love.

She closed her eyes, breathing deeply, and I knew that I could not waste another moment.

My *pyroki*, Okan, raced toward me, as if sensing my need for him. When I swung onto his back, as my *darukkars* swarmed around us, I ordered Valavik, "Stay here. Find a break in the fog toward the west edge and get the horde out, *lysi?*"

He knew better than to argue. He understood that he was responsible for the horde in my absence.

"I will, *Vorakkar.*"

"And watch over her!"

Those words ground out from me as I looked at my Mina for the last time. Her green eyes seemed to glow as they met mine, knowing mingling with her pain.

"Go," she whispered. But I heard her voice as if she'd whispered it into my ear.

"*Darukkars!*" I bellowed, wheeling Okan around toward the Dead Mountain, the Dead Valley spread before us, clear and open. It was a straight path, unhindered by fog. "*Vir drak!*"

The war cries rose up.

Fierce determination, unlike anything I'd felt before, rose up in me with them.

And we rode for the Dead Mountain.

CHAPTER 51

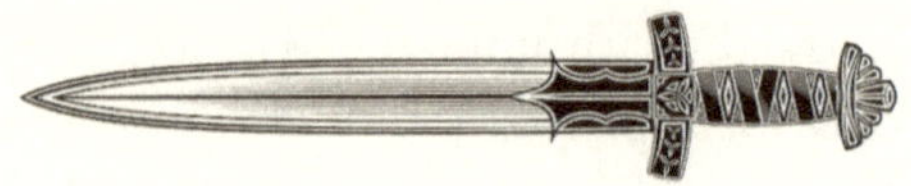

"Do not harm the *vekkiri*," I growled, "unless they threaten your life. We need to be quick. Find our *darukkars* and then get them back to the horde!"

The thunderous booms of dozens of *darukkars* dismounting from their *pyrokis* momentarily shook the earth. Before us lay the entrance to the Dead Mountain, that yawning, gaping mouth that led to blackness.

I cast a look over my shoulder though I had lost sight of Mina with the widening distance. All I saw was night behind me.

Yet the fog had not returned. That alone told me she still stood strong. It lingered, high over our heads, even beyond the top of the Dead Mountain, like a thick band of clouds. I saw one or two *darukkars* casting it wary looks, but I could *see* the strength of Mina's barrier as it kept the fog back.

"Hurry," I bit out, scraping the blade of my sword over my *Vorakkar* cuffs, as Okan stomped beside me, discomforted by being so close to the Dead Mountain. As if my beast could sense something sickened about the place.

We surged into the entrance tunnel, silent and quick, heads

constantly moving, eyes constantly scanning for the barest hint of motion.

I didn't know what to expect. I didn't know what we would find. Neither did the *darukkars*.

The lower levels of the Ghertun's kingdom were a mystery to me, though I remembered the path Mina had taken when she led me from the darkness. And so I retraced it, veering left toward a long tunnel to access the stairs that led us down. And down. And down.

One of the *darukkars* dragged a torch across the wall with a quick snap, and a small flame burst to life, lighting our way. Dozens of booted feet on stone sounded and echoed, but I didn't worry that it would give us away.

Let them hear us, I thought.

Determination filled me. Every beat of my heart reminded me that precious time was wasting away. Every second we lingered was another second that my *Morakkari* would suffer. *That* was motivation enough to end this quickly.

A familiar floor greeted me. A familiar hallway, though it was deathly silent. I motioned for my *darukkars* to follow, and we charged quickly down it, moving as one, inspecting every darkened space and empty room we came upon with efficiency and speed.

Soon, I saw the door that once led to my prison. The door was wide open, hanging off one of its hinges. I peered inside, my jaw tightening when I saw the dark stain of *vekkiri* blood, where Benn had bled and pissed on the floor. I saw the table I'd been chained to, toppled over on one end since I'd cut through the stone leg with the blackened Dakkari-steel chain.

No one was in sight.

With a churning gut, I motioned the *darukkars* forward, leaving that empty prison behind. I caught a multitude of different scents as we went farther down the hall, which led to a dead end. When we went back, I traced the scents up the staircase and down another long corridor. We passed a well, where I saw mold-ridden clothes tacked to the walls, as if they'd been hung to dry after washing. A basin was toppled over, and when I peered into the well, I saw that it had run dry.

The scents I caught led to a room. A room where I saw torn hides and thin furs spread on the rocky floor. Another room just beyond that smelled of rotting meat.

"There's no one here, *Vorakkar*," came Besik's voice, who I hadn't even realized had been among the *darukkars* to join us. "They've left."

He kept his gaze averted, however, his voice low.

"*Nik*, they are here," I said. "There's another place I think they might be."

And I cursed myself for not checking there first. Precious moments. I pictured Mina with blood trailing from her nostrils, with her bloodshot eyes, and the excruciating pain that had flowed into me, however briefly. And *that* was the pain she was feeling now. Right this moment!

"Let's go," I ordered, taking them to the next stairwell that led to the upper levels.

The witches had wanted to sacrifice me in the Ghertun's throne room, hadn't they? Because that was where this all began. While they didn't have *me* anymore, it was possible they believed that specific place still possessed *power*. Remnants of Kakkari's power that would help channel and strengthen their own.

We climbed up endless flights of stairs, taking them two or three at a time in our haste. When we reached the upper level, the one we'd started on, I roved down the long hallway to my right, orienting myself. I remembered the detailed sketches that a member of Drokka's horde had made when the *Vorakkar* had tasked her with it. The Mad Horde King had believed they would prove useful. They already *were*.

As such, I knew the top floors of the Ghertun's fallen strong-hold well.

The Dead Mountain was like a maze. It was a series of hall-ways, of twisting, tight stairwells and darkened tunnels. The scent of death and rot clung to the place like skin. I sensed the unease of my *darukkars* as they followed close behind me.

I tried to imagine Mina living in this place, and I couldn't. In my mind's eye, all I saw was her walking in the sun, Hukri close to her side, enjoying the breeze as she walked through the horde. Her flesh was darkening from Kakkari's sun. She was becoming stronger from Kakkari's nourishment.

But here...

In this place full of darkness and death, she had lived for weeks, longer even than she'd been at the horde.

I wondered if she'd felt the unease I felt as we neared the throne room. I wondered if she'd avoided the top floors like a plague. Could she feel the sickness? Could she smell the decay?

The doors were closed. As we neared, I saw two human males slumped against them. And I knew we had the right place. We were *close*.

Striding up to them quietly, I saw that they still breathed. I recognized one of them. His arm was still broken from when I'd snapped it, when a group of humans had swarmed me to read-just my chain in my cell.

Rising, I kicked open the heavy doors, snapping whatever lock had been secured on the other side. Immediately, my *darukkars* flooded into the throne room as the scent of death hit us like a wall.

The Ghertun were still *here*. There were piles of bodies that had fallen the day that Rath Drokka's *Morakkari* used the heart-stone here.

Up on the dais, next to a toppled throne, I saw who I could only assume was the *Setava Terun*. Dressed in white furs tipped in black blood, she was drawing a blood marking onto the floor.

"*Bevir*," came a *darukkar's* growl from next to me, shock in his voice.

With my jaw tight, with my chest aching, I saw the lifeless body of the *darukkar* next to the witch. She watched me, her wild red eyes outlined in black paint, as she dipped her claws into the wound in his chest and dragged fresh lines of blood across the floor.

Natevik's brother. A member of the horde.

Gone.

Slain.

My gaze flicked, assessing the rest of the room quickly. That wasn't all the death within, I realized. A Dakkari female was lying close by, a similar wound in her own chest. As if her heart had been taken too.

One of their own, I thought, my throat tightening with the realization. They'd killed one of their own. Why?

But I thought I knew. For *sacrifice.*

Had it been *her* life that caused the fog to surge? Or had it been my *darukkar's?*

A dozen Dakkari females were within the throne room, all dressed in thin furs and pelts and stained hides. The *sarkias*. And it looked like time out in the wildlands had not been kind to them. They were almost as malnourished as the *vekkiri* were.

And the humans...

They were here too. Mina had told me there were over thirty people that remained of her village. Though I only counted twenty-two present, and most of them were slumped over, lying next to the sludge of Ghertun bodies that littered the throne room.

Were they dead too? Or were they unconscious, like the two males outside the doors?

My eyes scanned over them, catching on familiar faces. Benn, though his eyes were closed and he was lying on his back, the bandage covering the stump of his arm dirtied.

And *Tess*.

I recognized the dark-haired female. Mina's friend. She was sitting on the floor, staring at us with wide, solemn eyes as tears streamed down her dirtied cheeks. She was in shock, I knew. There were others awake as well. Like Jacques. A pregnant female. And a small boy, who couldn't be older than some of the children in the horde. The boy was staring down at a woman close to him, her limp, dark hand clutched in his own.

"*Vorakkar*, there," came an urgent voice. Teiro stepped forward, his sword flashing in the low light as he gestured to the remaining three *darukkars*, very near where the line of *sarkias* were standing. "They breathe. They're *alive*."

"Take them," I growled, my gaze flitting back to the *Setava Terun*.

The twelve *sarkias* were whispering together. An eerie sound, spoken in their language, that filled the throne room as the wet sound of blood dragged across the floor. Using my *darukkar's* blood as ink.

Were they praying to Kakkari? As if our goddess would heed their prayers.

"Enough," I bellowed out, trudging through the thick piles of bodies, my eyes only on the *Setava Terun* as more than a dozen of my *darukkars* made for the *sarkias*, tightening into a phalanx, swords drawn, their movements one.

"You will not take them," the *Setava Terun* rasped, her eyes flickering to the *darukkars*. "The markings are not yet complete. There is more work to be done."

"Markings for what?" I growled. "The fog has spread even farther across the land with your blood magic!"

I heard a few of the humans gasp and sniffle.

The *sarkia* leveled me a cold look. "There is no fog here. Just look around. Breathe in the air. Kakkari is giving us her blessing. The mark is working." She looked at the group of humans. "He lies. Continue in your prayers!"

"There is no fog because my *Morakkari* is using her own power to ward it off from these lands," I told her, glancing at the group of remaining humans. "Your Mina."

My eyes connected with Tess's as I said my wife's given name, knowing that humans had no such misgivings about them, not like Dakkari.

"*Mina?*" Tess whispered, tears still falling down her face. A face that was bruised. A split lip, a rough scrape across her cheekbone. Her hair was tangled, her face pale and ashen, her lips dry.

"She is saving you all even now," I said softly. "She is saving all of us!"

In Kakkari's name, what had *happened* here since Mina and I left? Was *this* why my wife had felt such a need to return? As if she knew this was the fate that would fall on her villagers?

My palm tightened on my sword.

Turning to look back at the *Setava Terun*, I said, "Cease now, or I will *make* you." My *darukkars* were nearing the *sarkias* along the east wall. The witches had never once faltered in their whispered prayers even as their death loomed. "I will cut your head clean from your shoulders. And I will wipe out the entirety of your coven in a single instant. *Cease!*"

The *Setava Terun* smiled, revealing sharpened teeth, darkened with decay. "You forget that it was *sarkias* who ruled this land long before a king came. A male king," she spat, "who took Dakkar from us and made us bend to *his* will. When it was *us* made from Kakkari's own image!"

Twisted lies. Ones she actually seemed to believe.

"But no longer, Horde King," she hissed. She pointed a sharp claw at me as she spat, "I know who you serve. I know who *your* knee bends for."

"I serve my horde," I growled. "I come to reclaim my warriors you took and the humans you've preyed upon. And to end this madness before the East is completely consumed with the fog you just spread over it!"

With a whisper, the *Setava Terun* spoke in her own language, flicking her claws in a gesture toward the line of her *sarkias*.

That was when I felt it.

A familiar energy, building up against my skin.

When my gaze snapped to the line of *sarkias*, I saw one who stood out, whose yellow eyes began to glow as she stepped forward. Her exposed flesh was a riddle of deep cuts and bloodied scrapes, not yet healed. Her hands were tipped in black blood, and I watched as she cut a line across her chest, her claws as sharp as blades.

As blood began to seep from her wound, her eyes closed and the room seemed to hum. The back of my neck prickled. In an instant, as dread churned in my belly, I knew what had to be done.

I had talked to Mina of the prices paid for power. The price Kakkari asked for her given gifts. The price Mina was paying now.

All the prices Kakkari asked seemed to be *pain*. Suffering.

I'd believed that there *were sarkias* with actual power among the *Setava Terun's* coven.

Now here one stood.

"Kill her now!" I bellowed to my *darukkars*, who were closing in on her, as I darted for the *Setava Terun* on the dais, my sword drawn. "Before she—"

But it was too late.

It felt like an explosion went off within the room. Out on the plains, I remembered that pivotal moment when the fog had seemed to retreat into the Dead Mountain before it hurtled across the land. As if the mountain had been breathing it in, nourishing it, giving it power.

It felt like that. Only this time, it felt like the *sarkia* was breathing *us* in. And when she screamed her exhale, we all went hurtling across the throne room.

The cries of the *vekkiri* echoed.

The grunts of my *darukkars* sounded.

I felt the snap of my forearm as I landed on top of it. I felt my sword slice into my side, drawing even more of my blood, when I fell.

I exhaled sharply, feeling the pain explode through my limbs. When I looked up, I saw we'd all been pushed against the far wall, thrown like we were weightless.

The *sarkias'* whispering intensified. I dragged my gaze to my *darukkars*, scented the metallic stench of blood, and I wondered if others had been injured too.

When I stood with a pained grunt, when my warriors began to rise too, I caught the eye of the *sarkia*, whose blood seemed to pour down her chest. She was looking straight at me, her expression mirroring my own. *Determined.*

I had thought it was the *Setava Terun* I needed to kill. Kill the leader of the coven, and the rest would fall. Only it wasn't the *Setava Terun* that had the power here.

It was *her.*

I drew my sword out from underneath me, feeling blood leak over my hip.

Mina, I thought, casting my gaze briefly over the humans. Had Mina felt that surge of power?

Mina's villagers had been pushed up against the far wall too. Tess's eyes found mine. With a furrowed brow, I watched as she slid a dull dagger from Benn's own pocket, where he'd been flung next to her. The male wasn't breathing anymore.

"*Vorakkar,*" came Besik's voice. I cast a glance at the *darukkar* who, up until this moment, I hadn't trusted I could depend on. Only now, as blood dripped into his eyes from the wound at his temple, I saw the fierceness of his expression. I saw the strength of his will. "What are your orders?"

I risked too many lives in this throne room. The humans, my *darukkars'*. My own.

How much longer could Mina hold the barrier?

How much longer before her own strength would begin to wane?

I felt that energy rising again. Much too soon. I felt it spread over my skin, but it felt warm and soft. Just like it had felt when my wife used her gift on me, when she told me that she'd cast it unknowingly over me because she'd only wanted to keep me *safe*.

This wasn't the *sarkia's* power. The *sarkia* whose blood was the price she had to pay.

It was Mina's.

And it was *here*.

CHAPTER 52

There was a strange place in the folds of my gift where the pain disappeared entirely and there was only beautiful *relief.*

It filled my body with lightness. I felt like I was floating. My limbs weighed nothing. And though streaks of light filled my vision, they no longer felt like daggers spearing into my mind.

It had taken a long time to reach these heights. It had taken endless suffering where I felt like I was screaming, wailing into the night, and yet I made not a single sound.

My bones seemed to creak. I tasted my own blood as it ran from my nostrils, as it coated my tongue.

And I focused on breathing. *Breathing.* One moment into the next. That was all I needed. *Just one more moment.*

A moment for Wrune. A moment for Tess. And then I thought of the countless members of the horde, who I knew Valavik was shepherding beyond the new stretch of the fog, a place that it could not reach. They'd found a break in it, toward the western edge. Hukri had been the last to leave. And only when I begged her, with tears streaming from my eyes, had she finally left.

Safe. They were safe.

Yet Wrune had not returned.

I just needed to be patient. Which was so difficult when it felt like one's soul was being plucked from one's body. Piece by piece. Bit by bit.

But then I reached that place where I felt nothing at all. Only relief.

Then came the whispers. Whispers in an ancient language that I could somehow understand, though I had never heard it before in my entire life.

Whispers that sounded like they came from thousands, if not millions, of voices, joining as one. And I understood what they asked of me. They asked for my sacrifice. They *asked* me to suffer. Because I had to. In their voices, I had the realization that Wrune had been right: I had been *chosen* for a reason. I had been given this gift for a reason, though at this moment, my gift felt more like a curse.

I had been chosen for a greater purpose. I had been chosen to *protect*.

A protector.

All I'd ever wanted to be.

The voices asked me to endure. They *asked* me if I could endure it.

And though my own sob nearly choked me, as an inkling of the pain began to trail down my arms, sliding into my veins and funneling into my stiffening body, I gave them my answer.

The relief faded. Piece by piece.

Nausea rose. My mind throbbed. My limbs felt like they'd been pulled apart.

But something strange happened. Though there was pain, there wasn't *strain*. The strain and stretch and the *limit* placed on my barrier, which kept the fog at bay, had vanished.

My breath whooshed out of my lungs. And I understood. I understood that if I could endure the pain, my power would be strong. It would be strong enough for the horde. It would be strong enough for Wrune.

A voice was speaking to me, but my eyes were unseeing.

"*Morakkari*," came the word again. That familiar word. "*Morakkari*, where are you going?"

My head turned. Through the blur of my tears, I saw a figure take shape. Familiar.

Valavik. And he was on his *pyroki*.

"The horde?" I rasped.

"All have made it beyond the fog's edge. It stretches a mile west and then stops, just like before."

I closed my eyes as it felt like a dagger was twisting in my mind. A small relief. At least the horde was safe.

"Where are you going?" he demanded.

"*To him.*"

It was then I realized that I was walking, though it didn't feel like my feet were connecting with the ground. I saw I was already halfway to the Dead Mountain. How long had it been?

The expression on the *pujerak's* face was grim. He reached down his arm. "Then I will go with you."

"You cannot touch me," I told him through gritted teeth. "Or your *pyroki*."

His brow was furrowed. Whatever he heard in my voice, he insisted, "Try."

His arm was right there. I could hurt him, just like I'd hurt Wrune. My power was endless, and it flowed wherever it could.

And yet...when I reached out to take his hand, he didn't flinch.

Only Wrune, then. Only Wrune suffered with my power.

Why?

Because he was my mate? My *fated* one?

Because Kakkari had bound us together, for whatever reason?

"Let's hurry, *Morakkari*," Valavik said. "Though he will kill me for bringing you there."

I didn't remember getting on Valavik's *pyroki*. I didn't remember racing across the plains in that quiet, quiet night.

I didn't even remember stepping *into* the Dead Mountain, with Valavik at my side, his sword drawn and glinting.

What roused me from my stupor was the smell.

"*No,*" I breathed.

It was familiar. Only I had grown used to the fresh air in Wrune's horde. I had grown used to the smells of smoking meat and the hard soil of the earth, of the breeze that sometimes blew in from the southwest, of the freshness of bath crystals, of Hukri's hair, and of my husband's scent mingled with my own in our furs.

All wonderful things.

Yet I had forgotten *this*. The endless darkness. The stench of rot and desperation, cloying and diseased.

And somewhere, Wrune and his *darukkars* were here. Somewhere, Tess and the others were too.

I needed to find them. I couldn't be cowed by the pain I had *agreed* to take. Knowingly, I had made a deal. Perhaps even with Kakkari herself.

And in exchange, she gave me the power to *save*.

"This way."

The words came from me, and I felt myself being pulled toward another energy. An energy I sensed within the Dead Mountain. Strange and roving, like a beast on the prowl.

I recognized the path my feet took. It led toward the throne room, the place we'd always avoided whenever possible.

As I neared, I felt a chill run up my arms. Fear prodded at me. Something was rising. Building.

Just like on the plains.

And when that energy broke, it seemed like the whole mountain shook with it.

Up ahead, I heard the pained cries. The thud of dozens of bodies hitting something *hard*.

Underneath it all, I singled out Wrune. I could actually *hear* his breaths. I could hear a bone snap, a blade slide.

No.

I took Valavik by surprise when I started to run. The pain was forgotten. I just needed to *reach* him. I needed to reach him before something terrible happened, before something terrible *took* him!

Kakkari, please, I pleaded in my mind, tears streaming down my face. *Please protect them.*

And yet...

I could protect them.

Without realizing it, as we neared the doors of the throne room, I had begun to build up a barrier. A *second* barrier, within the first, within the one that held the fog away, high above this cursed mountain.

"Protect them all," I rasped, feeling my pain heighten. The price was higher now. Because the power was *more*.

It nearly brought me to my knees. I trembled underneath the weight of that pain, but I could not fall. I *would* not.

When we reached the throne room, I saw Jos and Kyl slumped in the doorway. Valavik stepped over them without a second glance. And so did I. I could not waste another moment.

Even before I stepped inside, I unleashed the barrier. I could sense Wrune near. I swore I could hear his heartbeat. I could hear dozens and dozens of hearts beating, both Dakkari *and* human.

And when I stumbled into the throne room and cast my gaze wide, I strengthened my barrier, running it along the walls. I saw Tess, I saw Jacques, Kaila, Hassan. I saw Benn, though I could not hear his heart. Others among the villagers were alive, but they had slipped into unconsciousness. Like Farah, whose hand Hassan scrambled for, even though they'd fallen into a heap. Like Emmi, who Kaila had gathered close to her.

And Tess. Her wide eyes were on me. So familiar, and yet even under the tumultuous pain, I felt stronger than she was. She looked broken. A shell of who she'd been. Like me. Like how I'd been. Surviving one day into the next.

I pushed my barrier over them, quick and so fast that I saw Tess's hair blow back from the wave of it. And to my right...

Wrune.

His red eyes fastened to me. His left arm was hanging, the bone snapped clean. Blood dripped down his side. Beyond him, his *darukkars* had risen, though most were nursing similar injuries. Two warriors had not risen, knocked unconscious from the tumble.

"*Morakkari,*" came Wrune's guttural rasp.

Relief spread through me once they were all encased under my protection.

"Nothing can touch you now, *sailon,*" I told him.

Even still, nothing would *dare* touch him.

In that moment, I realized I would sacrifice anything for him. He'd talked of love once, and I'd been afraid. But I didn't feel afraid any longer.

I felt *strong*.

When my eyes caught on the *sarkias,* my gaze was dragged like a magnet to the one I knew I felt the energy emanating from. She looked even younger than me. Thin and bony. Her black blood dripped. Her lips were painted gold, though it had smeared along her cheek. Her claws were encased in crusted blood.

She'd been born with power too.

Only I didn't think she'd ever heard the voices of Kakkari.

I didn't think she'd ever *answered* to them.

Next to her, I spied the *darukkars* that had been taken,

including Hukri's mate. In a flash, I whipped out the barrier, encasing them fully at her feet. I pulled, bringing them away.

The *sarkias* hissed and made a mad scramble for them, but when they struck my barrier, it flung them away, the force of which surprised even me. Again and again, they clawed at it, striking, scrabbling like ravenous beasts.

With one final tug, I shot the unconscious *darukkars* across the throne room and laid them gently at the feet of their warrior brothers.

Only three. Where was the fourth?

Wrune's sword rang as he whipped it up.

"Who are you?" came the voice. Soft and rasping. Familiar.

My gaze landed on the owner of the voice.

The *Setava Terun.*

"Don't you recognize me?" I asked, though my voice sounded far, far away. A moment later, my gaze strayed to her side. A Dakkari female lay to her left. And on the other side of her...my breath hitched when I saw the fourth *darukkar*, and my chest ached where his own had been torn open.

Her eyes narrowed before they widened. "*The servant girl.*"

Yes, that was how she'd seen me. As Benn's servant.

"The girl from a village in the North Lands," I corrected, striking out my barrier again, tethering it around Natevik's brother and lifting his limp body. He came easily, and he would return to the horde. Where he belonged. I laid him next to the others as Wrune's warriors gathered close. "And the *Morakkari* of Rath Rowin."

"You have the gift," came her growling, astonished, angered voice. "You belong with *us*! Don't you see that? Instead you whore yourself to a *Vorakkar*!"

Out of the corner of my eye, I saw Tess rise and begin to walk toward the *Setava Terun.* What was she *doing*?

Wrune was already moving, his sword leveled in front of

him. I recognized the look in his eyes. It told me that whatever happened, he would finish what he'd come here to do.

"He's my husband," I said. "And I would choose him again, if given the choice."

The *Setava Terun* stepped down from the dais, her eyes locked on me.

"*Sullied,*" she bit out. "It is too late for you."

"And why would I join you?" I whispered, though I knew she heard me. Next, a hissing sound rose from the *sarkias,* and I felt the tension of the energy in the throne room snapping tight. "You only take. You only destroy."

Another wave was coming. I could sense it.

That was when I saw what was in Tess's grip. A dull dagger. One I recognized.

"Cease, *Vorakkar,*" the *Setava Terun* ordered Wrune when she saw he was coming too close. "You think my coven will let you touch me?"

Out of the corner of my eye, I saw the *darukkars* begin to follow their king's lead. The soft padding of their boots on the stone floor was like a whisper. Swords were raised. They formed a tight pack, approaching the line of *sarkias*. I rippled my boundary just to be sure it was still strong, though I tasted blood as I did.

The Dakkari female wasn't even looking at Tess. To her, a human was nothing. Forgotten. As expendable as air. And yet my oldest friend crept along the far wall, keeping to the shadows until she had gotten behind the witch.

But it was my husband that had her full attention. I heard his grip tighten on the worn hilt of his sword.

"You are nothing without your coven," Wrune's voice rang out, clear and strong. "You have no power. Only *she* does. The cuts all over her body tell me that you have used her mercilessly. A tool for you, a desperate grasping for power, and nothing more."

The *Setava Terun*'s lips curled into a snarl.

"Are you not the same as me?" she asked him.

She flipped her fingers in a quick motion, and I watched the *sarkia*—the one Wrune had spoken about—run a long cut down her arm. The hush seemed to settle in the room.

And then she unleashed her power, striking at Wrune and the approaching *darukkars* that never faltered in their steps.

I gritted my teeth, nearly crying out in torment, as I felt the lash of her power. It hit my barriers, blue sparks flying into the air at their meeting point, sizzling and burning and cutting *into* me.

And yet I held them strong.

Wrune's grin was dark as he regarded the unease that flitted over the *Setava Terun*'s face. Again I felt that crash of energy. The *sarkia* unleashed her power again, hitting my barriers a second time. And then a third time. I heard her breath heaving. Though, so was my own.

Tess was approaching from behind. Closer and closer. When I saw her eyes, I saw the glimmer of her tears. When she raised the dagger, I saw that it already had blood on it. *Red* blood.

The *Setava Terun* finally heard her. She turned, and Wrune sped, jumping over the Ghertun bodies that lay between them.

It all happened so fast. Tess's hand flashed out. I felt my barrier pierced from the inside as the dagger slid forth. The wet squelch of it as it thrust into the very center of the *Setava Terun's* chest echoed in the throne room.

A break in the barrier.

I felt another wave of power from the *sarkia* unleash at that precise moment, and it flashed out at Tess.

She was unprotected.

"No!" I cried out.

But then Wrune was there, bounding forward into its path.

The wave struck his barrier as a bubble of blood rose from the *Setava Terun's* lips.

"*Lik Kakkari srimea tei kirtja,*" he growled.

May Kakkari watch over you, he'd said.

And then with a grim expression, I watched as my husband became an executioner. His sword—the one his own father had laid next to him after his birth, the sword he was made to wield —flashed out. It cut through flesh and sinew and vein.

I didn't watch as the *Setava Terun's* head fell from her shoulders, but I heard the thud of it as it rolled to the floor.

Cries from the *sarkias* sounded.

Wrune turned to them, his sword stretched out before him, dripping in black blood.

"Yield," he ordered, his voice unbending. "Yield, and you will be sent to *Dothik* to answer for your crimes. Yield now, or you choose death. Right here in this place that is only too hungry for it."

No one moved. At least for a moment.

Then one by one the *sarkias* circled the Dakkari female who still thrummed with power. They laid their hands on her, pressing their blood-stained palms into her flesh. Their expressions were defiant.

In that moment, I wondered about their lives and what they had been before. Where had they grown up? Where were their fathers, mothers, families?

What had led them to *this*?

But as I watched, I feared I understood. Had I not also felt lost and powerless? After my father died, I thought I had no one.

And feeling *connected* with others was better than being alone. If the witches had found me in my weakest state, if they'd promised that they could help me with my gift, would I have gone with them?

I shuddered, thinking about the possibility.

"You don't have to do this," I whispered, meeting the eyes of the head *sarkia*, who regarded me as her enemy. *"Hanniva."*

She stood tall and impassive.

Then, with dread in my belly, I watched as she dragged her claw across her skin. The price that needed to be paid.

Wrune's head inclined in answer.

"So be it," he rasped.

Her power unleashed, quick and unexpected, fueled by the support of her coven. I cried out as I felt the raw ferocity of the strike.

And that was what it was, I realized.

It was then that I realized what her power *was*.

It was an aggressive, *offensive* force. A weapon, meant only to hurt. Like a whip, it snapped with quickness, but it retreated just as swiftly. A *sword*.

It was like a sword.

Yet I was a shield.

It was my *husband* that was the sword.

And as the *sarkia* struck at Wrune, I protected him, defending against her blows as he strode closer and closer.

And together, we became a powerful thing. We became one.

The *sarkias* had begun to retreat at Wrune's—and his *darukkars'*—approach. Even when cornered, they were fierce. They struck out at the barrier with daggers they pulled from their waistbands, daggers of Dakkari steel. Unbreakable.

Still, my shield did not falter.

Wrune was within a sword's length of the *sarkia*, with her cut skin and glowing eyes. The *Vorakkar* waited until she struck out with her power again.

And when it retreated, he struck out with his own sword.

My gut churned, but I steeled my spine as the blade penetrated. It cut through the shield, but her power came in waves. She had nothing left. She was depleted. She could do nothing as he landed that fatal strike, with a speed that she could not defend against, right into her heart.

In that moment, I witnessed her despair. Her grief. Her shock. It widened her eyes as Wrune slid his sword from her. A moment later, she fell. He'd been merciful at the very least, delivering a killing shot where she would not suffer. Though his *darukkar*, Natevik's brother, had no doubt suffered. Though her coven had preyed on us, though they had played with something they didn't truly understand with blood magic.

They had killed one of their own. One of their sisters. And for what? For power?

And yet Wrune hadn't allowed her to suffer, though I wondered if a part of him wanted her to.

I felt it when she died.

The pain of it bowed my back as a deep rumbling from underneath the mountain seemed to erupt.

No!

"*Rowin!*" I bellowed, panic infusing my veins, mingling with the tightness of my limbs and the light bursting in my vision. "The shield! Get everyone out!"

I felt the barrier keeping the fog at bay *cracking*.

Like cracks that tunneled under my own skin, splitting apart my flesh and veins and muscle.

The *sarkia's* death had triggered it. And I knew why.

Balance.

Balance in all things.

Her death had tipped the scales again, a powerful force gone from this world, and my own gift was reacting to it.

It was *weakening* from it.

The deal I had made with Kakkari was done. Ended. I only wondered if she would allow us *time*.

When my eyes met Wrune's, for the first time, I saw fear in his gaze. But not fear for himself. Fear for me. And I wondered what it was he saw.

"Get out!" I screamed, just as my vision started to darken. "Get out now!"

CHAPTER 53

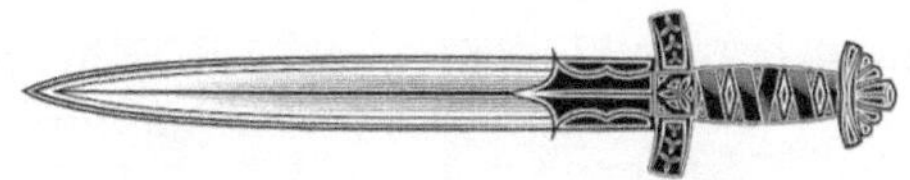

The *darukkars* were carrying humans from the throne room, slung over their shoulders. The humans that were still conscious ran behind them, trying not to fall to the ground as the mountain trembled.

As tears of blood streamed from Mina's eyes.

"*Rei Morakkari,*" I rasped, going to her, cupping her face within my hands.

Immediately, the flow of her power entered my body and my back bowed with the pain, my eyes going wide, my heart tripling in speed. Pain so extreme that I wondered if it would stop our hearts entirely.

"G-Get everyone," she started, sobbing, "*out. My barrier is weakening.*"

She took my wrists and flung them from her.

And I roared to the ceiling because I could not take the pain from her. My wife suffered, and I was *powerless* to stop it.

In the corner, the *sarkias* huddled around their fallen members, pulling them close. Their whispered prayers started up again, praying over their bodies, even as the Dead Mountain rumbled.

"*Vorakkar,* the *sarkias,*" Besik said, and I saw that Natevik's brother was in his arms. We would bring him back to the horde, give him a proper burial.

"Leave them to the mountain," I growled. "It is what they want."

Besik inclined his head and then ran from the throne room, heading toward the entrance where the *pyrokis* waited. If the barrier was breaking, we needed to reach the edge before it crumbled, before the fog rushed back in and fed from us all.

When I turned back to Mina, I scooped her up in my arms, gritting my teeth against the pain.

"Stay with me, Mina," I ground out. "Stay with me."

With one last scan of the throne room, I saw that it had been cleared. Of the humans, of my *darukkars*. Only the *sarkias* remained.

Just then, a large rocky shard, bigger than Okan, fell from the ceiling, crashing into the dais, splintering it with a loud *boom*.

Vok.

The mountain was *falling*.

With my queen in my arms, I turned from the room and raced through the doors. Behind me, more pieces of black rock fell, quaking the ground. My teeth gritted so hard I was surprised they didn't crumble into dust.

Underneath us, I swore I felt the lower levels caving in, violent and loud. I narrowly dodged a large boulder that crashed just before us, managing to dodge it but never breaking in my sprint to the entrance.

Her head lolled against my shoulder.

"*Nik,*" I growled out, shaking her until her eyes peered up at me. Softening my voice, I rasped, "Hold on, *rei kassiri*. Just hold on for me."

"*Rei kassiri?*" she asked, her voice sounding more brittle by the moment.

"*My love,*" I translated for her, the words growling from my throat. "So do not fall, Mina, or I will surely fall with you."

More tears of blood streamed from her green eyes. A sob burst from her throat, and I fought through the dizzying wave of pain that accompanied it.

"*Rei kassiri,*" she whispered, reaching up her hand to touch my jaw.

"*Lysi.* Yours," I told her, my voice guttural and husky. "And you are mine. *Lo rune tei'ri.* Remember?"

I felt the surge of her power at the words.

Mina screamed, her body tightening in my arms.

Fighting.

She was fighting against the pull of sweet relief, of darkness. She was fighting to *feel* the pain because it was the only thing that was keeping us all safe.

I saw the open darkness up ahead, saw my *darukkars* as they jumped onto the backs of their own *pyrokis* with the human villagers. Though, they lingered at the entrance, as if waiting for me.

"*Drak!*" I bellowed out. *Ride!* "Ride hard for the western edge!"

The command in my voice was unmistakable, and they didn't hesitate. Right then, I heard a crack, like *thunder*, reverberate across the plains, making my *darukkars* crane their heads up, looking toward the sky. Whatever they saw spurred them into motion.

"Wrune," Mina breathed in my arms.

"Just a little while longer," I promised, my arms tightening around her.

Then we burst from the mountain's mouth. Above us, I saw what the *darukkars* had. For a moment, I thought it was lightning. Blue lightning streaking across the sky, never striking the ground.

But then I saw the red fog just above it, swarming *into* the streaks. And I realized what it was. It was Mina's shield. It was fracturing, cracking, weakening above us.

My lips parted, seeing the depth of her power. I had not known she was capable of *this*.

"You're holding it, *rei kassiri*," I told her, though her eyes were peering up at the cracks too.

Okan raced toward us, stomping into the ground wildly, tossing his head as if he sensed the danger that would soon fall over this land. And yet my *pyroki* had waited. My loyal beast.

"*Kakkira vor*, Okan," I growled, catapulting onto his back with Mina still safely cradled in my arms. In the sheath at my *pyroki's* side, I slid my sword, freeing my other hand to clutch her to me more readily. "*Vir drak ji vorak!*" I told him.

Immediately, he raced into motion, the jolting beat of his clawed hooves digging deep into the earth, throwing us across the land as dust kicked up behind us.

A rattling, deep boom nearly toppled Okan over. A boom so loud that it rocked the plains. When I turned, I watched with grim disbelief as the top of the Dead Mountain began to cave inward, its weight crashing toward the very center of that fallen mountain kingdom. A storm of dust and debris raced at our heels, but Okan managed to keep in front of it, riding hard and fast, nearly catching up with the last of the *darukkars*, who still charged across the Dead Valley.

Overhead, I tracked the fog. With a wave of relief, I saw that the edge had retreated *backward*. To right over the encampment where my warriors had been taken. Where it had originally been before the *sarkia's* blood magic had spread it far and wide, as if the *sarkia's* death had erased whatever spell she'd cast.

That meant the horde was untouched.

Another thunderous crack came. I thought it was the Dead Mountain, but I felt a rush of wind blow at our backs. With grim realization, I saw Mina's barrier, a section right over us, begin to splinter.

Then it caved in.

The fog was waiting. It tumbled and swirled and raced through the open break, heading right toward us. A tidal wave that was reclaiming its land.

"*Draki,*" I growled to Okan. *Faster.*

Yet he was already sprinting at his top speed. I felt him begin to falter. I eyed the line of the western edge. We were so close, I could see the fire flickering in the basin.

Just a few moments more!

Just a few moments and we would—

Red consumed us with such force it nearly toppled me off Okan's back. A sound, unlike any I'd ever heard before, roared in our ears as the last of Mina's shield fell.

She went limp in my arms.

Immediately, that excruciating pain I shared with her lifted from me, but instead of relief, I felt only dread.

"Mina, *nik!*" I roared. I was unable to see in front of us. All I saw was the red. Red, like the color of my queen's blood. Her head lolled, her body slack. "Mina!"

Okan's pace began to slow. The fog began to thread into his own lungs too. How long would it be before he fell?

Only a little farther, I thought, blinking away the mist when it began to sting my eyes. Because that was what I had to *believe.* I had to believe we would reach the edge.

A few breathless moments later, golden light broke through the red. A fire roared in the basin, growing and growing. I could *see* it. We were there!

When we catapulted through the fog's boundary, I dragged in deep lungfuls of clean air, clearing the remnants of fog from my throat.

"*Rowin!*" came Valavik's voice, relief evident. When I looked up at the clearing, I saw all the *darukkars* there, though their *pyrokis* sagged with exhaustion. "In Kakkari's name, I thought—"

But I paid him no mind. I didn't even have time to feel relief that we'd made it beyond the edge.

"Mina," I whispered, my voice ragged as fear and panic clogged my throat. To no one, I roared, "Send for the healer!"

Valavik cursed but turned immediately, jumping onto the back of his *pyroki* without a moment's hesitation.

"Mina?" came an alarmed voice. "Mina!"

It was Tess. The frail, pale, dark-haired human was trying to make it past a *darukkar* who held her back.

I felt the earth quake before I heard the cracking sound that echoed into the night sky. Fearful gasps and sounds of alarm came. In the distance, I could see the stretch of plains that the fog had not yet reached.

In the distance, I watched as the Dead Mountain fell, crumbling to Kakkari's earth as if it had never been.

And as it fell, Mina's heart stopped.

My roar of agony and grief echoed deep and endless into the night.

Chapter 54

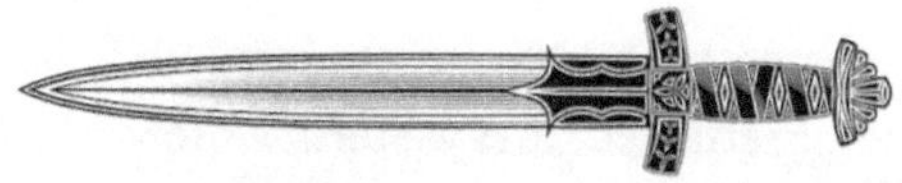

"Rowin," came the quiet voice.

I blinked, surfacing from a daze, as I watched Mina. I had pulled up a chair next to our bed. It was there I spent every free moment, when my horde did not demand the rest of my time.

Valavik stood at the entrance of our *voliki*. His lips pressed as he watched us. Sympathy, I knew.

"*Neffar?*" I rasped, my voice deep and husky, as if I hadn't spoken in a week. In some ways, I hadn't.

"The *Vorakkar* of Rath Drokka and his queen have arrived at our gates," Valavik said.

Looking back at Mina, I stroked my fingers down her smooth cheeks. They were still pale, though some color had returned to them, which filled me with hope.

It had been a week since the events of the Dead Mountain, and still she had not woken.

"Tess wants to stay with her while you go about your duties for the day," Valavik added.

"Only if Hukri accompanies her," I grunted, rising from my uncomfortable chair, loath to take my eyes off my *Morakkari*.

As I stared down at her, I was struck again by the impossibility of her state. It had been a week since she'd fallen into a deep, unshakeable sleep. Though her heart had stopped out on the plains, it had begun beating, though faint, a few moments later. As if she'd toed her way into death and Kakkari had cast her back to us.

In that week's time, it was like she'd been frozen. Though she didn't eat or drink, her body was well nourished. The rhythm of her breathing had not changed. And yet every day, more of her color returned. Just yesterday morning, as I held her in my arms after a restless sleep, I swore I saw her lips move. Though I thought that it was, perhaps, my own wishful thinking, my own dizzying *want*.

"I will let the *kalles* know," Valavik said, inclining his head and retreating. The past week, he'd given me a wide berth. All of my horde had. I went through the motions of daily duty, though I found my patience had been cut thin. My mind was with Mina constantly. The days dragged on, and yet she still would not wake.

When I strode from the *voliki*, I caught Tess lingering at the bottom of the slope.

She swallowed when she saw me but cast her gaze down. "How is she?" she asked.

There was a part of me that still didn't trust Tess, though truthfully, my complete trust in someone came rarely. Yet I had witnessed her deep concern for Mina. A few days after we returned to the horde, Tess had confessed to me her torment after Mina had helped me escape the Dead Mountain. She confessed to me that she'd believed the worst about my wife and that every moment since it had haunted her.

Cracks among the human villagers had only widened since we'd left. Benn had become even more of a monster, even as he recovered from his injuries and his wounded pride.

The wells had dried up shortly after Mina left. They sent scouts far and wide to bring back whatever water they could find, however dirtied or unclean. Some of the villagers had left the Dead Mountain, escaping into the night, and they hadn't heard from them since.

When the witches came, Tess told me their blood magic restored the well, however briefly, but it came at a price. Benn had chosen an older male named Ian to give to the *sarkias*.

As *sacrifice*.

To use his blood and his life's force for their runes.

Tess had protested. Half of the remaining group had protested. Benn had beat her for it, nearly killing her in the process, and given Ian to the *sarkias* anyway.

"But we didn't protest enough," Tess had told me, with tears in her eyes. "And it made me realize what monsters we'd all become. All I could think about was Mina. How horrified she'd be if she saw us now."

Then came her next confession that night, but she'd looked me squarely in the eyes as she said it. "I killed Benn. I killed him in the throne room when he lay next to me unconscious. I took the dagger from his waist, and I plunged it into his still body because I wanted to make sure that he'd never wake up again."

"Why do you tell me this?" I'd asked her.

She'd shrugged. Her face had been washed. She was clean and well fed among the horde. All the humans that remained were. But there was still a deep ache I sensed within all of them. An ache that might never heal, though it would get better with time.

"Because it is like I am telling *her*," Tess had said, surprising me. Her eyes had glittered as she said the words. "And because she is not yet awake, I will tell these things to you. And I want her to know all the terrible things I've done, all my sorrow and grief and guilt. But I will never be sorry for killing him. I am only sorry it took me so long."

Now, as the morning sun rose steadily in the sky, I recalled that tense conversation as I stared down at Tess. In the distance, I saw Hukri approaching.

"Go to your friend," I told Tess. "Her *piki* will join you soon. And remember—"

"Yes, if she so much as twitches, I will send for you," Tess finished for me. I let her interruption slide. She was not a member of my horde, and as such, I was not her *Vorakkar*. She had rejected my offer to join the horde, as had many of the humans that came from the Dead Mountain, though I knew she had her own reasons, reasons she would explain to Mina once she woke.

Because I had to believe she would, that Mina *would* wake.

That was the only way I would survive.

I inclined my head and passed her on the slope, nodding to Hukri in greeting before I set forth, toward the front of my horde. In the distance, I saw the flags of Rath Drokka waving in the breeze. A small encampment had been made for his traveling party, an area cleared within the gates. They would stay for a week or more, as we waited for the others to arrive.

Inside my council's *voliki*, I saw Rath Drokka's red eyes glow as I entered and I watched his white-haired queen bow her head. Valavik was there too, but it was only the four of us for now. Rath Kitala was on his way, as was the newest of the *Vorakkar,* to ride out into the wildlands—and at such a tumultuous time.

The *Vorakkar* of Rath Serok.

The alleged son of the *Dothikkar* himself, though it was rumored that Dakkar's king ignored his birthright. A bastard son, born from the womb of the king's servant. An unwanted son, whom the *Dothikkar* had banished from his great halls at the time of his birth.

Now Rath Serok was a king in his own right, the path to his power paved with his own blood.

"Rowin," the *Vorakkar* of Rath Drokka greeted.

"We are sorry to hear about your *Morakkari*," his white-haired queen said next, her gentle voice seeming to soothe some of the tension in the *voliki*. Dust from the plains was still settled on her high cheekbones as her violet eyes watched me closely. "We came as soon as the *thesper* arrived."

"I appreciate your haste, *Morakkari*," I rasped as a wave of exhaustion came over me. The long nights were creeping up on me. "And we have much to discuss."

Drokka didn't waste any time.

"Did you receive news of Rath Okkili?" he asked.

My brow furrowed. "*Nik*. His *thespers* ceased weeks ago. I assumed he had begun passage toward the North Lands."

"The Orala Pass is frozen over," Drokka told me. "He could not even traverse the north river."

Vok.

Which meant the priestesses couldn't be reached. Not until it thawed. Not until the height of the warm season, which was *months* away.

I raked a hand through my hair, peering behind Drokka at the map of Dakkar. The one Mina had painstakingly memorized. My eyes darted to the village she'd grown up in.

We would still have to endure months of the fog, which grew every passing day. Even if the priestesses finally came, there was no assurance they'd know *what* it was or how to defeat it.

"We cannot stay in the East Lands much longer," I said, my tone grim. "The fog grows too unpredictable. Especially now."

"Is it true, then?" Drokka asked quietly. "Has the Dead Mountain fallen?"

"I saw it myself," I told him, my jaw clenching. "I *felt* it myself."

And afterward, I felt my queen's heart cease beating. I could *still* feel that raw, scraping agony as it clawed at me from the inside out.

The *Morakkari* was still looking at me. I had the strangest feeling that she heard exactly what went unspoken, that she heard all the thoughts swirling in my mind.

"After I used the heartstone under the Dead Mountain, I slept for a long time too," she murmured softly. Next to her, Drokka rumbled, reaching out a hand to press to her lower back, as if he was loath to remember that time. "I slept and I dreamed and I healed. Your queen is still alive. Her heart beats, does it not? Every day, she grows stronger. And soon she will wake too. Kakkari is within her now. The goddess will not abandon her. Just as she did not abandon *us*."

She cast a long look at her mate, and I saw the way Drokka's harsh face softened for her.

"Tell us about her," the *Morakkari* requested after she cleared her throat. "Tell us exactly what happened under the Dead Mountain. *Hanniva*."

Seeing no reason not to, I did as the human *Morakkari* asked.

And I started from the very beginning.

I started with Mina and the fog.

<hr>

Okan was restless beneath me, but I did what I did every night. I patrolled the edge of the fog, guiding Okan against its barrier.

And as always, I was *still* looking for answers. Nothing had changed. Only now I was more desperate for them than ever. I thought that I could find what I was looking for within the depths of it. The answer that would bring my *Morakkari* back to me.

The last of the sun's rays faded from the cloudless sky. Soon the stars would make themselves known. The moon was almost full, however, so their bright light would be dimmed.

I will do anything, I thought, staring into the endless sea of red before me.

"I will do anything you ask of me, if only you bring her back," I rasped.

But like always, my pleas went unanswered.

I wanted to roar my fury and frustration and longing and grief far and wide across the plains. I wanted all of Dakkar to hear me. I wanted to wake the *Dothikkar* in his gilded halls with it. I wanted—

I blew out a sharp breath.

I just wanted *her.*

Leaning down, I spread my palm down Okan's long, scaled neck. His head shook in pleasure, preening into my touch.

I would never know the true extent of her pain that night under the Dead Mountain. I would never truly know what she had sacrificed for the horde, for her villagers, for *me.* I had only felt a remnant of it, a piece.

"She is strong."

Those words rose from me.

"She is strong, Kakkari," I murmured. "And you will not take her from me. I forbid it."

Perhaps it wasn't wise to command a goddess, but I was growing desperate.

A breeze kicked up and sent a chill racing up my spine, curling underneath my furs. Though we were approaching the warm season, the nights were still cold. Bitterly cold.

Return to the horde, came the thought.

I would not find the answers I sought out here. I needed to be with Mina. That was the only place I wanted to be.

And so I turned from the red fog. I turned my back on the thing that had not only brought me to my wife but that had caused so much pain. An emotional duality that was difficult to come to terms with, that was difficult to fathom: the purest of joys in finding her and the bone-aching grief of knowing it had taken so much.

I made for my horde.

But as I neared the gates, I saw Valavik riding out to meet me, his *pyroki* sprinting at full speed, kicking up billows of dust in his wake.

That was when I saw the fires of the horde being lit, though they had already been dimmed for the night. I heard the voices, the startled commotion. Okan sped, sensing my sudden haste. My heart seized in my chest as my *pujerak* neared.

What had happened? Was it Mina?

Hope speared through me when I saw the expression on Valavik's features.

"Tell me."

"She's awake, Rowin!" Valavik called out. "The *Morakkari* is awake!"

Warmth.

And Wrune's scent.

Icy like the North.

I heard a gasp as my hand moved, searching for him, as if I was waking from a dream in the middle of the night and needed to feel him near.

The dream was thick, however. It wanted to keep me pulled under, but I didn't want to sleep anymore. I wanted *him*.

All I felt was the softness of furs—empty and Wrune-less—and then came a voice, soft and drawn out. A familiar voice.

"Mina! Mina, can you hear me?"

Tess.

"Is she waking?" came another voice.

When my eyes dragged open, my vision was blurry, but I spied two familiar figures, standing next to the bed I lay on. *My* bed. *Our* bed.

The Dead Mountain.

The power.

The *sarkias*.

Wrune.

It all came rushing back, in a merciless stream. I remembered the blue lightning, like streaks in the sky, a storm I'd created. And the fog, it had been chasing us, just at our heels! The *fear*, the fear for Wrune.

"It's all right," Tess said as Hukri took my hand, squeezing. "You're safe. It's over."

I followed those words as reality began to sink back in, infusing in my chest and awakening my limbs. I moved my fingers. My toes. My lips parted, but no sound came out.

When I tried again, I rasped, "*Tess?*"

Her smile was wobbly. There were faint bruises on her face, but she looked healthier than I'd seen her under the Dead Mountain. In the throne room.

Oh gods, how long had I been sleeping?

"Where's my husband?" I asked, my eyes going to Hukri, my voice alarmed. "Is he all right? Did everyone make it through the fog?"

The questions came pouring out from me in a rush. Hukri said, "*Lysi, missiki.* Your *Vorakkar* is unharmed, though he has not been himself with you gone from us. They all made it through the fog. Your barrier held until the very last moment."

Pure relief made me want to float from the bed. I sagged as tears rushed into my eyes.

Hukri pulled away from me for a brief moment. I watched as she ducked her head underneath the *voliki* entrance. Though muffled, I heard her voice, strong and certain, as she called out, "Find the *Vorakkar*! Tell him our *Morakkari* has awakened!"

"You saved us all, Mina," Tess murmured to me when my eyes returned to her. I had very rarely seen her cry in our lifetime, but the tears tracked down her cheeks now. "I'm so happy you've come back to us!"

My nostrils stung. How often had I envisioned this moment? To see her *here*. To see her *well*. Or, at least, as well as she could possibly be.

When Tess pressed her face into my neck, hugging me tightly, I embraced her back.

"And I'm so sorry," came her ragged whisper. I stilled. "I'm so sorry, Mina."

I knew why she was apologizing. It brought a lump to my throat.

"Let's not speak of it now, Tess," I told her softly. Everything was still so jumbled. Like the pieces of a puzzle that weren't yet fitting together. Not until I saw Wrune. I didn't think I'd be right until I saw him with my own eyes, until I processed everything that had happened under the Dead Mountain...and afterward. "But you know I love you. My sister. You always have been."

When she pulled back from the embrace, I saw her guilt, her sorrow at my words, as if they deepened her own shame. That hadn't been my intention. I scrambled for her hand, squeezing when I felt a small portion of my strength surge within me.

I said, "I'm just so happy you're here. I've missed you so much."

It seemed to soothe some of her sudden tension. She squeezed my hand back. "And you're a queen now, Mina. The queen of a horde."

The words came out whispered and soft. We stared at one another, as I sensed Hukri lingering at the entrance, giving us privacy.

"So much has changed," Tess whispered again, though this time the words came out ragged. "Hasn't it?"

I thought she meant *us* too.

I thought she meant *we'd* changed. And she'd be right.

The girl she'd known before...I couldn't remember who she was. As for Tess...gone was the headstrong, optimistic, and courageous girl I'd known nearly all my life. She was a quiet, solemn creature now. And scarred, though they were unseen scars. She knew that she'd hurt me too, which only added to her pain.

We had both changed. Nothing would ever be the same between us. Then again, since our village burned, nothing had truly been the same, had it?

I recognized that, and Tess did too.

And I wondered what that meant for our future.

"Soon," I promised her softly, placing my other hand on top of her own.

Soon we would have a long conversation. We would see where it would lead. And that was the only thing we could ask for.

"Right," she whispered, wiping at her cheeks. "I'm sorry. I know you just woke up. I've just been thinking all these things for much too long, and I..."

"It's all right—I understand," I told her, giving her a small smile before I started crying again. "Will you help me up? I need to stand."

"I don't think that's wise, *missiki*," Hukri finally cut in, worrying her lip. "You just woke. And you've been sleeping for over a week now."

A week?

That long?

That was when I remembered. My breath hitched. "Your mate. Is he—"

"*Lysi*," she said, coming to the side of the bed. "*Kakkira vor, Morakkari. Kakkira vor.* You brought him back to me."

"No, the *darukkars* did. The *Vorakkar* did, and..."

"We know what you did, *missiki*," Hukri said. "The whole horde knows that you saved the *darukkars* under the Dead Mountain, that you pushed back the fog from the horde. And you have their gratitude. You have their loyalty. As you deserve."

Hearing that made my throat tighten. I didn't know what

to say.

Instead, I focused on pushing up from the bed. I slid my legs out from beneath the furs. For being bedridden for nearly a week, I felt oddly...*good*.

Energized. Light. I didn't feel any soreness or pain. When I touched my face, my fingers didn't come away with blood. My skin was smooth, my limbs were unbruised.

I pressed a hand to my waist as Tess helped me sit up. And though she had protested, it was Hukri that helped me stand from the bed.

And just when I stood, when I straightened to my full height, I heard the entrance flap whip back, hitting the hide with a violent crack.

And then...

There he was.

When his red eyes found mine, the *voliki* seemed to fade away. Everything seemed to quiet, even the crackling of the fire basin and the cheers of celebration I heard outside. For me?

I drank him in *deep*. He was safe. *Whole*, though his arm was wrapped tight in a bandage. He'd broken the bone, I remembered. I had heard the snap of it.

I felt a distant squeeze on my hand, and out of the corner of my eye, I watched Hukri and Tess leave us in peace. They shifted around Wrune to leave the *voliki* though he didn't even seem to see them. He was only looking at me.

And when we were alone, he strode forward, his footsteps quick and light.

"Wrune," I whispered, feeling a smile begin to break over my face though I had the strangest sensation that I was about to cry as well. "Wrune."

"Mina," came his growl, deep and guttural and rough and husky.

Just from his voice alone, I heard the strain that this week

457

had been on him. It made my throat tighten, wishing I could take that strain away.

He caught me up in his arms. Unlike Hukri, he didn't seem to believe I would break. He embraced me tightly, and I embraced him right back with every bit of my own strength, feeling the tears pool in my eyes, but I willed them away. I knew he didn't like to see me cry, though these were happy tears. Tears of *relief*.

Digging my hands into his hair, I turned his head. His hand slid under my jaw, cradling it gently as he lifted my face.

Then his lips met mine. I dragged his scent into my lungs, finding peace and comfort and desire and warmth in his kiss.

It was soft at first. Soft and deep and mind-meltingly wonderful.

"I've missed you," came his whisper, peppering kisses over my face, the bridge of my nose, my cheekbones, my eyelids. "*Vok*, how I've missed you, *rei kassiri*."

Rei kassiri.

Then his kiss returned to my lips, dragging me in deep as one of my hands clutched his hair and the other was steady on his thick shoulder.

I wasn't worried I would fall. He would never let me fall, and so I gave myself up to him. I gave into him. Then again, I felt him giving into me too.

The longer he kissed me, however, the more I sensed his need. His need to make sure I was *here*. Alive. With him.

What had he thought while I slept?

What terrible things had gone through his head?

"Wrune," I whispered, pulling back, placing my hand on his lips when he moved to kiss me once more. "Tell me."

As if he knew what I asked, he bit out roughly, "You *died*."

My breath hitched.

"You died right in my arms," he rasped out.

And I had never seen Wrune cry, but right at that moment, he was the closest to tears I thought I would ever see.

Hearing the anguish in his voice nearly undid me.

His hand stroked through my hair, and he took a steadying breath. He didn't close his eyes, he didn't look away. He met my gaze fully. Head on.

"You died, and I thought I'd died with you," he continued. "For that brief moment, when your heart no longer beat, I felt my soul wither. I felt darkness. Unlike anything I'd ever felt before."

My vision blurred. Taking his hand, I led him to our bed. I wanted to hold him. I wanted him to hold me too.

And only when I was wrapped in his arms did he seem to relax. Ever so slightly. A long, deep sigh threaded up his throat, but his grip on me never loosened.

"I'm here," I told him, pressing my hand to his chest, leaning up on my elbow so I could press a kiss to his cheek, to his jaw. "Wrune, I'm here."

"Are you?" he rasped, looking at me. "Because it feels like a dream. It is the only thing I've dreamt of when I've slept—you coming back to me."

My lips trembled.

I wondered how I would react, had our positions been reversed. Likely in the same exact way.

I took his hand, pressing it to my heart. I could feel the thud of it against his warm palm. I watched a shudder race through his large body, as if he was remembering when it was still.

"You feel it now," I whispered to him. "It beats. For *you*. Because of you. Never forget that."

"Mina," he growled.

But I saw him beginning to understand. I saw him beginning to accept that this wasn't a dream. This was real. I was here. *With him.*

And it was here I would remain.

"I need to hold you," he rasped, his arms sliding tighter around me. "I need to feel you."

And for a long time, he did just that.

Late into the night, as the celebrations of the horde began to die down and the moonlight speared through the venting hole at the top of the *voliki*, we continued to lie side by side. Looking at one another, for we had not taken our gazes off one another once.

His arms were wrapped around my waist, his knee pushed between my thighs. Every now and again, he smoothed his hand through my hair.

And when the time felt right, I whispered, "Wrune, what's happened? What happened after my shield fell?"

Though I felt his muscles tense at my request, my husband did not deny me.

And so I listened.

I listened as he told me that the Dead Mountain fell, though the reality of that *magnitude* of power—power required to topple a mountain—whether it was my own or the *sarkia's* or both, left me reeling.

I listened as he told me about the wariness of the horde, that many wanted to leave the East Lands after the fog surged.

I listened as he told me about the *Vorakkar* of Rath Drokka and his queen, who had arrived earlier that morning.

"Will I meet them?" I asked him.

"Of course you will," he murmured. "When you wish."

I listened as he told me about the Orala Pass being frozen over, the grim confession in his voice when he told me the priestesses could not be reached for another season. Our calls for aid would be unheard...or knowingly unanswered. They couldn't be certain if the priestesses had received messages from the *thespers*.

Then he told me that the majority of the *Vorakkar* were on their way to our horde. To reevaluate. To reassess. To formulate a new plan. And he told me the *Dothikkar* had called them all back to meet in *Dothik*, that he would have to heed the summons within a month's time.

"So soon?" I murmured, worried for the journey. Worried for his absence from the horde.

"*Lysi*," he murmured. "But I am here now. And I will make sure the horde is settled in a new territory, far from the East, before I will journey to *Dothik*. Perhaps we will go to the North?"

My breath hitched. He'd mentioned something about returning to the North Lands before.

"Toward your grandfather's *saruk*?" I questioned.

"If you would like to see it," he murmured.

"I would," I told him. I wanted to see where he'd grown up.

"And along the path we take to journey there, we can find your father's grave. So you may visit him."

The sentiment behind the words made my throat tighten.

"Really?" I whispered. I knew, from my studies of the maps of Dakkar, that that path would add days, if not a full week, of travel.

"*Lysi*," he murmured, sliding his hand through my hair. His brow furrowed. "Of course."

"I—I would like that very much," I told him, trying not to cry again. Only it seemed my tears, even happy, came much too easily these days.

"It is done, then," he said. "Once we leave this place, we will journey north."

"Time away from the fog, from the East Lands..." I started, unsure how to voice what I was thinking without sounding too selfish.

But Wrune finished the sentence for me, unafraid. "It will be good for us."

By *us*, I knew he meant the entire horde.

Being so near to the fog, I knew it caused tension and turmoil. After the fog had burst forth from its western edge and swallowed it up, I knew there was even more fear than before.

Being away from this place...it would feel like a fresh start. At least for one season we could rest and recover. Recharge. So that when we faced whatever came next, we would be ready.

We would be *strong*.

Leaning forward, I brushed a kiss against Wrune's lips. Sealing our agreement and the hope I felt rising within me at the prospect of leaving this place behind.

There was so much uncertainty rumbling over Dakkar. Now more than ever.

But being in Wrune's arms, it made me remember that I needed to savor these small moments. Because it was moments like these that I had fought so hard for.

"When the moon is full, Mina," came his voice as his eyes recaptured mine, "I want to marry you again."

"What?" I breathed, blinking in surprise. That was only in two or three days' time. "You want another *tassimara*?"

"*Nik*," he said, his lips quirking. The first hint of a smile all night, and I was extremely gladdened to see it. He had begun to relax. The longer he held me in his arms, the more his muscles loosened. "Just you and me. Under a bright moon. And I want to speak the vows to you, instead of simply having them marked into your skin."

For a brief moment, my eyes flashed to my *Morakkari* markings, glittering gold in the fire's light. I held my breath, realizing what he was asking of me.

"Our *tassimara*..." He trailed off, swallowing, regret flashing in his eyes. "You only joined yourself to me because I gave you no choice."

"And I forgave you for it, Wrune," I reminded him softly. "We moved past that."

"But I want to marry you knowing that *you* choose it too," he said. "That it is *your* choice. Because you already know my choice, and it has been you."

A warmth was building in my chest.

"*Rei kassiri*," he whispered. *My love.* "I want to give you those sacred vows, untouched and pure."

I gave him a grin as my cheeks warmed and my eyes glittered. "Are you asking me to marry you, *sailon*?"

"*Lysi*," he growled, sensing that I teased him. His hands clutched me closer. Between us, I could feel the pounding of his heart. It matched the rhythm of my own. "Please say that you will."

I kissed him, and I knew he felt my smile against him. Who knew that this horde king, who I'd once thought as cold and unfeeling as a statue, was actually a *romantic*?

"*Lysi, rei kassiri*," I whispered into the kiss. "I will marry you again. I would love nothing more."

His shoulders loosened. I swore I felt a relieved grin, and when I pulled back, I caught a last glimpse of it.

Softly, sobering slightly, I told him, "But just so you know, I *already* chose you."

"Oh, *lysi*?" he murmured, his eyes seeming to glow. A small smile lifted his lips. "When?"

I blew out a breath, not even certain I could answer that.

"Maybe when you first laughed for me," I teased softly.

Just as I knew he would, he chuckled. Low and deep.

"That's it. That's definitely it," I murmured, grinning, unable to resist pressing my hands to his chest, feeling the tantalizing rumble of it. "Or maybe it was when you told me about the *orala sa'kilan*. The frozen haven. When you comforted me about my father."

His chuckle slowly died down, but I could feel the warmth

of his gaze. I could *feel* the warmth of his palms as they began to trail over me.

"Or maybe it was those moments in the fog," I told him, my voice catching. "Maybe it was how you looked at me, like you're looking at me right now."

"And how is that?" came his voice, thick and rich.

"Like I'm the only one for you."

"Because you were," he said. "You *are*."

I grinned. Wrune growled and caught my lips in another dizzying kiss, one that had me breathless and clinging to him.

We were *strong*.

I was the shield, and he was the sword.

Together, we could do anything.

"You're the only one for me too," I told him.

Epilogue

One moon cycle later...

"**M**orakkari,*" came Wrune's voice.

I smiled, though I did not turn to face him as he approached from behind. My gaze was glued to the expansive view laid out before me like an offering. All glittering ice and frozen valleys.

That late afternoon, I'd climbed up this small mountain, Hukri and my ever-present guard, Revia, staying at the base of the incline to give me some privacy. Wrune had been busy meeting with Valavik, plotting our way on the maps to ensure that our route was as efficient as possible.

Yet he'd found me. As he always would.

When his arms encircled me from behind, I leaned back into the wide expanse of his chest. His hand moved, his palm pressing just over my heartbeat as it thrummed for him. Even five weeks after the Dead Mountain, he still did that and *often*. It brought him comfort, as if he still could not shake the memory of that night.

I felt him lean down and press a kiss to the side of my temple before nuzzling his head just below my ear.

"*Leika,*" he rasped. "I never tire of the North Lands."

Beautiful.

"And majestic," I told him, "though harsh. Brutal, even."

"Deadly in their beauty," Wrune agreed. "Though we are both northerners, are we not? The ice is in our blood."

I chuckled, tracing my fingers over his *Vorakkar* cuffs, warmed from his wrists.

This high up, we could see a fair portion of the North Lands in their entirety. This high up, my eyes immediately tracked to the tall, blue-tipped mountains and the valley that they bracketed. The Orala Pass.

The mountains were so high that I couldn't see the tops of them. I recognized them, of course, had seen them nearly all my life. Only I hadn't known what the Dakkari had named them. I hadn't realized that there was a road between them. And I certainly hadn't known that the road led to a fortress.

"Why do you think the priestesses chose the North Lands for their temple?" I asked him, my gaze pinned to the last bit of valley I could see. I wondered how much longer one would have to travel to reach them.

Wrune's warm breath tickled the base of my neck. "Maybe they see the majesty here too. Maybe this is where they feel Kakkari most."

I sighed. His lips came to my neck.

"But truthfully, their temple has been here for as long as I can remember," he told me. "For hundreds, if not thousands, of years."

"And do you think they'll help us?" I asked, swallowing.

Wrune's arms tightened around me.

After the Dead Mountain, ever since I'd woken, my gift was weakened. I could still a create a shield, and yet it was small. I couldn't hold it for long.

The *Morakkari* of Rath Drokka—Vienne was her name—told me that her powers had eventually returned to her, though they had never been the same. After she used Kakkari's heartstone, she'd never been the same.

And I understood what she meant. Sometimes, at night, I heard those millions of voices in my dreams. Kakkari's voice. And when I woke, I swore that I could feel my powers surge, but when I tried to make a barrier, I couldn't.

My gift had become unpredictable. In the tumultuous times we were living in, that frightened me. Because what if Wrune or the horde needed my protection again and I wasn't able to save them? Just the mere thought gave me nightmares.

"We will not know until the warm season," Wrune said. "The ice is thawing, you see?"

I looked to where he pointed. *Orala* in Dakkari meant *frozen*. The frozen pass. And it lived up to its name, though Wrune told me that the ice should've thawed last month, as it always had before.

"With Okkili taking our place in the East Lands," Wrune murmured, "it will be the *Vorakkar* of Rath Serok's responsibility to find the priestesses."

The newest *Vorakkar*. The one I heard whispers about through our horde.

"You think he will?" I asked quietly.

"I think he *must*" was what Wrune said. Then, quietly, he confessed, "When we met, he was not what I expected."

"Because he's the king's son, you thought he'd be pompous and arrogant?" I teased.

His chuckle warmed me from the inside out. My cheeks stung with the bitter cold, but I nestled myself more deeply into my husband's arms. This felt nice. We'd been traveling for over a week now. And traveling with a horde was more intense and stressful than I thought it'd be. There was so much that Wrune had to account for, so much that he had to oversee.

I helped him whenever I could, and I liked to think I was doing a good job of it. Wrune seemed proud of me, at the very least, but anything that would take a load off his shoulders, I would do gladly.

But with the stress and travel, we barely had time to *be* with one another. We barely had time to talk. Just like this. And so I savored the moment, knowing that I could be patient. Soon we would settle near his grandfather's *saruk*, the *saruk* of Rath Rowin, and we would have all the time in the world together once Wrune returned from his summons in *Dothik*.

"I think Rath Serok was made to be a horde king," Wrune said. I considered that a high compliment, coming from him.

"Like you," I murmured, finally taking my eyes off the glittering north and turning in my husband's arms.

Going to my tiptoes, I pressed my lips to his, weaving my hands into his cold black hair. A rough sound came from his throat, and he responded to my kiss eagerly. Traveling had also not given us much time for *this*.

When his hands began to roam, I broke the kiss and laughed. "Your horde is just down the mountain, *Vorakkar*," I reminded him. Whispering, I said, "And I'm pretty sure Hukri and Revia can hear us."

"It wouldn't be anything they haven't heard before," he grumbled, his hands sliding over my thick, fur-lined trews to squeeze my backside.

Knowing I needed to distract him before he had me bent over the ice-covered boulder next to us, I asked, "Are we camping here for the night?"

"*Lysi*," he said. "So we can take our time up here."

"Insatiable male," I teased, pushing at his chest a little when he dragged me toward him. He stole another kiss as I grinned.

Then he sighed, dropping his forehead to my own as his tail

trailed up my leg. I felt it wrap around my ankle, holding me to him.

"We near your old village, *rei kassiri*," he told me.

Slowly, my grin died. I looked at him and said, "Yes, I know."

"The bog you lived near is likely still frozen over, but tomorrow, I'll take you there. You think you can navigate from there to where you buried your father?"

"I know I can," I whispered, feeling confident. "Will the rest of the horde be..."

"*Nik,*" Wrune said. "Just you and me, *lysi?*"

Relief and gratitude flowed through me. "Thank you. *Kakkira vor.*"

"Valavik knows that I am taking you there tomorrow. We'll ride out on Okan once the sun rises. The horde will rest here another day, and then we will move on."

I nodded, swallowing.

"Will you be all right with this?" Wrune asked gently. "We will likely pass your village as we navigate toward the bog. At least, where it used to be. You might see the ruins of it."

"I'm all right, *sailon,*" I told him, though his worry and concern made soft affection bloom in my chest.

Just when I thought I couldn't love this male any more, he always found new ways to wiggle into my heart.

"I'm not afraid," I told him. "And I want to see my father's grave again. I want to be near him. I want to remember him."

Tomorrow would be difficult, but it would be worth it. So incredibly worth it. And something I'd only dreamed of for a long, long time.

Wrune pressed a kiss to my forehead, sliding his hand up and down my back in comfort.

"Tess's mother is buried somewhere nearby too. And my aunt," I told him. "I need to find their graves too. To pay my respects to them."

Though my aunt and I had always had a difficult relationship, blood was blood. She was my father's sister. And I knew she'd loved me, in her own way. And I had loved her in my own way as well.

As for Tess...she would be happy to know that I'd visited her mother. I'd had the weapons master craft gravestones for all of them. Onto them, Hukri had helped me paint patterns in gold, each one unique and beautiful. There had been many graves dug after our village burned though. With all the gravestones the *mitri* had given me, I thought I could mark all of them. In memory.

Tess had decorated her mother's gravestone, carving her given name into it meticulously, though it had taken her nearly a week. And before Tess and the majority of the villagers left our horde, she'd given it to me. She'd entrusted me to find her mother, and I had promised her that I would.

"Of course, Mina," Wrune replied. The soft pelt of his furs tickled my cheek when I pressed my face into them. "And when you visit her in the new settlement after the warm season, you can tell her all about it."

I smiled into his chest, though I still felt a pinch of sorrow whenever I thought about Tess.

As promised, we'd had our long conversation after I woke. It had been a difficult one—turned even more heart-wrenching when Tess told me she'd rejected Wrune's offer to join the horde, as had many of the humans.

I'd been dumbstruck by the decision. But Tess told me that she was determined. She'd had a multitude of reasons, but the biggest one was that she needed to stand on her own feet again. She'd lost who she was under the Dead Mountain, with Benn and the others and all the terrible things they'd witnessed or *done.*

She'd lost herself. She didn't recognize who she'd become.

But she'd been resolute in her decision to build herself back *up*. To build the others back up. Because she *needed* to.

With Wrune and Valavik's help—and with the other *Vorakkar*'s support—Tess had come up with a plan.

She wanted to build a new human settlement.

The largest one that had ever existed on Dakkar, though it would take time, of course.

A settlement where any of the displaced humans could live. Any of the humans from under the Dead Mountain or the ones that the Ghertun had stolen or the ones who had no home left.

The *Vorakkar* had all reached an agreement with her—that they would send two trusted *darukkars* from each horde to help build the settlement. Instead of *volikis*, since the settlement would be permanent, they would model the housing structures on that of a *saruk*. Homes and buildings made of stone and steel and insulated with thick hide. The *mitris* of the hordes would help craft them fire basins and cooking pots and furniture and chests. The tanneries of the hordes would give furs and pelts. The seamstresses would give clothing. And the hunters would help with the game.

Most surprising of all was that many Dakkari volunteered to help with the building of the settlement, whether it was for a couple weeks or for an entire season. A few *bikkus* offered to teach the humans how to properly prepare a variety of food. Another few would teach them about crops and the season cycles and the nutrients of the soil.

It would become a *saruk*. A *saruk* of the *vekkiri*, though I wondered once it was all said and done if there wouldn't be Dakkari living among them as well.

I was proud of Tess. In the week when she presented her plans to the *Vorakkar* that had all met at our horde, she reminded me of the girl I used to know. Confident and determined, like nothing would stand in her way.

That was how I knew that she would succeed. The building of a new settlement was no easy feat. But if anyone could do it, it was Tess. With what the humans had learned living among the Dakkari, I thought that they would flourish. They'd witnessed the rhythm and flow of a horde, the rhythm and flow that Wrune had once spoken to me about. They now knew what it took to survive on the wildlands, when before the humans had been woefully unprepared, failed by the Uranian Federation and the *Dothikkar*.

With the aid and support and knowledge from the hordes, I knew that they would thrive.

And after the warm season, after our time in the North Lands, we would journey south to visit the budding settlement. I would see Tess again. And the rest of the villagers. Like Jacques. Farah and Hassan. Kaila, who'd given birth to a healthy son a couple weeks ago. Emmi, who had never quite been able to look me in the eyes after the Dead Mountain, just like many of my old villagers.

It didn't matter, however. That part of my life was over. I only wanted to move on and not linger on old pains and wounds. Life was hard enough as it was without the prick of bitterness and anger.

But I knew that Tess would lead them well. And I had promised her that as Wrune and I traveled north, I would look for signs of Jacob and the other villagers that had fled from our group. I didn't have hope that I would find them, but I still looked every moment I could. Even Wrune had assigned a few *darukkars* to search for them when they went out on patrols.

Maybe one day, all of them would be reunited once more.

I could only hope.

In my ear, Wrune whispered, "The healer told me that you have been getting sick these last few days. You never said anything about it."

Licking my lips, I pulled back to look at him and asked, "Keeping an eye on me, *sailon?*"

He chuckled, low and deep. "Only because I worry for you. I wish you would ride with me at the front of the horde."

Impossible male.

"*Setovan.* You told me to ride toward the middle," I reminded him. Because, supposedly, it was one of the safer places to be. Not at risk of drifting away toward the back and not at risk should they come across anything dangerous in the front.

"I know," he said. "We can rest here for another few days if you'd like."

"No," I whispered, nibbling on my lip. I knew we needed to push forward. I was also anxious to have Wrune all to myself again, nestled in our *voliki.* Peering up at him, I asked, "What else did the healer tell you?"

Wrune made a rough sound in his throat. The black strands in his eyes swirled with contentment, and my lips parted in realization when I saw that he *knew.* Or at least, he *suspected* what I did.

"Nothing," he purred, the maddening male. "Nothing at all."

The glittering in his eyes told me otherwise.

My cheeks flushed. Swallowing, I told him gently, "It may be nothing, Wrune. I don't want to get our hopes up."

"I know, *rei kassiri,*" he murmured, dropping his head to give me a sweet kiss. One that made me melt into him and made my head spin. "Yet I think Kakkari has heard us and has blessed us. I feel it."

"Oh?" I asked, my heart fluttering with the sentiment. "You have been praying to Kakkari for a child?"

"Only every time I am deep between your thighs, *rei Morakkari,*" he rasped.

My gasp shot icy air into my lungs, almost making me cough.

Wrune laughed—loud and booming and wonderful—but soon it died down. He sobered, though the expression that came over his face was soft and vulnerable and warm. And so full of his love that I was struck, frozen by it, as I often was when he looked at me like this.

"*Lo kassiri tei,*" he rumbled.

And like always, I would never tire of hearing those words.

"I love you too," I whispered back, feeling tears begin to prick my eyes.

"And whatever happens, we have been blessed already beyond imagining. For simply finding one another," he told me.

"I couldn't agree more," I said as a grin took over my face. "But should there be a child now, I know what name I would like to choose for our son or our daughter."

His nostrils flared. He stepped closer. His warm hands came to cup my cheeks, and he tilted my face up toward him.

"*Lysi?* Then tell me what you have chosen, *rei Morakkari.*"

"What's the Dakkari word for *new beginnings?*" I asked, seeing his eyes flash. I added, "Without the other attached meaning of *destruction.*"

His own name meant *new beginnings*, but it also meant *ruin.* The name his father had given him.

For our child, I only wanted one of those meanings.

A fresh beginning. A new start for all of us.

As Wrune's eyes softened, I saw that he wanted the same. Though he liked his name now—and had embraced the meaning behind it—I knew that it had been a point of tension between him and his father, a constant reminder of his mother. A burden that should never have been placed on him.

My husband's lips quirked up in a small smile as his hand slid from my cheek to curl around the back of my neck.

"*Allari,*" he murmured. "It also means *dawn.* That special moment when the sun rises at the start of each quiet morning and all of Dakkar is glowing with it."

My throat tightened. My nostrils stung. My vision blurred.

Thickly, I said, "I love that. It's *perfect*."

"It is settled, then."

I smiled through my tears.

Against my lips, Wrune murmured, "A new dawn for us all, *rei kassiri*."

THRONE OF THE HORDE KING
HORDE KINGS OF DAKKAR #6

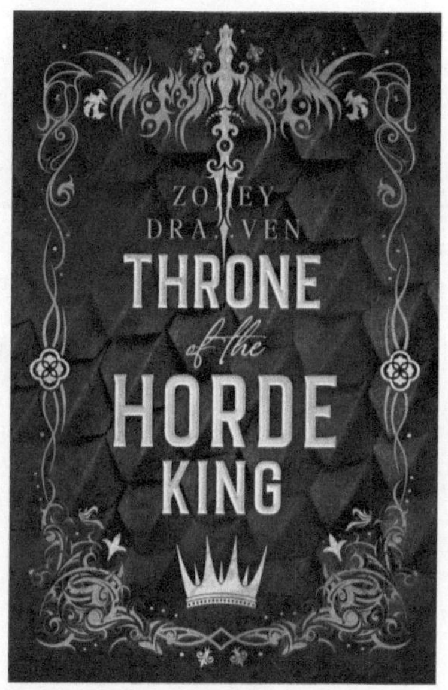

OUT NOW!

The final book of the *Horde Kings of Dakkar* series is here...

High in the icy northlands of Dakkar, I've lived a sheltered, predictable, and safe life. My days are spent caring for an ancient temple and staying out of the priestesses' way. My nights are spent pouring over the great stories of warrior kings and the queens that stole their hearts.

But I have a secret.

I'm a hybrid female. Half-Dakkari, half-human, the first of my kind. The priestesses have risked everything to keep me hidden from the dangerous hordes that roam the wild lands and the greedy king that sits on the throne in *Dothik*. I am the secret they could never let free.

Then a horde king—with molten eyes and the body of a battle god—shows up at the temple's gates, demanding entry.

He's the one I see in my dreams, all ruthless, merciless strength and a tempting smirk to match. Only, he's not the gentle male I always imagined. He's cunning, sensual, cruel…and he thinks that everything has a price. Even me.

With a growing danger in the east and a precarious throne in the west, he steals me away from the sacred temple with daring plans all his own.

He thinks I'm a naive temple girl, who will bend easily to his demands. Instead, I fight him at every turn, showing him claws of my own. Instead of fear, lust begins to rise between us—hot, addicting, and *forbidden*. His teasing touch makes me tremble. His stolen kisses make me weak.

But the horde king of Rath Serok is as mysterious as he is devilish.

And he has his own secret…one that will forever change the future of Dakkar.

Want to hear about new releases, exclusive giveaways, and get access to **bonus content,** like extended epilogues and character art?

Sign up for **Zoey Draven's newsletter:**

www.ZoeyDraven.com/newsletter

If you're already subscribed to my newsletter, access all bonus content here:

https://zoeydraven.com/bonus-content/

Connect with Zoey

Scan the QR code with your phone to access her links:

ALSO BY ZOEY DRAVEN

<u>Horde Kings of Dakkar:</u>

Captive of the Horde King

Claimed by the Horde King

Madness of the Horde King

Broken by the Horde King

Taken by the Horde King

Throne of the Horde King

<u>Warriors of Luxiria:</u>

The Alien's Prize

The Alien's Mate

The Alien's Lover

The Alien's Touch

The Alien's Dream

The Alien's Obsession

The Alien's Seduction

The Alien's Claim

<u>Warrior of Rozun:</u>

Wicked Captor

Wicked Mate

<u>The Krave of Everton:</u>

Kraving Khiva

Prince of Firestones

Kraving Dravka

Kraving Tavak

Brides of the Kylorr:

Desire in His Blood

Craving in His Blood

Hunger in His Blood

Hordes of the Elthika:

The Horde King of Shadow

About the Author

Zoey Draven has been writing stories for as long as she can remember. Her love affair with the romance genre started with her grandmother's old Harlequin paperbacks and has continued ever since. As an Amazon Top 50 and USA Today bestselling author, now she gets to write the happily-ever-afters—with an otherworldly twist, of course! She is the author of Sci-Fi and Fantasy Romance books, such as the *Horde Kings of Dakkar* and the *Brides of the Kylorr* series.

When she's not writing, she's probably drinking one too many cups of coffee, hiking in the redwoods, or spending time with her family.

Website: www.ZoeyDraven.com
Facebook group: Zoey's Reader Zone

www.ingramcontent.com/pod-product-compliance
Lightning Source LLC
Chambersburg PA
CBHW061036310726
48969CB00004B/981